HER
LONE
WOLF

PAIGE TYLER

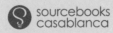

sourcebooks
casablanca

Published by Sourcebooks Casablanca, an imprint of Sourcebooks, Inc.
P.O. Box 4410, Naperville, Illinois 60567-4410
(630) 961-3900
Fax: (630) 961-2168
www.sourcebooks.com

Printed and bound in Canada.
MBP 10 9 8 7 6 5 4 3 2 1

With special thanks to my extremely patient and understanding husband. Without your help and support, I couldn't have pursued my dream job of becoming a writer. You're my sounding board, my idea man, my critique partner, and the absolute best research assistant any girl could ask for.

Love you!

Prologue

Buffalo, New York, 2008

CLAYNE BUCHANAN SAT ON THE LONE COT IN THE holding cell of the Erie County Jail, trying not to think about how completely screwed he was. But since he was probably going to be spending the rest of his life in prison, it was hard not to think about it.

This is what you get for taking that freaking job, dipshit.

It was supposed to be simple. All he'd had to do was play guard dog for a shipment of merchandise going across the U.S.-Canadian border. He'd done it before and it had always been a piece of cake. This time though, things hadn't worked out the way he'd expected, and now there were three dead men to explain. Not just a little dead, but big-bloody-mess-on-the-floor dead. Sure, the pricks had deserved it, but he doubted the system would see it that way.

The cops were out there right now trying to figure out what the hell had happened in that warehouse last night. And how three guys as big and badass as those bums had ended up looking like they'd gone twelve rounds with a pack of rabid wolves.

Unfortunately for Clayne, the cops had found him standing over the bodies with blood on his hands, his clothes, and everywhere else. It might take a few more hours for them to piece everything together—if they could find all the pieces, much less get them to fit—and explain how three men had been slashed when they hadn't found a knife on him. But they'd connect the dots at some point, and when they did, he'd be done.

Shit.

Clayne clenched his hands into fists to keep from punching something. Maybe he'd luck out and the district attorney would offer him a deal. But who the hell was he kidding? This case was a DA's wet dream. All the evidence the DA could ask for and a bad guy who looked the part, with a rap sheet to match. It was a slam dunk. But for him, there really wasn't a difference between ten years behind bars and life. Someone—a guard or another inmate—would piss him off at the wrong time or look at him the wrong way, and a lot of people would end up dead, including him.

But that'd be a small price to pay for stopping those assholes he'd killed from getting their merchandise across the border. At least that's what he kept telling himself.

The door at the far end of the hallway opened, then closed. Footsteps echoed on the concrete floor. That would be his public defender. Clayne could smell the crappy cologne from his cell. No doubt the guy had a cheap suit to match.

But the man who came to a stop in front of his cell wasn't wearing a cheap suit. Clayne had seen enough cheap suits—and expensive designer knockoffs—when he'd moved them on the black market a few years ago to know the difference. The one this guy wore was $800, easy.

Okay, so the average-height, average-weight,

average-everything man who studied him thoughtfully through the bars wasn't his public defender. The district attorney, then?

"Who the hell are you?" Clayne demanded.

The guy regarded him silently, taking in Clayne's six-foot-six-inch frame in the county jail jumpsuit as if he were some prized piece of livestock he was considering purchasing. "I'm the man who can change your life."

Clayne snorted. "You mean like my fairy godmother?"

The man chuckled. "Your file didn't mention you had a sense of humor. But if I'm your fairy godmother, that would make you Cinderella."

"Ef-you."

"No, not Cinderella. More like the Big Bad Wolf, I'd say."

Clayne swore softly. He wasn't sure whether the man was simply playing a game of name-that-Grimm's-fairy-tale-character for fun or if he actually knew something.

"Yes. Definitely the Big Bad Wolf. Complete with claws, fangs, and an extremely poor choice in business associates. Not to mention a serious problem with anger management. That would just about sum you up, wouldn't it, Mr. Buchanan?"

Heat swirled in the pit of Clayne's stomach the way it always did right before he was about to lose control. He hated it when people acted like they had him all figured out. Because he was damn sure this guy didn't know him at all, regardless of all the wolf innuendo.

Clayne doused the fire coursing through his veins before getting to his feet and approaching the bars. He stopped just short of them, afraid if he didn't, he might reach out and choke the crap out of the guy.

"I'm not in the mood to screw around. What do you want, Suit?"

If the man on the other side of the bars picked up on the low growl underlying Clayne's words, he gave no indication of it. "I don't expect you are, Mr. Buchanan. The possibility of a lifetime in prison can do that to a person. So I'll just say what I came here to say—I can make your problems go away. If you cooperate."

Clayne narrowed his eyes at the guy. Maybe he *was* the district attorney.

"Why would you want to make my problems go away?" Clayne demanded.

"Because I know you're a shifter."

Clayne had been called a lot of things in his life, but that wasn't one of them. "What the hell is a shifter?"

"Someone who's part human, part animal."

Clayne stared. Even if he'd been capable of speech at the moment, he wouldn't have known what to say.

On the other side of the bars, the man in the suit smiled smugly. "I see that I have your attention now."

Damn right he had Clayne's attention.

"I know exactly what you are. In fact, I probably know more about your wolf side than you do."

"How do you know so much about me?" Clayne practically growled.

"Because I work with other shifters like you."

Clayne's head spun. How could this guy possibly know what he was? He'd spent most of his life on the move, never letting anyone get too close to him, never allowing anyone to learn his secret. The only people on the planet who knew what he could do had died in that warehouse last night.

Yet this guy said he knew all about him. And if he was telling the truth, there were others like him out there. That struck a nerve Clayne hadn't even known existed. He wasn't the only freak like this?

The man put one hand on the bars, casually leaning against them. "I have a simple deal for you. The organization I work for would like to offer you a job. If you take it, the charges against you go away."

Clayne wasn't so off-balance that his bullshit meter didn't spike at that. Who the hell did this guy work for that he had that kind of power? "How can you possibly cover up three dead bodies?"

The man sighed. He actually sounded bored. "Look, I'm not going to give you the full recruiting pitch. You don't have a lot of options. You can take my offer, or you can rot in prison for the rest of your life. Because that's what's going to happen. Trust me, I've seen the evidence they have on you."

Clayne was this close to telling the suit to go screw himself just because he didn't like it when people gave him ultimatums. But the guy went on before he could say anything.

"I will tell you this—if you take the job, you'll be working for a very particular branch of the U.S. government."

What the hell was he being roped into? "Which branch?"

"The branch no one's ever heard of." The suit eyed him coolly. "So, are you in?"

"Depends." Clayne might have his back to the wall, but that didn't mean he was going to roll over easily. "What kind of work will I be doing?"

"Don't worry about what you'll be doing. The work

will suit you. But if it will help you make up your mind, rest assured you'll be making the world a better place."

Clayne hesitated. "You really have the power to get me out of here?"

"I just said I did."

Not good enough. "How do I know you won't turn me over to the cops when you're done with me? It's not like there's a statute of limitations on murder."

The guy muttered a curse. "You don't know. But what other choice do you have? It's not like you have a lot of options."

Clayne pinned him with a hard look. "I just don't want to go from the frying pan into the fire."

"You'll find this out if you come to work for us, but I'll give you the distilled version now—if we want something done, it happens. You accept the offer and the murder charges go away, along with all the evidence, forever. In return, I'll expect you to bust your ass for us. You get a job, a paycheck, your freedom, and the chance to do something for someone other than yourself. Does that just about answer all your questions?"

Clayne had a whole lot more, but he was already pushing his luck. There was one more thing that was eating at him, though.

"You said there are others like me. If that's the case, why recruit me after knowing what I did? Why the hell would you want someone like me working for the U.S. government?"

When the suit didn't say anything, Clayne figured maybe that was one question he wasn't going to get an answer to.

"Because I have plans that require a certain kind of

shifter, and I've decided that shifter is you. That's all you need to know." The man pointedly checked his watch. "Now, what's it going to be? You in or not?"

Instinct told Clayne there was something going on here he didn't fully comprehend. His gut said the man in front of him was a total sleazebag who couldn't be trusted. But he'd heard it said that a drowning man will grab on to an anvil if you throw it to him. And right now, he was in over his head and barely treading water.

Clayne reached his hand through the bars, offering it to the other man. "I'm in."

The suit stared at his outstretched hand for so long Clayne thought he wasn't going to take it, but then he grasped it and gave it a shake. "Dick Coleman. Welcome to the DCO, Mr. Buchanan."

Chapter 1

Five Years Later, Somewhere Near Sacramento, California

DANICA BECKETT DIDN'T HAVE TO HEAR WHAT THE two Sacramento police officers were muttering about as they followed her and her partner, Tony Moretti, into the warehouse to know they were pissed off. Local cops didn't like it much when the FBI swooped in with their federal jurisdiction and took over their cases. And that was what had happened last night. After four deaths in the area—three of which had erroneously been ruled animal attacks—the governor had called someone high up, who'd called someone else higher up, and just like that, a whole lot of hides had been rubbed the wrong way. It wasn't her fault, or her partner's, but that was the way these things worked. Big shots at the top made the decisions, and the field agents had to deal with the mess on the ground.

Finding a serial killer was hard enough. The local PD could have run down the anonymous call that had come in this morning about another possible victim, but Roger Carhart, the new senior agent in charge who'd recently transferred from the New York office, wanted the FBI following up on every tip. He'd said he wanted someone on the scene who knew the difference between a murder and a bear attack, but what he meant was he wanted the FBI preserving the evidence before the locals messed everything up. That was going to get old quick, and definitely wouldn't help to smooth any ruffled feathers.

Even though the warehouse looked deserted, Danica took out her weapon and held it down at her side, finger near the trigger but not on it. Beside her, Tony did the same. One of the cops snorted. She ignored him. It was standard Bureau procedure. If the locals didn't like it, tough. No wonder the governor had called in reinforcements.

The smell of fresh blood assaulted her the moment she stepped through the open door, and she and Tony simultaneously lifted their guns to the ready position. That got the attention of the two cops with them. They pulled their own sidearms and immediately started checking the darkened building.

Danica did a quick survey of the room as she and Tony cautiously made their way across the big, open space to the body lying on the floor. It was a white male, somewhere between twenty-five and thirty, though he could have been younger. He was naked from the waist up and there were dozens of jagged wounds crisscrossing his chest. On their own, they might not have been enough to kill him, but whoever had attacked him had ripped out his throat.

Shock gripped Danica, making her feel light-headed. It wasn't the blood and carnage that bothered her. It was the fact that she knew exactly what type of person had done this. She'd seen this kind of kill before.

"Looks like our serial killer's MO," Tony said, jerking Danica back to the present. "These tears and lacerations look exactly like the ones in the photos of the previous victims."

Behind them, one of the cops made a gagging sound. She looked over her shoulder to see him covering his mouth with his free hand, like he was trying not to throw up.

Tony swore under his breath. "Get him out of here before he fouls up the crime scene," he ordered the second cop.

That guy didn't look much better than his partner. He stared at Tony for a few seconds before the words sunk in. As the two men left, Danica turned back to survey the body again, hoping against hope she was wrong about who'd done this. She'd almost convinced herself when she heard a noise above her. She raised her Glock, aiming it in the direction of the sound. A metal catwalk ran from one end of the warehouse to the other, and her gaze darted over it just as a man up there hauled ass in the other direction.

"We've got a runner!" Danica shouted. "Cover the outside exits."

She didn't wait to see if Tony obeyed as she ran for the other end of the building. God, she hoped there was a stairwell that would get her up to the catwalk.

Behind her, Tony ordered the cops to get on the outside escape routes. Knowing her partner would be coming to back her up, Danica ran as fast as she could and slammed into the set of double doors at the far side of the warehouse.

As she'd hoped, it was a stairwell. Somewhere above her, a door banged against a wall, followed by pounding footsteps. She kept both her eyes and her weapon trained on the next landing as she hurried up the steps, fully expecting someone to come racing down the stairs.

But she got all the way to the top of the fourth floor without catching sight of anyone. The door that led out to the roof had just swung closed, so the guy couldn't be far ahead of her.

Footsteps echoed on the stairs below her. Tony. Danica knew she should wait for him, but she'd never been the type to hang around for backup. Instead, she kicked open the door to the roof and darted her head out for a quick look. When no one took a shot at her, she stepped outside and did a slow sweep of the gravel-covered roof before moving around the stairwell, ready to take down the first threatening target she identified. She didn't know for sure that the man she was chasing had murdered anyone—he might be some poor homeless guy for all she knew—but she'd assume the worst until she knew better. It had saved her butt more than once.

She saw him running away from her across the roof as she rounded the corner of the stairwell. He was bigger than she'd first thought—at least six two—and could run as fast as an Olympic sprinter.

"FBI!" she shouted as she took off after him.

Danica didn't have a chance of catching up to him. Until he ran out of roof, at least. Unless there happened to be a fire escape. As the man picked up speed, she had a sinking feeling. She ignored it and ran faster.

She was at least fifty feet behind him, so far away that she could do little more than confirm he was in fact male, dressed head to foot in black, and that he had shaggy, sandy blond hair. But all of that became irrelevant when the man got to the edge of the roof and jumped.

Holy crap.

Danica skidded to a stop at the edge of the roof seconds later and peered down at the street below, expecting to see the man in black on the ground. But there was no sign of him. She looked around wildly for another way off the roof. There were some heavy-duty electrical conduits running along the side of the building almost all the way to the ground, as well as a set of guide wires that attached a big antenna to the corner of the warehouse. The man could have used one of those as an escape route, but it would have taken him a few minutes to get down to street level. Which meant he hadn't gone down that way.

So where did he go?

The door leading to the stairwell on the building across the alley banged against the wall, then slowly swung closed. That really bad feeling she had in her stomach suddenly got a whole lot worse.

Dammit.

She eyed the gap between the roof she was on and the other warehouse. It had to be twenty-five feet at least, maybe thirty. The roof over there was about ten feet lower than the one where she was standing, but there weren't any normal humans she knew who could make that leap. She knew some not-so-normal humans who could, though. If she was right, this wasn't the kind of guy she and her partner should go after by themselves. Hell, she wouldn't want to go after him with four or five agents for backup.

Danica holstered her gun and turned to head back downstairs when Tony rushed onto the roof. She waved him off.

"All clear. It was a homeless guy. He slid down some electrical conduits and disappeared. I'm pretty sure he's not our guy."

Tony's dark eyes scanned the rooftop as he shoved his gun in his holster. "Maybe he saw who dumped the body."

"Maybe," she said. "I'll give a description to the locals and see what they turn up."

She hated lying to Tony. They'd been partners for the past two years and friends even longer—since all the way back at Quantico. But what the hell was she going to say? That there was a not-quite-human guy out there who could jump thirty feet in a single bound? Tony was a good FBI agent—a great one even—but he was practical to a fault. He'd think she'd lost her marbles. She had to keep her partner in the dark for his own good.

Luckily, the two Sacramento police officers had been so busy covering either side of the long warehouse they hadn't seen what had happened on her end. Good. She hadn't been looking forward to trying to convince them they hadn't seen something they really had. Since that wasn't an issue, she sent them off on a wild goose chase after an imaginary homeless guy. Yet one more thing to feel bad about, but she'd gotten used to living in a morally gray world long ago.

While Tony called in the situation to the task force command center, she crouched down and checked the body once more. As she surveyed the mutilated remains, she desperately wanted to convince herself this wasn't what she thought it was. But that would be a crock of crap. She'd seen this more than once—back when she worked for the Department of Covert Operations.

She stood up and walked around the warehouse looking for anything that might give them a clue as to who'd
dumped the body. And it had definitely been a body
dump. She didn't need a crime scene tech to tell her that.
Unfortunately, the killer hadn't left so much as a piece
of lint behind. That sucked. It would be so much better
for everyone if forensic evidence and old-fashioned detective work led them to this killer. But it wasn't going
down that way. And delaying the inevitable wasn't
going to make that call to the super-secret organization
she used to work for any easier.

Danica walked outside to find Tony briefing the lead
crime scene investigator. She gave her partner a wave as
she held up her cell phone and moved off to the side. She
dialed as she walked, her finger flying over the keypad
from memory. Two years and she still remembered the
number. God, that was sad.

She held her breath as she waited for the person on
the other end to pick up. When she'd walked away from
the DCO, it hadn't been on her terms, and it had been
ugly. Getting involved with them again was going to
open a lot of old wounds. But stopping a serial killer was
more important than hurt feelings and a broken heart.

———◇———

This wasn't going to end well.

Clayne squatted behind the sandbag barricade as live
rounds of ammunition buzzed over his head. It wasn't
the live-fire training exercise out at the DCO training
complex in Quantico that worried him—he'd taken part
in hundreds of these stupid things. Other than someone
screwing up and drilling a round through your forehead

while you moved from one covered position to the next, there wasn't much to get jazzed about. Occasionally, you might have to return fire against various pop-up targets. If the training officer running the op was really feeling his oats, you might get to engage in a little hand-to-hand combat at specific designated no-fire zones. Again, no big deal.

But today was different. Because today, he'd been paired up with Tanner, the Hybrid from Hell. Maybe it wasn't the nicest way to describe a guy who was trying to get his life together, but Clayne couldn't think of anything better to label the man-made shifter. The drugs that had been used to turn him into a shifter had come with some nasty side effects. While Clayne might have anger management issues, Tanner went stark-raving mad at the drop of a hat. And when he did, the ragged claws, long fangs, and strength beyond that of any shifter made him the most dangerous and uncontrollable creature the DCO had ever dealt with. That's why everyone in the DCO called Tanner and those like him a hybrid instead of a shifter.

Some things just didn't make sense from the get-go. Like ordering a Diet Coke with a monster burger. Or giving a guy who had more issues with anger management and impulse control than Clayne did a loaded weapon and putting him in a combat scenario.

Oh yeah. This *really* wasn't going to end well.

Clayne swore under his breath as he moved out from behind his covered position and hauled ass for a pile of logs fifteen feet away. The gunfire over his head sounded a whole hell of a lot closer than before. If the machine gunner on top of the hill was doing his job right, the bullets would be ten feet above his head. But it was hard not to duck anyway.

As he dove behind the barricade, Clayne caught sight of Tanner out of the corner of his eye. The hybrid was right there beside him.

Thirty minutes earlier, Clayne had been getting ready to run the exercise with Trevor Maxwell, one of the other shifters he'd worked with a few times. He wasn't exactly friends with Trevor—though that could be said about almost anyone at the DCO—but he respected him. The coyote shifter and his industrial-espionage-slash-counter-intelligence team—humans, or norms, though they may be—were damn good at their job.

Then Dick Coleman had shown up with Tanner Howland in tow. That should have clued Clayne in that something screwy was up. Dick rarely came out to the live-fire training area. Probably because he was afraid one of the dozens of people he pissed off on a recurring basis would "accidentally" shoot him. And if that hadn't been enough to let Clayne know something was up, the fact that the Russian doctor, Zarina Sokolov, was hurrying after them with a concerned look on her pretty face sure as hell should have.

"Howland is taking Maxwell's place," he'd told Todd Newman, the training officer for the exercise.

When Todd had attempted to point out it wasn't a good idea to introduce Tanner to DCO training in the middle of a live-fire exercise, Dick waved away his concerns.

"He was an Army Ranger. This stuff is child's play for him."

So Todd had given Tanner a loaded M4 carbine and told him to follow Clayne's lead.

Clayne had to admit that so far Tanner was doing damn good. He covered Clayne when necessary, reacted quickly to pop-up targets in his sector, and didn't hesitate to move under overhead fire. The tactical exercise was still talking a toll on the guy. Tanner's eyes were a bit too wide, he was sweating a bit too much, and his jaw looked like it was clenched so hard that dental damage was a definite possibility. Worse, his heart was racing a hundred miles an hour. Clayne knew because he could hear it.

But despite all that, Tanner was keeping it together.

The end of the live-fire lane—the base of a squat, wooden tower atop the shallow hill where the machine gunner was positioned—was only forty feet away. A couple more sprints and they'd both be there.

Maybe this would turn out okay after all.

Suddenly, the ground in front of them exploded.

Clayne leaped for the next covered position before the pressure wave of the detonating plastic explosives reached him. Tanner didn't react as fast. The blast hit him right in the face, throwing him back on his ass. The demo charge had been small, probably no more than a quarter pound, and it had been buried several feet off the course for safety, so while the explosion might not technically have been dangerous, there was nothing like having shit blow up right near you to convince you otherwise. Even Clayne's heart was thumping pretty hard now.

From his crouched position, he leaned forward to take a quick look around the sandbags and saw four enemy combatants coming his way. Guess Todd had decided it was time for the hand-to-hand portion of the exercise.

This was one of those training scenarios you didn't

see anywhere but in the most serious special ops organizations, like the SEALs, Special Forces…and the DCO. Because combining live weapons, live explosives, pumping adrenaline, and hand-to-hand fighting was usually a recipe for disaster. People were known to get killed doing this kind of shit.

As if on cue, Tanner let out a roar. It wasn't the sound a soldier made as he readied himself for a charge. It wasn't even the growl a shifter made to intimidate an opponent. It was the sound a hybrid made when he lost his freaking mind.

Clayne spun around to see Tanner throwing someone—one of Maxwell's team members, former Navy SEAL Jake Basso—fifteen feet into the woods. In a fraction of a second, Tanner turned and casually blocked a flying kick from another opponent—this time Air Force Pararescue Jumper Ed Vincent—then swatted the man like a cat taking down a humming bird. Ed hit the ground hard and didn't get up.

Tanner stood over him, his claws shoved out so far his fingertips were bleeding from the force they'd exerted as they ripped through his skin. His upper canines were extended an inch beyond his other teeth, which had grown as well. His freaking jaw had actually pushed out to accommodate the sudden growth spurt. And his eyes were glowing scarlet.

Clayne had seen plenty of shifters change, but never like this. Tanner wasn't a man shifting into a lion. He seemed more like a lion that was trying to claw its way out of a man. And the result was freaking creepy.

Tanner reached for Ed Vincent, fangs flashing as if he intended to eat the guy.

Clayne ignored the DCO agent who was supposed to be his enemy in the exercise, and instead launched at Tanner. If he didn't jump in, somebody was going to get killed—probably more than one somebody. He could have shifted, too, extending his claws and fangs to gain an advantage, but he resisted the urge. Two shifters going at each other was never pretty. The end result would only be bloody. And that's what he was trying to avoid.

He hit Tanner as the shifter was about to sink his claws into Ed's chest. Clayne was the biggest shifter in the DCO next to Declan MacBride, but when he slammed his shoulder into Tanner's ribs, the hybrid barely noticed. Clayne wrapped his arms around him, hoping to take him down that way, but Tanner only shrugged like he was trying to brush off an irritating mosquito.

Clayne ground his jaw. He hadn't wanted to get rough, but Tanner wasn't giving him a choice. He balled his hand into a fist and punched Tanner across the jaw with everything he had. His hand felt like he'd rammed it into a brick wall, so Clayne knew Tanner had to have felt it. But while Tanner's head rocked back, it didn't seem to have fazed him. He glared at Clayne, then took a swipe at him. Clayne ducked just in time. If Tanner'd raked anything important with those long-ass claws, the DCO would be looking for a new wolf shifter.

Clayne punched Tanner hard in the ribs, then danced out before the counterstrike came. That was when the cavalry arrived. Trevor jumped on Tanner's back, while someone else got him around the knees. The next thing Clayne knew, there were a half-dozen men piling on top of the enraged hybrid. But Tanner still wouldn't go down.

Clayne slammed his shoulder into Tanner's solar plexus with enough force to send the hybrid tumbling to the ground. He grabbed a fistful of Tanner's long hair and twisted, doing everything he could to keep those fangs away from anything soft and squishy. On the other side of him, Maxwell was using all his strength to keep one of Tanner's arms pinned to the dirt. The other men were wrestling to hold his legs down. Even with all of them, Clayne wasn't sure they were going to be able to restrain the DCO's pet hybrid. Tanner was insanely strong, and it was damn near impossible to stop a guy like that when no one wanted to hurt him. But it was starting to look like that wasn't going to be an option for much longer.

Someone else jumped on Tanner's chest. Clayne caught a glimpse of blond hair and realized it was Zarina.

"Dammit, Zarina!" Clayne snarled. "Get back before you get yourself killed."

Instead of obeying, she put her face close to Tanner's and whispered softly to him. Clayne could barely hear anything over the growls, grunts, and cussing going on, but when he finally tuned his exceptional hearing in to what she was saying, he realized the doctor was speaking Russian, which he didn't understand a lick of. Although *cooing* was probably a better word for it. Like she was comforting a child. Whatever she said, it worked. Tanner relaxed and stopped struggling. The red eyes, the fangs, and the claws—along with the really bad attitude—disappeared.

Clayne wasn't ready to release him yet, though. The other DCO agents holding him down clearly weren't, either. If anything, they used the opportunity to get a firmer grip on Tanner.

"You can let him go." Zarina's voice was almost as soft as it had been when she'd comforted Tanner. "He won't hurt you."

Clayne hesitated. Tanner seemed as if he were back in control of the beast inside him. Besides, they couldn't sit on him the rest of the day. Hoping he was doing the right thing, Clayne relaxed his grip and sat back on his heels. The other men looked unsure but slowly did the same. Clayne frowned as they checked each other for injuries. Jake seemed to have gotten the worst of it if the way he was holding his side was any indication. He had broken ribs for sure. Ed was standing a little funny, too. Maxwell was the only member of his team who looked like he was still in one piece. No surprise there. Shifters didn't go down easy.

Clayne turned his attention back to Tanner. If the look of horror on his face was any indication, the man was torn up over what he'd done. Clayne knew where he was coming from. There'd been a shitload of times in his life when the animal inside him had taken over and he'd been forced to live with the consequences afterward.

As he watched, Zarina gently brushed Tanner's hair back from his forehead, completely unconcerned that moments ago he'd been a raving monster. She seemed to be the only one who could control Tanner—or at least get through to him—when he went into a rage.

"You injured, Buchanan?"

The question came from Todd Newman. Clayne had been so focused on Tanner he hadn't even heard the training officer walk up. He shook his head. "Nah. Not a scratch on me."

"Good. Because John wants to see you."

Clayne started to ask what he wanted, but Todd turned and walked away before he could. If the director of the DCO wanted to see him, Clayne had either done something to piss someone off or John Loughlin had a mission for him. Since Clayne didn't remember pissing anyone off lately, it was probably the latter. John liked sending him on short-notice jobs that required little planning and a whole lot of direct action. It usually meant dropping what he was doing and leaving right away, but that suited him just fine. He much preferred punching things to sitting in meeting after meeting, planning shit.

He turned to leave, but Tanner's voice stopped him.

"I'm sorry," Tanner said. "About losing it like that."

"Don't worry about it," Clayne told him. "No one got hurt. It's all good."

"But—"

"But nothing," Clayne cut in. "Keep working on staying in control and you'll get there. You were ninety percent done with the course before you blew a fuse. That's better than you would have done two months ago."

When Tanner opened his mouth to say something, this time it was Zarina who interrupted him.

"I told you so…"

Clayne practically ran into Kendra Carlsen as he walked into the administrative building. The behavioral-scientist-slash-training-officer stumbled back a few steps to catch her balance. He almost reached out to steady her, but thought better of it.

"Sorry about that," he mumbled.

"No problem." She chewed on her lip, her blue eyes looking anywhere and everywhere but at him. "Um, I gotta run. John's looking for you by the way."

"Yeah, I know. Todd told…"

But Kendra was already out the door. Which was kind of a relief. Because having a conversation with her would probably be awkward as hell considering the date they'd recently gone on had been a train wreck. Okay, maybe that was an exaggeration. It'd be more accurate to say they hadn't hit it off, which in his book was the same thing. Why the hell had he let Ivy talk him into going out with Kendra? Because the feline shifter could be very persuasive when she wanted to be.

John was on the phone when Clayne stuck his head in. The director glanced at him over the top of his wire-rimmed glasses, motioning for him to have a seat on the leather couch. Clayne dropped onto the sofa, stifling a groan as he sat back on the soft cushions. Damn, he was sore from that impromptu wrestling match with Tanner. He needed a long soak in a hot tub, preferably with a couple beers.

"I completely understand," John said to whoever was on the other end of the line. "I'm sending one of my best agents to help out. He's very discreet and will blend perfectly with the team you've already assembled out there." John glanced at Clayne, his mouth twitching. "Well, perhaps that's a bit of a stretch, but he's damn good, I can tell you that. I can't guarantee he won't ruffle a few feathers, but if he does, call me and I'll smooth them out."

Clayne almost groaned again, except this time it had nothing to do with physical discomfort. No doubt John was talking with one of the hundreds of powerful people he knew about inserting him into someone else's operation. He hated working with other federal organizations, but that's exactly what was in store for him. And from what John said, he'd be leaving ASAP. So much for the beers and hot tub.

John hung up and walked over to sit in the wingback chair adjacent to the couch. "There've been five murders out in Northern California," he said as he handed Clayne a manila folder. "The FBI has assembled a standard serial killer task force, but our intel indicates we may be looking at a rogue shifter at work. Maybe even a hybrid."

Clayne frowned. He wasn't usually assigned the rogue shifter cases. He wasn't sure why. Possibly because most people at the DCO considered him just a hop, skip, and a jump from being one himself.

"Why aren't you sending Tate and his team?"

Bringing in rogue shifters was one of their specialties. Over the years they'd brought in ones who'd gone nuts and started killing people, apparently like this one in California, but also ones who were scared and didn't understand what was happening to them when they started shifting. Tate Evers and his guys were good at knowing how to handle shifters. Clayne wasn't much good at anything but the nuclear option when it came to that kind of thing.

"What? You have a date you don't want to miss?" John asked.

Clayne shifted on the couch, trying to find a more comfortable position. "Tate's team is just better at this stuff, that's all."

"Maybe so, but they're busy." John held up his hand. "Before you ask, Ivy and Landon are in Japan. And Tucker and Ramsey are both still in the hospital recovering from their last mission. You're the only agent I consider qualified and available for this kind of job.

This shifter's already murdered five people, and I need someone who can track him down before he kills again."

"How about Lucy? If you want someone killed, she can do it."

John shook his head. "She's busy with something else."

Clayne sighed. Damn. She was perfect for a job like this.

"Kendra has you booked on a flight out of National. It leaves in two hours," John continued.

"Who's my team member?"

God, he hoped it wasn't Foley. Or even worse, that asshole Powell.

"No one. You're going solo on this."

That was a first. The DCO always sent a norm along in case the shifter part of the team got compromised and had to be taken out. They must be stretched even thinner than he'd thought.

"I've gotten you assigned to the task force as a liaison with the Department of Homeland Security. The director of the FBI here in DC knows I'm inserting you, so he'll cover for you as much as necessary."

Clayne wondered if the guy had any idea who John was really assigning to the task force. Probably not. Plausible deniability and all that.

"Got it."

"Oh, and one more thing," John said as Clayne started for the door. "The director asked that you be as discreet as you can."

Clayne almost laughed. John knew who he was sending on this mission, right? He didn't do discreet.

But he gave his boss a nod. "They'll never even know I was there."

Chapter 2

CLAYNE STIFLED A YAWN AS HE SAT BACK IN HIS CHAIR and surveyed the conference room in the FBI's Sacramento field office. Thanks to the time change, he'd gotten there early enough to make the scheduled afternoon task-force briefing, but between the o'dark-thirty start that morning for the training exercise and the flight out from the East Coast, he was dog tired. If it wasn't for the caffeine he'd been mainlining since getting off the plane, he probably would've been asleep right in his chair.

He sipped his coffee, watching people filter into the room and take their seats. A few of them glanced his way but didn't come over to introduce themselves. He ignored them and reached for the folder John had given him. He'd already reviewed the case file on the plane, but it was either that or sit there and try to figure out who was FBI, who was from the state's Bureau of Investigation, and who was Sacramento PD. And he didn't give a rat's ass.

As he opened the folder, his shifter senses suddenly heightened. He didn't know why, but damn, he felt twitchy. Like he'd left the stove on at home. But he hadn't turned his oven on in forever, so it wasn't that. He swept the room with his gaze to see if someone was giving him the evil eye, but no one was looking his way. And since he was sitting in the back corner of the room, he didn't have to worry about anyone behind him. Maybe he was just more exhausted than he'd thought.

He dismissed the funny feeling and started reading. Over the past month, the killer had kidnapped five men in the Sacramento area and torn them to shreds. The coroner had mistakenly called the first three murders animal attacks. Looking at the photos, Clayne could see why. And if the bodies hadn't been found within the city proper, maybe he'd cut the coroner more slack for the error. But when three bodies showed up on your slab, all killed in the same manner with similar ligature marks around the ankles and wrists, even the most incompetent coroner should be able to see those men hadn't been savaged by an animal. At least not the four-legged kind.

The first two bodies had been discovered at construction sites, while the third had been found on a loading dock behind a convention center, and the fourth in an alley behind a club. Even though the file didn't have any details on the fifth murder, Clayne was willing to bet it'd been a body dump as well. Most wild animals Clayne knew didn't go to that kind of trouble to cover their tracks.

The coroner was obviously an idiot. It was bad enough he'd missed the body dump angle, but he should have at least noticed that none of the victims had been fed on. No wild animal goes crazy and kills without taking a nibble here or there.

Thank God some curious reporter had started nosing around when the fourth body showed up or the governor's office might never have stepped in and asked for FBI assistance. Who knew how many more murders would have gone unnoticed?

Of course, it would have been nice if the Bureau hadn't spent nearly a week putting together a task force just in time to find the fifth victim. Now the other media outlets in Sacramento had gotten wind of the story and were sniffing hard. Grisly murders like this were exactly the kind of thing that got a place spattered all over the national news for all the wrong reasons. The governor would be thrilled.

Clayne looked up just as a thin, balding man in a gray suit stepped behind the podium. About damn time they got the briefing started.

"Afternoon. For those of you who don't know me, I'm Senior Special Agent Roger Carhart, and I'll be heading this task force. We'll get into the reason we're all here in a minute, but we have some administrative things to cover first."

There was a serial killer out there and this idiot wanted to talk admin crap? Clayne smothered a curse as Carhart launched into a presentation about reimbursable expenses, which forms to use for filing situation reports, how to file for overtime, where to park, which kind of gas to use in the federal vehicles and where to buy it. The list of asinine topics never ended. The guy even had freaking PowerPoint slides to go with the briefing.

After that, Carhart moved on to the task force's command structure, then went on to introduce the members of the Bureau of Investigation, several detectives from the local PD, and a lieutenant in charge of the patrol officers assigned to the task force. Who was next, his mother?

Clayne didn't bother remembering anyone's name. He wasn't going to be around long enough to need that information. He'd find this killer, figure out if the guy was a human, shifter, or hybrid, then deal with him accordingly. Without a lot of talking and thinking, and sure as hell without filling out expense reports.

He was just about to walk out and get more coffee when Carhart motioned to someone standing in the back on the opposite side of the room.

"Now I'd like to introduce Danica Beckett, one of the lead agents on the case. She'll brief us on what we know up to this point in the investigation."

Clayne stiffened at the name, sure he must have heard wrong. But then he smelled a scent so familiar, so intoxicating that he knew he hadn't. The air left his lungs and he suddenly couldn't breathe. He gripped the folder in his hand in an effort to keep his claws from coming out. Danica-freaking-Beckett. He felt as if he'd just been kicked in the balls.

He didn't dare look at her as she walked to the front of the room and took her place at the podium, afraid if he did, he might completely lose it. Not that he needed to look. He knew every inch of her body from her full, luscious lips to the tiny beauty mark on her right hip, and everywhere in between. Her face had haunted him every moment of every day and night for the past two years until he thought he'd go insane.

But one memory seared hotter than all the others. When the woman he'd loved more than life itself had looked at him with cold, hard eyes and told him she never wanted to see him again.

"Thank you, Agent Carhart."

Her voice might as well have been that of a siren's call for all the power he had to resist it. Unable to help himself, Clayne lifted his head to look at her. She was dressed in a dark pantsuit with a blue blouse underneath, her silky brunette hair up in that twist thing she always did when she was working.

It had been two years since Danica had dumped his ass, and she looked even more beautiful than she had the last time he'd seen her. That only made it worse. It would have been easier if she'd let herself go to hell. It hurt to gaze at her. Getting away from him had clearly done wonders for her.

She nodded to whoever was manning the projector, and the screen changed from the dumbass authorized gas locations to a photo of a man with claw marks on his chest and his throat ripped out.

She slowly scanned the room, making momentary eye contact with each person as she told them about the most recent victim.

"Tom Robbins disappeared from a gym parking lot approximately forty-eight hours before his body was discovered at a warehouse this morning, but according to the coroner, he'd only been dead for six hours by the time we found the body. We have no idea where he was during those missing hours, and no idea where he was murdered."

When her gaze met Clayne's, her eyes went a little wide, but her voice never wavered as she described the number of lacerations the victim had sustained. Obviously, she wasn't as affected by seeing him again as he was seeing her. No surprise there. He knew first-hand what a cold bitch she could be.

Clayne barely listened to the briefing she gave. Torn-up body with over thirty slashes ranging from minor surface penetrations to cuts all the way down to the bone. The FBI had no idea what kind of weapon had caused the wounds, but they appeared to match the previous victims. They had no worthwhile forensic evidence so far, no idea why the men had been murdered, no obvious connection between the victims, and no idea when the killer would strike again. They hadn't even generated a profile of the killer or his victims yet.

When Danica was done, she took questions and gave detailed answers to each one, regardless of who'd asked it or how stupid it was. Clayne didn't want to listen, but he couldn't resist losing himself in the sound of her husky voice. The soft tones and the way she drew out certain vowels—her northeast upbringing coming through—had always gotten to him.

The longer he sat there inhaling her delicious scent, the more pissed he got. She had no right to make him feel like this, dammit. She'd dumped his ass and had made no secret about why. She'd gone out of her way to end their partnership in the most complete and total way possible. He should be thinking of all the different ways he could make her suffer, but instead he was remembering what it had felt like to hold her in his arms and make love to her. And that pissed him off even more.

Something else pissed him off, too. Something that made him want to get up and walk straight out of the Sacramento field office and right back to the airport: John had set his ass up. True, John hadn't known he and Danica had been sleeping together—at least Clayne didn't think so—but he'd known their partnership hadn't ended on a good note. Understatement there. John had to know Clayne would rather take on a whole pack of hybrids by himself than work with his old partner again.

There was no way he didn't know Danica was on this
case. John clearly wanted them working together again.
But why?

Clayne didn't know, and he didn't care. The blatant
manipulation was enough to make him unleash his inner
animal right there in the middle of the conference room,
witnesses be damned.

Somehow, he kept it together until Danica was finished with her briefing. The moment she was done, he
was out of the room and heading for the elevator. He
punched the down button with his thumb, wishing
he could put his fist through the wall instead. Down the
hall, feds and local cops poured from the conference
room. Dammit. He'd hoped to be long gone before
anyone came out. And they were heading his way, too.
Shit.

While most of them regarded him curiously, one of
the suits wearing a visitor's badge extended his hand.
Clayne knew it'd be too much to hope they'd ignore him.

"Jeremy Weathers from BI," the man said. "I didn't
catch your name."

Because I didn't give it, smart-ass. The words were
on the tip of his tongue, but Clayne bit them back. John
had told him to be discreet, and even though he felt like
killing his boss at the moment, the DCO director was
right about playing nice with these people. Growling at
them and shoving them up against the wall wasn't going
to improve this screwed-up situation anyway. So he put
on his happy face and shook the man's hand.

"Clayne Buchanan. Homeland Security."

Weathers's eyes narrowed. "What's DHS doing
working a serial killer case?"

Clayne gave the man a shrug. "Just lending a hand, that's all."

"Does DHS think the guy we're after is a terrorist?"

The question came from a stocky blond-haired man with an FBI badge. Where the hell was that elevator?

Clayne shook his head. "No, nothing like that."

Senior Special Agent Carhart had joined the group and was eyeing him with the same interest as everyone else.

"If the killer isn't a suspected terrorist, why is Homeland Security wasting its resources helping us look for him?" Carhart asked.

Clayne ground his jaw. What Carhart really wanted to know was whether the Department of Homeland Security—the DHS—was going to swoop in and take over his investigation. Kind of like the FBI had done to the locals.

"I just go where I'm told," he said.

"Is that so?" The superior look Carhart gave him probably would have been a lot more intimidating if Clayne wasn't a foot taller and outweighed him by seventy pounds. "What exactly do you add to the team, Agent Buchanan?"

Clayne barely suppressed a growl. He'd been willing to stick to the script and play nice like John wanted, but he didn't need some pencil-pushing prick getting in his face because he was worried someone might steal his glory. It had been a really bad day already, and it'd feel damn good to rip off this asshole's face.

The thought made his fangs tingle in that pleasant way they did before they elongated. He still had enough control to prevent it, but that didn't stop him from forming a nice visual in his head of making this jerk piss all over himself in fear. Then he'd see what Clayne added to the team.

Carhart was oblivious to the ass whooping Clayne was about to lay on him, but the people around them must have picked up on the hostile tension because they were eyeing him and the fed warily.

"He hunts people." Danica's words effectively stuck a needle in the balloon that had been the only fun this day was going to provide. That was the second time she'd snuck up on him since he'd gotten there. He was seriously off his game. "He has the unique ability to track down bad people."

The men and women gathered around him and Carhart turned to look at her. There wasn't a room that Danica couldn't command when she wanted to. Clayne used to think he was the only one she had that effect on because he'd been so in love with her, until he'd seen her do it to heads of state and foreign military leaders. It obviously worked on FBI agents, too.

Carhart frowned at her. "You two know each other? I didn't see anything in your file saying you worked interagency with DHS, Agent Beckett."

"We worked together a few years ago," she answered smoothly. "I think you'll discover Agent Buchanan is a valuable asset to the team."

Carhart's mouth tightened. "That remains to be seen. Since you worked with Buchanan in the past, he stays with you at all times. I don't want anyone going rogue on this task force. I don't care what agency he works for."

Danica looked about as thrilled with that order as

Clayne was, but Carhart strode down the hall before either of them could say anything.

The elevator doors finally opened. Damn things.

Clayne would have jumped on, but the BI guy he'd been talking to earlier beat him to it. The rest of the people waiting hurriedly crowded on, leaving Clayne with Danica and a tall, dark-haired man. Clayne waited for the man to bolt like everyone else, but he stayed where he was.

"Good to see you haven't let those valuable social skills of yours deteriorate in the last two years," Danica said when the elevator doors had closed. She glanced at the man beside her. "This is my partner, Tony Moretti. Tony, Clayne Buchanan."

Moretti offered his hand, but Clayne didn't take it. The fed studied Clayne with dark eyes, as if he didn't know exactly what to think of him. Clayne, on the other hand, knew exactly what he thought of Danica's partner—he hated him.

Danica sighed. "Some things never change, do they?" She shook her head and glanced at her watch. "We have a little bit of daylight left. I assume you'd like to see the most recent crime scene?"

Ten minutes ago, Clayne wanted to be anywhere but in this building. Now he wasn't sure he wanted to leave, not if it meant going with Danica and her partner.

"Give me the address," he said. "I'll check it out myself."

Danica shook her head. "Uh-uh. You want to see it, you get an FBI escort. And thanks to my big mouth, Carhart's decided that's going to be Tony and me. So, let's go."

She pressed the button for the elevator, then stood there with her eyes focused on the doors and her arms folded underneath her perfect breasts. Damn, he hated her with a vengeance right then.

Clayne swore under his breath. He didn't care what it took, he was going to find this killer in record time, then get his ass the hell out of California. Because there was no way he was spending one minute longer with his ex-partner-slash-lover than he had to.

—⁓—

If looks could kill, Danica knew she'd be dead right now. Clayne's dark eyes had been boring a hole in her head from the backseat of the sedan since they'd gotten in the car. She refused to squirm. She'd almost lost her lunch when she'd seen him in the conference room at the FBI offices. She thought she'd been mistaken at first. But there was no mistaking the square jaw, sensuous mouth, and arching brows. Or those liquid brown eyes. And while his dark hair was longer than it had been, she'd known it was most definitely him.

She'd come that close to saying the hell with the briefing and bolting, but then got a grip on herself. She couldn't run away again. She'd already done that, and there wasn't any place left in the continental United States that was farther away from Clayne than where she'd run to. So, she'd gritted her teeth and finished the briefing, only screwing up about every third or fourth word.

She'd known she was going to regret calling John. She just hadn't known how much. Why the hell had he sent Clayne? If there was one person from the DCO she hadn't wanted to see, it was him.

She'd thought Clayne was already long gone when she'd walked into the hallway. Instead, she'd found him in a pissing contest with Carhart. She'd thought he was going to bite the head off her new boss. It was like he hadn't matured a day since she'd left him. He was still letting his inner animal handle every situation.

But while there hadn't been any growth in the maturity department, she couldn't miss the fact that Clayne had definitely filled out in other areas. Her ex-partner looked like he'd put on fifteen or twenty pounds of muscle since she'd last seen him. He'd always been broad in the chest and shoulders, but he'd seriously bulked up. She had a thing for well-built guys and Clayne looked damn fine in his suit. She knew from experience how fine he looked underneath it, too. She wouldn't go there. *Right*. Like that was going to help. The heat he was generating from the backseat was enough to make her feel hot all over.

It wasn't just memories of mind-blowing sex seeing him again had brought back. It was the little, everyday things she and Clayne had shared—things she'd convinced herself she could live without. Like running to the bakery on the corner for fresh bagels on a Sunday morning, then going back to his apartment and eating them naked in bed. Spending a lazy weekend cuddling up on the couch so they could catch up on all the TV shows they'd DVR'd. Getting out of the city and going for a drive in his mint-condition 1976 Dodge Charger to nowhere in particular.

"Earth to Danica."

Crap. How long had Tony been talking to her?

"What?"

He glanced at her. "I asked if you wanted to come over for dinner after work."

Clayne let out a low growl from the backseat. It was a sound Danica was all too familiar with. That was his way of saying he was this close to sinking his claws into someone. Her gaze darted to her partner, hoping he hadn't heard, but Tony was giving him a strange look in the rearview mirror. With the kind of mood Clayne was in, he'd yank Tony into the backseat—regardless of the fact that he was driving—so he could smash his face into the side window a few times.

"Maybe," she said to Tony. "If we're not pulling an all-nighter."

Behind her, Clayne made what sounded suspiciously like another growl. If she didn't know better, she'd think he was jealous. But that was insane. It didn't take a genius to know he wanted nothing to do with her. After what she'd done to him, why would he?

Tony mumbled something in agreement as he pulled up outside the warehouse where they'd found the body that morning, but Danica barely heard him. She got out of the car and breathed in some much-needed air. Maybe it'd clear her head because it was spinning right now. It helped, at least until Clayne stepped out. Man, she'd forgotten how tall he was. She wasn't short by any means, but he towered over her. She stepped back to put some distance between them.

"I'm going to check-in with the local PD. Let 'em know we'll be looking around," Tony said, jerking his head toward the two cops leaning against a parked patrol car a few yards away.

Clayne's eyes were hard as they followed her partner. "Are you screwing him?"

Danica stared at him, her mouth open. She knew better than most that Clayne Buchanan could be ruthless and brutal when he wanted to be, but having it directed at her hurt.

His lip curled. "That's what you do, isn't it? Screw your partner, then screw him over."

The fact that his voice was cold and flat only made the things he said worse. If he was furious, that would be one thing. It was as if he wanted his words to hurt her as much as possible.

Well, it worked. But she wasn't going to let him see that. She wasn't going to slap his face, either, even though her hand was itching to. Because while Clayne's barbs stung, they were no more than she deserved. She couldn't simply walk away from a confrontation with him, though. The best way to deal with Clayne's in-your-face attitude was to get right back in his. He'd see anything else as weakness. Her old boss at the DCO had told her that the day he'd hired her.

"Tony is a happily married man, and his wife is one of my closest friends."

Clayne growled. "That doesn't answer my question."

He never did know when to quit. "No, I'm not screwing Tony," she said, somehow managing to keep her voice even. And if she left it at that, maybe it would have been enough to soothe the savage beast inside Clayne. But he might think that was her way of trying to reconcile, and she couldn't risk that. So she lifted her chin and fixed him with a frosty look. "Not that it would be any of your damn business if I was."

The pain on his face brought tears to her eyes, and Danica quickly turned and hurried toward the warehouse before he could see them. Dammit, she hadn't wanted to hurt him again. She hadn't wanted to hurt him two years ago, either, but she had.

Danica tried to focus on the crime scene, but it was worthless. There could have been a forty-foot monster outside the warehouse and she would have walked right past it. Two years was a long time to remember something. Or maybe it wasn't. Not when the thing you remembered was the night that changed your life and that of the man you loved forever.

She and Clayne had just gotten back to his apartment. They'd been at the training complex all day and were both exhausted. Not too exhausted to make love, though—they'd never been too exhausted for that. When Clayne had tossed his duffel bag of gear on the floor and wrapped his arms around her, it had taken everything in her to push him away. She knew if he kissed her, she'd never be able to walk away from him. The confusion on his face had broken her heart.

"I can't do this anymore."

"Do what?" he asked.

"This." She gestured with her arm, sweeping the apartment. *"Us."*

He'd wanted to talk it out, figure out what was wrong. What he'd done wrong. But she'd just kept shaking her head. She couldn't give him a reason, not the real one anyway. Clayne wouldn't let her go until she did, though. So she'd said something she knew would completely sever their partnership, both professionally and personally.

"What did you think, Clayne? That I'd spend the rest of my life with a freak like you and bear your pups?"

The words had been beyond cruel, but they'd done their job. Clayne hadn't tried to stop her from leaving after that.

He brushed past her now and strode into the warehouse without saying a word. He didn't have to. The hatred coming off him in waves said more than enough. Danica stopped and leaned against the metal siding of the building to compose herself. This case was going to be tough enough, but working with her former partner was going to make it ten times worse.

She had seriously screwed Clayne over when she'd left. She may have done it for his own good, but she'd still hurt him worse than he'd ever been hurt by anyone. Clayne had spent the years before they'd met building a fortress around himself. The only reason she'd been able to damage him as badly as she had was because he'd let those walls down for her. And she'd used that precious gift to cause him pain. It had been the only way to get him to let go.

———————

Clayne knew he was dealing with a shifter the moment he walked into the warehouse, but he prowled around the interior anyway, both to confirm what his nose told him and to make sure there was only one killer. He didn't know exactly what kind of shifter it was yet because he couldn't pick up enough scent molecules from a few footsteps. The killer had walked in, dumped the body, then walked out. No big surprise there. The victim Danica and Moretti found this morning had been the shifter's fifth kill—that they knew about anyway. He'd moved past the tentative and careful stage a while ago. Now he was simply cold, confident, and calculating.

He saw Danica and her partner watching him. Danica knew what he was doing, but Moretti had an irritated look on his face. He probably thought Clayne was wasting his time. Maybe he'd rather be at his place with Danica—having dinner.

Clayne bit back a growl and deliberately took his time walking back to the spot on the floor where the body had been just because he knew it'd piss off Moretti some more. It was juvenile, especially since he'd grudgingly accepted Danica probably wasn't sleeping with the man. She'd sounded sincere when she said his wife was her best friend.

Then again, she'd said a lot of things to him before she'd dumped him that had sounded sincere too, so maybe he just had a shitty lie detector.

He stopped screwing around and went down on one knee beside the big bloodstain on the concrete floor.

"It's hard to believe the murder didn't happen here with all that blood," Moretti said.

"This isn't a lot of blood," Clayne said.

The fed snorted. "Looks like a lot of blood to me."

"That's only because you haven't spilled enough of it to know better."

"Clayne," Danica warned.

Clayne ignored her. She'd given up the right to be in charge of his attitude a long time ago.

He leaned in close to the stain, trying to separate the scent of the victim from the scent of the killer. It was tough. There'd been so many cops and crime scene investigators around the body he was having a hard time picking up the shifter's scent. He finally got down on his hands and knees and put his nose close to the floor.

"What, Homeland Security can't afford a blood-hound?" Moretti said.

Clayne looked up at Moretti with a growl. Not a serious growl that would make the guy's hair stand on end. Just a soft I-don't-like-you growl. While Moretti might not be sleeping with his ex-partner, it would still be satisfying to punch him. Fortunately for Moretti, there wasn't time for fun and games like that.

Moretti shook his head. "I'm going to go call the coroner's office and tell them we'll be swinging by in a few," he said to Danica. "Maybe we'll learn something worthwhile there."

Clayne waited until Moretti left the building before leaning closer to the bloodstain. Now that he didn't have to worry about the fed, he could really get his nose into the mishmash of scents. This close, he could finally separate them and find the one that belonged to the shifter. It smelled a little like Ivy—without all the good parts. Which meant the killer was a cat shifter of some kind. Good. After seeing the photos of the victims, he'd been worried it was a hybrid.

As he stood up, Danica caught his eye, a question on her face. Since she'd called the DCO in on this, she already knew it was a shifter attack, but she wanted confirmation. He considered keeping the answer to himself, just to be a prick, but that would be beyond stupid. People were dying here. He threw a glance toward the door. Moretti was out by the car on his cell phone.

"It's a shifter. Probably a cat of some kind. A seriously messed-up one at that."

"Dammit." She sighed. "Guess that means we're stuck with each other."

"I'm not thrilled with that any more than you are, believe me." He checked on Moretti again. The fed was still on the phone. "Want to tell me what clued you in to the shifter angle before your partner comes back?"

Danica told him she'd first suspected when she saw the wounds, but wasn't sure until the guy she'd chased on the roof had leaped across thirty feet of empty space to the neighboring building.

"Show me the catwalk," he said. "And the roof."

Danica led Clayne up the stairs, detailing the chase and how it ended. All he could think about was how stupid she'd been to go after the guy while her partner played babysitter for a couple of rookie beat cops. But that'd always been the way Danica operated. Damn the torpedoes, full-speed ahead. That's what came from growing up with three older brothers and a determination to do everything they did, he supposed. And while it was something that infuriated him, it was one of the things that had drawn him to her.

Following the shifter's trail, Clayne jumped to the other roof while Danica waited on the roof of the warehouse. It was one hell of a jump. The shifter he was after was ballsy, that was for sure.

He followed the trail down to the street, but the killer's scent disappeared within a block. He growled in frustration. What the hell good was his keen sense of smell if he couldn't track someone when they got in a car?

Swearing under his breath, he took the stairs two at a time to get back up to the roof, then leaped across to the warehouse where Danica was waiting impatiently.

"He must have gotten into a car," Clayne told her. "Not surprising. The only thing I can't understand is why the killer came back after he dumped the body."

"What do you mean, came back?"

"The scent up on the catwalk is six or eight hours fresher than the scent down by the body."

Danica frowned. "Maybe he was the one who called 9-1-1. Maybe he was watching to make sure someone found the body."

"Maybe," Clayne agreed.

It seemed risky, though. Hopefully, it meant they were dealing with an idiot who'd make a mistake. But Clayne didn't think so. Whoever this shifter was, he was smart enough not to have slipped up yet. Then again, he hadn't had his own kind hunting him.

Moretti was waiting for them downstairs with an impatient look on his face. "Where'd you two go?"

"Clayne wanted to check out the roof," Danica told him.

Her partner frowned, but then shook his head. "Forget it. I don't even want to know. If you're done wandering around, Agent Buchanan, we can head over to the coroner's office. He's waiting for us."

So let him wait. Considering this was the same coroner who'd said the first three victims were attacked by an animal, they weren't likely to learn anything from him anyway. But there was a hell of a lot Clayne could learn from taking a look at the body of the most recent victim, so he nodded.

The coroner was a short, heavyset man with a bushy mustache and a stutter that became more pronounced when he set eyes on Clayne.

"This ain't a damn p-petting zoo, you know," he said after Danica told him they were there to see the body that had been brought in that morning.

Muttering something even Clayne's ears couldn't make sense of, he waddled over to the wall of refrigerator units, opened the one marked Robbins, then pulled out the stainless-steel table and yanked back the sheet covering the body.

Danica said Robbins had been at the gym when the killer grabbed him, but Clayne hadn't expected him to be in such seriously good shape. Why the hell would a shifter go after a guy who could fight back?

"Can you give us a minute?" Danica asked the coroner.

The man waved his hand. "Take all the time you need. I got paperwork to finish up anyway."

She waited until he was out of earshot, then reached down and lifted the victim's upper lip with a gloved finger. The right canine tooth was gone.

"We kept this out of all the briefings and reports, but the killer likes to take a trophy. The same tooth is missing on every victim."

Weird, but it wasn't unheard of for a serial killer to take a trophy. Beyond the slashes and gouge marks that could be contributed directly to shifter claws, there were dozens of shallow scratches all over the victim. Clayne turned the man on his side so he could take a look at the back of the body. There was a horizontal slash behind the left knee. It was deep, too—damn near to the bone. The guy had been freaking hamstrung.

"He was hunted," Clayne said.

Moretti frowned. "What do you mean, hunted?"

"These scratches are the kind you get from thorns and branches when you're running for your life through the underbrush." Clayne pointed to the jagged claw marks. "These are from the killer. See how he struck different places on the victim's body? Chest, upper back, lower back, arms, thighs, stomach? They would have hurt like hell, but they aren't nearly deep enough to be fatal. The killer was playing with the victim, hitting him fast and hard, then slipping away to come back from another direction. He wanted the victim to run so it'd make the hunt more interesting."

Moretti made a face. "That's sick. How the hell could a person hunt another human being like this?"

"The killer played with Robbins for a while, but at some point he got bored with the game," Clayne said instead. "That was when the killer sliced through the guy's hamstring. Robbins wouldn't have been able to do more than crawl after that. That was when the murderer came in for the kill and tore out his throat."

"But what the hell did he tear it out with?" Moretti wondered.

Clayne saw Danica give him a warning look. She should know to give him more freaking credit than that.

"Something sharp," he said.

Moretti sighed. "Okay, so what does all this tell us?"

"At this point, not much," Clayne admitted. "We can have the coroner look at the previous victims, but I'm assuming they'll all bear wounds that support the hunting angle. All we know for sure is that the killer is fast. And that this is a game to him. A game he's damn good at playing. Which means one thing for sure."

"What's that?" Danica asked warily.

"That we'd better work fast. Because if the killer doesn't already have his next victim, he soon will. The adrenaline rush from a good hunt is like nothing else, but it goes away fast. This guy will be looking to hunt again—soon."

Danica couldn't overcome the emptiness she felt as Clayne drove off in his rental car. When they'd first gotten back to the FBI offices, she'd had this crazy urge to ask him to grab something to eat, but she knew that would only make things harder for both of them.

"Your invitation for dinner still open?" she asked Tony as the taillights of Clayne's car disappeared around the corner. It was late and his wife probably didn't feel like having company, but Danica didn't want to go home to her tiny apartment just yet. She'd only end up thinking about Clayne.

"Definitely." Tony pulled out his cell phone. "I'll call Beth and tell her you're coming."

"Tell her not go to any trouble," Danica said.

"I'm sure she'll just grab a couple pies from Masullo's or something."

Danica doubted that. Beth Moretti was a classically trained chef with a very successful catering company. If she knew Beth, her friend would have a four-course meal waiting for them by the time they got there. While it was guaranteed to taste amazing, Danica'd almost certainly have to go for an extra-long run afterward just to work off all the calories. It'd be worth it, though. Besides, it wasn't as if she was going to get much sleep tonight anyway with Clayne prowling through her psyche.

She was right. Beth had cooked a big Italian dinner. The mouthwatering aroma of garlic and oregano hit her the moment she walked through the door. Her stomach growled, reminding her she hadn't eaten since the soup and sandwich she'd had for lunch almost eight hours ago. She groaned softly when she thought of all those extra calories again, but she never could say no to Beth's food.

Her blond friend hurried over and hugged her like she hadn't seen her in ages even though Danica ate dinner at their house at least once a week. Danica felt a little guilty for taking advantage of their hospitality, but if it weren't for Beth, she'd never eat a home-cooked meal. That wasn't her fault—the oven in her apartment didn't work. Even if it did, she hated cooking for one person.

"Go wash up," Beth said. "The chicken parmesan is just about done."

Danica took her time in the guest bathroom, giving Tony time to say hello to his wife in private. While Beth might be outgoing and bubbly, Tony was reserved to the extreme. The only time Danica could remember seeing him kiss his wife in public was at their wedding.

By the time she walked into the dining room, the parmesan was out of the oven and Beth had drizzled the salad with Danica's favorite dressing.

"Beth, you didn't have to do all this," Danica admonished as she sat down.

Her friend waved her hand dismissively. "It was

nothing. I had some leftovers from the bridal shower I catered today. If we don't eat it, I'd have to throw it away."

Danica didn't believe her, but didn't call her bubbly friend on it. Instead, she took a bite of salad and sighed. Beth wouldn't tell her what was in the homemade dressing, which only made it that much better.

"I don't know how you stay so fit, Tony," she said as she speared a tomato. "If I ate like this every night, I'd be as big as a house."

Beth laughed and gave her a wink. "I make sure Tony gets plenty of exercise before we go to bed. Sometimes twice on Saturdays."

Her partner flushed and ducked his head, examining his salad like it was evidence at a crime scene. Danica shook her head. Reserved didn't even begin to cover it.

Beth handed Danica a bowl of freshly grated parmesan cheese. "So, fill me in on this new case you two are working."

Danica almost laughed when Tony sagged with relief. Serial murders weren't exactly dinner conversation, but her partner obviously preferred talking about that to his sex life. He avoided the gory details of the investigation, but told his wife about everything else, including what a jerk Special Agent Carhart was. Thankfully, he left Clayne out of it.

The pasta stuck in her throat at the thought of her ex, and she gulped some water. It was hard being around him and pretending she didn't care. While she'd walked out on him for all the right reasons, not loving him hadn't been one of them. It had been two extremely long years. Her feelings should have subsided. But if anything, they were even stronger. She didn't know how the heck she was going to keep it together long enough to deal with this serial killer. But she had to. She couldn't risk slipping up, even once.

"Danica, honey," Beth said. "Don't you like the chicken parm?"

Danica looked down and realized she'd been pushing her chicken around the plate without eating it. "Oh no, it's great. I was just thinking about the case."

Across from her, Tony snorted. "More like thinking about your ex-partner." He glanced at his wife. "DHS sent him to help out with the investigation."

Beth's eyes went wide. "Clayne is here?"

Danica could have smacked Tony. While she hadn't told him much about Clayne—nothing really—she'd told Beth plenty, except the real reason she'd broken up with him, of course. And from the way her friend's blue eyes were twinkling, she wasn't going to let something this juicy go until Danica told her everything.

"It still doesn't make sense." Tony helped himself to another piece of chicken. "I know what Clayne said to Carhart, but why the hell would Homeland send him to help catch a serial killer? Don't get me wrong, he seems like a sharp guy. The way he came up with the hunting angle was damn impressive. But you have to admit, he's kind of strange. All that time he spent checking out those blood stains? I swear he was sniffing them. He's a freak, if you ask me."

"He's not a freak," Danica said sharply. "He just approaches situations from a completely different angle than the rest of us. And he's damn good when he does it."

She hadn't realized she'd raised her voice until she saw Tony staring at her from across the table, a forkful of chicken halfway to his mouth.

"Tony, honey," Beth said quietly. "I have three souf-flés in the warming oven. Could you heat up the choco-late sauce that's in the fridge?"

Tony stared at her, then looked down at his plate. "I'm not finished eating."

Beth smiled. "Take your plate with you. That way you can eat while you stir."

He made a face. "You know I suck at that stuff."

"Keep the flame turned down and you'll be fine," she said. "Just remember to stir it continuously or it'll scald."

Tony sighed but picked up his plate and stood. "Okay, babe. Three soufflés with chocolate sauce, coming up. I'm sure you two can come up with something to talk about while I'm in the kitchen."

Danica actually felt a little bad Tony had been rel-egated to KP duty. But that was what he got for spilling his partner's secrets.

The moment Tony was out of earshot, Beth turned to her. "So, how does he look?"

Danica stabbed fiercely at a piece of chicken and stuffed it in her mouth. "How does who look?"

"Your ex, you dummy! Who did you think I was talk-ing about?"

Danica shoved another piece of chicken in her mouth, mumbling around it. "I knew who you were talking about."

"And?"

Danica hoped Tony was having a really hard time in there with that chocolate sauce. "Unfortunately,

Clayne looks good. Better than good, actually. In fact, he looks like a six-foot-six ripped Adonis crossed with that actor who played in the remake of that barbarian movie."

"I know who you're talking about, and damn." Beth frowned. "So, what's unfortunate about that?"

Danica put down her fork and flung herself back in the chair, arms folded. "Call me shallow, but a woman likes to think a man might have a hard time moving on when she walks out on him. But Clayne looks better now than he did when we were together. And believe me, he looked amazing back then."

"Honey, it's not shallow at all. In fact, it's completely understandable." Beth sipped her water. "So, does he still have a thing for you like you do for him?"

Damn, did her friend know how to get down to the brass tacks or what? "I don't still have a thing for him."

Beth lifted a brow.

"Okay, maybe I do," Danica muttered. "But as for him, that would be a big hell no. He hates the idea of working with me, much less being in the same room with me."

And God, did that hurt.

"Well, you did break up with him, you know."

Danica frowned at the reminder. "I didn't have a choice."

"Because Homeland Security has some stupid policy about partners not hooking up, right? You're not his partner anymore. If you and Clayne want to rekindle the flame, what's stopping you?"

The part that Beth knew nothing about, that's what. And Danica couldn't explain it to her. As far as she knew, Danica had broken up with Clayne because she hadn't wanted to jeopardize her career.

"Did you miss the part where I said Clayne looks at me like I'm something stuck to the bottom of his shoe?"

Beth picked up a slice of garlic bread and nibbled on it. "I heard you. But if you ask me, that just means he still cares about you."

Danica wished. "Let's just agree that it's complicated and leave it at that. Suffice to say, the things keeping Clayne and me from getting back together are the same things that split us up in the first place. And it was more than some stupid policy about not getting involved with your partner."

"Like what?"

"Nothing that I want to talk about. I'm going to focus on this case and catch this psycho so Clayne can go back to DC and I can go back to my life."

Beth nodded. "That's very mature of you. But you're forgetting one thing."

"What's that?"

"That six-foot-six ripped Adonis you mentioned. You seriously think you're going to be able to stay away from him?"

"I have to," was all Danica said.

Not for her sake, but for Clayne's.

Chapter 3

"HAVE YOU HEARD FROM LANDON AND IVY YET?"

Kendra looked up from her computer to see John poking his head in her office. "Yeah. Ivy called me last night. Their whole return trip was a nightmare. They got hung up in Manila for two days. They'll be in later this morning."

John shook his head. "I'm starting to think they're cursed. I've never heard of anyone having so many problems. If their plane isn't breaking down, they're getting bumped from the flight. Remind me to never travel with them."

Kendra laughed, but as soon as her boss left, she immediately felt guilty about lying to him. Again. But what was she going to tell him? That his two best co-vert agents were running their own operation behind his back, and that his senior behavioral-scientist-slash-training-officer-slash-personal-assistant was helping them do it?

John had Ivy and Landon, along with a dozen other agents, looking into any lead that might tell them where Klaus and Renard, the doctors who'd developed the hybrid process, might be hiding. But as far as Ivy was concerned, they weren't doing it fast enough. So she and Landon were slipping away in between legit missions to check out possible sites that John thought weren't strong enough to waste DCO assets on. John would freak out if he knew, but Kendra couldn't refuse to help her best friend. Especially since Ivy would do the same for her if some demented doctors were using samples of her DNA to create whacked-out hybrids. So Kendra did what she could by slipping into the agency's intel databases and sniffing out leads on possible labs, then getting Ivy and Landon into those places without the DCO knowing about it. It was dangerous work—well, not as dangerous as actually going to those places—but it made her feel like she was contributing to the cause.

It was also a hell of a lot more exciting than observing training exercises and analyzing data. She loved her job, but after ten years, she was tired of sitting on the sidelines. She wasn't asking to become a full-fledged operative, but she wouldn't mind going on a few missions now and then. Unfortunately, John wouldn't even think about sending her into the field.

All that being said, her job was still more satisfying than her social life. Which—thanks to her epic fail of a date with Clayne Buchanan—sucked right now.

After years of crushing on the big, handsome wolf shifter, she'd been thrilled when he'd finally asked her out. So she'd put on her sexiest little black dress and gone to the steak house determined to seduce him.

She should have realized they weren't going to hit it off when Clayne gave her one-word answers to every question she asked during dinner—even the ones that required more than that. She'd told herself that wasn't unusual—he'd never been much of a talker. Hoping he'd loosen up if they were alone, she'd invited him back to her place. She'd been sure the moment they hit the sheets, they'd be on fire.

She'd been wrong. It hadn't been the worst sex she'd
ever had, but it definitely hadn't been the earthshaking
experience she hoped it'd be. Maybe she simply set un-
realistic expectations no man could live up to. If Clayne,
the man she'd been sure was The One, didn't rock her
world—in bed or out—that didn't give her much hope
for the rest of the male species. Then again, maybe she
just had lousy taste in men. But that wasn't fair. Clayne
was a great guy. They simply hadn't connected.

Kendra sighed as she turned back to her computer.
But instead of working on the report she was writing,
she opened the matchmaking program she'd created—
the one she'd used to pair up Ivy and Landon. She almost typed in her own name, hoping to find her perfect
mate, but chickened out. What if it said there wasn't a
guy for her? She cringed as she remembered writing the
default response the program was supposed to give if it
couldn't find one: *Sorry, no match found. It's hopeless.*
She typed in Clayne's name instead.

After a few minutes of sorting, the software spit
out a name—Danica Beckett. Well, damn. Clearly, the
program wasn't as foolproof as Kendra thought. It had
been dead-on with Ivy and Landon, but had missed by a
mile with Clayne and Danica. Because, in Danica's own
words, she and Clayne had been a train wreck.

Kendra had always suspected the two had been
more than partners, but she didn't know for sure until
Danica confessed during the exit debriefing that she
and Clayne had violated department policy by getting
involved with each other and that it had ended badly.
Kendra tried to persuade Danica to stay, explaining she
could get John to team her up with someone else, but

the woman had refused, saying it would be too painful for both of them.

Which was why Kendra supposed the DCO had a nonfraternization policy. The downside to having partners get romantically involved was that you ended up losing one of them when things didn't work out.

"Promise me you'll keep an eye on Clayne," Danica had said before she left.

Kendra blushed. Somehow, she doubted the other woman had meant keeping an eye on Clayne's naked body while they had sex.

A knock on the door interrupted her thoughts. She looked up, smiling when she saw Ivy and Landon. Both tall and dark-haired, they were dressed casually in jeans and T-shirts. With Ivy's exotic beauty and Landon's rugged good looks, they made a very attractive couple.

"Hey!" She closed the matchmaking program with a quick click. "Man, am I glad you're back. John's been looking for you and I was starting to run out of excuses."

Ivy's dark eyes filled with alarm as she exchanged looks with her husband.

"Don't worry," Kendra added. "I told him you got hung up in Manila. He doesn't suspect anything."

Her friend visibly relaxed. "Thanks for covering for us. Again."

"I'll go talk to him," Landon said. "He's probably interested to know what happened in Japan." He glanced at his wife. "Stay and catch up with Kendra."

Kendra smiled as the two newlyweds went through their little I-love-you-ritual before Landon left. When they were at home or on a mission, the two could act like any other couple in love, but it was a different story at the DCO offices. They had to stay in their we're-just-partners mode every second because if anyone suspected anything, they'd both be fired. Or at the very least, split up.

So the feline shifter and her ex–Special Forces husband had come up with some simple coded gestures to say "I love you" without anyone else knowing it. Ivy would touch the engagement and wedding rings she wore on a necklace under her shirt. And Landon rubbed his ring finger on his left hand, as if he were rotating an invisible wedding band around and around in circles. There were some people who'd probably think it was mushy, but Kendra thought it was romantic.

"Did you and Landon find anything in Batan?" Kendra asked as Ivy sat down in the chair beside her desk.

The small island in the Philippines was the latest in a string of locations where Klaus and Renard, the creeps who'd kidnapped Ivy and harvested her DNA all those months ago, had supposedly set up a lab.

Ivy threw a quick glance out the open door, her waist-length hair swinging over her shoulder.

"Dick's at the DC office this week," Kendra said.

Hiding stuff from John was one thing, because he was a trusting man. Dick wasn't. He'd been suspicious of Ivy and Landon from the moment they'd teamed up, and his suspicions had only gotten stronger after what had happened with the hybrids. Dick refused to believe events had gone down the way Ivy and Landon claimed. He'd stopped one step short of accusing them of lying about it—at least in front of the rest of the DCO. But whenever he cornered them alone, he made sure to let them know he was watching.

"Yeah," Ivy said in answer to Kendra's question. "Dead bodies of people they experimented on and an empty lab."

Kendra felt as much as heard the despair in her friend's voice. She hadn't seen the makeshift labs the doctors set up, but from what Ivy and Landon described, she knew they were horrific places. Rooms with metal beds and bug-infested mattresses with shackles to hold the test subjects in place while they were injected with the serum that was supposed to turn them into hybrids. Blood on the floor and sometimes the walls. Implements that looked like they'd be better suited for torture than medicine.

"They dumped the bodies in a mass grave." Ivy's eyes shimmered with tears. "I couldn't even bring myself to look at them this time. I felt awful making Landon do it alone, but every time I see the twisted things Klaus and Renard turned those poor people into, I feel like I'm going to be sick."

"At least this lead wasn't a dead end like the other places." There'd been a lot of those. Kendra leaned forward and covered Ivy's hand with hers. "We're going to find those doctors and we're going to stop them."

Ivy wiped her cheeks with her free hand. "It's just that we never seem to get any closer. We're not a step behind them; we're a whole mile back. Sooner or later, they're going to get the hybrid formula right."

By "getting it right," Ivy meant using her shifter DNA to create the perfect hybrid—one who would have all the attributes of a feline shifter, but with none of the nasty side effects, namely the uncontrollable rage that made them all but useless—and a potential liability.

"They'll slip up long before that," Kendra said. "When they do, you and Landon will be there to take them down."

Ivy's lips curved into a small smile. "You should really think about adding shrink to your list of duties."

Kendra laughed. "And kick poor Marlon out of a job?" she asked, referring to the DCO's resident psychologist.

That got a laugh out of her friend. Ivy hadn't done much of that since the mess in Washington State. "So, what did I miss while Landon and I were away?"

Kendra picked up a stack of papers from her inbox and thumbed through them. "Nothing."

Ivy lifted a brow. "Nothing, huh?"

Sometimes, Ivy's feline intuition was annoying as hell. "Not a thing."

"Did you and Clayne ever go on your date?"

Kendra tossed the stack of papers back in the inbox and straightened her desk. Unfortunately, she was a neat freak when it came to her desk, so there wasn't much that needed straightening. "We did."

"And?"

"And nothing. We went out to dinner, then he took me home."

She hoped that would be enough to satisfy Ivy's curiosity. She should have known better. Her friend sat there with her arms folded and a look on her face that said she'd stay there all day if she had to. Kendra opened her pencil drawer and began reorganizing it.

"Seriously?" Ivy said. "You've been fantasizing about Clayne for years, and that's all you're going to say?"

Kendra didn't answer as she carefully picked up the

thumbtacks that had been rolling around in the drawer for ages and put them back in the container from which they'd escaped.

"I think Marlon would call this avoidance," Ivy mused.

Kendra dropped the last thumbtack in the container and pushed the drawer closed with a curse. "You aren't going to let this go, are you?"

"Nope."

Kendra was afraid of that. "The fact is, Clayne and I didn't hit it off that well."

"Oh." Ivy looked taken aback. And more than a little chagrined that she'd pushed. "Well, first dates are always kind of rough. Maybe when you sleep together…" Her voice trailed off as Kendra shook her head.

"We already slept together. That's what I meant when I said we didn't hit it off that well." Kendra blushed. Ivy might be her best friend, but admitting she and Clayne were dullsville between the sheets was embarrassing.

Ivy's dark eyes went wide. "You and Clayne had sex on the first date?"

"You don't have to say it like that. This isn't the eighteen hundreds, you know. You and Landon had sex on the first date."

"Actually, our first date was in a tent in South America, and we just kissed."

Kendra pinned her with a look.

"Okay. I get the point, and I didn't mean it that way," Ivy said. "I just didn't think things would move that fast. I figured Clayne would need some persuading before he jumped into bed."

"He did, and I provided it." Kendra picked up a pen

and doodled in the bottom corner of her desk calendar. "Turned out not to be one of my best ideas ever."

Her friend regarded her thoughtfully. "So, you two didn't…you know…spark at all?"

"Not even a little. After all this time chasing him, I finally catch him, only to find out we're completely incompatible in the sex department. Talk about a downer."

"That means he isn't the right guy for you." Ivy chewed on her lower lip. "You know, you could think about saying yes when Declan asks you out again."

Kendra fought the urge to roll her eyes. Ivy'd been trying to get her to go out with the bear shifter for months. While Declan was cute in a cuddly sort of way, and she was sure his dark blond hair and electric blue eyes made some women melt, he just didn't do it for her. She kind of wished he did, since he clearly had a crush on her—as was evident by how many times a week he asked her out.

"You know he's not my type, Ivy. He's so quiet and shy."

"It's the shy, quiet ones they say you have to watch out for." Ivy winked. "Maybe Declan does all his talking in the bedroom."

Kendra laughed. She tried to imagine the big, gentle bear that was Declan turning into an animal in bed, but couldn't.

Fortunately, Landon chose that moment to return and save her from any more embarrassment.

"Who does his talking in the bedroom?"

"No one," Ivy told him. "Everything cool with John?"

Landon leaned back against the filing cabinet. The casual pose made his muscles flex under his shirt. "Yeah. He just wanted to debrief me after Japan."

Kendra completely forgot to ask about the real reason they'd gone overseas. She'd get the details from John later.

Ivy nodded. "Does he have anything else for us?"

"Other than training, no."

"Good."

Kendra reached for her coffee mug. "You guys doing something special?"

Ivy made a face. "Not unless you count laundry. Although we might repaint the bedroom." She gave her husband a teasing smile. "For some reason, Landon isn't crazy about the lavender walls. Oh, and we'll probably go visit Jayson. We haven't been to see him in a while."

Kendra tried to place the name as she sipped her coffee. *Oh, that's right.* He'd been Landon's second-in-command back in Special Forces and was currently rehabbing from a devastating injury at the Walter Reed National Military Medical Center in Bethesda. He was super sweet and cute as hell, and while he'd gotten around with a cane at the wedding, it looked like every step was pure agony.

"Tell him I said hello." Kendra put her coffee mug down. "And stop worrying about those doctors. We'll track them down."

"I know." Ivy gracefully got to her feet. "And you think about what I said."

Kendra wanted to ask which part of their conversation Ivy was referring to, but had a sneaking suspicion she knew it had something to do with going out on date with the DCO's teddy bear.

It might have been the endless procession of experts Senior Agent Carhart had lined up to brief them on the task force's investigative approach that had him dragging, but Clayne suspected it had more to do with the lack of sleep he'd gotten the night before. After dinner, he'd used the hotel's workout facilities for two hours in the hopes he'd wear himself out, but instead, he'd lain in bed staring up at the ceiling in the dark, alternating between being pissed off at John for manipulating him into working with his ex-partner again and being furious with Danica for pretending they didn't have a history together. More than once, he'd almost packed his things and gotten his ass on the first flight out of California.

But regardless of how he felt about Danica and the messed up situation he was in, there was still a psychotic shifter out there killing humans at an alarming rate. As much as he wanted to, he couldn't leave until this was over.

Even if he'd gotten a good night's sleep, he'd still be tired of this endless talking. He'd been sitting there for three hours listening to people who'd never left the safe, comfy confines of their offices tell them how to catch a killer.

The profiler from the FBI was the worst. The guy looked like he was twelve, for crying out loud. Clayne wondered if he'd ever seen a murderer outside the pages of a college textbook. His deeply insightful addition to the investigation? The killer was likely a male between twenty-five and forty-five who hated his father. Well, that was useful. Clayne could walk around the streets of Sacramento asking middle-aged men if they liked their daddies.

After the profiler finished, the forensic expert took his turn at the podium. He didn't have a lot to say, either. This killer hadn't left anything behind beyond common dirt and a few tiny pieces of forest mulch. There was nothing to lead them to where the actual murders had occurred—other than somewhere in the woods of Northern California—and no hairs, fiber, trace material, or DNA that might give them a clue where to start looking for the killer. At least the forensic guy was able to confirm that all the victims had sustained some kind of debilitating injury to their hamstring or Achilles prior to their deaths. Which meant Clayne had been right about the hunter angle.

Clayne swore under his breath. He'd just handed the feds their first lead, and they all sat around and stared at each other. It was aggravating as hell and he couldn't suppress a growl. The female agent from the state's Bureau of Investigation turned around to give him a startled look. He bit his tongue and smiled at her. Apparently, his smile must have been just as terrifying because she quickly turned back around.

Damn. He had to get a grip on himself. He'd be the first to admit he wasn't the most patient guy, but he usually didn't let petty bullshit like this get to him so quickly. After being in the DCO for six years, he was used to it. He did a few head rolls to relax and caught a whiff of Danica's scent.

This was definitely one of those times he hated having a superior sense of smell. He'd been subconsciously attempting to push her pheromones to the back of his mind from the moment she'd walked into the room, but it was no good. While he'd been successful in keeping his human half from obsessing on the scent, his animal side had been taking it in the whole time.

After everything she'd done to him, the smell of her body still had an effect on him. It was like they'd never been apart. If anything, her scent was more powerful than it had ever been. He found himself taking those small, short breaths to capture even more of her delectable fragrance.

He bit back another growl. He shouldn't be reacting to her like this. After everything she'd done to him, he should hate her. Her scent should make him physically ill. But instead, it made him remember things he didn't want to. Things he'd wished now had never happened at all. Like walking into his boss's office at the DCO that day four years ago and finding her waiting for him.

Washington, DC, December 2009

Clayne was at the shooting range when John called him in. Despite all the smoke fumes he'd been breathing in for the past hour, he couldn't miss the tantalizing aroma lingering in the air as he headed down the hallway. It was so exquisite he stopped walking and inhaled, letting his wolf out just enough to pinpoint where the smell was coming from. After a few slow circles, he figured out it was John's office. Hot damn.

He picked up his pace, suddenly eager to get there. Usually getting called to John's office meant something bad was coming his way—a reprimand, an attempt at a motivational pep talk, a briefing for a mission he didn't

have any interest in, a partnership pairing that had no
hope of succeeding. But if that delicious scent was coming from John's office, he didn't care what the hell the
man wanted.

He walked in without knocking and almost fell to his
knees as the full impact of the fragrance hit him. As
sweet as peaches mixed with the unmistakable—and
delectable—touch of feminine musk. Which meant it
could only belong to the woman John was talking to.
She was seated on the couch at a slight angle to the doorway, so he couldn't see her face, but the sleek column of
her neck exposed by her upswept hair made him lick his
lips. Another minute and he was going to start drooling.

He'd smelled a lot of humans in his life, and none
of them had come close to the intoxicating scent this
woman was putting off.

"Clayne, there you are." John rose from the wingback
chair. "Sorry to drag you off the range, but there's someone I want you to meet."

The woman got to her feet and turned to face Clayne,
and he had to force himself not to stare. *Daaaammn.*
Whoever she was, she not only smelled amazing, but
looked it, too. With big, brown eyes; smooth, creamy
skin; and wide, full lips—not to mention one hell of a
body—she was the stuff fantasies were made of. His,
anyway. And though he couldn't tell how long her dark
hair was since it was up in a bun, he'd guess it reached
past her shoulders. His fingers itched to pull the clip free
to see if he was right.

If meeting this fine woman was the reason John had
yanked him off the range, he'd have to tell his boss to
do it more often.

As she walked around the coffee table and came closer, Clayne realized she was taller than he'd thought, maybe five ten or eleven. That still made her small compared to him, but at least she could look him in the eye without craning her neck.

Up close, her scent was even more powerful and it was all he could do not to bury his nose in the curve of her neck and breathe deeply. Yeah, he might want to control that particular urge.

He tried to focus on John instead, but he couldn't take his gaze off her. There was a rebelliousness in her dark eyes and a stubborn line to her jaw he hadn't noticed before. His gut told him she wasn't the kind of woman who backed down from anyone, and that made her even more attractive in his book.

"Clayne Buchanan, meet Danica Beckett," John said. "You're going to be her partner."

Clayne was so busy thinking how beautiful her name was that he almost missed the last part. He jerked his gaze away from her to scowl at John. Unlike everyone else at the DCO, his boss didn't even blink.

"What the hell do you mean—partner?"

John regarded him the same way he would a dog who'd just figured out the thing he'd been chasing for the last few minutes had been his own tail. "Partner. As in someone you'll work with on a permanent basis to accomplish the DCO mission. That kind of partner."

Clayne clenched his jaw to keep from letting out his inner wolf and biting John's head off—figuratively, of course. This was the tenth time the DCO had tried to set him up with a partner. And it would be the tenth time he showed them he didn't want or need a partner.

He hated working with other people, especially humans. And while the idea of spending some quality time between the sheets with Danica Beckett appealed to him, the idea that they could be partners was ludicrous. Men couldn't put up with him. What chance did a woman have?

"Forget it," Clayne said firmly. "I've told you before that I don't need a partner. They're dead weight and just get in the way. And if you think that I'll get along better with this one, just because she's a woman, you're wrong. It takes more than a pretty face to get the job done—or get on my good side."

He turned and headed for the door, suddenly having an urge to get back to the range. Shooting something seemed like a really good idea at the moment. But a hand caught his arm and jerked him around. Thinking it was John, he bared his teeth, ready to snarl, only to snap his mouth shut when he saw that it was Danica. *Shit*. Most men were too busy trying not to piss themselves to put a hand on him, much less glare at him with fire in her eyes like she was doing.

"I think you heard John wrong." It was damn hard to even comprehend what she was saying because her scent was so overpowering this close. "He didn't say I was going to be your partner. He said you're going to be mine."

Clayne stared. Obviously, someone had had their Wheaties this morning. What the hell was with this woman?

"John told me that you had problems working with your previous partners and that it affected team performance." She went up on tiptoe so she was almost eye level with him. Not quite even, but almost. "Well, those issues aren't going to hurt our team." She smiled at him, and damn if it didn't make his heart beat faster. "Fortunately for you, I'm good enough at my job to carry your dead weight for a while. But I won't do it forever, so you better get your crap together." She leaned closer, and he damn near passed out from the pheromones she was putting off. "Pay attention, wolf boy. From this moment on, we're a team, so get used to it. Because you don't want this pretty face pissed off at you."

She brushed past Clayne and stormed out of the office. He stared at her retreating back in disbelief. Damn, hadn't he been the one who was going to do that? The woman had just punked his ass in front of his boss, and all he wanted to do was chase after her.

A soft chuckle from behind him brought him back around, and he turned to see John regarding him with the same amused look he'd had on his face earlier.

"What the hell just happened?" Clayne asked.

His boss smiled. "I'd say you just met your match."

Clayne shook off the memory to realize he had a stupid-ass grin on his face and a hard-on in his pants. Thinking too much about Danica always had that effect on him.

He smothered a snarl and picked up his pen. Maybe taking notes would help him think about something other than Danica. But Carhart was already breaking people into investigative focus groups. Another waste of time. Where the hell had this guy gotten his badge?

"Buchanan, you're with Beckett and Moretti," Carhart said.

Yeah, he figured that.

By the time Clayne grabbed his coffee and notepad,

Danica and Moretti were already heading out the door. Apparently, they assumed he'd follow like a good dog.

―◦◦◦―

"I'm going to throw up if I look at these crime scene photos any longer."

Danica glanced up as Tony tossed the pictures on the table in the conference room they'd commandeered. Carhart had assigned them the task of profiling the victims to see if there was any connection between how they were selected. Danica knew right off the bat that Carhart considered this busywork. Her new boss was putting most of the assets on tracking the serial killer. That's where everyone thought the big break in the case was going to come. Profiling victims was backup work, but ever since Clayne showed up, she and Tony had been relegated to the B-Team.

"You're welcome to the witness statements from the friends, neighbors, and relatives." Clayne sat at the end of the table with his boots propped up on an adjacent chair, a tall pile of folders in front of him that was in serious danger of toppling. "I can distill them down into four simple words: I. Don't. Know. Shit."

Danica knew Clayne and Tony had gone through their respective stacks twice already, but so had she. She didn't know what they were complaining about. Thanks to them, she'd gotten stuck with the coroner's reports. Her stack was twice as high as both of theirs put together, full of gory autopsy photos.

"Going over this stuff again and again isn't getting us anywhere." Tony got up and walked over to the whiteboard in the front of the room. "Let's try something different. How about we start with what we know and see where we get?"

Danica expected Clayne to veto that suggestion with a snort and some snarky comment, but to her surprise, he told Tony it was a good idea.

As Clayne moved to sit on the edge of the table, she thought about joining in the discussion, but that meant sitting beside her ex-partner, so she stayed where she was. What the hell did it say about her that she'd rather look at pictures of mutilated people than be close to him?

After a while, even the gruesome photos weren't enough to distract her. No matter what she looked at or read or took notes on, she kept sneaking glances at Clayne. He'd traded in a suit and tie for jeans and a button-down shirt. The material stretched tight across his broad shoulders, reminding her how muscular he was under there. As if she needed a reminder. Her hands practically ached with the need to touch him.

It was so sorry and pathetic that she should have been angry with herself for having these thoughts—especially since he obviously hated her—but it wasn't her fault that her body betrayed her whenever she was around him. Clayne was the only man she'd ever met who could make her forget her own name just by looking at her. Which she nearly did when John had first introduced them years ago.

She smiled at the memory in spite of herself.

The DCO director had wooed her away from the FBI with a promise of more hands-on work at an organization that was at the pointy end of the spear when it came to dealing with the bad guys. She wasn't being challenged

in her job at the New Haven, Connecticut, field office
and had already been thinking about a change of scenery
anyway. Jumping to an ultra-secret covert organization
with domestic and international responsibilities sounded
like just the thing she'd been looking for. The pay and
benefits had certainly been enticing—the agency had
even been willing to find her a place in DC and cover
the cost.

But the thing that had finally swayed her was hearing she'd be teamed up with another agent who'd been
selected specifically to complement her personality
and abilities. While she'd had a partner at the FBI, they
hadn't ever really clicked. If she was going to be doing a
job where she put her life in another person's hands on a
daily basis, she wanted it to be someone who was good at
what he did. John had assured her that her partner at the
DCO was one of the best. What her new boss hadn't told
her—at least until after she'd taken the job—was that
her new partner was a shifter or, as the DCO referred to
them, an Extremely Valuable Asset. Oh, and that she'd
have to eliminate him if they were ever compromised.

She hadn't been sure what to think about the whole
shifter thing, but the kill-your-partner-crap had just
about ended her minty-fresh employment with the DCO.
Only a great deal of tap dancing and assurances from
John that it was simply policy and that no one expected
her to ever have to do it had stopped her from walking
out. She'd still thought she might be making the biggest
mistake of her life and considered backing out of the
job anyway.

Then John had introduced her to Clayne and everything changed.

Okay, so Clayne had been rough around the edges when she'd first met him, and he sure as hell hadn't been thrilled—understatement there—to be paired up with her as a partner. Maybe the reason they'd rubbed each other the wrong way in the beginning was because they were so much alike. Neither was good at hiding their emotions or holding their tongues. So yeah, it had been tough the first six months or so. There were times she'd thought the DCO had been crazy to pair them up.

But once they'd gotten past that rough patch, damn did they click. She smiled at the memory.

—~~~—

Mexico, June 2010

Danica brought the small, silencer-equipped automatic up to cover Clayne as he moved across the courtyard toward the guesthouse behind the main building of the estate. The Beretta .380 felt unnatural in her hands, and she would have given anything to have the familiar grip of her Glock instead. But this had been a true come-as-you-are mission, so all their gear had been supplied by a local DCO contact.

The mission had been thrown together with about ten minutes' worth of planning and even less thought. Some big shot in the Metarone drug cartel had kidnapped the daughter of the U.S. ambassador to Mexico barely more than six hours ago. Understandably, the ambassador was losing his mind, especially when he learned the kidnapper wasn't interested in money but instead wanted the next shipment of high-tech weapons the United States was scheduled to deliver to the Mexican Army to be diverted to his cartel militia within the next twelve hours. If not, the kidnapper would send the ambassador's daughter home in pieces.

Unfortunately, there were several problems with that plan. One, the weapons weren't scheduled to arrive for more than a week, if Congress and the State Department got around to clearing them. Two, the ambassador didn't have a damn thing to do with the weapons, so he couldn't divert them.

While the State Department, CIA, and U.S. military had immediately gotten involved, they'd been more interested in arguing about who should be in charge instead of mounting a rescue. That was when someone called in the DCO. Thirty minutes later, she and Clayne were on a private plane headed for Mexico City, armed with only the kidnapper's identity and the girl's location. The DEA had been watching the cartel closely for over a year and had immediately known the identity of who'd grabbed the ambassador's daughter. All Danica and Clayne had to do was get into a heavily guarded compound, find her, then get back out. It sounded like a simple enough snatch 'n' grab—if they were working from a plan.

But Clayne wasn't really big on plans.

Danica kept her weapon trained on the two balconies overlooking her side of the house. It was dark inside, so she didn't think the risk of detection was very high, but she stayed alert anyway.

Clayne covered the open space at a speed she could never hope to match without the aid of a motor. Once he reached the house's wall, she watched him sniff the air for a while. The concrete and stucco structure would prevent him from getting a good read on any scents coming from inside, but she trusted his nose to tell him if anyone was lurking around outside.

He must have liked what he smelled—or didn't smell in this case—because he waved her over. While Clayne kept an eye—and a nose—out for anyone coming around the corner of the house, he spent most of his time watching her jog toward him. With his shifter-enhanced night vision, she had no doubt he was getting quite the show. Thanks to the clothing their contact had provided, there was a lot to see.

She and Clayne were supposed to be there for the cocktail party the drug lord was throwing. The bastard was ballsy enough to actually entertain guests—including the ambassador—in the main house while his thugs held the girl a few hundred yards away in the guesthouse. The ambassador didn't know the man hosting the gala had his daughter, of course. He only knew his attendance at the party was critical to getting her back—and for getting Danica and Clayne inside. Which meant they had to dress for a party instead of a hostage rescue. When Clayne sprinted across the meticulous lawn, he did it in a tux. When she ran, it was in three-inch heels and a black evening gown with a slit up to her hip and a plunging neckline that stopped a few inches short of her belly button. She was lucky to keep everything where it belonged when she walked, much less ran.

For some reason though, Clayne's more than casual observation didn't bother her as much as it might have if it had been any other man looking. Probably because sexual tension had been brewing between them for months.

After they'd gotten over the initial awkwardness and made it through the hell that was the DCO team certification process, they'd started to notice each other in a different light. How could they not when they were together almost around the clock? She'd already seen Clayne nearly naked a few times and knew he possessed one hell of a body. Although he looked damn yummy in the expensive tux he was wearing now, too. She was having a hard time deciding which way she liked him better—bare-ass naked or dressed to the max.

She opted for naked. She was shallow like that.

Danica almost laughed when she came to a stop in front of her partner, who at the moment looked more like the Big Bad Wolf that wanted to eat her up than a highly skilled undercover agent.

But while Clayne might appreciate her body, he wasn't stupid enough to let it distract him for long. He dragged his gaze away from her cleavage and sniffed the air.

"Still clear."

"You pick up the girl's scent yet?" Danica asked.

"Yeah. At least the trace amount she left behind before they took her inside. I won't know exactly where she is until we get in there."

He gave her a nod, then led the way toward the back of the guesthouse. According to the floor plan, there was an entrance to the kitchen on that side. Danica only hoped it wasn't guarded. John's orders had been simple—this wasn't a shoot-'em-all-and-let-God-sort-'em-out kind of mission. They were to avoid engaging the guards, slip inside quietly, grab the girl, and get her off the estate before anyone knew they were there.

They weren't supposed to go anywhere near the drug lord or kill his men in retribution. Get in and get out, nice and quiet.

Right. If John wanted a nice, quiet mission, why the hell had he sent her and Clayne? They didn't exactly do quiet.

Clayne peeked around the corner of the guesthouse. "You gonna take the lead once we get inside?"

Danica fought the urge to lean around him to take a look. It was better if he did it. His nose and ears would alert him if anyone was coming long before she'd ever know it. He was good at recon and attack; she was good at data processing and on-the-fly planning. That was why he wanted her to lead once they got inside. She was better at directing them through a close-quarter situation. He preferred to follow her lead and cover her back. It had taken them a while to come to that conclusion, mainly because Clayne liked being in charge, but once he saw how much better they worked as a team, he gave in.

"Sounds good," she said.

Clayne edged around the corner and headed for the kitchen entrance. Danica kept an eye on their six and their flank. They were almost there when he stopped in his tracks and spun around.

"Incoming," he whispered.

Crap. Someone was coming out the kitchen door. There was no way they could retrace their steps and get back to the corner in time.

Danica tensed, ready to pop whoever walked out the door. *So much for nice and quiet.*

But instead of dropping to his knee to cover their backside while she dealt with the person coming out of the guesthouse, Clayne swore and pressed her back against the wall. She barely had time to register a what-the-hell before his right hand—the one with the pistol—slid behind her back and his mouth came down on hers.

Danica didn't think. She simply trusted that Clayne knew what he was doing and instinctively pushed her gun under his arm. If she had to, she could shoot through his jacket. Her line of fire would be limited, of course, and Clayne would have some serious flash burns, but it might just save their lives.

She twisted his body, pressing her hip against his groin as she tried to aim her weapon at the door. Clayne growled and shoved back with his thigh, moving her weapon off the door and pressing her harder against the wall, his mouth moving insistently over hers.

Danica was still trying to figure out what he was doing when the kitchen door opened and two women stepped out. They wore plain black dresses with white aprons—maids. They were maids, not armed guards. That's what Clayne had been trying to tell her with his impromptu make-out session.

Realizing she wasn't playing her part as convincingly as he was, Danica buried the fingers of one hand in his hair and parted her lips under his with a loud moan. God, he tasted better than chocolate. And she had a serious weakness for chocolate. His tongue slipped in to tangle with hers, and Danica had to remind herself they were supposed to be pretending. Because there was nothing pretend about her body's reaction to what they were doing.

Behind Clayne, one woman said something to the

other in Spanish, then they both laughed and walked toward the main house. Danica's familiarity with the language was limited to two years in high school. She couldn't be sure, but she thought they said something about horny Americans needing to find a room.

Clayne had his back to the women, so he was probably depending on her to break the kiss when the coast was clear. Danica didn't pull away, though. Not even after the maids had disappeared inside. It wasn't her fault. Clayne was a damn good kisser. Besides, she had to make sure the women didn't come back, didn't she?

But they had a job to do, and a teenage girl to rescue. She reluctantly slid her hand from his silky hair to lightly push against his rock-hard chest. He got the message and lifted his head. His eyes flared in the darkness and she saw a flash of gold before he turned to look over his shoulder in the direction the women had disappeared.

"Sorry about that." His voice was soft and a touch ragged. "I realized they were maids when I heard one say they had to clean up after the party. I was afraid you'd shoot them, and kissing you was the first thing I thought of."

Because he'd been thinking of doing it before? The idea made her pulse skip a beat and she licked her lips. "Don't worry about it. It was good improv. The women didn't suspect a thing."

Clayne's molten gaze dropped to her mouth, and for one crazy moment she thought he was going to kiss her again. But he only jerked his head toward the guest-house. "You ready to do this?"

The double entendre almost made her moan. Not

trusting herself to speak, Danica nodded and followed
him across the lawn.

The rest of the mission hadn't gone as smoothly—or
quietly—as they'd planned, thanks to the uncooperative
bastards who'd been holding the girl hostage. But they'd
rescued the ambassador's daughter and that's what
mattered. And when they got back on the plane for the
States, neither of them mentioned the kiss in Mexico.
She and Clayne had grown more as a team in that one
mission than in all the other missions and training exercises they'd done since getting paired up, and she
couldn't help but wonder if it was because of that kiss.

"Are you just going to stare at those photos all night,
or help us?"

It took Danica a moment to realize Tony was talking to her. She looked up and was surprised to see that
he and Clayne had filled two entire whiteboards with
names and random pieces of information. She must have
zoned out longer than she thought. She scratched a quick
note on her pad to make it look as if she'd been doing
something other than daydreaming.

"Sorry. What can I do to help?"

"Maybe you can look at this and tell us what we're
not seeing," Tony said.

She read over the collection of notes scribbled on
the whiteboard. Damn, Tony had crappy handwriting.
Thinking about the past wasn't going to help solve these
murders. Staring at the coroner's reports wasn't getting
her anywhere, either.

Clayne gestured to the board. "We've written down

every piece of information we have on each victim, and we can't find anything connecting them."

Danica scanned each list. Something had to be buried in that mess connecting the men—they just weren't seeing it. She wished they could call up the DCO and have their analysts come up with the answer, but unfortunately, their computers weren't any better than the FBI's. Without something to put in the search engine, they were worthless.

"What do these guys have in common?" she asked. "Don't think about it. Just say it off the top of your head."

"They're all men," Clayne said.

That was obvious, but she nodded anyway. "What else?"

"They all live in the Sacramento area," Tony added.

"I don't suppose any of them worked together?"

Clayne and Tony shook their heads. *Of course not. That'd be too easy.*

"Any chance they dated the same people?" she asked.

They shook their heads again.

"Okay, so no connection there, either," Danica said.

"They were all athletic," Clayne pointed out.

She didn't need to check for facts in the files on that. She'd looked at their dead bodies enough to know that all five men had been in great shape.

"Yeah, but none of them worked out at the same gym," Tony added. "Hell, they didn't even go to the same grocery store."

Danica leaned back against the table next to Clayne and folded her arms. She could feel the heat coming off him through the thin blouse she wore, and she scooted a little farther away.

"So, other than the fact that the men were in good

shape, I don't know if they have anything in common at all," Tony said. "Maybe the serial killer is simply picking his victims at random."

God, that was a frightening thought. If the killer didn't have a type, they couldn't narrow it down to a particular demographic, which meant he was going to be even harder to catch. She was about to point that out when she realized Clayne was fixed on the whiteboard.

"Clayne, you got something?"

He didn't take his eyes off the board. "Why were they in good shape?"

Tony looked at Danica as if Clayne were mental. "Because they worked out."

Clayne shook his head. "No. I mean, why did they work out so much?"

Danica wasn't following Clayne any better than Tony, but she recognized when he was onto something. Clayne did everything by instinct, even reasoning. If he thought he'd found a connection, he probably had.

Clayne walked over to the board on the left and pointed to it. "Victim one was a boxer. Not just any boxer, but one known for being a punishing hitter." He gestured to another part of the board. "Victim two was an enforcer for a loan shark. He liked to break kneecaps. Three was an ex-cop turned private detective. He had a string of lawsuits against him when he was a cop for excessive force. Victim four was an ex-soldier working as a bouncer. Multiple combat tours with awards for valor in every one of them."

"And number five taught martial arts but was also a competitively ranked fighter as well," Danica finished. She was starting to get an idea where this was going.

Tony frowned. "So they worked out because they had

physically demanding jobs that they excelled at? That's the connection?"

Clayne shook his head. "It's even simpler than that. I think the thing that ties these five men together is that they're all basically guys you wouldn't think of as a serial killer's victims—unless that serial killer was interested in a challenge. I mean, who's going to go after a mob enforcer who breaks bones for a living?"

Danica instinctively knew Clayne was right. Beside her, Tony still looked skeptical, but then he slowly nodded.

"Holy shit," he breathed. "We should have realized it the moment the coroner confirmed what you saw at the morgue yesterday—that the killer chased every one of the men and ran them into the ground. They were prey for this sick prick."

Clayne gave Danica a pointed look. "A soldier, a cop, a boxer, a bouncer, and a martial artist. All aggressive and violent. And the killer took all of them down without them laying a hand on him. He's more dangerous than anybody on this task force has even begun to realize."

What Clayne really meant was that the men and women on the task force were in over their heads. And that no one—except for the two of them—was suited to deal with this killer.

"Now that we have this prey angle, what do we do with it?" Tony asked.

Clayne glanced at him. "I'll talk to some intel analysts I work with at Homeland who are good at finding specific types of people and wait for them to give us a list of suitable prey living in the Sacramento area. Then we use that list to figure out who the killer is going after next, and we get there first."

Danica waited for Tony to point out that the FBI had analysts who could do that, but she was surprised when he nodded.

"Sounds good. Let me grab a couple of other agents and we'll set up a victim—or prey—profile, so Homeland will know what to look for."

Danica opened her mouth to tell Tony she'd go instead, but her partner was already out the door. *Great.*

She braced herself for whatever snide comments Clayne had probably been waiting all day to get her alone to say, but instead he walked up to the one whiteboard that still had open space left and began listing the character traits that made a good victim. Being ignored by him hurt almost more than all his anger and bitter words. She swallowed hard, watching as he scrawled across the board. When they'd been together, she used to do most of the strategizing—and note taking—and he'd been happy to let her. Now, he did it on his own. Then again, she hadn't really given him any choice, had she?

What if she had given him a choice that night in his apartment? What if she'd told him the truth instead of lying to him? Would he have agreed to let her go if he'd known it was for his own good?

More likely, he would have gone off half-cocked and done something that would have landed him in prison.

Tony came back with three other agents in tow and his cell phone to his ear. He was ordering pizza. That turned out to be a smart move because they ended up working through the night. Coming up with the list of character traits and physical abilities they thought would make the victims attractive to the killer didn't take long, but everyone wanted to hang around to see what both the

FBI profilers and the intel analysts Clayne knew came up with. Danica knew her former employer kept a full team of capable people on duty twenty-four hours a day, so they'd get the information together quickly and immediately send it to Clayne.

She wasn't wrong. Within an hour, Clayne was downloading a list from the DCO's secure server. Unfortunately, it was big. Apparently, there were a lot of men in Sacramento who fit their initial profile. They still had over two hundred names to work with, but it was the best they could do at this point.

"Should we go brief Carhart?" Tony asked a little after seven thirty the next morning.

Danica winced. She'd rather not, but they had to keep him in the loop.

"You spent the whole night working and all you came up with is a list of a hundred people you think this psycho *might* want to kill?" Carhart practically shouted when they told him. "Are you out of your damn minds? The governor didn't ask the FBI to step in and take over this case so we could waste time tracking down possible victims. He wants us out there finding the killer."

"Sir—" Danica began, but Carhart kept talking.

"Which is why I'll be briefing the task force this morning on the profile we've come up with for the Hunter."

Tony exchanged looks with Danica. "Hunter? That's what we're calling this guy?"

Carhart waved his hand. "That's what the media has started calling him. And right now, it's as good a name as any."

Danica bit her tongue. She wouldn't be surprised if Carhart had leaked the name to the press. Nothing grabbed the media's attention like a good serial killer name. And her new boss was all about making a name for himself.

"When did they come up with a profile for the killer?" Tony asked.

Carhart gulped his coffee. "After we broke up into focus groups. It's a broad list—survivalists, gang-bangers, hunters—but it's a place to start."

More like a waste of time. Even without seeing the list, she knew there'd be thousands of potential suspects on it. The task force could work twenty-four hours a day for months and still not be able to check all of them out.

"Sir, Agent Buchanan thinks we'd be better off looking—"

Carhart thumped his mug down on the desk so hard that coffee spilled onto his hand. "For the Hunter's prey, I know. But Buchanan isn't in charge of this investigation, Agent Beckett. If I had my way, he wouldn't be on the task force at all. I contacted everyone I know, called in every favor to get him tossed from the team—I mean I called all the way up the chain. I don't know who the hell he is, but he isn't just Teflon-coated; he's bulletproof. I can't touch him."

No wonder Carhart's list of suspects was so damn brainless. He'd spent his night trying to get his best asset kicked off the team. *What an idiot.*

"If we can't get him out of the way, we're going to have to marginalize him," Carhart continued. "I need you to help me do that."

Okay. Idiot would be a step up for this guy.

"I know neither of you want to babysit this jerk, but

I want him kept away from the investigation. This is an FBI operation and we don't need outsiders from the Department of Homeland Security getting in the way." He held up his hand when Danica opened her mouth to protest. "I know you two want to help catch the Hunter, but the best way you can help is to keep Buchanan on the sidelines. So if he wants to scour Sacramento looking for people he thinks might be the Hunter's next victim, let him."

Danica had to fight to keep from laughing. "Let me get this straight. You want us to keep Agent Buchanan busy while the rest of the task force rounds up suspects?"

"That's exactly what I'm saying." He eyed her and Tony. "So, how about it? Can I count on the two of you to take one for the team?"

Obviously Carhart's finely tuned detective skills had yet to inform him that few people kept Clayne Buchanan in check. Her least of all. She didn't answer his question right away. She'd been planning to help Clayne regardless, only now she wasn't going to have to sneak around behind her boss's back to do it. But she couldn't give in too easily. So she sighed loudly and put on her best resigned look.

"Yes, sir."

Carhart turned to Tony. "Agent Moretti?"

Beside her, Tony nodded.

"Good," Carhart said, sounding pleased with himself. "That'll be all."

Danica wondered how pleased her boss'd be if he knew they'd catch the killer way before the rest of the task force did. At least she hoped they caught him. Because if not, things were going to go from bad to worse for the city of Sacramento.

Chapter 4

WHEN DANICA EXPLAINED HE'D BEEN EXILED TO the periphery of the investigation, Clayne almost laughed. He was going to do his own thing whether Carhart.approved or not. Although if he didn't know better, he'd think Danica had manipulated the fed into ostracizing him so he could go after the shifter without being under the watchful eye of the Bureau. Because he knew for a fact that the woman had a way of getting what she wanted.

He swore under his breath as he followed her and Tony to the car. It had taken him a good portion of yesterday to get his head to a place where he could push all personal thoughts about his ex-partner to the back of his mind and focus on the case. He'd be damned if he was going to slip up and get distracted again. He was here to do a job, and once he did it, he was leaving. End of story.

He had to admit the previous night had been like old times, though. He was never as sharp and instinctive as when he was with Danica. She had a unique way of suggesting possibilities and ordering his thoughts that made him better at his job.

Damn, he'd said he wasn't going there and yet he was doing it again. Thinking about her, letting her invade his every thought. Why the hell was he doing this? This was a one-time deal. He'd do fine once she wasn't around, just like he had the last two years.

Clayne distracted himself by watching Danica and Tony argue over who was going to drive.

"You drove yesterday," she pointed out.

Tony put his hands on his hips as he squared off against her. "I didn't know we were keeping track."

"We always alternate."

"Since when?"

She lifted her chin stubbornly. "Since now."

Clayne resisted the urge to chuckle as the fed shook his head in obvious exasperation. Besides coming up with a list of potential victims last night, Clayne had also come to the conclusion that Tony wasn't the asswipe he'd pegged him for. The guy was okay and seemed like a good agent. It wasn't his fault he was Danica's rebound partner.

The longer Danica and Tony argued, though, the more amusing it got. Clayne couldn't remember her ever caring about who drove when they'd worked together. He'd driven and she'd navigated. But what'd worked for them obviously didn't work for her and Tony. Clayne was just about to grab the keys and say he'd drive just to put a stop to the argument when they solved the issue with a game of rock, paper, scissors. Danica won.

But before they could get in the car, someone across the parking garage called Tony's name. He muttered something under his breath. "Hold on. I'll be right back."

Clayne's phone rang as he opened the back door of the car and got in. It was Kendra.

"Hey, Clayne. I continued working on the list of prey suspects I gave you this morning, hoping I could narrow it down."

"Hang on and I'll put you on speaker." He thumbed the button. "Go ahead."

"I think I have something, but I'm not sure," Kendra said. "Regardless, it's really weird. All the victims had the same rare blood type—AB. Can you think of any reason a shifter would select his prey based purely on what kind of blood they had?"

Clayne swore. "I can think of a really good reason. AB blood smells better."

In the front seat, Danica arched a brow. "Shifters can tell one blood type from another by scent?"

He nodded. "Yeah. It's just something I never thought about. But if all the victims had AB, I can almost guarantee it's because it matters to the killer."

"How would he even know what blood type they have?" Danica asked.

"I don't know," Clayne said. "Like you said, AB blood is really rare. Maybe all these guys were on a blood donor registry."

"That makes a lot of sense," Kendra agreed. "Anyway, if you think this is a good lead, it'll narrow your list of names to less than twenty people. In the meantime, I'll see if the victims were on a donor list and see who had access to it. It might help find the killer."

Clayne circled the names of the AB blood types as Kendra read them off. She was right. There were eighteen people to focus on now. By the time Tony got in the car, he and Danica had already worked out the order in which they would talk to them. They filled Tony in on the new lead and headed to the first address. He was skeptical about the blood thing, especially since they couldn't tell him the killer was able to smell it, but he agreed it was too much of a coincidence to overlook.

As they worked their way through the list, they asked each man the same questions. Have you seen anyone hanging around, checking you out, watching your house or your routine? Has anyone talked to you about your exercise regimen or what you do for a living? Have any of your family or friends mentioned seeing anyone or asking them those same questions?

Checking names off the list made for a long day running around the city from one possible target to the next, but as much as Clayne hated admitting it, he liked spending time with Danica. She was fun to be with, dammit. On the downside, being trapped in the car with her meant he couldn't avoid inhaling her scent. He tried putting his window down, but without sticking his head out like a dog, it didn't do any good. He had to sit there and deal with it.

The sun was already well down behind the trees as they pulled up to an apartment complex in the El Dorado Hills. The next guy on their list lived in a unit toward the back, where the buildings butted up against the rolling hills that gave the community its name. Danica had just parked in one of the visitor spaces when Clayne caught sight of movement off to the right as he got out of the car. He jerked his head in that direction, eyes narrowing.

He caught the shifter's scent at the same moment he saw movement near the separate garages that lined the back of the complex. The shadowy figure of a man dragging something—make that *someone*—toward the hills behind the apartment buildings.

Clayne gave Danica a shout before he sprinted across

the parking lot. He couldn't shift completely in the middle of the apartment complex, but that didn't stop him from growling softly. The shifter must have heard because he froze, his gold-green eyes wide in the semi-darkness. He cursed and dropped his prey, taking off.

Clayne paused long enough to make sure the man on the ground was alive before going after the shifter again. The guy was out of it, but otherwise didn't seem hurt. Footsteps echoed behind Clayne, then stopped at the exact spot where he'd left the shifter's would-be victim, just as tires squealed on pavement. Clayne knew without looking back that Tony was the one on foot, while Danica had sped past him into the hills so she could try to get ahead of the killer. It was a herding technique they'd used before. Good to see Danica remembered it.

Once he got behind the garages, he fought the urge to shift completely and let the wolf take over. But in this case, having long claws and fangs wasn't going to help him. He only needed the superior sense that came with a partial shift. The darkness disappeared around him, and he knew that if someone saw him, his glowing yellow eyes would freak them out. Luckily, his enhanced sense of smell and hearing never came with any physical changes. He would have hated having furry ears and a long snout.

He cleared the eight-foot privacy fence that surrounded the apartment complex and took off at a run the moment he landed on the other side. Even with his natural night vision, he couldn't see the other shifter ahead of him in the trees. But he could sure as hell hear him, smacking aside branches and kicking up rock. *That's right, asshole, see how it feels to be the one getting chased for a change.*

Clayne heard a thud behind him, quickly followed by a whole lot of cussing. Apparently, Tony wasn't having such an easy time with that fence. Clayne felt bad for the fed, but not bad enough to slow down. He wasn't about to let the shifter get away. Besides, it was better if Tony was otherwise occupied for the moment. Having to explain to the fed why he could clock speeds of twenty-five miles an hour over rough ground might be a little difficult.

He tried to use both his sense of smell and hearing to predict which way the cat shifter would go, then take the shortest path to intercept him, but the asshole didn't make it easy. The cat shifter was fast. Maybe faster than Clayne. And he obviously knew these hills a whole hell of a lot better. While Clayne stayed with him, he wasn't catching up. In fact, if it wasn't for the scent the shifter left, Clayne would have lost him more than once already.

Clayne growled and shifted completely, allowing the claws on his hands and his fangs to slide out. It was a risky move in such a heavily populated area, but he didn't have a choice. He had to let out his inner wolf and everything that went with it if he hoped to catch this son of a bitch.

A heightened sense of smell, better night vision, and an extra burst of speed weren't the only things he felt when he shifted this time, though. As bizarre as it sounded, he swore he could sense Danica. She was somewhere on the hill directly above him, moving fast in a line that would cut right across the killer's escape route. He didn't get how he knew she was there. Maybe it was his senses going a little nuts from spending so much time with her the last few days. But what the hell? Maybe they'd all get lucky and Danica would run the murderous piece of shit over. Save everyone a lot of trouble. Not to mention get him back home faster.

Then he heard tires squeal, followed by a crash.

He stopped cold, his boots sliding across the rough ground. Something clenched deep inside his chest.

Danica.

He took off running again, faster than before. When he reached the top of the hill, he saw a car smashed into a tree and his heart stopped beating. Then he realized it wasn't Danica's sedan and his heart started up again.

Thank God.

But if it wasn't her car, where was she?

Clayne looked around wildly and spotted her sedan a few hundred feet away from the other vehicle. He immediately headed toward it only to stop when he caught sight of her kneeling down beside the other car. She was checking on the driver and talking on her cell phone at the same time.

A part of Clayne wanted to go after the shifter, but he knew it was too late. The killer would have had a getaway vehicle parked somewhere nearby to transport his prey. This little distraction was all it'd take to give the shifter enough time to get to his car and drive off. Chasing him would also mean leaving Danica, and he didn't know for sure she hadn't been injured.

He glanced over his shoulder, searching for Tony. But the fed was still way back there somewhere. He wasn't going to be any help.

Swearing under his breath, he ran over to Danica, retracting his claws and teeth as he went. Inside the car, a young woman leaned back in her seat, blood running down her face. The airbag had inflated, but the impact with the tree must have bounced her head off the side window.

Danica finished calling in their location, then glanced at him. "The suspect ran into the middle of the road and darted right in front of her. She went into the tree and I had to choose between helping her or going after him. I'm sorry."

"You did the right thing." Clayne searched her face. "You okay?"

She nodded. "Yeah. Did you get a good look at him?"

Clayne shook his head. "You?"

"No. I didn't see crap. He was lightning fast, though."

"Yeah, no kidding. Something to keep in mind the next time we catch up to this bastard. Don't let him get close to you."

Danica opened her mouth to say something, but Tony came stumbling over the crest of the hill, gasping like he'd run a marathon. He took one look at the woman behind the wheel of the car and mumbled something that sounded like a curse before collapsing on the ground. He leaned back against the car and eyed Clayne in amazement.

"How the hell can someone as big as you run so freaking fast?" he demanded.

"Good shoes," Clayne told him.

The fed looked down at his feet. "You're wearing boots."

Clayne looked, too. "Yeah. But they're the right boots."

Tony just shook his head and put his head between his legs, gasping for more air.

Even though he knew the trail was cold, Clayne had followed the shifter's scent anyway. He'd been right. The trail had disappeared in a subdivision one street over from the apartment complex.

Clayne would rather have kept the whole event quiet and not let the rest of the task force—especially that prick Carhart—know how close he and Danica had been to the killer, but that turned out to be impossible. Within the hour, the crash site turned into a three-ring circus. As soon as the press found out the FBI was on the scene, they put two and two together and came up with *Hunting the Hunter: Drama in the El Dorado Hills*.

The man the killer had tried to kidnap—an up-and-coming MMA fighter—was talking a mile a minute by the time Clayne, Danica, and Tony got back to the apartment complex. Unfortunately, he hadn't seen much more of the killer than Clayne had. It had been dark in the shadows where the rogue shifter had made his move, and he'd attacked from behind, so the target never saw his face. The would-be victim had no problem using his imagination to fill in the gaps in his fifteen minutes of fame, though. He went to great lengths to describe how he'd fought the killer, saying his attacker was muscular, freakishly strong, and growled like an animal. Clayne wished he'd left off that last part, especially since the media clearly ate it up.

He glanced over to where Danica stood talking with Carhart. He probably shouldn't be eavesdropping, but that had never stopped him before.

"How the hell did Buchanan stumble across the Hunter? You were supposed to be keeping him away from the investigation, Agent Beckett."

Danica gave him a contrite look that Clayne couldn't have managed in a hundred years. "I'm doing my best, sir. But Agent Buchanan is tough to control."

Clayne snorted. If only Carhart knew. She'd never had any problem wrapping him around her finger when they'd been together, that was for sure.

The task force leader didn't look quite as amused. Actually, he looked as if he might just blow a gasket.

Clayne swore. If he listened to any more of this, he was going to jump to Danica's defense and punch Carhart in his smug face. Turning his back on them, he took out his cell phone and called John so he could get him up to speed. He didn't have a lot of info to pass along, but he wanted the DCO to have everything there was. You could never tell what might be important.

"The witness said he was a white guy," he told John. "And based on what I saw, he's about six three or so, at least two hundred and twenty pounds. Probably somewhere between twenty and forty years old."

That wasn't much to go on, but the DCO had spent more than a decade finding shifters within the general population, so Clayne hoped they might already have someone matching that description in the database.

"We'll add what you've given us to the search criteria and keep looking," John said. "But right now, we don't have very much. Zarina was able to look at the wound patterns and confirm you're looking for some kind of cat shifter, though."

That was a big help. "Yeah, I've already figured that

part out," Clayne said dryly. "Any chance you can get Ivy and Landon out here to help? It might be good to have another cat on this. Maybe she can figure out what this psycho is going to do next."

John sighed. "I'd like to. But I've still got Ivy and Landon trying to find something on Klaus and Renard. If I send them out to help, I'm only going to have to yank them again the second something pops."

Clayne understood. He knew how important it was for Ivy to find those doctors—and the DNA samples they'd taken from her.

"Regardless," John added, "we'll search our database for a cat shifter that meets your description, one with serial-killer tendencies. Since we don't already have something on this guy, we'll extend the parameters outside the U.S. border. We might be dealing with a foreign national who slipped into the States recently. I'll be in touch as soon as we find anything."

"One more thing," Clayne growled. "You could have told me I'd be working with Danica."

There was a slight hesitation on the other end of the phone. "I thought I did."

Clayne just grunted and hung up. He turned back around to see if Danica was still getting chewed out by her boss only to find Carhart giving a quick field briefing.

"Based on the information our profilers have gotten from the witness—most especially the abnormal strength and animal-like growling—we're most likely dealing with a drug user, probably someone who abuses steroids. Which makes perfect sense since the previous victims spent a lot of time in the gym."

Tony leaned over to Danica. "Now we're not only

looking for a survivalist who's a hunter and a gangbanger, but one who works out at the gym and takes steroids?"

"And who growls," she whispered back.

Their words were too low for Carhart or anyone else to pick up, but Clayne chuckled. What wasn't so funny, however, was that Carhart hated the idea of giving the "guy from DHS" any credit. He'd completely dismissed the fact that Clayne had been right with the prey angle and that they'd almost caught the killer. Or saved the next victim. How the hell Carhart had ever been put in charge was beyond Clayne. Then again, Dick got ahead in the DCO by being so stupid that people thought he was brilliant. Maybe that was this guy's MO, too. Hell, maybe they taught the technique in the academy or something.

"So, do we go back to the list of possible victims?" Tony asked when they got in the car.

Clayne leaned against the backseat as Tony pulled out of the parking lot. "That's all we have to go on right now."

"Let's hope the killer doesn't change his tactics now that we know his preferred target demographic," Danica said from the passenger seat.

She reached up with one hand to rub the back of her neck. Some of her hair had come loose from her bun to hang down her back, and Clayne had to resist the urge to lean forward to gently sweep it aside so he could massage the tension from her shoulders. Damn, she looked beat. None of them had slept in thirty-six hours, so they probably all looked like crap.

But she was right about the killer possibly changing up his script. If he did, it wouldn't be because he knew the feds were onto his favorite target group. It'd be because the killer knew there was another shifter after him. If the guy was smart, he'd blow town. That'd solve the city of Sacramento's problem, but it'd make life hard on Clayne, because he'd have to figure out where the asshole had disappeared to. That'd be a pain in the ass.

On the upside, he wouldn't have to work with Danica anymore.

That should have had him doing freaking cartwheels, but for some stupid reason, it didn't. And that irritated him just about as much as not catching the serial killer did.

Chapter 5

THANKS TO THE MEDIA BUZZING WITH NEWS ABOUT "The Sacramento Hunter," it was damn near impossible to get anything useful out of anyone. Everyone freaked the moment someone with a badge showed up at their door. For all Clayne knew, they'd spooked the killer off last night and he was now prowling another part of the state—or continent—looking for some poor, unsuspecting husband-slash-boyfriend-slash-father to sink his claws into. On the other hand, the cat shifter might already have grabbed someone who wasn't on the list and was hunting him while Clayne wasted his time driving around town with Danica and Tony.

Clayne ground his jaw. If it were up to him, he'd have surveillance on the most likely targets, but unfortunately it was up to that asswipe Carhart. Instead, he had every member of the task force out on the street, rounding up every drugged-out, steroid-using gym rat and hunting freak who had a police record. And while they did that, the rest of the FBI field office was spending their time trying to determine if there was some new drug that could account for the animal-like behavior and exceptional strength. The media had put that in their story, too, saying the FBI was searching for a serial killer who was high on bath salts or some other hallucinogenic drug. Like they needed to freak people out even more than they already were.

Danica and Tony had attempted to convince Carhart the FBI should put agents on the other possible victims on their list of AB blood types—the fact that they'd almost caught the Hunter proved they were on the right track. But Carhart didn't want to waste agents on what he thought had been dumb luck. He'd rather drag in every juicer and drug addict in the city than do anything useful. Maybe the idea that they were facing a drugged-out wacko was less terrifying than the truth—that they were after a seriously deranged, but smart, serial killer.

"How the hell are we supposed to find the killer if we're doing this stupid shit all day?" Clayne growled to Danica as they dropped off another suspect for interrogation. This guy was the owner of a local gym who was known for selling steroids to the local high school football players. He was scum, but being scum was a long way from being a serial killer.

Clayne clenched his hands into fists to keep his claws from coming out. God, he felt like punching someone—preferably Carhart. But truthfully, right then, anyone would work. Which was unfortunate for the uniformed officer who appeared with another rap sheet of yet another suspect to bring in for questioning. Clayne's claws pushed out from beneath his nails. *Screw this*. He was done playing these silly-ass games. He ignored the folder the young cop held out to him and instead reached for the front of the man's uniform. He wasn't that idiot Carhart, but he'd do.

But Danica's hand intercepted his, her fingers closing over the folder just in time. "Thanks, Officer," she said smoothly as she stepped between Clayne and the cop. "I'll take that."

The man blinked like he'd just been pushed out of the way of a moving truck and nodded his head nervously as he stepped back and darted for an opening in the crowd filling the room.

Danica turned and gave Clayne a pointed look. "O-kay. Time to get you something to eat."

Huh? She wasn't going to lecture him about keeping his cool and playing nice with others, or some other stupid crap that wasn't any of her damn business?

"Eat?" he repeated stupidly.

Way to go, genius. But she was standing so close to him that he couldn't think, much less speak.

"Yes, eat. Before we pick up this next suspect," she said. "It's a little early for dinner, but you tend to get hangry when you don't eat."

He glanced at his watch. Three o'clock. It was early to eat, but he was hungry. He fell into step beside her as she walked toward the exit. "Hangry? What the hell is that?"

She led the way to the four-door sedan that he was starting to think of as his home away from home. He spent more time in it than he did in the bed at the hotel. "You know, when you get angry because you're hungry. Hangry."

He couldn't help chuckling. "Cute. Did you come up with that?"

Danica laughed. "No, but I wish I had. I saw it on some website." She jerked her head toward the backseat. "Get in. We'll grab something to eat, then pick up this next guy."

Tony was leaning against the side of the car waiting for them, and he got in the driver's side as Danica went around to ride shotgun.

"Where to?" Tony asked as he put the car in gear.

When Danica named a fast-food place known for their monster burgers, Clayne almost laughed. Danica knew him pretty damn well—maybe better than he knew himself. She knew when he was frustrated, when he was pissed off, when he was hungry, and apparently what he liked to eat. And as the past few days had reminded him, she knew how to keep him calm and focused on the task ahead of them, and she knew what to say to keep him from losing it. She brought out the best in him—like any good partner would.

Only Danica wasn't his partner anymore. And working with her again reminded him of how good they'd been together.

She'd been the first woman—the first person—to really get him. It made no sense, especially since she was a norm, but she understood him like no one he'd ever met before. Within weeks of teaming up with her, he'd felt this connection between them, almost a bond. It should have scared the hell out of him, but it hadn't. Instead of pushing her away with baleful glares and subtle growls like he had everyone else, he'd allowed her to get inside his defenses and get close to him. It had been so easy to trust her, and even easier to fall in love with her.

Clayne looked out the window, not seeing half of what went by as he replayed the memory of that first time they'd both decided to let their partnership slip beyond the bounds of a professional relationship into something more. And though the memory was rather bittersweet now, it still made him smile.

Upstate New York, July 2010

They'd been watching the Chinese diplomat's house for a week. According to their intel, the guy was supposed to be buying information from a high-tech computer company in the United States and sending it back to China. He and Danica weren't sure what technology was trading hands, but their orders had been simple. Don't touch the Chinese diplomat. Wait until he made the transfer, then apprehend the person who picked up the package. Problem was, no one had shown up for the drop, which was supposed to have happened a week ago. Clayne's gut told him they'd missed it, but John insisted they sit tight, that their source might have been wrong about the date.

Hanging out with his partner certainly wasn't a problem. They'd been working like a well-oiled machine ever since that hostage rescue in Mexico City a few weeks earlier. Any time he spent alone with Danica was in the category of quality time as far as he was concerned. The problem was that it was the middle of winter in upstate New York, and only place the DCO could find that had a view of the Chinese diplomat's house was a fancy home in foreclosure across the street. They had no lights, no power, and no heat.

If they'd been stuck there only a day or two, it wouldn't have been so bad, but a whole week? It was shitty, even for Clayne, and the cold weather didn't bother him. They had food and water, as well as plenty of blankets and cold-weather gear. But you could only pile on so much clothing. Danica looked like she was about to turn blue. And it was supposed to get colder tonight than it had since they'd holed up there.

Clayne peered through the nightscope at the house across the street again. The place was completely dark inside. "This is stupid," he muttered. "No one's coming tonight. And even if someone does, I can handle it. Go back to the hotel where it's warm. You're going to freeze to death if you spend another night out here."

He looked at Danica—or what he could see of her. She was sitting on their sleeping bags buried under a pile of blankets, shivering.

She shook her head. "I'm fine."

Right. Her teeth were freaking chattering.

He swore under his breath. Danica was just being stubborn now. But there wasn't much he could do about it. He wasn't going to drag her out of the house against her will, and he couldn't find another blanket or scrap of clothing to pile on her. Hell, he'd already given her his coat.

With a growl, he got to his feet and went over to her. Dropping to one knee, he yanked off the blankets, leaving her exposed to the subfreezing temperature in the room.

Danica clutched at it like her life depended on it. "What are you doing?"

"I'm trying to keep you from freezing to death."

"By taking all the stuff that's keeping me warm?"

Clayne sat down behind her and rearranged the blankets around both of them. "By doing this."

Danica hugged herself. "I think this kind of thing only works in the movies."

He pulled her back against his chest and wrapped his arms around her. "Stop talking and keep your eyes on the house next door. You're the one who wanted to stay here, so you watch for a while."

Danica might be slender, but she wasn't petite compared to most women. She fit nicely between his legs all
the same, and he pulled his knees up so she was completely enveloped in his body heat. She muttered something under her breath again about this never going to
work, but he noticed she stopped shivering. He opened
his mouth to point it out to her, but had to clamp it shut
to avoid letting out a groan as she wiggled against him.
His cock took notice despite the room's arctic chill.

"Why didn't you volunteer to do this four days ago?"
she asked as she grabbed his arm and wrapped it around
her shoulders like a shawl. "You're like a freaking
muscle-bound electric blanket."

Why the hell hadn't he thought of it four days ago?
"I didn't think you'd appreciate it as much then as you
do now."

That was probably true. Just because they'd gotten a little hot and heavy in Mexico didn't mean she
wanted him putting his paws on her. He might not be the
sharpest tool in the shed when it came to understanding
women, but he knew that.

"Shows what you know," she muttered.

He chuckled. Okay, so maybe he didn't know anything about women.

She looked over her shoulder at him. "What's so
funny?"

"Nothing. I was just imagining you trying to shoot
me if I had tried this on Tuesday."

She considered that, but then she nodded. The movement made her hair brush against his jaw. It felt nice.
And smelled seriously delicious. "Maybe you're right
about that."

Clayne shifted slightly, easing his increasingly hard-ening cock away from her perfect ass. He'd finally found a partner he clicked with. He wasn't going to mess it up by letting his mind—and other parts of his anatomy—wander where it shouldn't.

But it was tough. Sitting with her like this, he couldn't help but notice Danica had all kinds of curves in all kinds of places he hadn't really noticed before. Okay, that wasn't true. He had noticed. But a man noticed curves in a whole new light when they were pressed up against him. Especially when Danica wiggled around and pushed those curves back even more in search of the warmest spot to snuggle into.

He closed his eyes and bit back another groan. When she did that, it was hard not to think about what had happened between them in Mexico City. Sure, the kiss had only been a ploy to keep their cover intact, but it had also been hot, especially when she'd started kissing him back. It'd damn near been enough to make him forget about the two innocent maids or that the next people who came out very well could have been the drug lord's goons. It hadn't been his fault. He was a man, after all. And Danica was the type of woman who could bring him to his knees if she wanted to.

His dick stiffened to new and painful proportions at that. He quickly turned his attention to the house across the street. Maybe keeping his mind occupied would make him stop thinking about the very warm, very soft body he was cuddling up with. This close together, Danica was going to notice that he had a hard-on.

"I'm sorry," she murmured.

Clayne tipped his head to one side to look at her

face. Her cheek was resting against his forearm. It was the first time he realized her complexion was so much lighter than his, almost creamy in comparison to his naturally tanned skin.

"About what?"

"I should have told you earlier that I was having an issue with the cold," she said. "I was being stupid and stubborn. If the contact had shown up, I probably would have been too cold to be of much use to you."

Clayne doubted it. "I don't know about that. You feeling better now?"

He felt pretty damn good, that was for sure. He especially liked the part where his arm draped across her soft breasts. Which, now that he thought about it, was a dangerous place for his arm to be. He tried to relocate it to a safer spot, but she wasn't having any of it. If anything, she pulled him even tighter.

"Much better," she said in answer to his question. "I wish I knew your body was this warm before. I would have cuddled up with you every night." She stiffened suddenly, as if realizing what she'd just said. "Um, that didn't quite come out the way I intended it. I just meant…"

"Forget about it," he said softly. "I know what you meant. It's completely understandable that you'd want to cuddle up with me. I'm pretty irresistible."

Danica laughed, relaxing against him again. "Yeah, right. You're just a big, strong guy with a soft, gooey center."

His mouth twitched. "Exactly."

"Then tell me something. If you're so soft and gooey, why is there something hard poking me in the butt?"

It would have been Clayne's turn to stiffen, but he

wasn't sure he could get any harder without exploding. But hell, it'd been a long time since he'd been this close to a woman this beautiful and sexy. Check that. He'd never been this close to a woman this beautiful and sexy—ever.

"Um…sorry."

He was so embarrassed he could barely get the word out. He would have backed away some, but Danica still had a firm grip on his arm and didn't seem inclined to let him go.

"Forget about it." She tilted her head to look at him, her dark eyes half hidden beneath her lashes. "It's completely understandable that cuddling up with me would do that to you. I'm pretty irresistible."

When she said it, the words weren't nearly as outrageous as when he'd said them because they were true. She was damn hard to resist. Especially the way she was looking at him right now. It was all he could do not to cup her chin in his hand and taste that mouth of hers again. The thought only got him more turned on and he swore.

Shit.

She'd said that to make light of the whole thing so he wouldn't feel more uncomfortable than he was, not because she was trying to come on to him.

As the silence stretched on, he fumbled for something to say that wouldn't make him sound like an idiot. Or like he was trying to get in her pants. While he'd never been any good with words, he'd never been shy around women. But this was different. He had no idea what the hell was happening between them or where this was going. If it was going anywhere. But if it did go somewhere, he was damn sure going to enjoy the ride.

"You're right," he agreed. "About being irresistible, I mean."

Danica smiled up at him and wiggled closer. "Good answer."

Clayne inhaled sharply. Was she trying to kill him? If she thought there'd been something hard poking her in the ass before, she was about to get a big surprise now. He was like a freaking fence post.

God, this was torture. It was one thing to look at a woman's ass and imagine how firm and delicious it would feel. It was a completely different thing to have that ass in your lap, moving around in the most tempting way. He had to put some distance between them before he lost his mind.

He pulled his arm from around her shoulders so he could get a good grip on her hips, but once he had a hold on her, he hesitated. He'd intended to lift her off his lap, but what he really wanted to do was yank her down even harder. Preferably while he buried himself inside her.

Danica turned to look at him over her shoulder again. "Everything okay?"

"Yeah. I just, um, thought you might still be cold."

Which explained why he was holding on to her hips like this. What was he going to do next—ask what she thought about the weather they were having this time of year?

She gave him a sexy smile. "I'm not cold at all."

He could attest to that. And his body's response to the scorching heat she was putting off was immediate and all consuming. Whether he wanted to admit it or not, this is where the two of them had been heading for weeks now. From the moment he'd kissed her in Mexico City, he had wanted it to go here. Hoped it would go here. Prayed it would go here.

Clayne gazed into Danica's big, dark eyes, knowing he had a decision to make. If he let this go where he thought it was heading, things between them would never be the same. If he didn't, he knew he'd miss a chance at something his gut told him only came along once in a lifetime.

It wasn't an easy choice. If he went down this path, he'd be risking their partnership. Was he willing to give up what he had for what was behind door number two?

He tightened his hold on her hips and lifted her off his lap, but instead of setting her down on the sleeping bags like he should have, he spun her around and settled her back down on his lap so that she was facing him. Then he reached down and pulled the blanket around her shoulders again.

"Thanks," she said. "I'm much warmer now."

He leaned closer, letting her sweet scent fill him. It was exhilarating. Like HALO jumping from twenty-five thousand feet. But even the high-altitude-low-opening jump wasn't this much of a rush.

"Let's make sure you stay that way."

"I don't think that's going to be a problem," she whispered.

He'd been wrong. She *was* coming on to him.

The small gap between them closed by mutual consent, then Clayne's mouth was on hers. Danica sighed, the sound soft and sexy, and a growl vibrated deep in his throat before he could stop it. Another woman might be frightened by the animal lurking beneath the surface, but not Danica. She was the one woman he didn't have to hide the wolf from.

He deepened the kiss, his tongue going in search of hers. He slid his hands up her sides to cup her breasts, lingering there a moment before reaching for the zipper of her coat. He'd intended to unzip it slowly, but he was too impatient for that. He yanked. Metal flew. Cloth tore.

Danica pulled back, her eyes wide with shock.

Shit. He'd blown it. Damn his animal side.

"I'm sorry," he mumbled. "I didn't mean to—"

She pressed a finger to his lips, silencing him. "Don't be sorry. You surprised me, that's all."

He caught her hand, gently pulling it away. "Danica, are you sure about this? Really sure?"

When he had sex with a woman, he'd always been careful to keep the wolf in check, but he wasn't certain he could do that with Danica. There was something about her that made him think he might very well lose control.

She leaned forward to kiss him long and slow on the mouth before trailing her lips across his jaw to whisper in his ear.

"I'm absolutely sure."

—∿∿—

"You still like chili on your burger, right?" Danica asked from the front seat.

Clayne nodded, not sure what he'd just agreed to. But then he looked around and realized they were sitting at the drive-through window of the fast-food restaurant. He was still trying to reposition the painful hard-on in his jeans when Danica handed him two chili-smothered cheeseburgers, onion rings, and a Coke. He hoped she didn't notice the tent he was pitching.

Apparently she hadn't, because she turned around without a word and settled back in her seat as Tony pulled away from the window and parked in the first available space.

Clayne covered up the evidence of his excitement with the wrapper from the first burger. He was still so lost in the pleasant—and painful—memory of making love to Danica for the first time that he barely tasted the food. They'd lain in that pile of blankets and sleeping bags the whole night and most of the next day, making love like they needed it to survive. The contact who was supposed to meet the Chinese diplomat never showed, and he and Danica couldn't have cared less. Once they'd gotten past the thing that had been holding them back, it was like a dam bursting. They hadn't been able to get enough of each other.

For Clayne, it had been… Well, a moving experience was probably the best way to put it. He'd felt things that night he'd never felt before. He'd had sex with other women—okay, plenty of other women— before her, but what'd happened that night with Danica made all the others nothing more than a vague and distant memory.

Which was why before they had left that cold, dark, beautiful stakeout location, Clayne had opened up and shared things with Danica that he hadn't told anyone. Not John, not Dick—nobody. And she had listened to him talk, never once unsettled about the things he told her and the life he'd led, about the man he used to be. She'd held his soul in the palm of her hand, and he knew without a doubt he'd found the thing that had been missing from his life.

Clayne shoved a few more onion rings in his mouth and chewed them along with a big bite of burger. In the front seat, Tony was saying his wife would kill him if she knew he was eating this stuff. Clayne sipped his Coke as he watched Danica eat. Damn, she even made eating a cheeseburger a sensual experience.

He shook his head and focused on his own meal. That night had been the first of many nights—and days—that convinced him that he and Danica would be together forever. But that wasn't the way it had worked out. Danica had dumped him. Not simply dumped him, but just about cut his heart out and fed it to him.

That's what a man like him got for being stupid enough to think soul mates really existed.

He'd lain awake countless nights since she'd walked out, wondering what he'd done to mess things up with her and drive her away. If he asked her now, would she tell him? Probably not. What would be the point anyway? He and Danica couldn't pick up where they left off and expect everything to go back to the way it'd been.

———

After eating, they talked to a few more people on their list—or tried to anyway—then did as Carhart had ordered and picked up yet another suspect. This time it was a guy who'd been arrested a few years earlier for hunting deer out of season up in the mountains. Danica guessed that qualified him as an extreme hunter or something, but it seemed like a big leap from there to being a serial killer. They brought him in for

questioning anyway, even though it was a complete
waste of time.

Thankfully, there weren't any more suspects left to
pick up by the time they got back to the field office. After
dropping off their guy, they headed to the main conference room to see if anyone was around. If they were
lucky, someone on the task force had learned something
that might be useful. If not, they'd probably be pulling
another all-nighter poring over the files, looking for anything they might have missed. Beyond waiting for the
killer to strike again, there wasn't much else to do.

She glanced over her shoulder at Clayne. He hadn't
said more than two words since they'd stopped to get
something to eat, but she knew he was frustrated. She
was frustrated, too. But she couldn't let it show. She
might not work for the DCO anymore, but she still considered it her responsibility to keep Clayne calm and
focused on the case. It was the only way they were going
to catch this killer.

Unfortunately, Clayne'd never dealt well with ob-
stacles. When he got exasperated, he usually ended up
punching someone. Her ability to keep those violent
tendencies in check—until it was the right time to release them—was one of the things that had made them
such a good team. In fact, John had told her that was the
main reason he'd recruited her. She never figured out
how the DCO had known they'd work so well together,
but they'd been right. She and Clayne had developed
an almost instinctive understanding for how the other
person operated. He recognized her need to plan and
think everything out, and she respected his need to kick
down doors rather than knock on them.

It wasn't surprising Clayne had developed his attack-first-and-ask-questions-later approach to solving problems. He'd had a rough life before the DCO recruited him. Clayne had been abandoned by his mother when he was five. She'd taken him into a church and just left him there. Clayne had never had much use for churches after that—or mothers. As someone who'd grown up with loving parents and three protective older brothers in the suburbs, Danica couldn't even begin to understand what he'd gone through living in foster care, shuffled from one place to the next.

It didn't help things any when his shifter side came out in his teens. He'd had no idea what the hell was happening to him and didn't know how to handle it. After getting thrown out of high school at sixteen for fighting, he'd lived on the streets doing what he had to in order to survive. The petty crimes he committed turned into other, more serious offenses, which had landed him in jail on more than one occasion.

But that didn't stop Clayne from doing things his own way. He followed a code that didn't make sense to anyone but him. He'd rarely carried a gun, even in situations where someone might shoot him. He wouldn't take things from people he considered weaker than he was, and he never did what other people told him to do.

That code had both kept him out of trouble, and gotten him into it. More often than not, people viewed a man as independent as Clayne as a problem. No one could tell where his loyalties lay, and that scared them.

Clayne's bizarre code of ethics was ultimately what put him on the DCO radar. At the time, he'd never told her what he'd done and she hadn't asked, but she'd gotten the impression he would have gone to prison for a really long time if they hadn't recruited him.

It wasn't until later that she'd finally learned what kind of trouble he'd gotten into. She'd wondered so many times since then how Clayne's life—and hers— might have been different if she'd met him before he'd gotten mixed up in the things he had. They probably wouldn't be chasing serial killers, that's for sure.

"Agent Beckett!"

Danica turned to see a blond man running down the hall to catch up with them. She thought his name was Collins. Or was it Foster?

"Thank God I found you," he said breathlessly. "Carhart wants you and Agent Buchanan in the command center ASAP."

Crap. What had they done now? Or had her boss simply come up with a new form of torture to keep them occupied and out of the way?

"The Hunter made contact, and he's demanding to talk to Agent Buchanan."

Watching Ivy cry tore at Landon's gut. And he couldn't do a damn thing to comfort her because no one in the DCO could know they were husband and wife because workplace romance was against the rules. So he stood there outside the abandoned farmhouse in Saskatchewan, Canada, and cursed the stupid rule that forced them to keep it a secret.

They'd been visiting Jayson when John called saying he wanted them to check out another possible hybrid research lab. The DCO had tracked several large computers perfect for handling the huge amount of data that came with modeling and simulating DNA strands, as well as various medical equipment, to a rural community outside of Saskatchewan. He and Ivy would have been here weeks ago, but now that the doctors knew the DCO was on to them, they'd started covering their tracks. The farmhouse was one of at least twenty different places all over the globe that had come up as possible locations in the past week. Almost all of them had turned out to be bogus, which meant the doctors were deliberately leaking false information, knowing the DCO had limited resources to cover all of them.

John wasn't the only one at the DCO who was concerned. While everyone knew the doctors were out there somewhere, they'd all thought Stutmeir had been the driving force behind the hybrid research. With him dead, the DCO assumed the program would fall apart. Clearly, it hadn't. While they hadn't stumbled on any more nests of vicious man-made shifters, they'd still found evidence of research. And now they had decoy labs popping up all over the world. Even if the doctors weren't actually in all of them, it took a huge amount of money to make the DCO think they were. This wasn't some small-time operation. It was large, well-funded, and growing.

Landon swore under his breath as the two scientists who'd come with them examined the body of the teenage girl they'd found. She was a pretty girl, or had been before the doctors had experimented on her. But while she bore the telltale signs of hybrid research—the horribly twisted body and expression of incredible pain permanently etched on her face—they'd found something else that was both different and disturbing. The finger-nails of one hand were elongated and curved—almost like Ivy's, but not quite.

Up until now, all the hybrid claws they'd seen had been straight and rough, regardless of the shifter breed they were trying to mimic. Even Tanner, who sometimes seemed more shifter than hybrid, lacked Ivy's perfectly shaped and curved claws. But the claws on this poor dead girl's right hand were eerily close in appearance to Ivy's.

That was why his wife was taking it so hard. The knowledge that they may have used her stolen DNA to warp the pretty girl's body was tearing her up inside.

Landon wished again he could take her in his arms, but he couldn't risk it, not with the two scientists a few feet away. All he could do was watch as tears ran down his wife's face.

"I'm sorry," she whispered.

"Don't be," he said softly.

"I'm just not used to seeing children like this." She tried to wipe the tears from her cheeks, but more took their place.

Landon threw a glance at the scientists. They were kneeling beside the body of the girl, not paying any at-tention to him and Ivy.

Screw this.

He took his wife's hand. "Come here."

He yanked her away from the dreadful scene and be-hind the Yukon they'd rented, both so that she wouldn't have to see the kid anymore and so they'd be away from prying eyes. Then he pulled her into his arms and held her tightly.

"You never get used to it," he whispered in her

ear. "I saw more than my fair share of this kind of thing—not the hybrid part—but children lying broken, beaten, and dead. Afghanistan, Iraq, the Sudan…it's always the same and it's never easy to deal with. The day it stops bothering you is the day you know there's something wrong with you." He ran his hand over her long, silky hair. "We'll get those bastards, sweetheart. I promise."

Ivy rested her head on his shoulder, her gaze going to the back of the farm where the scientists were busy taking pictures and collecting samples. She would forever blame herself for letting those doctors get her DNA. It didn't matter that it wasn't her fault, that she couldn't have done anything to stop them, or that they'd be conducting their twisted experiments with or without her DNA. The way Ivy saw it, if they'd never gotten her DNA, this kid might still be alive.

Landon opened his mouth to say something comforting when the satellite phone rang. He swore under his breath and dug it out of his pocket.

"Donovan."

"Landon, it's John. We've got another possible research lab in Norway I need you to check out. Kendra's already got you and Ivy booked on a flight. She's sending you the details now."

Landon was tempted to tell John he'd have to find someone else to handle this one. Ivy needed time to deal with what she'd just seen, and he didn't want her walking into some makeshift lab filled with more dead bodies. But one look at his wife stopped the words in his throat.

She'd obviously heard what John said—that wasn't

a shock since her hearing was ten times better than Landon's would ever be—and was nodding her head.

"Landon, you there?" John asked.

"Yeah. We'll check it out and call you."

He hung up without waiting for a reply and shoved the phone back in his pocket. "You sure about this?" he asked Ivy.

She nodded. "I shudder to think what we're going to find in Norway, and pray that it's not another little girl, but if there's even a chance we might find something that leads us to Klaus and Renard, I want to be there."

When that happened, Landon knew Ivy was going to make them sorry they'd ever been born—for what they'd done to her and that innocent little girl. And Landon swore he would do everything it took to help his wife get that chance.

Chapter 6

CLAYNE WALKED INTO THE ROOM TO FIND CARHART waiting for him, along with a dozen other agents, tech people, and profilers. He couldn't help but notice Carhart looked like someone had pissed all over his Wheaties. And from the way he was glowering at Clayne, he was giving him all the credit.

Foster—the fed who'd been sent to fetch them—leaned over to fill him in since it was obvious Carhart sure as hell wasn't going to do it.

"The Hunter's called several times over the last hour or so demanding to speak with you." He glanced at Danica. "I tried your cell phone repeatedly, but it kept going to voice mail."

The man kept his voice low, as if he was afraid Carhart might overhear. Clayne didn't think he was wrong. Carhart seemed like one of those vindictive pricks who'd go after the low guy on the totem pole just because he was mad at Clayne.

"What did he say?" Danica asked, not bothering to explain the reason she hadn't answered the phone. Clayne suspected it had something to do with not wanting to round up any more of Carhart's suspects. He couldn't blame her.

"Not much, really, once Carhart told him you weren't around," Foster said. "He threatened to kill someone else tonight if you weren't here the next time he called."

Clayne could have said something snide about the stupid-ass suspects he'd been running around all day picking up, but why take it out on a guy who had nothing to do with giving those orders?

"You're telling me even though he's called half a dozen times, you still can't get a fix on his location?"

Clayne glanced up to see Carhart intimidating some poor techie working the phones. Shit, he was practically foaming at the mouth. To his credit, the computer geek didn't flinch.

"I'm sorry, sir, but whoever this guy is, he's smart as hell. I think he's calling from a bootleg satellite phone, which is completely untraceable with the technology we have. Plus, he's bouncing the calls through phone service centers throughout the federal government. I don't even know how to do that."

Carhart swore and turned away to stare out the window. Clayne ignored the fed as a freckled-face, redheaded guy hurried over. The profiler who looked like he was twelve, Wayne Hobson.

"The first call came through around noon, and he's been calling on the half hour every hour since then. The guy knew every detail, including the missing canine teeth. That immediately red-flagged his call and routed him to us. He said he won't talk to anyone except the big, angry guy who chased him out in El Dorado Hills." Hobson gave him a sheepish look and adjusted his glasses. "We figured he had to mean you."

Guess that explained why Carhart was so pissed. Knowing the killer'd only talk to the outcast from the DHS instead of the head of the task force must really be sticking in his craw.

Clayne glanced at his watch. Almost four o'clock. If the killer was true to his word, he'd call soon. The rest of the men and women in the room were obviously aware of the time, too. Everyone seemed to be holding their breath. Well, everyone except Carhart. He looked as if he'd sucked on a lemon.

The phone rang, putting an end to any and all conversation.

The tech manning the phone looked to Carhart, who nodded.

"This is Senior Agent Carhart," he said in his best I'm-in-charge-here voice when the tech thumbed the button on the speakerphone in the center of the conference room table.

"You again." There was a snort on the other end of the line. "I told you that the next time I called, I'd only talk to the leidolf. If you don't put him on the phone in ten seconds, I'm going to walk outside and kill the first person I come across."

Clayne ignored the baffled looks he was getting. The damn killer not only knew he was a shifter, but he knew he was a wolf shifter. Leidolf was an old Scandinavian word for hunting wolf or fighting wolf, or some stupid shit like that. Luckily no one else in the room—except maybe for Danica—understood the significance of the word.

Between his knowledge of the old Norse term, and the trouble he was giving the FBI computer techs, Clayne's opinion of the guy was changing drastically. A shifter who enjoyed killing was bad enough, but a smart shifter who enjoyed killing was even more dangerous.

Clayne stepped closer to the table. "I'm right here.

What the hell do you need to tell me? Any one of the agents working the case could have escorted you to jail. Hell, if you were that eager to turn yourself in, you could have done it at any police station."

Clayne saw Carhart's mouth tighten. It probably wasn't something the fed would have said, but that was tough. He wanted to provoke some kind of reaction from the shifter. Nut jobs like him typically took themselves extremely seriously and usually didn't like people making a joke of their handiwork.

The shifter laughed softly, as if he was genuinely amused by the jab. Clayne had to admit, it was one menacing sound. If the fact that the guy killed people for pleasure wasn't enough to convince him the cat shifter was insane, that laugh sure did.

"I'm glad to see you have a sense of humor." Clayne didn't know how it was possible, but the tone in the shifter's voice dropped the temperature in the room a few degrees. "I was a little worried you were one of those serious alpha dogs. But it's good to know you like having fun. It will make the game much more interesting."

"Game, huh?" Clayne let out a snort of his own. "Should I go get a ball of yarn?"

On the other side of the room, Carhart's eyes narrowed.

"Touché," the killer said. "As much as I'd like to sit here and one-up you, I did call for a reason. I have a special game I want to play with you. I think you'll like it."

"There's only one kind of game I'm interested in," Clayne snarled. "Tell me where you are and I'll show you how to play it. I promise I'll come alone."

The cat shifter laughed again. "That's tempting. But I like my game better. I'm going to grab another rabbit, then hunt him twelve hours after I do. All you have to do to save the rabbit is stop me before I rip out its throat."

The entire room went a few shades paler as he detailed exactly how he was going to hunt his rabbit and what he was going to do to the man when he caught him.

"This guy is a complete fruitcake," Tony whispered to Danica.

Understatement there.

Clayne rested his palms on the table, leaning closer to the phone. "You've clearly thought this out, so I'll play along. Go ahead and give me the cryptic clue you spent all day coming up with so I can get started."

"I'm not giving you any clue," the killer said. "That'd make it too easy for you. What fun would that be?"

When Clayne caught this psycho's ass, it was going to be anything but fun. For the cat shifter anyway. "If you want me to play this kind of game, you have to follow the rules. And everyone knows the rules say you have to give me a sporting chance. If not, I might as well go home and catch a game on TV."

Clayne knew he was taking a chance. The killer could tell him to screw off and hang up. But he was counting on the cat shifter's arrogance.

There was a distinct feline hiss on the other end of the phone. "Fine. But since I'm making this so easy on you, I'm going to give you less time to find me. The hunt will start at ten p.m. Of course, now I have to go collect my rabbit much faster, but I still think that's fair. Hope you FBI pogues have those recorders going, because I'll only say this once—Zero…Nine…N…Zero…Nine." He paused, then added, "Don't be late, Leidolf. That would be a tragedy."

Then he hung up.

Carhart looked at the tech working the trace. "Anything?"

The man shook his head.

"Dammit! Get working on the code he gave us." Carhart rounded on Clayne. "Where the hell did you get your negotiation training? You should have played up to the Hunter's ego and let him think he was running the show so you could drag more information out of him. If you would have taken control of the conversation and asked the right questions, we might have been able to stop him before he kidnaps his next victim."

Clayne wondered if grabbing the head of the task force by the shirt and ripping him a new one would be crossing the line. Probably. "What kind of information? The victim's name and address? That asshole wasn't going to give us shit."

Carhart's face turned so red Clayne thought he was going to explode. He might have if Hobson hadn't jumped in.

"Agent Buchanan's right, sir," he said. "The Hunter doesn't simply act like a predator; he thinks of himself as one. He's a type A dominant personality in the extreme. He'd see any attempt to cozy up to him as a sign of weakness. That's why he wouldn't talk to any of us. He doesn't consider us worth his time." He gestured to Clayne. "The Hunter sees Agent Buchanan as different from the rest of us because he chased him and scared him off his kill. That's what probably piqued his interest. That word he used—*leidolf*—I've heard it somewhere before. It means hunter or wolf or something like that. He thinks of Agent Buchanan as an equal. When Agent Buchanan challenged him over the phone, matching aggression for aggression, it only confirmed what the Hunter already knew. He's now more interested in playing this game with Agent Buchanan than he is in killing. It might cause him to make a mistake."

Well, damn. Clayne might have to adjust his opinion of profilers. Not all of them were oxygen thieves.

Carhart didn't look as if he was buying what Hobson was selling, but at least he didn't look like he was going to have a coronary anymore. After a moment, he nodded. "Okay, Wayne. I see your point. But we're still in a bad tactical position on this one."

Which was a nice way of saying Carhart didn't want his ass hanging in the breeze if and when this next victim turned up dead. But Clayne couldn't disagree with the part about this being a clusterfuck. The shifter had given them a clue, but it was so damn vague, there was no telling what it referred to. Six hours to stop a killer wasn't much time when he'd probably been planning this hunt for days. Which was what the cat shifter was counting on. It was why he'd given them that hint. He knew they'd still be spinning their wheels regardless of what he said.

Carhart looked around the room at the agents, profilers, and techies. "All we have to go on is this code without any context as to what it might mean. We don't know if it's related to the victim or where this hunt is supposed to take place. We need to ask ourselves how the hell we're going to stop the Hunter from grabbing his next victim."

"We can't," Clayne said.

Carhart gave him with what would have been a withering look if Clayne gave a shit what he thought. "I don't know how they do things at Homeland, Buchanan, but the FBI doesn't give up. This is a man's life at stake here."

"Don't you think I know that?" Clayne fought the urge to bare his teeth. "But we're not going to be able to stop the killer from grabbing him. Not this time."

"Why the hell not?"

"Because he already has his victim," Danica said before Clayne could answer. He turned to give her an appraising look. She always was one step ahead of him.

Carhart frowned. "How can you possibly know that?"

"Because the killer detailed exactly how he was going to chase this rabbit down," Clayne said. "He said his victim would trust his feet and try and outrun him instead of standing up to him in a fight like the others had. He knows the guy will head uphill and through the thickest parts of the brush, trying to lose the killer on the rough terrain. Those weren't guesses. He's stalked this victim long enough to know exactly how he's going to react. I wouldn't be surprised if this victim is a runner—probably cross-country."

Which was one demographic the DCO hadn't included in their search parameters.

"That doesn't mean he already kidnapped his victim," Carhart insisted. "He could be on his way to grab him right now."

"Maybe, but I don't think so," Danica answered before Clayne could reply. Which was probably just as well. Carhart didn't seem willing to listen to anything he said anyway. "The killer wouldn't have bargained away his time if he didn't already have his victim ready to go. He's not stupid. He didn't give up anything."

More than one FBI agent looked a little ill at that.

Carhart looked to Hobson for confirmation. The profiler nodded.

"Agent Beckett is right. And if we accept that the killer has his victim already, our only hope of saving him is to stop the hunt before it starts."

Carhart swore. He looked completely out of his element on this one. If he wasn't such an a-hole, Clayne might feel sorry for him.

He turned to Clayne. "You seem to have some kind of connection with this killer. How do we stop him?"

Clayne didn't like what he was implying, but this wasn't the time to get in another pissing contest with the head of the task force. If Carhart could put aside his animosity, so could he. "Assuming we're correct about him already having his prey, that means the clue he gave us has to be related to the location where the hunt will take place. We need to figure it out and get there first."

Carhart considered that, then nodded. "Okay, that's what we do." He gave the other people in the room a nod. "Make it happen, everybody. And see if local PD got any missing person reports within the past twenty-four hours."

Half the room immediately started typing furiously on computers, while the other half worked the phones. It was pure chaos, but with a single purpose—figure out what that string of numbers and letters meant so they could save a man's life. But while they were diligent, they weren't the DCO.

Clayne turned to Danica. "I'm going to make a call."

He pulled his cell phone from his pocket and went into the hallway. When Kendra answered, he explained the situation, then gave her the code.

"I'll call you when we have something," she said.

Not "if" but "when"—that was one thing Clayne liked about the DCO. He put his phone away and went back into the room.

"We're not coming up with anything obvious," Danica told him. "That string of letters and numbers doesn't correspond to any known address, building code, company, organization, city zoning district—anything."

Clayne knew it couldn't be that easy.

"I think I figured out who the victim is," Tony announced.

Everyone froze.

"Sacramento PD got a report of a kidnapping this morning—a high school track and field coach named Joshua Vender. Witnesses saw a man drag Vender into a van outside the school's gym." Tony gave Clayne a nod. "You were right. Vender's specialty is cross-country running. He's won dozens of awards for races he competed in."

"Did they get a description of the guy who grabbed him?" Danica asked.

Tony shook his head. "No. Just a big guy, wearing a hoodie and sunglasses. Nothing on the van, either. Cops found it a few blocks away, wiped clean."

Carhart singled out a female agent. "Jansen, take Anders and talk to the witnesses. See if one of them remembers something that'll help."

As the woman hurried out, Danica turned to Clayne.

"Why change his MO and grab a runner this time?" she asked softly. "Why not go after the guys on our profile, the ones who'd put up a fight?"

Clayne shrugged. "Maybe he got bored. Maybe he thought it'd be more fun to chase someone who could run fast. The other ones weren't much of a challenge for him."

Around the room, people had separated into smaller groups to pursue their own interpretations of the clue the killer had given them. This was the part of the job Clayne hated. He was lousy at this kind of stuff. So he stood hovering over Danica while she listened to the recording of the telephone conversation on a pair of headphones. In the front of the room, Carhart and several other agents studied the killer's clue that had been enlarged and projected onto a screen. Clayne didn't think much of Carhart, but he hoped the bastard could come up with something soon.

Two hours later, Danica pulled off the headphones. "I might have something."

Everyone stopped what they were doing to give her their full attention.

"I think the killer gave us an additional clue. Listen to what he says right before he hangs up."

She played the recording on speaker so everyone could hear it.

"You mean the part where he says it'd be a tragedy?" Clayne asked.

Danica nodded. "He puts emphasis on the word. It's too deliberate and precise to be a coincidence. It has to mean something."

"Yeah," Tony agreed. "But what?"

While half of them kept trying to decipher the code, the other half focused on the word *tragedy* and what it might mean. Clayne put in a quick call to Kendra to give her the new information, then sat down with Danica and Tony to work on it. Unfortunately, there were dozens of locations in the Sacramento area that could be associated with the word—and that was just in the literal sense. When they started looking at tragedies that had occurred in the area, the possibilities jumped astronomically.

Clayne stared at the computer screen they were crowded around until his eyes went blurry. They had less than three hours until the deadline and all this searching was getting them nowhere.

He got to his feet and walked over to stare out the window. The view wasn't much, but in the distance he could see trees and, beyond that, mountains. That's where they needed to be focusing their search. Behind him, Danica pushed back her chair and got up.

"You okay?" she asked.

Clayne gave her a sidelong glance. The concern on her face almost looked genuine. He turned back to the window. "As much as I hate your boss, I'm wondering if he was right. Maybe I shouldn't have antagonized the killer."

"You got a clue about where his next hunt is going to take place. That's more than any of us could have done." When Clayne didn't say anything, she sighed. "Now that he knows who you are, he's more interested in challenging you."

Clayne looked at her, a wry smile curving the corner of his mouth. "Don't you mean what I am?"

Something flickered behind her eyes, but she turned

away before he could figure out what it was. "Come on. Let's get back to work."

Was that what she was calling it? He called it wasting time. He was just about to suggest to Danica they go check out some of the places while the rest of the task force kept looking, but Carhart beat him to it. Clayne waited impatiently as the fed divided up the locations among the agents.

"Beckett, you and Moretti take the house in Rancho Cordova," he said. "There was a home invasion there a few years back. The whole family was murdered. Papers called it a tragedy. It also had a few of the numbers in the address."

Danica took the piece of paper he held out, then showed it to Clayne. "It's close to a wooded area."

But it wasn't nearly remote enough. Clayne didn't mention that, though. Maybe he'd think better outside in the open air. Not that the four-door sedan was all that open, but at least it made him feel as if he was doing something other than sitting on his hands. And for once, being in the tight confines of the car with Danica and her sweet scent didn't distract him. If anything, it made him focus.

He pulled out the map of the Sacramento area he'd grabbed from the field office, hoping something would jump out at him. Regardless of the clues, going to a residential area didn't feel right.

"This is the wrong way," he said. "Turn the car around."

Danica did a U-turn and headed east without batting an eye. Tony, on the other hand, didn't have as much faith in him.

"Where are we going?" He glanced over his shoulder

at Clayne and frowned. "Are you reading a map? How the hell can you even see in the dark?"

Clayne didn't answer. Why he could see in the dark was need-to-know. And as to where they were going, he wasn't sure. He only knew it wasn't Rancho Cordova.

He studied the map again, looking at it more closely. If he was a psycho shifter serial killer, where would he go to hunt? A big-ass forest would be nice. And look, there was one to the east of town. Why the hell hadn't someone mentioned that before? Because they were all focused on that damn string of numbers the shifter had given them. Which didn't have anything to do with the Eldorado National Forest.

Hang on.

There was a picnic area called Tragedy Springs.

"The Eldorado National Forest," he said. "There's a picnic area there called Tragedy Springs. If he's going to hunt someone, that's where he'll do it."

Danica's gaze met his in the rearview mirror. "That's almost two hours from here."

"If you're wrong, we won't be able to get back to Sacramento before the deadline," Tony added. "You know that, right?"

Clayne nodded. "I know."

Tony turned around in his seat. "Why didn't the computers flag this place?"

Clayne's cell phone rang before he could answer. He pulled it out and checked the screen.

"Kendra," he said as he held it to his ear. "Tell me you've got something."

Preferably something to confirm his gut was right.

"Maybe," she said "That combination of letters and numbers you gave me correlates to a small road in the Eldorado National Forest near a picnic area called Tragedy Springs. It's the only place I could come up with that had both of those parameters. I'm sending the directions to your phone, but it's still going to be hard to find. Especially in the dark."

"I'll find it," he said. "Thanks, Kendra."

Tony glanced back. "Was that Homeland?"

Clayne nodded. "There's a road near the picnic area that corresponds to those numbers. Kendra's sending me the directions."

Danica gave him a grin in the rearview mirror. She'd never doubted him, he realized. Despite everything that had happened between them, she still trusted him. The knowledge did strange things to him. Analyzing what those things were now wasn't an option, though. He needed to focus on stopping the shifter.

Danica made the two-hour drive in an hour and a half with her lights and siren, scaring the hell out of both him and Tony, as well as everyone else on the highway.

Clayne glanced at his watch. They weren't quite there yet, but they were damn close. For the first time, he honestly thought they might make it.

But the moment they entered the national park area, his hopes plummeted. There were dozens of paved roads with hundreds of smaller dirt roads and trails crisscrossing them. Clayne had a hard time reading the tiny signs in the dark. He didn't know how the hell Danica and Tony managed. And the directions Kendra gave him were worthless.

"This is going to take all night," he muttered.

"Maybe not," Danica said.

She'd always been a glass-half-full kind of woman. Clayne opened his mouth to remind her of that when she suddenly spun the car into the path of an oncoming pickup truck and slammed on the brakes.

Clayne jerked forward in his seat belt. "What the hell?"

But Danica was already out of the car and running toward the other vehicle. It had to be the shifter. Why else would she stop?

Clayne jumped out, ready to protect her against the crazy-ass killer, only to skid to a stop when he realized the truck belonged to a park ranger. Behind him, Tony did the same. Danica already had a map spread out on the hood and was asking the gray-haired man if he could help them find the road they were looking for.

The old guy pulled out a flashlight and squinted at the map. "Yeah, I can take you to it. But there really isn't anything there. It just dead-ends at a trailhead."

"If we don't get there in less than twenty minutes, a man's going to die," she said.

That got the ranger's attention. He snatched the map from the hood and yanked open the door of his truck. "I hope that car of yours is insured because it ain't going to look so good by the time I get you to that road."

"Just get us there," Danica told him.

The ranger might look like he was on the downward slope toward retirement, but when he started driving, he didn't mess around. Danica was hard-pressed to keep up with him. Clayne thought more than once that maybe he should have driven. His reflexes and night vision would have helped. Driving also would have given him something else to do besides check his watch every five seconds.

Danica switched on the siren to accompany the lights that were already flashing in the grill of the car. The screams filled the heavily wooded surroundings and bounced back at them.

"Maybe the sound will make the killer bolt if he thinks we're close," she told him and Tony. "Or at least give Joshua Vender something to run toward."

What she said made sense, but something told Clayne it wasn't going to matter. They still had ten minutes until the deadline, but his gut was saying they were already too late.

Clayne slammed into his seat belt again as Danica slid the car to a stop inches from the rear bumper of the park ranger's truck. Clayne opened the door and immediately jumped out. The old guy'd been right about there being nothing up here. Except for an opening in the overgrown bushes that some adventurous hikers might call a trail.

Behind Clayne, Tony ordered the ranger to stay in his truck even as he leaped out, gun in hand.

"Can you find him?" Danica asked.

Clayne had gotten the shifter's scent from the first time he'd chased him. Even now, he picked up a slight trace of it on the breeze. They'd been fortunate to come in downwind of the hunting sight.

He gave Danica a nod.

"Then go," she said. "We'll be right behind you."

Clayne ignored the startled expression on Tony's face and took off at a sprint into the trees.

He shifted as he ran. His sense of smell immediately exploded, and he was assaulted by the thousands of scents that made up the forest. Rabbits, deer, squirrels, and mice predominated, but somewhere nearby, a black bear prowled about. And overlaying all of it was the overpowering scent of humans. This national forest probably saw hundreds, if not thousands, of visitors per day, so if he'd been trying to find Joshua Vender out here, he might have been in trouble. But he wasn't tracking Joshua Vender—he was hunting a shifter.

Luckily, shifters possessed a distinct scent all their own. Once Clayne sniffed a particular shifter, he never forgot the scent. Hell, he could pick it out of a crowd at a football stadium. Out here in the forest, with the thousands of powerful scents coming at him, he could still pick out the shifter as easily as if he were standing beside him.

The breeze carrying the scent was coming from the right. Clayne turned that way and put on more speed. The smell was strong enough to make him think it was coming from the shifter himself, not a trace he'd left behind on the ground.

That was good. But also freaking weird. The shifter's scent seemed to be all over the place. Like he'd been pacing his prey at a distance, watching and playing with him.

Clayne ignored the side trails and focused on the primary scent he picked up on the wind, not worrying about where the shifter had been and where he'd run. He only cared about where the killer was at the moment.

But as Clayne ran toward the source of the scent, unease gripped him. The shifter wasn't moving anymore. Did that mean the hunt was already over? Praying he was wrong, Clayne growled and pushed himself harder.

While he was focused on reaching the killer—and the victim—Clayne couldn't deny he was worried about Danica. And Tony, too. But mostly Danica. They might not be partners anymore, but he still didn't like the idea of leaving her alone in the pitch-black forest. What if she got turned around in the dark and ran off a cliff or something?

He slowed a little, straining his ears for sounds of movement behind him—sticks snapping underfoot, someone crashing through underbrush or over rolling rocks, even cursing. Anything that would let him know where Danica was.

But as he pushed his senses out, he was shocked to discover he knew exactly where she was—behind him and a little to the south. He must have subconsciously picked up some sound that let him pinpoint her location. But he immediately dismissed that thought. He hadn't *heard* anything. He'd *felt* something—that same twitchy sensation he'd gotten right before Danica had walked into the conference room that first day at the FBI field office.

He would have dwelled on what that meant, but he didn't have time. While he'd been distracted, the shifter's scent had started to fade. The killer was on the move again. Which meant Clayne needed to stop screwing around and focus. He didn't want the bastard pulling a fast one and doubling back to set an ambush. Or worse, circle around to attack Danica, Tony, or the park ranger.

Clayne didn't get more than a hundred feet before the overpowering smell of fresh blood assaulted his nose.

Shit.

Clayne raced toward the smell of the blood, praying he was in time but knowing he wasn't. The stench was strong, which meant there was a lot of it.

He found Joshua Vender wedged up against a tree, his throat ripped out, his head at a funny angle, his body limp and draining fast. Unlike the other victims, there were no other wounds on the body. The cat shifter hadn't had time to play with his prey. The guy had only been dead for two or three minutes. If Clayne had gotten there a few minutes earlier…

He took off with a growl, running so fast now that the trees around him became a blur. It wasn't hard to follow the killer's trail this time because it moved in a straight line. Clayne was still downwind of the bastard, too. If he was lucky, he'd catch up to the psycho before the other shifter knew what was happening.

But the trail stopped cold at a paved road. The asshole had jumped in a car. Clayne tried to remember where this particular road came out. Shit. It'd take twenty minutes to go back to Danica's car and get back here. And he sure as hell couldn't catch up to a speeding car on foot. He roared in frustration, not caring that it echoed through the forest and probably scared the shit out of whoever heard it.

By the time he got back to the crime scene, Danica and Tony came running up out of the trees, weapons at the ready, flashlights swinging around wildly. Not that Clayne wasn't relieved to see them, but how the hell had they managed to stumble across him in the middle of the freaking forest? He thought for sure he'd have to corral them. He let the wolf inside go, retracting his claws and allowing his fangs to disappear back into his jaw as he walked over to meet them. Darkness closed in around him as his eyes returned to normal.

"Shit, you were right," Tony muttered, glancing at Danica as he shined the beam of his flashlight on the body. He looked at Clayne. "I didn't think we were going to find anything out here in the dark, but she led us right to him."

Clayne lifted a brow. Damn. He didn't remember Danica being that adept at finding her way around in the woods before.

Danica ignored the remark and walked over to take a closer look at the body. Tony followed, his eyes scanning the darkness.

"He hasn't been dead very long. Any chance the killer is still in the area?"

Clayne shook his head. "I followed his trail. It dead-ends at a road about a half mile from here. He had a vehicle waiting."

Tony looked at him in disbelief. "You found the body in the dark, then trailed the killer through the woods, all without a flashlight? What are you—half Native American, half bloodhound?"

"Something like that," Clayne murmured. "We need to get the task force up here. We might be able to block off the roads and catch this son of a bitch if we're quick."

Tony studied the body for a moment longer, then holstered his gun and took out his cell phone. He muttered a curse. "No signal. I'll go back to the car. See if I can get one there."

"You okay finding your way back in the dark?" Clayne asked.

God, he hoped so. He really wasn't in the mood right

now to play chaperone. In fact, he felt like going off and punching a few trees.

"I got it," Tony said. "I'll see you down there."

Clayne watched as he disappeared into the trees. At least he was headed in the right direction.

"This wasn't your fault, you know," Danica said softly.

He didn't look at her. He didn't ask how she knew he was thinking that exact thought, either. They'd been partners long enough for her to be able to read his mind.

"Yeah, it was. I didn't get here in time, and that got this guy killed."

"You figured it out as fast as you could." She rested her hand on his arm. Her touch was a reminder of everything he'd been missing since she'd left him. He wanted to pull away but couldn't. "The killer made sure we didn't have enough clues to give us a fighting chance. He was screwing with us all along, you know that. He was going to kill this poor guy whether we got here in time or not. You got here faster than anyone else on the task force could have."

"Tell that to Joshua Vender's family, and the families of this asshole's other victims." Clayne jerked his head in the direction of the car. "Come on. Your boss'll be here soon."

She fell into step beside him. Clayne swore as he inhaled the shifter's scent. Shit, that bastard had been all over the place up here. Maybe Danica'd been right. Maybe the killer had started his hunt earlier than he'd said. Maybe he never intended to give Clayne a chance to stop him. That was the only thing that explained why his scent was scattered so far and wide.

Carhart had the roadblocks in place long before he arrived by helicopter. Then he sent the bird back up to help with the search while he set up a mobile command post and tried to establish a perimeter around the whole park. As much as Clayne prayed the FBI would find the Hunter, his gut told him it was too late. This shifter was smart. He would have had an exit strategy planned. He would be long gone by now.

Clayne let Danica and Tony fill Carhart in on the details of what had happened. He could hear what was being said from where he stood, but since he wasn't in the mood to play nice, he decided to stay out of it. He swore that if Carhart gave Danica one second of grief, he was going to walk over and knock the fed out cold.

But Carhart kept his mouth shut as Danica explained how they'd come up with the sudden inspiration to check out the National Forest but had gotten there too late. Carhart threw a suspicious glance in Clayne's direction as he listened. It was obvious the fed was angry as hell, but there wasn't really anything he could say since their hunch had been right. That was good. Because between thinking about the dead track and field coach and all the people in his life who would miss him, and the smug, arrogant bastard of a shifter who was probably laughing at all of them right then, Clayne was getting more pissed off by the minute.

Chapter 7

Danica's groan echoed in the break room as she poured coffee into her Tweety Bird mug. Being so close to Clayne was damn near killing her. Every time he looked at her with those hurt-filled eyes, she wanted to throw herself in his arms and beg for his forgiveness. And when he smiled at her like he had yesterday after she'd made that silly joke about him getting hangry, she'd almost cried.

Leaving him the first time had hurt so much she'd thought she would die. And when he was the one who left this time, she knew it was going to be even worse.

Clayne was leaning against the wall outside her office when she came back from the break room. He looked beat. Not surprising. It was one thirty in the morning. They'd driven straight back here from the park, hoping the whole time to hear that the Hunter had been apprehended. It hadn't happened.

She was about to ask if he wanted to get something to eat when Wayne Hobson ran down the hall. The profiler didn't look as if he'd slept any better than her and Clayne. "Agent Buchanan, the Hunter's on the phone. He wants to talk to you."

Clayne muttered something under his breath and pushed away from the wall, leaving her and Wayne to catch up as he stalked down the hall in that predatory way only he could pull off.

Everyone in the command center eyed him warily, as if they weren't sure what kind of mood he was in. Or maybe they were just wondering who the hell this Homeland agent was and why the serial killer had fixated on him.

Wayne pressed the speaker button on the phone.

"I'm here," Clayne said.

He might have sounded calm, but Danica knew he was close to boiling over. Tony must have been getting a bead on Clayne by now, too, because he threw her a worried look. If he only knew how bad it could get when Clayne got seriously pissed, he'd really be concerned.

"Took you long enough," the killer taunted. "But that really doesn't surprise me. You're not nearly as quick as I thought you'd be."

Clayne growled. Danica stepped closer to him. She didn't know why—it wasn't as if he was going to go all shifter right in front of everyone. But still…she figured she should be close, just in case.

The Hunter ignored the rumble. "I even took my time catching that runner. I let him get away half a dozen times, but you no-showed on me. What kind of game is that?"

Clayne went from furious to code red in the blink of an eye. She saw his fingernails go ragged as he leaned over the teleconference phone. Oh crap, maybe he would shift in front of everyone. Could she fix something like that? Could John?

"You want to know what kind of game this is?" Clayne snarled. "This is the kind of game that ends with me ripping your throat out. I know it, and you know it. Before, it wouldn't have been personal. Just work, you know? But now, I'm going to enjoy listening to you scream when I end you."

As if he wanted to give the shifter a preview, Clayne slammed his fist down on the phone, breaking it and splintering the table underneath. Everyone around it almost fell over each other as they scrambled to get away from the flying wood chips and plastic fragments.

Danica cringed. That was one way of hanging up.

Even Carhart wasn't stupid enough to say anything as Clayne stormed out of the room.

She started to follow, but Tony caught her arm. "I know you two have a past and that things didn't end well—I get that," he said softly. "But we both know he's the only one who can catch this guy. I don't have a clue what the hell is going on between them, but he and the Hunter are playing a game we're not meant to be part of. You get that, right?"

She nodded. She got it, all right.

"Good. Then go out and get him drunk, get him laid—whatever. But get his head right. Because we need him."

Danica caught up with Clayne in the parking lot. She thought about trying to talk him down right there, but changed her mind. Instead, she grabbed his big bicep and steered him toward her car. She practically had to shove him in the passenger seat, but once she put him inside, she ran around and got behind the wheel, then squealed out of the lot before he could bolt on her.

"Where are we going?" he demanded.

"To a bar."

"Why?"

She didn't answer him. Tony had suggested getting him drunk or getting him laid. It went without saying that alcohol seemed the safer of those two options. She drove to a bar a few miles down the road. It didn't look too seedy, so she figured it'd do.

Clayne got out and scowled at her over the top of the car. "What the hell are we doing here when we have a killer to catch?"

She motioned toward the bar. "Just go."

The place was almost empty except for a young guy wiping down the bar. The chairs were already up on tables. The guy behind the bar glanced up as they walked in.

"Sorry, we're closed."

Danica flashed her badge as she led the way to a table in the back corner. "You're open."

The guy squinted at the badge, then shrugged. He probably figured if two FBI agents wanted to obliterate their livers after closing time, it was their business.

"Whatever," he said. "What'll it be?"

"Two glasses of whiskey." She glanced at him as she took one of the chairs off the table. "And bring the bottle."

Clayne lifted a brow but didn't say anything as he took down the other chair and sat. He looked even more pissed off now than when he'd taken his fist to the phone back at the field office.

The bartender thumped two glasses on the table and poured a healthy shot for each of them, left the bottle, then went back to wiping down the bar as if they didn't exist.

Danica turned her attention back to Clayne. He was glowering at the glass of whiskey like he was trying to intimidate it.

"Drink," she told him.

He ignored her. "How the hell is this going to help catch that son of a bitch?"

"By getting your head screwed back on straight."

"I'm fine," he said.

"Bullshit." She pushed his glass closer. "You forget—I know you. We didn't get there in time and Joshua Vender paid for it. Now, you're eating yourself up inside. As harsh as this sounds, you're going to have to get over it. We need you fully in the game. If you're still thinking about the last victim, the next guy doesn't have a chance."

Clayne looked sideways at her. "You know me, huh? So you're the lucky one who got stuck playing shrink? Or did you volunteer hoping you'll get a promotion if you close this case?"

Danica didn't know whether to get up and leave or smack him. She didn't do either. So she went for option three—she picked up her glass of whiskey and downed half of it. Then grimaced. God, she hated the taste of whiskey. It burned like fire on the way down, numbing everything as it went. Numb was good. She could do numb.

She lifted the glass to her lips, ready to finish the rest, but Clayne got there first. He pulled it out of her hand and slammed it down, sloshing its contents on the table.

"What the hell are you doing?" he demanded. "You never drink whiskey."

"I just started."

She reached for the glass again, but he moved it out of the way. "What's going on here, Danica? Really."

She considered reaching for his glass but changed her mind. Instead she sat back in her chair and folded her arms with a shrug. "You need to talk, and I'm here to listen."

He let out a harsh laugh. "Now you're playing the concerned ex-partner?"

"I'm more than your ex-partner, and you know it. And I am concerned."

"Right. I'm sure that sounded really sincere before you said it." He shook his head. "Your act would work a hell of a lot better if you hadn't pissed all over me in your rush to get out of the DCO two years ago."

Clayne pushed back his chair and headed for the door. Danica watched him walk away, knowing if she didn't stop him, he was going to go do something stupid or reckless, or both.

"Dammit, Clayne! It's not like I had a choice."

He stopped and Danica had a second of terror as she realized she'd said the one thing she shouldn't have. The agony of the entire situation hit her all at once and she choked back a sob as Clayne turned and strode back to the table.

"What the hell does that mean?" he demanded, his voice dangerously low.

On the other side of the room, the bartender was eyeing them like he was wondering if he should call the cops. Danica couldn't blame him. Clayne looked like he was on the verge of tearing the place apart.

Crap, she'd really put her foot in it. "I just meant that there really wasn't any easy way to break it off. With you, I mean."

God, that sounded lame even to her.

"That's bullshit, Danica, and you know it. You leaving never made any sense at all, so what did you mean just now when you said you didn't have a choice? You make it sound like someone held a gun to your head, and I want to know who. And don't bother lying to me again—you've turned into a shitty liar since we've been apart."

Danica swallowed hard. She couldn't tell him. If she did, all the sacrificing she'd done for the past two years would have been for nothing. But the longer Clayne stood there looking at her with those puppy dog eyes, the harder it was to remember that.

She opened her mouth to lie again, but stopped herself. She'd been lying for so long that she simply couldn't do it anymore. The load was too heavy to bear. Even if she could, Clayne wouldn't let it go, especially now that he knew she was hiding something. He was damn stubborn like that—like a dog after a bone, they'd always joked. Except now it wasn't so funny.

Clayne sat down and leaned forward, piercing her with those beautiful liquid brown eyes. "Neither one of us is walking out of this place until you tell me the truth."

She shook her head, fighting back tears. She wanted to tell him, she truly did, but the words wouldn't come.

Clayne reached out and took her hands in his big, strong ones. The warmth of his skin was like an old comfy shirt, reminding her of everything she'd given up.

"Honey, please talk to me."

The softly spoken entreaty was her undoing. "I

left to keep you from going to prison for the rest of your life."

There, she'd said it.

She grabbed her half-full shot glass and downed the rest of the vile stuff. It burned like hell but not nearly as much as it had the first time. She reached for Clayne's glass. If he wasn't going to drink it, she sure as hell would.

But Clayne moved faster than she did, snatching the glass away without spilling a drop, then taking her hand again. "That's enough whiskey. Now, explain what you meant. How did dumping my ass and leaving the DCO keep me out of prison?"

Danica couldn't look at him. She gazed down at his hands holding hers, drawing strength from them. "I made a deal with Dick. He agreed he wouldn't send you to prison if I left the DCO…and you. It was a one-time deal with a five-minute expiration date on it. I had to break up with you, and I had to do it fast. That was why I said all those horrible things to you—I knew you'd never let me go otherwise."

Just thinking about it made her feel sick.

Clayne was silent for so long she thought he didn't believe her. She lifted her head, half afraid of what she would see. But he only sat there with a frown on his face. He was taking this far more calmly than she would have expected.

"Why would Dick want to send me to prison?" he asked. "More importantly, how could he have done it? It's not like he could expose any of the less-than-strictly-legal missions I'd done for the DCO or he would have gone to prison right along with me."

"It didn't have anything to do with any mission you did. He has evidence on you…about those men you killed in Buffalo years ago."

"Buffalo? He was supposed to make that evidence disappear." Clayne's frown deepened. "Tell me everything."

She took a deep breath. In for a penny…

"It happened right after we came back from that mission in the Ukraine," she said. "You remember the one—when we took out that toxic nerve agent lab all by ourselves, incinerating the terrorists and their research at the same time?"

Clayne nodded, his sensuous mouth curving into a smile. They'd been beyond amazing on that job. Everyone at the DCO had been impressed. Everyone except Dick.

"The next morning, Dick called me into his office, and showed me a video…"

———

Washington, DC, September 2011

"Was there any part of that video you missed, Beckett?" Dick asked as he pressed the stop button on the video player.

His smug tone made Danica want to shoot him where he sat. "No, I don't need to see it again."

She'd seen more than enough. She knew about what had happened in Buffalo, but it was still hard seeing the man she loved with blood dripping from his hands. The angle of the camera had been wrong to catch him actually tearing the three men to pieces, but it had caught their bodies hitting the ground and Clayne walking away from them.

Clayne had told her about the way he'd screwed up and let himself get sucked into what he thought was a simple border-crossing job. He thought he'd be moving stolen merchandise. Electronics, cigarettes, maybe even maple syrup—yeah, there was even a black market business in maple syrup. But then Clayne had learned his partners in crime were moving something he really wasn't cool with: little girls. They had a buyer in Toronto who'd been ready to ship them overseas that same night.

The three thugs hadn't counted on Clayne's keen sense of smell—or his morals. Clayne had let the girls go, then confronted the men. The argument had gotten ugly, and Clayne had ended up killing them.

"Those men were pigs," Danica told Dick. "They were involved in human trafficking. Little girls."

"So Buchanan told you about it?" He shook his head as he took the VHS tape out of the machine. "I knew you and he were too damn close. But at least it saves me from explaining all the meaningless details. You see, the funny thing about those three men? Nobody has a clue they were involved in human trafficking. All anyone knows is that they were ripped to shreds by a vicious killer. No one is exactly sure how he did it, but they know he did it. This video is proof."

There was something going sideways here, and she didn't have a clue what it was.

"What are you getting at?" she asked.

"You're quick," Dick said. "I can see why John recruited you. Pair your brains with Buchanan's brawn and you make one hell of a good team. But all good teams have to be broken up at some point, and now is that time for you and Buchanan."

Danica's stomach dropped. Why would he want to split them up? It made no sense.

"So you're going to walk out of here and tell Buchanan that you're quitting the DCO," Dick said. "Then you're going to get as far away from DC as possible."

"And if I don't?"

He gave her a humorless smile. "I'll make sure this video—and all the rest of the evidence that implicates Buchanan in those murders—finds its way into the hands of the Eerie County District Attorney. And your partner will spend the rest of his life in jail."

The bastard was full of crap. "John won't let that happen."

"He doesn't have any say in this," Dick said. "Regardless of our titles, I don't work for him. I work directly for the Committee, and not all of them are as enamored with the EVA shifter program as John is. When I go to them with this information, do you really think they'll care what John has to say?"

Danica had never understood the inner workings of the DCO leadership, but what Dick said made sense. Most of the other operatives called him the Committee's mole. Now, she saw why. But she wasn't going to give in to his blackmail simply because he threatened her.

"You knew about this when you hired Clayne," she said.

He smiled coolly. "Did I? I'm sure this evidence just fell into my hands recently. And I was so concerned that I immediately contacted the Eerie County District Attorney. At least that's what I'm going to tell the Committee. Some of them might listen to you, but it won't matter to Clayne because he'll be in prison by then."

She lifted her chin. "You're bluffing."

Dick didn't say anything. Instead, he pressed the speaker button on his desk phone and dialed.

"Eerie County Attorney's Office," a female voice answered.

"Judy, this is Dick Coleman from Department of Homeland Security. Is Ron in?"

"Please wait while I connect you."

The phone rang once, then a man's voice came on the line.

"Dick, how're things down there inside the belt loop?"

Danica's heart plummeted. She reached out and disconnected the call before Dick could say anything.

"You're a bastard." She hated that her voice trembled, but she was so close to tears. "I'll give my resignation today. But I want the evidence before I go."

He laughed. "You'll give me your resignation right now. And you're never getting the evidence. It stays in my safekeeping to make sure you never come back or contact Buchanan ever again."

Her gut twisted. She had no leverage to make him do anything, and he knew it. "How do I know I can trust you?"

"You don't," he said. "But if you aren't out of DC by tonight, I'll send your boyfriend to prison, and it will be your fault."

Clayne drained his whiskey and thumped the glass down with a curse that drew another nervous look from the young bartender.

"Why the hell didn't you come and tell me that asshole blackmailed you?" he asked.

"Because if I told you, you would have killed him."

Clayne snorted. "You don't think I'm going to do it now?"

He reached for the bottle of whiskey. This time, she was the one to stop him. "That'd be a very bad idea. He still has the evidence on you, remember?"

"He can't use it if he's dead," Clayne pointed out.

"We don't know that for sure. He could have something set up to release the evidence to the police in the event of his untimely death. I made the deal with him because it was the only thing I could do that would definitely keep you out of jail." She sighed. "I know you don't want to hear it, but I did it for you, and that made it all worthwhile. Don't do anything stupid and make what I did a waste, okay?"

Clayne was silent as he mulled that over. "Okay," he finally said. "I won't do anything crazy. But don't think for a second I'm going to let that little prick get away with this."

Danica nodded. She knew that, for today at least, she didn't have to worry about Clayne killing the man.

"You know the thing I don't understand?" Clayne said. "Why go to all the trouble of blackmailing you? It obviously wasn't about getting me out of the DCO. If that was the case, he could have just turned over the evidence to the cops and let them drag me off to jail. Why go after you?"

She shrugged. "I think he simply wanted me out of your life."

"What, like the ultimate cock block or something?" Clayne asked, only half kidding.

Danica only wished it had been that simple. "I had a lot of time to think about Dick's motive over the past two years, and I think it all goes back to why he brought you into the DCO in the first place."

"Because he thought I'd make an excellent field operative?" Clayne's voice was sarcastic.

She gave him a wry smile. "Right. The guy who despises shifters and has never recruited another one since he brought you in."

"Why, then?"

"Don't take this the wrong way, babe, but I think the whole reason Dick brought you into the DCO was to sabotage the shifter program. I remember talking to some of the other operatives, and they used to tell me how Dick was constantly trying to get the program shut down. He probably figured he'd bring in a guy with a history of anger management issues and—"

"I'd blow up at the worst possible time," Clayne finished. "Giving Dick and people like him the ammunition they needed to pull the plug on the whole program."

She nodded. "Yeah. But with me in the picture, you were never going to blow up. Even Dick figured that out. Which was when he realized he had to get rid of me. Then he could go back to counting the days until you lost it."

Clayne rubbed his thumb over the back of her hand. "How did you know I wouldn't? What if he'd been right and you were the only thing keeping me from exploding right in the middle of the DCO?"

She gave him a smile. "Because I knew you weren't the person Dick thought you were. Those three men you killed in Buffalo don't define who you are. Those little girls you risked everything to save showed me what I needed to know."

He stared down at her hands for a long time, the muscles in his jaw working. "Thank you."

"For what?"

"For walking away from me." He lifted his head to give her a rueful look. "I mean, I hated that you did it, and I wish you hadn't, but I understand why you did it. I don't think I would have had the strength to do it if our positions had been reversed."

Danica felt tears start in her eyes again and she blinked them back. "Leaving you nearly killed me."

Clayne reached across the table to cup her face. "Dick's going to pay for what he did. I promise you."

Danica would simply be happy if they could get the evidence he had on Clayne, but she knew that wouldn't be enough for him. Once Clayne figured out how to get at the sword Dick was holding over his head, the man was going to regret being born.

She chewed on her lip, wondering if she should mention that she'd spent the last two years thinking about how to destroy the evidence Dick had on Clayne. She'd toyed with the idea of hiring a private investigator to steal the evidence a few times, but she'd never done it because screwing up would have put Clayne in prison, and she'd never risk that.

Now that Clayne knew about the evidence, they were going to have to find a way out of this situation sooner, rather than later. Clayne wasn't big on patience.

But they had a bigger problem at the moment. Like stopping the Hunter from killing again.

"I know," she said, answering Clayne's question.

"But right now, we've got a serial killer to catch. So we need to get your head in the game."

Clayne didn't answer. Instead, he pulled a twenty-dollar bill out of his wallet and threw it on the table. Then he grabbed her hand and led her toward the door.

"Where are we going?" she asked, hurrying to keep up.

He glanced at her over his shoulder. "Your place."

Her place? "Um…why?"

Danica thought she knew, but she didn't want to jump to any conclusions. That didn't stop her tummy from getting that funny flutter in it at the possibility of being with Clayne again. It had been a really, *really* long time.

Clayne stopped and gave her a look that almost melted her panties. "You said you wanted to help me get my head back in the game. I think we both know the best way to do that."

Heat pooled between her thighs. If he kept gazing at her like that, she wasn't sure they'd make it back to her apartment. Of course, now probably wasn't the time for this, but he wasn't the only one who needed to get his head right—she did, too. And nothing did that for them better than sex.

Clayne held out his hand. "Keys?"

He always did like to do the driving. She handed them over without hesitation. Her hands were shaking too much to drive anyway.

Clayne opened her door, then practically sprinted around to get behind the wheel. Danica gave him directions as he sped out of the parking lot.

"Um, unless you want to get pulled over, you might want to slow down."

She could just picture Clayne drumming his fingers

on the wheel as a police officer took his time writing them a ticket. Not that he'd get a ticket even if he got stopped. Clayne's DCO badge could get him out of just about anything.

He gave her a sidelong glance as he slowed down. "Sorry. I'm just…eager."

She grinned. "Me, too."

Although maybe impatient would be a better way to put it. She was practically bouncing on her seat, she was so excited. But as they got closer to her apartment, she realized they were both going to have to wait just a little bit longer.

"There's a shopping center with a twenty-four-hour pharmacy up on the right," she said. "Can you pull in there?"

Clayne did a double take. "You want to go shopping? *Now?*"

"I don't want to, but I'm pretty sure we're going to need condoms. Unless you have some on you."

Danica almost laughed at the look on his face. Clearly, he hadn't thought that far ahead.

"Don't you have any at your place?" he asked hopefully.

She shook her head. "I didn't really need them."

Surprise flickered in his eyes before he turned back to the road. She didn't know why he was amazed. She'd slept with a grand total of four men before she'd met Clayne. And after leaving him, she'd still been too much in love with him to have sex with anyone else.

The moment Clayne pulled into a parking space, she jumped out and ran into the pharmacy beside the grocery store. She grabbed a couple boxes of the thin, durable kind, then quickly paid the cashier and hurried outside. Clayne took off as soon as she got in the car.

Her apartment—thank God—was only a few blocks from the shopping center. The moment they were inside, she closed the door behind them and turned to Clayne. He was staring at her, his expression unreadable.

"Clayne?"

"I never gave a thought to how hard these past two years must have been for you until today."

"How could you have known? I said a lot of things that night I left to make you think I couldn't stand being near you anymore." She swallowed hard. "But the truth is that I spent the past two years wondering what the hell I was going to do with my life because it only made sense when you were in it."

"I'm sorry about the things I said when I first got here, and about…all the really shitty things I thought about you over these past two years." He shook his head. "But when you left…"

She reached out and cupped his cheek. "It's all right. I forgive you."

Clayne looked at her, his eyes wet with tears. The sight of them almost tore Danica's heart out. In all the time she'd known him, she'd never seen him cry.

"We've just lost so much time," he said, his voice rough with emotion.

She wanted to tell him it didn't matter, that they would more than make up for it, but all that came out was a muffled sob. She closed the distance between them and kissed him—hard.

Clayne gripped her shoulders in both hands and pulled her against him. She thrust her fingers into his

hair and opened her mouth to his, giving him an all-
access pass. This was what she'd given up—being in
the arms of the man she was meant to be with. She had
left him for the very best reason, but now she realized
it wasn't a solution that could have ever worked long-
term. She needed Clayne like she needed oxygen. How
had she survived the last two years without him?

Danica pulled away and rested her forehead against
his. "We have lost a lot of time, and for that, I am so,
so sorry," she said softly. "But we're together now, and
more than going to make up for it. Starting right now."

Clayne pressed her up against the wall and kissed her
so hard she couldn't breathe. She threaded her fingers
in his hair and gave as good as she got. Dear Lord, the
hair on her arms was standing up. She'd never expe-
rienced anything so intense—not even the first time
they'd made love.

Their weapon holsters hit the table by the door with
a thud, but she barely heard it over the impatient growl
Clayne let out as he shoved her suit jacket off her shoulders. This first time wasn't going to be slow and sensual. It was going to be raw and animalistic. And she
wouldn't have it any other way.

Danica wasn't sure who started ripping off clothes
first, but somewhere between playing tongue-twister
and grinding against him, she went for the buttons of
his shirt. Clayne wasn't quite so patient with her blouse.
Instead, he grabbed and yanked, sending buttons flying
everywhere. He went for her bra next, his fingers almost
snapping the front clasp in his haste.

She gasped as his big hands cupped her breasts and
his fingers tweaked her nipples. God, how she'd missed

this. Clayne was the only man she'd ever been with who understood that sometimes a woman needed it just as hard and fast as a man.

He bent his head, burying his face in her neck. She closed her eyes and let out a moan as his mouth worked its way all the way from her earlobe down her neck to her shoulders, kissing, biting, and generally driving her crazy. She was so into what he was doing to her upper body she didn't realize he'd unbuttoned her slacks and shoved them down until she heard her panties tear.

She'd gone through so much underwear during the time they'd been together she sometimes thought she single-handedly kept Victoria's Secret in business— but damn, she loved when he went all caveman on her like that.

He slid his hands between her legs with a groan. "You're so wet."

She let out a husky laugh. "You have a way of doing that to me."

Clayne chuckled and ran his fingers along her pussy lips, up one fold and down the other over and over until she thought she'd go crazy. To distract herself, she finished unbuttoning his shirt and pushed it off his shoulders, baring his chest.

He wouldn't stop what he was doing long enough for her to get the shirt all the way off, but that was okay. She still sucked in a breath when she got a glimpse of the parts she could see. *Daaaaammn*. He really had been working out a lot the past two years. He had muscles she'd never seen before, and he'd been unbelievably well built then.

She slipped both hands inside his shirt, reaching

around to run her nails down his back. Clayne lifted his head with a growl, his dark eyes turning molten gold as they shifted and locked with hers for a moment before he covered her mouth in another scorching-hot kiss.

It was her turn to growl as one of his long, thick fingers slid deep inside her. She clung to his shoulders, digging her nails in deeper as he moved his finger in and out. He didn't do it fast enough to make her come, but he teased her just enough keep her on the edge. She rotated her hips in time with his movements, grinding her clit against his hand.

He lifted his head, watching her face. She caught her lower lip between her teeth as she felt her legs start to tremble.

"You might need to get that condom on soon," she gasped. "It's been a really long time for me, you know?"

A slow smile spread across his face. "How do you know I don't want to watch you come like this?"

The way he was working her, he was pretty damn close already. "I don't mind if that's what you want to do. But I thought you'd want to be inside me with my legs wrapped tightly around you the first time you make me explode."

Clayne slid his finger out so fast she nearly fainted. His head whipped around to find the small plastic bag from the pharmacy. She almost laughed as he yanked the box of condoms out and tore it open. Most of them ended up on the floor, but he got what he wanted—one precious foil packet.

She yanked open his belt and together they shoved his jeans down to mid-thigh. She would have pushed them all the way down, but Clayne was in too much of a hurry. He'd barely pushed his straining underwear down far enough to free his cock before he was tearing at the packet in his hand.

Danica stared at his erection, almost overwhelmed by the urge to drop to her knees and take him in her mouth. But that would have to wait because she wanted Clayne inside her as much as he wanted to be there. She'd spent every night of the past two years remembering what it had been like to be with him, and she wasn't going to wait any longer. And as Clayne lifted her up and shoved her back against the wall, she realized she didn't have to.

She wrapped her legs around his waist as he found her wet opening with his shaft. He teased her by rubbing the tip along her slick folds once, then twice, before finally taking pity on them both and slamming into her with a single, hard thrust that stole her breath and convinced her that leaving him had been the dumbest thing she had ever done in her life. She buried her face in his neck, squeezing him with her thighs as he pounded into her.

Their joining was so amazing it almost moved her to tears. In between moaning, whimpering, and sighing, she probably did cry a little. Only a few short days ago, she thought she'd never see Clayne again, and now that he was with her, she was going to hold on to him and never let go.

Clayne must have felt the same because he gripped her ass in both hands and drove himself so deep inside her she wasn't sure where she ended and he began.

Pleasure spiraled through her, building steadily as Clayne moved in and out. She whimpered against his shoulder as she rode it out, her legs clenching more tightly around him, her heels digging into his well-muscled ass and yanking him harder into her, silently begging him to come with her.

He plunged his cock deeper but didn't climax. "Where's your bedroom?"

"Hallway behind you," she said huskily as she realized he wasn't nearly ready to come yet. "All the way at the end."

Danica started to unwrap her legs from around Clayne's waist so she could lead the way, but he stopped her with a growl. Tightening his hold, he turned and headed for her bedroom, the hands under her ass firmly keeping her impaled on his cock. The way he moved inside of her as they walked created some very interesting friction, and she squeezed her muscles around him, eliciting a low rumble from Clayne. *Mmm, a woman could get used to this.* Clayne clearly liked it, too, because he forgot about the bedroom and stopped in the kitchen to perch her ass on the edge of the counter. Pushing her back, he got a firm grip on both ankles and spread her legs wide, then began to plunder her pussy all over again. In this position, the tip of his penis thumped against her G-spot every time he thrust. The sensation was so overwhelming it threatened to take her breath away.

"Oh God," she moaned.

She dropped her head back, studying him from beneath her lashes. His muscles flexed and rippled each time he moved, mesmerizing her, and she was tempted to sit up so she could run her hands over him. But that would mean he wouldn't be rubbing her G-spot anymore. So she stayed where she was.

Clayne was just as focused on her. His eyes slowly caressed her naked body as if reacquainting himself with it. While he watched, Danica slipped one of her hands down between her legs and made lazy circles round and round her clit. His eyes smoldered.

Touching herself in front of Clayne had always gotten her hot as hell, and the two years apart hadn't changed that. Her orgasm washed over her in big, rolling waves and she had to grab the edge of the counter with her free hand when her head began to spin. She didn't bother to stifle her screams this time. She simply threw back her head and climaxed hard.

Clayne pumped faster, riding her the whole way and making her think he was going to come with her. But the moment the trembling subsided, he slowed his movements again.

She pried her eyes open to look at him. "You waiting for a special invitation or something?"

Clayne smiled down at her, his golden eyes glinting. "I've been waiting two years for this. Do you think I'm going to let it end this soon?"

She opened her mouth to tell him she wasn't going to let him get away with coming just once, but he reached down and pulled her to a sitting position.

"Wrap those legs around me again, woman," he ordered. "I'm getting you in that damn bed of yours this time."

That was the kind of order she had no problem following. She laughed and draped her arms around his neck as he slid his hands under her ass and picked her up again. She didn't know what she'd done to deserve this, but she could only thank God for giving her a chance to fix what she had screwed up so royally.

They made it to the bedroom this time, with only

one short pit stop in the hallway. Apparently, Clayne
couldn't control himself for the whole trip—something
Danica took as a compliment.

Once Clayne had her positioned in the middle of the
bed on her back, he pushed her knees up and drove himself into her. Danica had a moment of panic. After going
so long without sex, then having two orgasms right in a
row, she was afraid she'd be too sore, but to her relief,
her body welcomed him. She wrapped her legs tightly
around his muscular back and urged him to take her as
hard as he wanted.

Above her, Clayne's eyes glowed in the near darkness of the room. His canines were slightly extended,
and his face had taken on that leaner, more chiseled look
the way it did before a shift. Danica supposed a lot of
women would be unsettled by seeing him like this, but
she had always found Clayne's wolf form sexy as hell.
And after not seeing it for two years, those features seriously did it for her right then.

She reached up and buried her hands in his long hair,
yanking him down for a soul-searing kiss. His weight
pressed against her, holding her captive under him as he
pounded into her.

"I've missed this so much," she whispered.

The words were so soft that an ordinary man probably wouldn't even have heard them, but she was sure
Clayne had. He thrust faster and harder, his breathing
hot and heavy in her ear.

He was going to come soon. In her, where he
should be.

Clayne buried his face in the hair around her neck,
teasing her skin with those slightly extended canines.

She knew he was inhaling every trace of her scent, letting it fill every corner of his mind. She arched against him, giving him access to her throat. He groaned and grazed the vulnerable skin with the sharp points of his teeth, moving in and out of her in that ragged way that told her he was peaking.

"Come for me," she begged, wrapping her legs more tightly around him.

He nipped her neck, not enough to hurt, but she could still feel it. The sensation sparked another climax, and she went over the precipice of pleasure with him.

Clayne shoved his cock as far inside her as it would go and held himself there as the last tremors of his climax racked his powerful body. The way he pulsed inside her on top of the rippling aftershocks of her own orgasm was enough to bring tears of happiness to Danica's eyes. She had her wolf back. Everything was going to be okay as long as they were together.

"Don't you ever leave me again, Danica." The soft words were half plea, half sob. "Promise me."

She ran her hands from the damp hair at his neck down to the hard muscles of his ass and back up again to hold him tightly. She wasn't going to let him go—not this time.

"I promise," she whispered.

Chapter 8

NORWAY HAD BEEN ANOTHER DEAD END. AS MUCH AS Ivy wished the doctors had been there so they could finally end this, she was relieved they hadn't found any more dead kids. The one they'd found in Canada was horrible enough. Even so, she hadn't said more than ten words to Landon on the flight back to the States. The longer they went without finding the doctors, the better the chance of them creating a hybrid using her DNA. That possibility gnawed at her so much it was hard to think of anything else.

"None of this is your fault," Landon had told her.

Ivy had been too busy plotting what she was going to do to the two doctors when she and Landon finally found them to correct her husband.

Her silence hadn't been lost on Landon. When they got back to the DCO, he told John they both needed a couple days off to catch up on some much-needed sleep. Ivy let out a short laugh at that. She hadn't slept through the night in months. She didn't know what made Landon think she was going to start now.

Ivy grabbed her iPad from the coffee table and sat down on the couch. What she wouldn't give to go on a good old-fashioned mission that had nothing to do with mad scientists and hybrids. But she and Landon were officially on leave for the next few days, which was probably just as well. As preoccupied as she was, she could lose focus on a mission and get Landon hurt—or worse.

Ivy finally decided on an app and was about to click on it when the doorbell rang. Setting her iPad back on the coffee table, she uncurled herself from the couch and walked over to put her eye to the peephole. Layla's long ponytail bounced as she bobbed her head to the music on the buds in her ears.

Ivy opened the door. "Hey! I didn't know you were coming over."

Layla walked in, taking the buds out of her ears as she passed. "I didn't either. But I figured I'd take a chance and see if you were home." She looked around as she tossed her purse on the coffee table. "Where's Landon?"

"He ran to the store to pick up some milk."

Her sister lifted a brow as she flopped down on the sectional couch. "Since when do you drink milk?"

"Landon thinks eating cereal without milk is a crime against humanity." She still turned her nose up at drinking a whole glass of the stuff, though. "Do you want something? Iced tea, or a bottle of water?"

"No, thanks. I'm good."

Ivy curled up on the opposite end of the couch. "So, what's new with you and Jayson? Has he found a place to live yet?"

Layla had been with Jayson when Ivy and Landon had gone to visit him the other day. While the guys had caught up, she and her sister had gone to the cafeteria to grab coffee. As they waited in line, Layla told her Jayson was being released from Walter Reed soon and that he was terrified of the prospect. The former Special Forces lieutenant hadn't said it out loud, but since Ivy and Landon's wedding, Layla had hung out with him enough to know he was freaked out by the idea of leaving the protective confines of the military hospital. In there, he was just another wounded warrior. But out in society, he'd be handicapped, broken, someone to be pitied.

"Not yet." Layla kicked off her sandals to sit cross-legged on the couch. "We've been looking for apartments. Online, anyway. He's not much help. I think he's still hoping they'll change their minds and tell him he needs to stay longer."

"Does he need to stay longer?" Ivy asked.

Layla shook her head. "I don't think so. He's still in a lot of pain, but the doctors said that isn't going to change for a while. The rehab has taken him as far as it can. The rest is up to him."

Ivy understood that, but it still seemed harsh. She remembered how much pain he'd been in standing at the altar with the rest of the groomsmen at the wedding. That had only been a couple months ago.

"When are they booting him out?"

"They still haven't given him a firm date yet, but it'll be soon. Which is why he needs to find a place to live." Layla made a face. "It doesn't help that when I ask what kind of apartment he wants, half the time he agrees he should get one on the first floor. But then the other half, he acts like he doesn't have any injuries at all and wants to look at third-floor walk-ups."

If Jayson was anything like Landon, that's the kind of apartment he'd move into, just to prove to everyone he wasn't disabled. "He's definitely staying in DC then?"

Layla nodded. "He doesn't have any family left, so

there's no reason for him to go back to Indiana. And moving back to the Fort Campbell area would be silly, too, since his Special Forces buddies are deployed all the time. It just makes the most sense for him to stay in the area considering Landon and the other friends he's made in rehab are here."

"And you're here," Ivy pointed out.

Her sister blushed. "We're friends. I don't think he's going to make major life decisions based on what I want."

"I don't know about that. I saw the way he was looking at you when Landon and I stopped by. He really likes you. It's obvious."

Layla picked up the throw pillow beside her and plucked at the fabric. "I really like him, too. And I'd be lying if I said I didn't want him to stay. But I won't be selfish. If he wants to move somewhere else, I'll support him."

Ivy wasn't sure she could be as selfless if it were Landon. She didn't tell her sister that, though. Layla was pretty impressed with herself already.

"Has he talked about what he's going to do for work yet?" Ivy asked. "Landon told me the army offered Jayson a position at the Special Forces school at Bragg, but that Jayson wanted no part of it."

"Yeah. According to him, he doesn't want to be the guy who can teach it but not do it." Layla let out a snort. "I don't know what the hell that even means. What, does he think they're going to look down on him? Or that he got the job because he's disabled? So what if they do? That's their problem." Her sister tossed the throw pillow back on the couch. "He can be so damn frustrating."

Those were the exact words Landon had used to describe his friend on more than one occasion. She'd tell her sister the same thing she told her husband. "Just be patient with him."

"I'll try." Layla gave her a small smile. "Speaking of jobs, are there any openings at the DCO?"

"For Jayson, you mean?"

"No, silly. For me. You know, something in the psychology department." She pursed her lips thoughtfully. "Although now that you mention it, getting Jayson a job there might be a good idea. With his military experience—"

Ivy cut her off. "No. Absolutely not."

Her sister frowned. "Because he's disabled?"

"I'm not talking about Jayson. I'm talking about you," Ivy said. "There aren't any openings."

That wasn't true. There were always openings for shifters at the DCO. Just not for her sister. The thought of Layla going into a war-torn country with a partner who had orders to kill her if she was ever compromised made Ivy light-headed. And the image of her being strapped down to a table and tortured to get her DNA was enough to make Ivy sick. She'd been lucky to finally get teamed up with a partner like Landon. Her sister might not be as fortunate.

"How do you know?" Layla protested. "Maybe if you talk to your boss—what's his name, John—?"

"Forget it, Layla!"

Ivy jumped to her feet and made a beeline for the kitchen, hoping that would put an end to the conversation, but since the kitchen, living room, and dining room were all one big, open space, it didn't help.

"Why not?" her sister demanded from the couch.

Ivy ignored the question as she refilled her glass with more iced tea from the pitcher in the fridge. Her hands were shaking so badly she could barely get the drink in the glass without spilling it.

Layla let out a frustrated growl and stomped into the kitchen after her. "What the hell is up with you? You have a killer job you love at a place where you don't have to hide what you are. A place that provides you this unbelievable kickass apartment in one of the best parts of DC and pays you an unreal amount of money on top of that. Why wouldn't you want me to get a job there?"

Ivy thumped the pitcher down so hard on the granite counter it would have shattered if it'd been glass and whirled around to face her sister. Layla was standing there with her arms folded and her eyes gleaming like the cat shifter she was. Ivy's own inner feline came out in response, her teeth lengthening slightly, her eyes taking on that same green glow.

It was on the tip of Ivy's tongue to tell Layla about how her first partner had tried to rape her and how the second one had treated her like crap. About the standing order that Landon had to kill her rather than let anyone find out she was a shifter. About the hybrids and all the other monsters out there that she, Landon, and everyone else she worked with protected the world from every day. About being tortured and having needles shoved into her body over and over.

But she didn't say any of those things.

"You don't have a clue what the DCO does or what it thinks about shifters like you and me. To most of the

people there, we're nothing more than useful animals—
like two-legged K-9 sniff dogs."

Her sister snorted. "If it's so bad, why are you still there?"

"Because I don't have a choice, dammit!"

"What the hell does that mean?"

Ivy didn't answer. What could she say? That a pair
of mad genetic scientists had stolen her DNA to make
monsters and that she couldn't leave the DCO until she
found them?

Layla shook her head. "I don't even know why I
bothered asking you. Wait, I know. Because you're my
sister. I thought you'd want to help me out."

Eyes still gleaming, she turned and strode into the
living room to grab her purse. Ivy went after her.

"Layla, wait!"

"Forget it!"

Her sister jerked open the door so violently it nearly
bounced against the wall. She probably would have
slammed it shut just as hard if Landon hadn't been on his
way in with a bag of groceries in each arm. Layla stormed
past him without a word and disappeared down the hall.

"What was that about?" he asked as he closed the door.

Ivy followed him into the kitchen. "She wants a job
at the DCO."

Landon pulled out a half gallon of milk from one of
the bags. "So, what's the problem?"

She loved him, but sometimes he could be so dense.
"She's a shifter, that's the problem."

He put the milk away and closed the fridge. "Yeah,
but she has a degree in psychology, not criminology."

"And Declan was an engineer turned forest ranger,
but they turned him into an operative, didn't they?"

Landon frowned. "Okay, I see your point."

Ivy grabbed a box of cereal and started for the pantry, but her husband took it and set it down on the counter, then pulled her into his arms. She rested her head on his chest, surrounding herself with his warmth.

"Layla wants to join the DCO because she wants to follow in the footsteps of her big sister," he said. "With a résumé like hers, she's going to have so many job offers she'll forget all about the DCO soon enough."

"I hope so."

He kissed the top of her head. "I know so."

Ivy prayed he was right. Because if Layla got a job at the DCO, she'd be so worried about her sister she might never sleep again.

———

Clayne took one hand off the wheel to dig in his pocket for his cell phone. "Can you call John for me? I want to see if the DCO has a lead on this asshole yet."

Danica scrolled through his list of contacts. Her finger faltered when she saw he still had her number among them. Giving herself a mental shake, she continued scrolling until she got to John's number, then put him on speaker. Clayne didn't waste time with pleasantries when his boss answered, but simply asked if the man had any information for them yet.

"Unfortunately, not yet," John said. "There's no record of a shifter who even comes close to meeting the profile of the killer anywhere in our database, or even the older hard copy records. We've been searching for a link, but there's nothing. I think it's time I sent some backup."

"We don't need backup," Clayne growled. "We need a lead on who the hell this guy is."

"We're working on it," John said calmly. "But you're still going to need someone to help with cleanup."

The muscle in Clayne's jaw flexed. "Because you assume I'm just going to kill this bastard, right?"

Danica frowned. What the heck was that about? But if John noticed the anger in Clayne's voice, he didn't mention it.

"I'm assuming you're going to take him down however you have to. Dead or alive, the team will be there to help you clean up just like they always do."

Clayne muttered something unintelligible in reply as he pulled her car into the FBI parking lot. Danica hung up and handed him the phone.

"What was that about?"

"What do you mean?" Clayne asked.

"You got upset when John implied you might have to kill this guy," she said. "Since when do you have a problem with doing that? If there's one person who needs a bullet through the head, it's this sicko."

Clayne jerked the key out of the ignition. "Let's just forget about it, okay?"

She grabbed his arm as he started to get out of the car. "No, I'm not going to forget about it. Something's bothering you and we're not getting out of this car until we talk about it."

He shook his head, a hint of a smile on his lips. "I forgot how stubborn you could be sometimes."

She arched a brow. "Talk about the pot and the kettle. Seriously, what's bothering you?"

"If I hadn't been quick to kill those guys in Buffalo,

both our lives could have been completely different."
When she opened her mouth, he shushed her. "Just let
me say this, okay?"

Danica sat back and waited.

Clayne was quiet for a while before he continued.
"When John implied I was going to kill this guy, it
made me wonder if maybe I'm too quick to pull the
trigger sometimes."

She shook her head. "That's crazy. We were partners
a long time, and I never saw you kill anyone who didn't
deserve it. And as far as what happened in Buffalo, those
jerks deserved it more than most."

"But by killing them, I gave Dick the leverage he
needed to break us up. What if I do something like that
again because I shoot first and ask questions later?"

"Dick is a…well, a dick," she said. "If he hadn't been
able to use that against us, he would have found something else. And as for doing something like that again,
it's not going to happen. You're too smart for that."

Clayne was silent as he thought about that. She
waited for him to argue, but then he smiled. "Thanks.
You always know what to say to keep me straight."

"That's what I'm here for," she said.

"You're here for a hell of a lot more than that." He
leaned over and gave her a hard kiss. "Come on. Let's go
make sure this son of a bitch doesn't kill anyone else."

Tony and the rest of the task force were in the command center trying every angle to find the serial killer.
While they'd been gone, someone had replaced the
phone Clayne had ruined with a new one.

Tony did a double take when they walked in. "I thought
you'd be passed out somewhere," he said to Clayne.

"We just talked," Danica told him.

Tony lifted a brow. "Huh. Must have been some talk." He studied Clayne appraisingly. "I haven't seen you this chill since you got here."

Danica leaned over to look at the computer screen, pretending to be interested in whatever Tony'd been working on before they came in. Her partner was more perceptive than most men, but she didn't think he could tell she and Clayne had slept together simply by looking at them. Not that she cared if he knew, but still…

Thankfully, Clayne changed the subject. "What do we have on Joshua Vender? Any link to the previous victims?"

Tony shook his head. "Not that we can find." He glanced at where Carhart was standing in the front of the room, then lowered his voice. "Carhart hasn't officially come out and said he supports the idea of looking for the Hunter's potential victims, but he sent out some field agents as well as detectives and uniforms from Sacramento PD with the list we came up with. If they're lucky, they'll stumble on the killer when he tries to grab his next victim."

Danica saw Clayne's mouth tighten and immediately knew what he was thinking. It wouldn't be lucky for anyone involved if ordinary, everyday cops tried taking down a shifter. But instead of suggesting they go out and join the search, Clayne surprised her by saying they should try a new tack and focus on how and where the killer had grabbed his victims.

"I know it's a long shot," he said. "But right now, I'm willing to try anything."

Clayne tossed his pen down on the table with a muttered oath. "That asshole is going to grab someone in the next twenty-four to forty-eight hours and I'm sitting here wasting time."

He got up and walked over to stare out the window, not even bothering to suppress a growl. Danica cringed, but luckily no one noticed it. Or if they did, they probably figured it was Clayne just being Clayne. They had the resources of the FBI, as well as state and local law enforcement. How the hell could they have nothing to go on? Of course, the FBI didn't know about the shifter angle. But the DCO did, and they hadn't come up with anything, either.

Danica had just turned back to the file in front of her when movement in the doorway caught her attention. She looked up to see Beth standing in the hallway, a smile on her face and a huge paper bag bearing the logo of her catering company in her hand. Danica's stomach growled as the aroma of Italian food hit her. Over by the window, Clayne turned, his nostrils flaring appreciatively. Danica nudged Tony and jerked her chin toward the door.

He turned, his eyes widening when he saw his wife. Jumping to his feet, he went out to meet her. Danica couldn't hear what they were saying, but she hoped it had something to do with the bag of food in Beth's hand. Tony came back a few minutes later, a sheepish look on his face.

"Beth figured we'd forget to eat, so she brought lunch," he said. "Do you and Clayne want to take a break?"

Danica grinned. "You know I never pass up Beth's cooking." She glanced at Clayne, who nodded.

"Sounds good to me. I could use something to eat."

At the appraising look Beth gave Clayne when they

walked into the hallway, Danica suspected dinner might have been an excuse to get a peek at him. She knew it for sure when her friend turned to her after she made the introductions and silently mouthed the word *wow*.

"I think there's an empty conference room around here somewhere," Tony said.

He started to lead the way but his wife stopped him. "Let's eat outside instead. The weather's beautiful." When Tony frowned, she added, "Come on. I think it would do all of you good to get out of this building and away from the case, if only for a little while."

Beth was right, Danica thought as they walked over to the picnic area behind the building where a lot of agents, including her, ate lunch. It was nice outside. The fresh air would do them good.

As Beth set everything out on the table, a few of the other agents on the task force who knew her—and her famous cooking—came by to say hello and help themselves to her lasagna and homemade garlic bread.

Danica couldn't help but smile as she greeted each of them with a warm hug. It wasn't difficult to see why everyone loved Beth. She was like a ray of sunshine in the middle of this brutal case. Everyone had a bounce in their step to go with the plate of food in their hand when they left.

As Clayne got up to get a second helping, Beth sat down beside Danica. "I take it that things have worked out between the two of you?"

Danica looked at her in surprise. "Yeah. How'd you know?"

Her friend grinned. "Honey, you've been walking around with a forced smile on your face since you moved to Sacramento. The one you're wearing now is the real deal. Plus, you have a blush to your cheeks that only comes from the sun—or really great sex. And since you spent the whole day inside, I'm betting it isn't the sun."

Danica laughed, her face coloring. She should have known Beth would figure it out.

Beth nibbled on a piece of garlic bread. "What's going on with the investigation? Any closer to catching this psycho?"

Danica took a sip of water. "Unfortunately, we're stuck waiting around until the guy makes a mistake that'll lead us to him. Until then, more innocent people are going to end up dead."

Beth frowned. "How long before he makes a mistake?"

"It's impossible to say," Clayne answered. "The smarter they are, the longer it takes. And this guy is damn clever. He's killed six people in the span of a month, and we don't have a clue who he is, who he's going to grab next, or when."

Beth took another bite of garlic bread and chewed slowly. "How does someone just wake up one day and start killing people?"

Good question, Danica thought.

"They don't," Clayne said.

Tony paused, a forkful of lasagna halfway to his mouth. "They don't?"

Clayne shook his head. "I can't believe we didn't think of this before. Beth, you're a genius."

"I am?"

Beside her, Tony frowned. "Clayne, I'm not following you."

"We know this psycho didn't start killing this neatly and cleanly last week, right? The bastard's done this before."

"Yeah, the profilers already thought of that," Tony said. "They looked for similar cases after the fourth murder, then again after the fifth. They didn't find anything. These murders don't match any others."

Clayne grinned. "That's because they didn't know what to look for."

Danica returned his smile. But the DCO did.

Clayne knew it was crazy, but he actually felt a little guilty about leaving Tony out of the loop. But since he couldn't tell the fed about the DCO or what the hell a shifter was, he didn't have much choice. Tony'd given him a bewildered look when Clayne said he and Danica needed to check something out, but he hadn't asked any questions. He simply told them he'd cover for them with Carhart, and get police protection on the potential prey. Since they'd had to go back and add targets they'd originally thought weren't challenging enough, the list of men who had AB blood now had more than fifty names on it. Clayne didn't like the idea of abandoning that lead, but they just couldn't wait around any longer and hope to catch the Hunter the next time he went after a target. The shifter had already shown he was willing to adjust his target set to avoid fitting a pattern. They just had to hope the DCO would come through with a name.

Clayne considered heading to Danica's place to wait for the DCO to call, but decided that would probably be a bad idea. Two minutes after walking in the door, they'd be in bed for another round of hot, sweaty makeup sex. And while he wouldn't mind that one damn bit, they needed to focus on the case. Which was why he was sitting across the table from her with a hard-on at the Starbucks down the street instead. Crap, the woman even made drinking her nonfat latte sexy.

He checked his watch to give himself something else to do besides fantasize about Danica taking off an article of clothing every time she took a sip.

"It's only been a couple hours since you talked to John," she said.

"I know." He picked up his coffee and took a swallow. "I should have had the DCO look into the animal-attack angle before, dammit. If I had, maybe Vender would be alive instead of lying on a slab in the morgue right now."

"Maybe," Danica agreed. "Or maybe not." When he scowled, she added, "It's one thing to look for a shifter who's blatantly killing people. It's another to dig through every animal attack in the country to see if they were really murders instead. No one at the DCO thought of it, either. We were all looking for murders with this exact MO, not a shifter mauling his victims as he learned how to hone his technique. This isn't your fault."

It was his fault, but since he didn't want to get into an argument about it, he didn't say anything. He felt so damn stupid. Thank God Beth had said what she had or he'd still be thinking like a cop chasing a serial killer rather than a shifter going after another shifter. Instead of scouring old case files looking for murders where the killer had hunted his victims, then ripped out their throats and took their teeth for trophies, they should have been looking for animal attacks.

His phone rang, interrupting his mental ass kicking. He checked the call display, then thumbed the answer button. "Tell me you got something for us, John."

"I just sent you some files," his boss said.

Clayne looked around the coffee shop. The place was empty and the teenaged barista had her iPod blaring in her ears so loud even Danica could probably hear it across the room, so it wasn't like anyone was going to hear. He and Danica could have sex right there on the floor and the girl probably wouldn't have noticed, but he didn't want to take any chances.

"Hang on while Danica and I go someplace more private," he said to John.

The only place private was Danica's car. When they were both seated inside, he grabbed his laptop from the backseat and handed it to Danica. He'd never been good with computers and downloading stuff, especially from the DCO's website. The thing was a maze of passwords, folders, and acronyms.

"John sent us some files."

"What's your password?" she asked.

"Your name," he told her.

She blinked. "You never changed it in two years?"

"I haven't used the site since…well, you know."

Since she'd left. He couldn't say the words. He didn't want to remember that time in his life ever again.

Danica shook her head, her fingers dancing over the keys. A moment later, she had the files downloaded and open. The first several were newspaper articles about a series of animal attacks in Colorado two years ago.

Clayne took the phone off mute and put it on speaker so Danica could hear. "Go ahead, John. We're looking at the newspaper articles."

"Intel came up with over a hundred major animal attacks in the United States over the past ten years. After eliminating the obvious ones, they were left with three deaths in Colorado," John said. "The DCO looked into them when they first happened, but dismissed them because they looked like obvious animal attacks. The victims were completely mauled, and there was even a witness to one of them. It didn't look like a shifter kill the first time around."

According to the articles, three men—two late-night joggers and a hiker—had been killed on the trails outside Boulder. While mountain lion attacks were rare in Colorado, they weren't unheard of, so when the bodies showed up, the local authorities had jumped to the obvious conclusion.

Clayne frowned. Three deadly attacks in a three-month period would be a statistical fluke, but three attacks with no survivors? That wasn't a fluke; that was planning.

"When we went back and pulled copies of the medical examiner's reports, it wasn't difficult to figure out the wounds had been inflicted by a shifter," John continued.

"John, you said there was a witness?" Clayne shot Danica a look. "Did you see any mention of a witness in the articles?"

She shook her head.

"The articles are in chronological order," John said. "Read the ones with the most recent dates."

Danica scrolled down and found two articles that

detailed the last attack and the witness who'd stumbled out of the forest just in time to see the mountain lion mauling the victim. The man told the cops who'd responded to the scene that the animal had run off. But even more significant than the gory details of the last attack was the description of the witness and how he'd heroically tried to save the victim, getting blood on his own clothes in the attempt to save the hiker's life. Wasn't that convenient?

"Here's a picture of the witness." Danica pointed to a photo of a man in a plaid shirt with long, sandy blond hair and a beard. "Says his name is Ray McDermott."

Clayne couldn't say for sure the man was a shifter simply by looking at him, much less the shifter they were looking for, but the size was right.

"Based on McDermott's information, the cops tracked down a big mountain lion and killed it," John said. "No one else got attacked, so case closed."

"What do we know about this guy?" Clayne asked.

He could hear John's fingers clicking on the keyboard over the phone. "It's in one of the files I sent you. He grew up in foster homes, dropped out of high school, made some bad decisions, and ended up in prison."

Shit, Clayne thought as he scanned the file Danica had opened. It was scary how much he and McDermott were alike. If he'd gone left instead of right, he could have ended up exactly like this guy. Assuming McDermott was their killer, of course. Hell, if anything, the DCO—and Dick specifically—had set him up to be exactly that kind of beast. The only reason he hadn't turned into one was because Danica hadn't let him. She'd tamed the animal inside him without even knowing it.

"Where's McDermott now?" Danica asked John.

"According to our intel, he moved to—wait for it—Northern California."

That was too much of a coincidence.

"Unfortunately, we don't know where he is now," John added. "He fell off the grid after he moved, which means he changed his name, maybe even his appearance."

"Of course he did," Clayne muttered. "Otherwise, it'd be too easy."

They finally had a name and a face, and they were still back at square one.

Danica drummed her fingers on the dashboard, her neatly rounded nails tapping out a staccato rhythm as she thought. "We should put out a BOLO for this guy. Use his old photo, see if anyone might have seen or heard something."

Clayne shook his head. "Not yet. I mean, we can keep that as a backup option, but just because we have a suspect doesn't change the fact that this guy's a shifter or that we need to be the ones to bring him in." When she opened her mouth, he added, "We know what we're up against; the rest of the task force doesn't. Can you imagine what would happen if the local PD or an FBI agent—your partner—approaches this guy and tries to take him down without knowing what he was up against? It'd be slaughter."

"Clayne's right," John added.

She sighed, stirring the hair that had come free of her bun and was hanging down on either side of her face. "Okay. But at the very least we can tap into the NGI—the Bureau's facial recognition program—and see if we get a hit."

"Already on it," John said.

Even though John couldn't see her, Danica nodded anyway. "Good. But if we don't find him within
twenty-four hours, we try it my way. If we wait longer
than that, we're going to be finding his next victim before we find him."

She had a point. "In the meantime, send us everything
you dug up on this Ray McDermott guy," Clayne told
John. "School records, notes from his teachers, arrest
records, juvenile records, parole officer records, foster
home reports, everything."

Who the hell knew? Maybe there'd be something
in that mess that'd give them a clue where to find
this psycho.

———— ∿∿∿ ————

Back in the coffee shop, Danica was just about to ask
Clayne if he wanted a refill when a couple walked in,
followed by a trio of twentysomething women. Clayne
took in the crowd, then looked at her.

"Maybe we should take this investigation back to
your place," he suggested.

That was fine with her. She always did her best thinking curled up on her couch in her comfy clothes—not to
mention curled up with her comfy guy.

By the time they got to her apartment, everything
the DCO had on McDermott was waiting for them.
Danica downloaded the files, then went into the bedroom to change into shorts and a tank top. When she
came out, Clayne was so absorbed in what he was
reading he didn't even look up until she flopped down
on the couch beside him. He took one look at her bare

legs and his eyes went from their normal rich brown to gleaming gold.

"Anything helpful?" she asked, getting him back on task.

He turned back to the computer on his lap with a soft wolf-like whine. "Not really. The guy in here doesn't sound like he's smart enough to be the killer. Hell, he's barely smart enough to get out of his own way."

"Maybe, but he's obviously smart enough to get away with murder." She picked up one of the bottles of water Clayne had grabbed from the fridge and opened it. "He's also smart enough to have played us all—even you."

Clayne's mouth tightened. "Says something for street smarts, I guess."

She and Clayne disregarded the profile John had sent them on Ray McDermott. It was as worthless as a horoscope—right on target after the fact, but useless when it came to finding this guy. Instead, they built their own profile based on something they both knew very well—Clayne's life and what he'd do if he was on the run.

"You're joking, right?" Danica asked when he suggested it.

"I have a lot in common with him."

"No, you don't."

"Yeah, I do. He had a shitty childhood, hated school, turned to crime, ended up in jail—the list goes on and on." When she didn't say anything, he added, "Just go with me on this, okay?"

She wanted to argue, but when he put it that way, she supposed she could see the similarities. But the crappy

home life and criminal record was where it ended.
Clayne wasn't a murderer and never would be.

Danica took the laptop he held out and placed it on
her crossed legs, then opened a new document.

"The guy is a loner and seems to like nature, so he
probably lives somewhere outside the city," Clayne
said. "I'd put my money on a single-family resi-
dence. No apartment complex or subdivision for him.
Too crowded."

"Let's assume that while he probably created a new
identity, it wasn't a top-notch, professional job," Danica
pointed out as she typed. "He had no reason to think
anyone was after him, and nothing in his background
indicates he'd know how to do something like that. If
that's the case, he's probably renting a place because
he wouldn't pass the detailed review necessary to get
a mortgage."

Clayne nodded. "Good point. He'd prefer a cash-only
kind of deal, too, so real estate agencies are out."

"What about work?"

"Maybe a store that sells camping gear or hunting
stuff. He'd probably have a hunting license, too."

That made sense. A serial killer afraid of getting
caught wouldn't want to do anything that might get him
noticed by the cops, and hunting without a license would
be a red flag.

"How about a car? He'd need one if he lives outside the city. Let's assume he got a new driver's license
when he moved here."

"And while we know he stole a vehicle when he ab-
ducted Vender, it's not a stretch to think he might have
used his own vehicle at some point, especially in the

beginning," Clayne said. "Let's assume his registered vehicle is something big, like an SUV or a van."

Danica finished typing, then looked at Clayne. "Is that everything?"

"I think so. Or at least a good start." He pulled out his cell phone. "I'll call John."

"It's four in the morning on the East Coast."

Clayne paused mid-dial, frowning. "Is it? Damn, I didn't realize it was so late. I don't want to let this wait until morning, though." He went back to dialing, then waited. "Hey, Kendra, it's Clayne… Yeah, I know what time it is, but I need you to do something for me."

Danica leaned back on the couch, stifling a yawn as she listened to Clayne tell Kendra about the profile they'd come up with. She remembered Kendra, of course, but didn't recall her being involved with intel work.

"Good deal," Clayne said into the phone. "Danica's sending you the file now."

Danica sat up and pulled the laptop close so she could open Clayne's DCO email account.

"Yeah, she's here," Clayne said. "Hang on. I'll put you on speaker."

"Hey, Danica!" Kendra's voice sounded surprisingly wide-awake for someone who just woke up. "It's been forever. How are you?"

"I'm great." If Kendra was surprised she and Clayne were working together, she didn't let on. Danica met his gaze over the computer screen and smiled. "I'll be even better when we catch this killer."

"I hear that," Kendra said. "I'll rouse a few of the intel boys out of bed and have them help me. We'll get an address on this McDermott guy for you."

"I owe you one," Clayne told her.

Kendra laughed. "I'm going to remind you that you said that."

Clayne shoved his phone in the pocket of his jeans, then stretched out on the couch. "Now we wait."

Danica rested her hand on one of the jean-clad legs beside her. "We should probably get some sleep. We'll need to be fresh if Kendra finds anything."

"We could get some sleep." Clayne flashed her a wolfish grin. "Or we could do something else."

From the way he was looking at her, she guessed that by "something else," he meant have sex. If she had an ounce of willpower around him, she would have refused and insisted they go to bed, but as Clayne took her hand and urged her higher up his body, she decided sleep could wait a little while longer.

"What do you have in mind?" she asked, even though the hard-on poking her through his jeans answered that question.

He ran his hand over the curve of her hip, his fingers brushing her bare thigh and making her quiver. "I figured we'd both sleep better if we had a little exercise before we went to bed."

"What about all the exercise we got today?" Even as she asked the question, she shimmied her way up his body, pressing her stomach against his rapidly hardening cock. "Or yesterday, I guess, since it's already after midnight."

"That was hours ago. It doesn't count."

He gripped her ass in both hands and pulled her up until she was straddling his lap. She wiggled back and forth to get comfortable before she leaned in close for a kiss. As her lips came into contact with his, Clayne buried one hand in her hair and tugged. Mmm. She liked when he got all barbarian and held her captive while his mouth took possession of hers.

She moaned as his free hand roamed over her ass. No matter what they did or where they did it, Clayne's hands ended up there at some point. It was entirely possible he was obsessed with that part of her anatomy. That was fine with her. She was so happy to be with him again that she was more than ready to give him an all-access pass to any part of her body he desired. Because God knew she was going to do the same with him.

His canines suddenly sharpened, evidence of how turned on he was. She glided her tongue over those dangerous points, tantalized by the feel of them. That only made them extend even more, and he tightened his grip in her hair, trying to tug her back, but she resisted. Clayne was always so worried she'd hurt herself on his fangs, but that was silly. It was no different than kissing someone with braces. Well, that wasn't exactly true. Kissing someone with braces wouldn't be as thrilling as kissing Clayne.

She shoved more of her tongue in his mouth, forcing him to kiss her back or concede that she was in charge. That wasn't likely to happen, even with her on top. Clayne was way too alpha for that. But he did relax his hold on her hair.

When she finally ended the kiss—on her terms—she leaned back, grinding against him. Beneath her, Clayne let out a soft growl and slid his free hand down to rest on her other hip. She closed her eyes and wiggled herself back and forth over his erection. There were a lot of clothes in the way, but it still felt amazing. She'd forgotten how good it felt to behave like a normal woman, to enjoy a little teasing, get herself and her partner horny as hell, then get busy like bunny rabbits.

Yes, there was a killer out there, probably stalking his next target. And as soon as she and Clayne had more information from the DCO on how to find him, they'd put their romance on hold until they caught him—or killed him. But until then, it couldn't be wrong to enjoy being together. Nothing that felt this good could be wrong.

She opened her eyes to see Clayne watching her with an amused expression on his face.

"What's so funny?" she asked.

"Nothing. I just like watching you wiggle like that. I'm not sure if you know this, but your eyelids kind of flutter when you pleasure yourself. I think I could lie here and watch you do it all night."

There might have been a time when she would have blushed at a line like that, but instead of turning red, she ground harder against him, eliciting a playful groan from her lover.

She was tempted to sit there and wiggle all night just to see if she could make herself come like this—maybe Clayne, too—but they really needed to get some sleep. Clayne wouldn't think so, but he wasn't thinking with his big brain at the moment.

She gave him a languid smile. "I might just take you up on that someday, but right now, I think I'd rather skip the foreplay and get to the next part."

He flashed her a grin, showing off his gorgeous teeth. "You don't hear me complaining."

Clayne made a move to follow her as she crawled off his lap, but she pushed him back down. "You stay right there, mister. I like that position just fine."

"Is it just me, or do you tend to get bossy when you're tired?"

She pulled off her tank top. "I'm not being bossy. You can consider yourself completely in charge, as long as you don't move from that position. Unless it's to take off your clothes."

He chuckled. "Nope, not bossy at all."

Danica noticed he sure as hell wasn't complaining as he whipped off his shirt, then made short work of his jeans. And he did it all without taking his eyes off her. Something she found rather empowering. Which was why she couldn't resist teasing him by turning her back to him and slowly wiggling out of her panties. When she got them halfway down her hips, she looked over her shoulder at him.

"Are you sure you're not too tired for this?"

He moved surprisingly fast, lunging off the couch to grab her panties and yank them down. The sound of tearing fabric was unmistakable.

She stepped out of the small scrap of material puddled on the floor. "I'll take that as a no. Guess I'd better go get that condom."

When she came back, Clayne was lying on the couch in the same position as he'd been before he'd ripped off her panties, his erection jutting proudly between his muscular thighs.

She climbed on his lap and rolled the condom down

his shaft, then lifted up until his cock was perfectly in line with her pussy. She rocked back and forth a few times to get him well lubed, then gripped his shoulders and sat down hard, taking him all the way inside.

The sudden sensations took her breath away.

"Oh, shit," Clayne rasped. "You'll never know how good that feels."

Actually, she did, but his hands fastened on to her waist and tugged her down more firmly on his shaft before she could answer. Instead, she let out a long, low moan and contracted her pelvic muscles around him.

Clayne tightened his hold on her hips, lifting her up until she was almost all the way off his cock, then yanking her back down, sending shock waves through her body. God, that felt amazing.

She closed her eyes, ready to drift off into la-la land when Clayne suddenly moved his hands up her back and tugged her forward. Her breasts conveniently fell right in his face, and he latched on to one of her nipples with that perfect mouth of his.

She sighed and swiveled on his cock, grinding her clit against him while he suckled on her nipples. She threaded her fingers in his hair, holding him close while she moved closer and closer to orgasm.

He must have realized she was about to come because his hands slid down to her ass, squeezing her cheeks and helping her grind against him. Her climax hit her all at once, going from a flicker of light to a starburst in seconds. Danica squeezed her eyes shut, screaming his name as she came.

Clayne shifted his grip, thrusting up into her hard and fast. She flexed her thighs as much as her spasming body would allow, trying to make him come at the same time. He growled, throwing back his head and yanking her down hard on his shaft. She knew it wasn't possible with the condom, but she swore she could feel his warmth jetting inside her.

She didn't know how long they stayed like that, but at some point they untangled themselves and she led him to bed—to sleep, she told herself.

Chapter 9

KENDRA THOUGHT ONE OF THE ANALYSTS MIGHT actually kiss her when she showed up with a tray of hot coffee and a box of fresh donuts from a twenty-four-hour bakery as a thank-you for coming in so early.

Using the information Clayne and Danica had come up with, they searched through the database until they found suspects who matched the profile. Kendra was on her way to her office after uploading the list of names and addresses for Clayne when she noticed John's door was open. She stopped, knocked twice, then walked in, figuring he'd want an update.

Besides, if she ever hoped for her boss to see her as anything more than a glorified secretary, she needed to show him she could do other things for the DCO. Like track down serial killers.

John looked up as she entered. "Kendra, you're in early. What's up?"

Kendra quickly explained about Clayne's phone call and the information she helped find.

"Excellent work." John gave her an approving smile. "I appreciate you going above and beyond like this. Have you called Clayne yet?"

"I just uploaded the data to the server."

John glanced at her over the rim of his coffee mug. "Are Foley and Hightower back from that mission?"

Kendra frowned at the change in topic. "They got in yesterday."

"Good. I want them positioned in Sacramento for cleanup duty."

Clayne was going to love that. He and Foley didn't work well together. "Sure thing." She chewed on her lip. "You know, now that you mention it, maybe I could go with them and help out."

John froze, the mug halfway to his mouth. "Help out?"

"Yeah. You know, in case they need…help."

He sipped his coffee, then set down the mug. "I know you want to get involved in fieldwork, but I'm pretty sure this isn't the kind of work you'd be interested in."

"Sure it is." Actually, it wasn't. From what she'd heard, cleanup duty could get messy, and she wasn't really into messy. But she was committed now. "I could be a real asset to Foley and Hightower out there."

"You're more of an asset here."

"But—"

"Foley and Hightower aren't going out there to help Clayne and Danica work the investigation. They're going out there to make this shifter disappear after Clayne and Danica catch him," John said. "In some ways it can be the toughest part of a mission like this. Foley and Hightower won't even know whether the rogue shifter is alive or dead until they show up on the scene. And when they get there, they'll only have a short period of time to deal with the situation—we're talking minutes in some cases. That requires experience."

She felt like she was having a conversation with her dad. He knew best, and that was that. "What better way for me to gain experience than by watching Foley and Hightower?"

"Not this time, Kendra."

He turned his attention to the computer, putting an end to the conversation. Kendra wanted to argue, but what would be the point? John wouldn't change his mind, and if she pushed too hard, he might never let her in the field. She tried hard not to stomp in frustration as she walked down the hall to her office.

She called and woke up Hightower and told him that he and Foley were going to Sacramento. She glanced at her watch as she hung up and saw that it was a little past six thirty. That donut she'd eaten hours ago was long since gone. No wonder her stomach was growling.

Kendra usually drove to the cafeteria, but the weather was so beautiful she decided to walk instead.

She was at the corner waiting for the traffic signal to change so she could cross the street when someone jogged up beside her. She did a double take when she saw Declan. He was dressed in shorts and a T-shirt, the latter of which was soaked in sweat and stretched so tightly across his broad chest that it hugged every muscle—and he had a lot of them. Damn, his biceps were huge.

Had Declan always been this buff? Of course he had—he was six feet five inches of bear shifter. Perhaps the better question would be, why hadn't she noticed how ripped he was before? Because she'd been too busy crushing on Clayne to notice anyone else. But now that she finally had noticed, she had to admit he was hot—in that gentle giant kind of way.

The summer breeze caught her long, blond hair, whipping it around her face, and she reached up to tuck it behind her ear. Declan followed the movement with his sky-blue eyes. Or at least she thought he did—he had sunglasses on, so she couldn't be sure.

"Just starting your run or finishing up?" she asked.

He took a long drink from the water bottle in his hand. "Finishing up."

Finishing up, huh? Maybe she should ask if he wanted to grab breakfast with her after he showered. Or before. She'd never particularly considered sweat sexy, but Declan MacBride made it work.

But the light changed before she could say anything. Declan gave her a nod, mumbled something about having a good day, then took off at a run, leaving her to admire his great ass while she followed at a much slower pace.

There was a time not long ago when Declan would have been the one who invited her to have breakfast. Or lunch or dinner or even out for a cup of coffee. And every time he'd asked, she turned him down, silently praying he'd figure out she wasn't interested. It was just her luck he'd get the memo right when she realized what she might be missing out on.

She shook her head. *Really batting a thousand today, Kendra.*

It took longer than usual for Clayne to wake up. Which wasn't surprising since he'd had two mind-blowing orgasms last night and was currently curled up in bed with the amazing woman who'd given them to him.

What the hell woke him up anyway? Then he heard it—a loud, insistent ringing coming from somewhere in the apartment. His phone. He lifted his head and blinked at the small, red digits on the clock beside Danica's bed, trying to focus on them. Four o'clock. Crap, they hadn't been asleep for more than thirty minutes.

He crawled out of bed as quietly as he could, then stumbled out of the bedroom. Where the hell had he left his phone?

Clayne followed the irritating noise out to the living room and found his phone in the front pocket of his jeans, which for some reason were on the floor behind the couch. How had they gotten there?

He checked the display to see who it was, then put the phone to his ear. "Hey, John."

"I know it's early out there, but I figured you'd want McDermott's address as soon as possible."

Clayne grunted an affirmative as he walked back into the bedroom. Danica had wedged herself into a half-sitting position in bed and was busy shoving her hair out of her eyes as she looked up at him sleepily. Damn, she looked sexy in the morning, he thought as he climbed in beside her.

The sheet had fallen down past Danica's belly button, and Clayne was torn between what to focus on—her beautiful breasts or that taut stomach of hers. She solved the dilemma by pulling the sheet up under her arms and sticking her tongue out at him. Then she pointed at the phone.

"Kendra and the intel techs came up with three possibles," John said. "She sent you the addresses via secure drop already. Intel says the chances of one of them being your guy is eighty-three-point-six percent."

Clayne thanked his boss for the info, then tossed the phone on the nightstand.

"How the hell do they come up with that kind of probability?" he asked.

Danica threw back the sheet and jumped out of

bed. "I'm sure they can show you the math if you're that interested."

Right then, all he was interested in was watching her perfect ass as she walked out of the bedroom, but they had to get moving. She came back a few moments later, carrying her clothes. She held up her panties—or what was left of them—and shook her head.

"You have no idea how much these things cost, do you?"

The panties had a few rips in them, thanks to him. But as far as he was concerned, that only made them sexier. He grinned as he went into the living room to grab his clothes. "Not my fault you wear such flimsy panties."

She gave him an exasperated look as she walked over and dumped the panties in the trash can. He came back in time to see her pulling another pair out of the dresser that looked exactly like the ones he'd ripped. He wasn't sure what she was complaining about. He'd buy her a whole drawer full of panties if she let him.

He yanked on his jeans, enjoying the show as she pulled on her bra and panties. He could watch her get dressed all day. Maybe after the mission was over, he'd do just that. She could slowly pull everything off, then put it all back on, over and over. Well, maybe not all of it. He'd mostly prefer if she pranced around the place in her underwear all day, her hair all tousled like it was now.

As they raided the fridge a few minutes later, he asked if they should give Tony a call and let him know what they'd discovered. But Danica was against it.

"If the killer goes all shifter on us in front of Tony, what are we going to do then?"

Good point.

They headed to the first address on the list, a rental in the name of Jacob Garcia, in the hills west of Vacaville. Clayne was glad Danica had GPS in her car because the place was off the freaking map. As she navigated the small roads that ran through the low mountains, Clayne read the information Kendra had dug up on the three possible suspects. There wasn't much, which was part of the reason they'd come back as suspicious.

"All three names popped up in the system within the past two years," he told Danica. "Kendra said there'd been a lot more, but they focused only on the men who fit the parameters we gave them."

She glanced at him. "What else do we have on these guys?"

Clayne scanned the report. "Recently issued driver's licenses, registered vehicles are vans or SUVs, and they all have hunting licenses."

They were still discussing what the three suspects had in common when Danica pulled up in front of a Spanish-style home tucked into the trees at the end of a long canyon road. The place looked well-maintained and pricey. Clayne didn't want to be caught stereotyping a serial killer, but he crossed the guy who lived here off the list before they got out of the car. The place just didn't have the right feel to it.

But he and Danica did their due diligence and checked out Jacob Garcia. It took them all of thirty seconds to figure out the man wasn't their guy. For one thing, he didn't smell like a shifter. And for another, the guy had a serious limp and walked with a cane. No way this guy could chase down prey. Had he done something illegal? Probably, especially since he'd gone to all the trouble of creating a fake identity and living under an assumed name. But he and Danica were after a serial killer and didn't have the time or inclination to get bogged down in whatever Garcia's situation was.

The second address, rented by a Douglas Lister, was all the way over to the southeast of Sacramento, in Columbia. With the normal city traffic, it took more than an hour to get there. Danica pulled off into the woods a few hundred yards short of the house.

"What do you think?" she asked.

Clayne peered through the trees at the house. A simple one-floor, craftsman-style home, it had a red brick fireplace stack on one side and a big, plate-glass window in the front. While it might have been cozy and charming at one time, now it looked dilapidated and in need of some serious TLC.

"I think it's exactly the kind of place a psycho shifter could get comfy in."

Clayne stepped out of the car, his claws extending on their own. Danica took out her weapon, training it on the house.

"It's him," Clayne growled.

His canines slid out as the smell of cat shifter assaulted his nose. Score a point for the nerds at the DCO. Got it right in two. Douglas Lister was definitely Ray McDermott. They'd brought the game to this asshole's front yard now.

As they moved toward the house, Danica slid to the side to cover him. He knew from experience that she'd continue moving around so she could cover the back, leaving him to take the front. He hated letting her out of his sight, but with only two of them, he didn't have much choice. It was risky, but it'd been the way they'd operated the whole time they'd worked together in the DCO.

"Give me fifteen seconds," Danica whispered.

He counted to ten and headed for the house at a run, pulling his old Colt 45 out of its underarm holster. It didn't hold as many rounds as Danica's Glock, but the Colt more than made up for it. When he hit something with its .45-caliber, full-metal-jacketed bullet, whoever it was didn't get back up.

When he got to the front door, he slowed just long enough to kick it in. There was a time when Danica would have said something about warrants and illegal entry. But she'd stopped talking that nonsense a long time ago. There'd be plenty of time to discuss probable cause later—after the shifter was down

He swept the long, dark hallway that ran from the front of the house to the back, but didn't see anything. He darted a quick glance left, then right. Nothing. He started forward to begin clearing the place room by room, but then stopped. The shifter scent was older than he'd first thought. McDermott hadn't been here in a while.

Clayne holstered his gun as Danica cautiously made her way down the hallway.

"It's clear," he called out.

Danica still had her weapon out when she entered the living room. "You checked the whole house already?"

"Didn't have to. His scent is stale. McDermott hasn't been here for at least a day, maybe two."

She put her weapon away. "But this is our guy, right? Not another shifter in hiding?"

"It's him," Clayne assured her.

They quickly searched the place to confirm what he already knew. The guy's bedroom looked like a hunter's cabin—except in this version, the trophies on the wall were five framed pictures of his victims. On a shelf under each photo was a baby food jar with a tooth in it. McDermott's most recent victim was noticeably absent.

"Don't touch anything without gloves," Danica told him as he reached for a stack of photos on the nearby dresser. "I know how much you hate it, but we can't hide this from Carhart and the rest of the FBI. I don't want your fingerprints showing up everywhere when the crime scene techs dust everything."

Danica was right. He put on the latex gloves she gave him, then shuffled through the stack of pictures while she went through the dresser. To him, they looked like the kind of surveillance photos a private eye might take. But they weren't of cheating husbands or philandering wives. Instead, they were of the men McDermott had murdered. And some he hadn't yet had a chance to kill.

"Why hasn't McDermott come back here since killing Vender?" Danica asked as she opened the closet. "Did he think we were getting close?"

"Maybe. Or maybe he got spooked when he realized another shifter was on his tail."

"You don't think he left town, do you?"

"No. He likes playing this game with me way too much to skip out."

Clayne tossed the photos on the dresser and picked up the notepad beside them. He flipped through it, frowning as he realized it was a dossier to go with each of the men in the photos. McDermott not only had names to go with faces, but every other personal piece of information you could possibly think of. This wacko had been planning his kills for a long time. And from the list of names and faces, he was just getting started.

Danica tapped one of the baby food jars. "Why didn't he take his trophies?"

"I don't know," Clayne admitted. "That part doesn't make sense."

"Maybe he figured he could always get more." Danica turned to survey the room. "Do you think it'd be worthwhile sitting on the house in case he shows up?"

Clayne set down the notebook. "I don't think he's coming back here, but it wouldn't be a bad idea."

She took out her cell phone. "I'm going to call this in."

"You know that once you give them McDermott's name you're putting every FBI agent and cop who gets anywhere near McDermott at risk, don't you?"

"I don't think we have choice," she said. "If we don't find this guy, we're as good as giving him a free shot at his next victim. McDermott could be out there getting ready to kill someone else right now."

She was right, of course.

While they waited for the feds to show up, they checked the house one more time, looking for anything that might give them an idea as to where McDermott had gone.

"Look for anything that might give anyone a clue that he's a shifter while you're at it," Clayne said as he looked through a pile of old mail sitting on the kitchen counter.

Danica frowned. "Exactly what am I looking for?"

"I don't know. Just look for something that screams cat shifter."

"Like what? A human-sized scratching post?"

Clayne's mouth twitched. Somehow, he didn't think it'd be that obvious.

By the time Tony and Carhart showed up with half the task force and a CSI crew an hour later, he and Danica had already gone over the house twice. If there was anything there to find, they'd have found it.

Clayne wasn't too surprised when Tony didn't come over to find out what was going on. Clayne couldn't blame him. They'd essentially cut him out of the case at the most crucial moment. Danica was going to have to do some damage control to repair that bridge.

Carhart descended on both of them the minute he walked in, a scowl on his face. "What the hell do you mean not keeping me in the loop about something like this? You never mentioned you even had a lead, much less a prime suspect."

Clayne would have told him to go piss up a rope, but Danica merely gave him an apologetic look. "I'm sorry, sir. We thought it best to follow up on the lead first before involving you." She lowered her voice as if she was afraid someone might overhear. "I didn't want to embarrass the Bureau if anyone discovered what kind of angle we were pursuing."

"What the hell are you talking about, embarrass the Bureau?" he asked, automatically lowering his voice as well.

Damn, Danica was good at this manipulation stuff. Sometimes it wasn't fair how easily she could control the average man.

"Sir, we knew the task force had all the traditional bases covered, so we decided to look at the case from a different angle," she explained. "We wanted to make sure you and the FBI maintained plausible deniability if our idea proved wrong and the press learned about it."

Carhart eyed her thoughtfully. He was probably trying to figure out if she was feeding him a load of crap or not. But if there was one thing people like him understood and valued, it was covering the boss's ass.

"I understand." He surveyed the living room. "What's the story on this guy? I want to know who he is and what led you to him."

Danica gave him a sanitized version that was pretty close to the truth—at least a version of it. And she did it with a straight face that Clayne could never have managed.

Ray McDermott had witnessed a mountain lion attack in Colorado a few years ago and what he'd seen had apparently unhinged him. Ray had moved to the Sacramento area after that and changed his name to Douglas Lister. Along with his new name, he had a newfound urge to hunt people.

"Are you saying this guy thinks he's a mountain lion?" Carhart asked.

Danica shrugged. "We don't know that for sure, sir, but you can see why we wanted to check this out quietly before we put it out there."

Clayne's mouth curved. It sounded so good he almost believed it himself.

Carhart nodded. "Good work. If it got out that the FBI was tracking down a werecougar, it could be embarrassing. Any chance this guy was involved in those attacks out in Colorado?"

"We don't think so," Clayne jumped in. He didn't want the FBI sniffing around a case involving more deaths at the hands of a shifter. Although by now the DCO would have made sure those medical examiner reports were sanitized. "We checked the ME reports and they were legit animal attacks. McDermott is trying to recreate the violence he saw in the mountain lion attacks."

"Okay, let's get this guy's face in every newspaper and news channel," Carhart said.

Clayne exchanged looks with Danica. "That's not a good idea," he said. "If we back McDermott into a corner, he could do something crazy. Like go for multiple victims or take hostages or bolt."

That made the fed think twice. "Okay. Then get a BOLO out to all levels of law enforcement, but do it over the phone. I don't want someone with a scanner picking this up over the radio. And once we find this guy, I want to be on the scene when he's taken down." He gave Clayne a pointed look. "No more lone wolf crap."

―――

Tony stayed at McDermott's house to help search for clues while Clayne and Danica went back to the FBI offices. The moment they walked into the command center, Wayne intercepted them. "The Hunter called a few minutes ago. He knows you've identified him and he knew you were at his house. He's really pissed. Said that if you're not going to play by the rules, neither will he."

"What the hell does that mean?" Danica asked.

"No clue, but he said he's going to change the game, hunt someone who will make everyone more motivated to follow the rules." The profiler looked at Clayne. "He said you'd understand."

Right now, he had no idea what this psycho was thinking. In the command center, agents were running around like chickens with their heads cut off. Clayne jerked his head in that direction. "What's going on in there?"

"The Hunter left the phone off the hook instead of hanging up. We're trying to trace it. If it's like before, it's going to be useless, but we figured there's nothing wrong with trying."

Clayne frowned. McDermott hadn't left the phone off the hook by accident. He'd done it because he wanted them to know where he'd been.

"Number's coming through!" someone called out.

Clayne and Danica followed Hobson into the room. A phone number slowly appeared on the main computer screen at the front of the room, one digit at a time. He found himself holding his breath, along with everyone else, as each number emerged. The area code came first, followed by the local exchange. Then a longer delay as the last four numbers popped up, one after another.

There were still two numbers left to go when he heard Danica let out a strangled moan. "Oh God, no."

"What is it?" he asked.

She didn't answer, but just kept staring at the screen, whispering the word *no* over and over and really scaring the shit out of him.

"We have it," a curly-haired tech announced. "Running the address."

"I already know where it is," Danica said in that same anguished tone.

Everyone stopped what they were doing to look at her. But she only continued to stare at the screen.

"Danica," Clayne prompted.

She turned to him, her face suddenly pale. "It's Tony's home number."

———

Clayne drove this time. Mostly because he didn't think Danica was stable enough to get behind the wheel. He'd seen her face a lot of terrible stuff, but right now she looked about as devastated as he'd ever seen her. He'd only met Beth Moretti once, but he liked her. And now she was in the hands of a crazy shifter because her husband was working the case.

Clayne gripped the wheel tighter. He broke every traffic law on the books getting to Tony's place—a convoy of FBI vehicles and cop cruisers behind him. When they got to the sprawling ranch house, Clayne drove right up on the nicely manicured lawn and slammed on the brakes.

The moment Clayne saw the front door was open, he turned to tell Danica to stay in the car, but she already had her weapon out and was running for the house. He swore and chased after her.

She stopped in the doorway. "Is he still here?"

He inhaled deeply through his nose, then shook his head. "No."

She took a tentative step forward, then stopped again. "Is Beth…?"

Danica let the rest of the question hang, but he knew what she wanted to know. Was Beth dead? Clayne didn't answer right away, but instead took another sniff. "I don't smell blood."

He led the way into the house, his gun lowered. The couch in the living room was overturned, as were the two matching chairs. The coffee table was broken in two. The rest of the room was pretty trashed, too, books and knickknacks everywhere.

Clayne stepped over what used to be a statue of an angel.

"It looks like she put up a fight," he told Danica.

Behind them, federal agents and local cops poured in the door. They immediately split up and searched the house, hoping against hope they were wrong and that Beth was hiding somewhere in the house. But Clayne knew better. Beth wasn't here. So while they did that, he searched the house for something that'd tell him where McDermott had taken Beth.

He was still checking out the living room when Tony ran in, Carhart on his heels. Danica hurried to intercept Tony, but she couldn't hide the damage. The fed shook his head, mumbling something unintelligible over and over even as Danica tried to reassure him that Beth was still alive.

On the other side of the living room, Carhart was on his phone telling whoever was on the other end that one of their own was in danger and that he wanted every FBI agent and cop out looking for McDermott. Shit, he almost sounded like a worthwhile human being for once.

Clayne headed for the kitchen, only to stop in mid-stride when he heard a buzzing sound. He stopped and cocked his head, listening, but he couldn't hear anything over the FBI agents and crime scene techs and Carhart and Tony and Danica all talking at once.

"Everyone, shut up. Now!" he roared so loud the house shook. Even Danica jumped. "Listen!"

The entire room froze, falling silent as everyone listened for something they couldn't possibly hear with their ordinary hearing. But Clayne heard it. A vibrating cell phone. He followed the sound across the room to the sofa. The noise was coming from underneath it. He grabbed the leather couch and flipped it over on its side with one hand, not caring who saw his show of strength. He dug in between the seat cushions that had somehow managed to stay in place when McDermott had trashed the living room until he found the cell phone hidden there.

Clayne thumbed the answer button and put it to his ear. "Hello, Douglas. Or do you prefer Ray?"

There was a silence on the other end for a moment before the cat shifter laughed. "So you figured out who I am. And I always thought dogs were dumb."

Clayne caught movement out of the corner of his eye and glanced up to see Danica doing everything she could to keep Tony from grabbing the phone out of his hand.

"You took someone you weren't supposed to," he told the other shifter. "What kind of hunt do you expect to get out of a woman?"

On the other side of the room, Tony almost collapsed at the words.

"This isn't about good hunting. This is about you cheating," McDermott said. "We had a fun game going. I grab rabbits and you try to stop me. But then you went and screwed it up. Figuring out who I am and tossing my place isn't part of the game."

Clayne flexed his free hand, forcing his claws to stay put instead of extending like they wanted to. What he wouldn't give to get his hands around McDermott's throat right now.

"So, what kind of game are we playing now?" he asked.

"The same kind we were playing before. I'm going to release my fresh little bunny at midnight. You have until then to figure out where I'm going to do it." He laughed softly. "Something tells me you'll work even harder this time to get there since I've given you such motivation. Just remember, this game is between us. If I see anyone else, *smell* anyone else, I might be tempted to end the game before we start, like I did when you brought in that park ranger and those two feds. What fun would that be?"

Clayne clenched his jaw. "How do I know she's even still alive? This place is pretty trashed. For all I know, you could have killed her already. It's obvious you have control issues."

The shifter let out a derisive snort. "Coming from someone like you, that's rich. But don't worry, I'm keeping her safe for the hunt."

Like Clayne was going to take this asshole's word for it. "Put her on the phone."

The killer didn't answer and Clayne was half afraid the man had hung up. But he could still hear McDermott's even breathing on the other end of the line.

"I know you have her there listening to everything you're saying just so you can scare her more than she already is," Clayne said. "Hell, you're probably popping a boner right now from watching her tremble."

"Damn, we do know each other well."

The shifter let out a low, rumbling purr. There was a jumble of sound on the other end of the line, then Beth's trembling voice.

"Tony?"

Clayne thumbed the speaker button and gave Tony a nod.

"Beth?" Tony's voice was shaking as much as his wife's. He sounded like he was on the verge of tears. "Are you okay?"

"I'm okay. This jerk kicked in the door and—"

The rest was cut off as McDermott pulled the phone away. Beth muttered something that sounded like a curse, but it was quickly muffled.

"Beth!" Tony's face went red. "You sick son of a bitch! If you hurt her, I'll kill you! Do you hear me?"

Tony reached for the phone, but Danica caught his arm, pulling him back.

"There you go, Leidolf," the shifter told Clayne. "As you heard, the fed's fine rabbit is just that—fine. Whether she stays that way is totally up to you."

Clayne couldn't suppress the low rumble that came from his throat this time. He was going to make this jackass scream before he killed him. A few feet away, Danica gave him a warning look. That was when he noticed everyone in the room was staring at him like he was as much of a psycho as the guy on the phone. Clayne forced the animal inside down.

"So how's this going down? You give me another cryptic code, knowing there's no way I can figure it out in time?" he asked McDermott. "Why don't you just cut the crap and let the woman go, then tell me where to meet you? That way we can handle this one on one."

"Nice try. But I think I'll keep my hands on this particular rabbit." The cat shifter laughed. "This game is going to happen exactly the way I want it to. Which means no cryptic codes. I left you something at the

house to tell you where to find me. You're going to have
to follow that nose of yours to find it, though."

There was a click on the other end of the line. Clayne
resisted the urge to throw the phone through the wall and
tossed it on the couch instead.

Except for Danica and the few other agents who were
working to keep Tony calm, the house was quiet. *Keep
Tony calm. Yeah, right. Good luck with that.*

Carhart walked over to Clayne. "You sure you don't
have a history with this guy? Because for whatever reason, he's made this whole thing about you." He regarded
Clayne shrewdly. "And what the hell did he mean about
using your nose to find the clue he left for you?"

If it were anyone but the fed asking, maybe Clayne
could have kept his cool. But he really didn't like the
way Carhart kept getting up in his grill—well, as much
as the man could considering he was at least six inches
shorter. But the effect was still the same. Carhart was trying to bully him, and his inner beast wasn't in the mood.

Clayne clenched his hands into fists, ignoring the
way his claws dug into his palms. He took a deep breath
and closed his eyes, hoping his pupils weren't already
changing. If Carhart didn't back off, everyone in the
room was going to get a full-on shifter display in the
next ten seconds—quickly followed by flying lessons
for all of them.

"I think the killer was trying to say he left a clue
somewhere in the house and that Agent Buchanan is
going to have to sniff it out," Danica said softly. "Like
a dog or something."

Clayne felt his claws retract at the sound of his
lover's voice.

"Agent Beckett, sensible as always," Carhart said. "I didn't think of it that way. I'll get everyone searching the house."

Clayne heard Carhart walk away. Sensed Danica moving closer. Her sweet feminine scent surrounded him, washing away the last of his rage.

He opened his eyes to find her looking up at him with concern in her dark eyes. How had the DCO known they would be so perfect together when they'd teamed them up all those years ago? For the hundredth time that day, he thanked God she'd ended up back in his life.

"You okay?" she asked.

The urge to pull her into his arms and kiss her in front of everyone was hard to resist, but he did. Not because he gave a crap about how it would look, but because he knew Danica wouldn't have wanted that right then. She was as worried about Beth as Tony was. They had to focus on getting the woman back.

"Yeah," he said. "I'm good."

She jerked her head at the FBI agents, local cops, and crime scene techs already searching the house. "If there's a clue your nose is supposed to find, we better get to it before they completely muck up the place."

"Good point."

For his nose to work at its best, Clayne had to become blind to everything else going on around him. So, he shut everything else out, knowing Danica would run interference for him, and concentrated.

As Clayne moved through the living room, he saw Carhart pull Tony aside. Clayne didn't have to eavesdrop to know what he was saying. The defeated look in Tony's eyes told him Carhart was putting him on the bench. Probably telling him, "You're too close to this to be of any use. Trust me, we'll find Beth. We have the full resources of the FBI on this."

What a load of shit.

Clayne turned his attention away and focused on the shifter's scent, carefully following it from the front door he'd kicked in, then throughout the house. Clayne hoped it'd lead him directly from the living room to wherever this supposed clue was hidden. But it didn't. McDermott had been in every single room in the house. Worse, he'd rummaged through stuff—drawers, cabinets, pantry, closets, storage bins. Everywhere. Instead of grabbing Beth and running, the damn psycho had wandered around the place for no other reason than because he wanted to lay a difficult trail for Clayne to follow. Which meant something that should have been handled in five minutes took freaking forever. More than an hour later, he was still sniffing from room to room. Even Danica, with all her charm and personality, was having a hard time covering for a guy who was walking around like a drunk bloodhound.

Then he hit a fresh trail by the back door, one that was a mix of the shifter's scent and Beth's.

"Shit," Clayne whispered to Danica. "He went outside."

They earned a few more frowns and suspicious looks as they opened the back door, which had been sealed by the forensics team, and headed out across the well-manicured lawn. The scent was easier to follow out here—too easy. A scent this intense usually meant there was blood involved.

The trail ended at the edge of the woods.

Clayne stopped and looked around, sniffing the air.

There, stuck in the crook of a tree branch right at head height where it would be easy to find, was a bundle of fabric, tied with a strip of cloth. There wasn't a shifter around that'd have a hard time finding it—that much blood left a distinctive odor.

"What is it?" Danica asked, keeping an eye on the house as he reached for the bundle.

Up close, he realized the material had been torn from a piece of clothing. There was blood on it—a lot. He didn't have to sniff it to know it was Beth's. He untied the string and unwrapped the bundle of cloth.

Danica glanced over her shoulder. "What is it?"

"I don't have a clue."

She came around to take a look and made a face. "Is that Beth's blood?"

"Yeah. And that's a pinecone." He poked at a smeary-looking bit of something beside the pinecone. Identification wasn't made any easier by the fact that there was more of Beth's blood on whatever the thing was. "Not sure what the hell this is."

Clayne had a sinking feeling he was looking at a piece of Beth. He just didn't know which part.

"It's a strawberry," Danica said matter-of-factly.

"It is?"

He looked at it more closely. Sure enough, there were those little seeds that were always on strawberries.

"Yeah, a strawberry." She frowned. "What did you think it was?"

He didn't answer. Danica would think it was gross. "Never mind," he grimaced. "Figuring out what it means is more important."

Clayne followed the trail, but it led back to the

driveway where McDermott had most likely tossed Beth in his car.

The decision not to tell Carhart or anyone else about the clue wasn't difficult. It wasn't an option, not if they wanted to get Beth back alive.

Clayne made a show of looking around some more for a few minutes so no one would realize they'd found anything, but Carhart intercepted them before they could make it back out the front door.

"Did you find something?"

Clayne shook his head. "No. I'm going to get an assist from Homeland on this one. Maybe our intel people will have something to point us in the right direction."

Carhart's mouth tightened, but he nodded. "Okay. We'll let you know if we find something here. And I want you to do the same. I don't want you going after this guy on your own again. Got it?"

"Yes, sir," Danica said.

Clayne thought that'd be enough to satisfy the fed, but instead he pulled Danica to the side to talk to her in private. He probably thought they were too far away from Clayne to overhear. They weren't.

"I know you want to help Moretti, but don't forget who you work for," Carhart told Danica. "If you learn anything, call me ASAP. Is that clear?"

"Yes, sir. Very clear."

Clayne and Danica made it as far as the car before Tony caught up with them. He glanced at her, then back at Clayne.

"Can I talk to you privately?" he asked.

Clayne looked at Danica. She nodded and got in the car, leaving him alone with Tony. He had a feeling he knew what the FBI agent wanted to talk to him about.

"I know that you of all people understand what it means to have a woman mean more to you than your own life. If anything happens to Beth…" Tony's voice broke. He threw a quick glance at the house. "Carhart wants me to sit this out."

No surprise there. "Maybe that's a good idea."

"Like hell it is," Tony muttered. "I know they're going to do everything they can to get Beth back safely, but you and I know the FBI doesn't have a prayer of finding that asshole McDermott. I'm going with you and Danica."

Clayne's gut told him to say no. Tell Tony he'd get in the way, slow him and Danica down. But he couldn't do it. If he was in Tony's place and a psycho serial killer kidnapped Danica, no army in the world would be able to stop him from going after her.

He jerked his head toward the backseat. "Get in."

Clayne glanced at his watch as he got behind the wheel. Eight o'clock. They had four hours to find Beth.

Chapter 10

"YOU FOUND SOMETHING AT THE HOUSE, DIDN'T YOU?" Tony asked.

Danica looked at Clayne. When he nodded, she handed the bloody piece of fabric back to her partner—ex-partner, she supposed. Regardless of what happened between her and Clayne, something told her neither she nor Tony would be employed by the FBI after tonight.

"Oh God, what the hell is this?" Tony moaned.

She cursed herself for not telling him what was inside the little pouch before handing it to him. "Calm down. It's only a pinecone and a strawberry." She reached around to take them from Tony's trembling hand before he dropped them. "These are the clues McDermott was talking about."

"Is that…blood on them?"

"Yeah," Clayne said. "But not much."

That wasn't true. There was quite a lot of blood. But Tony didn't need to know that.

"What do the clues mean?" Tony asked as Clayne merged onto the interstate and headed east.

"We don't know yet," Danica admitted.

"Then why the hell aren't we on our way to the field office to talk to the profilers so they can figure it out?"

Clayne snorted. "Because they did such a bang-up job of it last time, right?"

"Clayne, stop it," Danica said.

He glanced at Tony in the rearview mirror. "Back at the house you told me the FBI didn't stand a chance of finding McDermott. What's changed since then?"

Tony didn't answer.

Danica turned in her seat as she dialed the DCO's number. Her partner's face was pale in the passing streetlights, his eyes haunted with fear. "We have other resources that can help us. Resources that are a lot better at this stuff than the FBI."

"You mean the Department of Homeland Security?" He gave her an incredulous look. "What the hell do they know about serial killers, strawberries, and pinecones?"

Danica saw Clayne give her a warning look. She ignored it. She needed to calm Tony down before he lost it. "They know more than the FBI. I'm calling them now, but I need it to be quiet, okay?"

Crap, she sounded like she was talking to a two-year-old.

Tony must have thought so, too. "Why?"

"Because I'm trying to save your wife, dammit," she snapped. "I'm sorry," she said quietly. "I know you're just afraid for Beth. I'm worried about her, too. She's my best friend. I wouldn't do anything that'd jeopardize her life."

Tony was silent for a long time. Finally, he nodded. "I know that. So, okay. We'll do it your way. But I'm trusting you with Beth's life, Danica."

"I know," she said softly. "And we'll find her."

Turning around in her seat, she waited for someone at the DCO to pick up. She glanced at her watch and did a quick conversion. Crap, it was the middle of the night there. They really didn't have time to drag everyone out of bed. She prayed there was someone manning the phones besides the normal on-duty staffer.

It was Kendra, thank God. "Danica, hey. I'm putting you on speaker so John can hear. What do you have?"

Danica thumbed the speakerphone button so Clayne could hear. "McDermott grabbed another victim and plans to start the hunt at midnight."

"Did he give you any clues?" John asked.

"He left us a bloody piece of the victim's clothing with a strawberry and a pinecone in it."

"Gross," Kendra said. "But we can work with that. Give us any other details you can think of. What kind of fabric was it?"

Danica held it up to get a better look. "Cotton. Pink cotton."

"What about the victim's name?"

"Beth Moretti."

"Your partner's wife?" John asked. "Why the hell did this whack job change his MO like this?"

"He thinks we cheated playing his game," Clayne answered. "He said we weren't supposed to figure out who he is. We were supposed to be happy trying to stop him from killing on the hunt. This is his way of upping the ante and showing us he's in charge, I guess."

John swore under his breath. "You need to end this. Sooner rather than later."

"I intend to," Clayne told him.

"Good. The cleanup team is already in Sacramento. You give the word and they'll be there."

"What the hell is a cleanup team?" Tony asked.

Danica snapped her head around to fix him with a glare.

"Who was that?" John demanded. "Is there someone else with you?"

Danica gave Tony her best shut-the-hell-up look as she answered. "Clayne was fiddling with the radio. I turned it off."

"I think I have something," Kendra said a few moments later. "There's a small town in the Stanislaus National Forest called Strawberry with a mountain nearby called Pinecrest Peak about three and a half hours southeast of you. Based on what you gave us, combined with the killer's previous MO, my best guess is that he's going to hunt Beth Moretti there."

Danica looked at Clayne and he looked back at her, a line of doubt clear on his brow.

"This isn't the time for guessing, Kendra," Clayne said.

"The analysts said that the probability of this being the—"

"I don't care what the analysts say," he told her. "I care what you say. Are we going to the right place? Because Beth is going to die if you're wrong."

There was silence on the other end of the phone, then, "It's the place. I'm sure of it."

"Give me the GPS coordinates," Danica said.

Kendra gave her the coordinates, telling her there were several small country roads—and a few trails—that would get them close to the peak.

"But none of them will get you all the way there," she added. "You're going to have to go the rest of the way on foot."

"Get the weather patterns for the area and bring us in from the downwind side of the peak," Clayne told her.

"Already did," Kendra said. "I'm sending the

directions to your phone now. But there's a lot of real estate in that area. How are you going to find Moretti's wife in time?"

"I'll find her," Clayne assured her, though Danica wasn't sure if he said it for Kendra and John's benefit, or for Tony's.

Danica hung up, then fed the coordinates into her GPS.

"You're not really from the Department of Homeland Security, are you, Clayne?" Tony asked.

------※------

As they drove deeper into the mountains outside the small town of Strawberry, Clayne could sense Tony's anxiety increasing by the mile. He had to be thinking there was no way they'd find his wife in this pitch-black wilderness. It probably didn't help that Clayne had never answered his question. But anything he told the fed would have generated even more questions that Clayne couldn't answer.

"The road should end just up ahead," Danica said as she checked the map on her phone.

It didn't exactly end, but instead turned into a dirt path leading into the forest. Clayne stopped the car and turned off the ignition, then got out. Danica and Tony got out and came around to stand beside him. Clayne stared into the pitch-black trees. Somewhere in the darkness, critters scurried along the forest floor in harmony with the ticking sound of the car's cooling engine, but he doubted anyone but him could hear them.

He closed his eyes and let his other senses take over. He picked up the scents of all the people who'd passed this way recently but couldn't smell Beth or McDermott. He roamed farther, picking up various odors carried on the breeze, listening for the chatter small animals made when something bigger came into their territory. Like a woman running for her life—or the crazy-ass shifter chasing her.

"What the hell have I done?"

Clayne looked over his shoulder to see Tony pacing back and forth in front of the car.

"I put my wife's life in your hands!" He jabbed a finger at the dark, unforgiving forest. "How the hell are we going to find them in that? There are thousands of acres out there. And we don't have a clue where to start, if we're even in the right place to begin with." His voice ended on a cry of desperation, tears welling in his eyes. "Beth's going to die, isn't she?"

"No, she isn't." Danica walked over to take both of Tony's hands in hers. "Clayne will find her in time. I swear it. And if you don't trust him, trust me." She turned to Clayne. "Go. We'll be right behind you.

The total commitment of the words was overpowering. With Danica by his side, there was nothing in the world Clayne couldn't face.

He shifted, letting the wolf inside take over. Hunting would be easier this way because his senses would be so much more alive.

He heard a gasp but ignored it. What Tony saw—or thought he saw—didn't matter now.

Clayne turned and entered the forest. With his built-in night vision, the darkness seemed almost inviting. He took off, letting the beast take over and guide him. He knew shifters like Ivy and Declan were afraid to lose themselves in their animal side like this because they were worried it would somehow diminish their control at the wrong time. But Clayne never had that problem. Probably because his wolf side handled situations the same way his human side did—violently.

As he raced deeper into the forest, he ignored the natural trails and man-made pathways, letting his nose and instincts tell him what line to follow. He went up steep inclines, jumped gullies and streams, leaping downed trees in his way. He wasn't necessarily following a scent yet, but he knew he was going the right way.

Danica and Tony would be forced to move slower up the mountain. They were falling farther back even now. He knew because he could sense where she was as easily as if she had a GPS tracker on her. If she ran into trouble, he could be at her side in moments.

On the flip side, Danica followed in a near straight line behind him, as if she was could see him ahead of her, which was impossible. Not only was he moving twice as fast as she was, but it was too dark for her to see anything. But something told him that if he stopped, she'd catch up to him.

That knowledge was comforting and he gave himself over to the chase, letting the wolf guide him.

He felt more than heard the sound of running feet. One set was unsure as if the person didn't know the terrain, while the other was quicker, surer.

He turned and headed in their direction. As he moved around the ridgeline into the oncoming breeze, the scents hit him all at once. First Beth's, followed by McDermott's. They were close by.

Clayne growled softly. According to his watch, it

wasn't yet midnight and the hunt was already on. Who was cheating now?

But Beth had a lead on McDermott, and the cat shifter didn't seem to be closing on her as quickly as he could have. He was playing with her, letting her think she might just get away.

Beth was headed downhill, probably instinctively knowing she could run faster that way. She wasn't screwing around, trying to swerve or hide, either. She was hauling ass straight down the mountain—straight at Clayne. And since Clayne was coming from downwind, the cat shifter was going to be in for one hell of a surprise.

"How the hell does Clayne even know where he's going?" Tony asked as he pulled himself to his feet. He'd taken a header over a fallen tree—again.

Danica threw him a look over her shoulder. "He just knows. This is what he's trained to do."

"Then how do you know where he's going?"

Danica didn't have a good answer for that. She couldn't see Clayne in the dark, and his quiet footsteps had been swallowed up by the trees before she'd even lost sight of him. But she knew he was out there, directly in front of her. She couldn't say how far away he was. He wasn't near and he wasn't far. He was somewhere…in between.

"I can't tell how I know where he's going," she finally said. "I just know."

Tony muttered something under his breath she couldn't hear. But he didn't stop, and he didn't fall over any more trees. Danica put on more speed, forcing Tony to push hard to keep up. She started up a small hill, but then stopped. Clayne had turned and was now heading left.

Freaky feeling, knowing that, but she wasn't going to argue just now.

"What did I see back there?" Tony asked so quietly she could barely hear him. "Right before Clayne took off?"

Danica was the one who almost stumbled that time. Why the hell hadn't Clayne waited until he was out of sight before going all shifter? Because he didn't give a crap about stuff like that when someone was in danger. Or when someone needed their ass kicked. Or whenever the situation required action before thought. It was one of the reasons the DCO had teamed her up with him in the first place. They'd wanted her to control his natural response in those situations.

She climbed over the trunk of a pine that must have been two feet in diameter before answering, "I don't know, Tony. What do you think you saw?"

When he didn't answer right away, she thought he might drop it. She should have known better.

"His eyes looked like they went yellow and his face…changed."

She opened her mouth to answer, then closed it again. That little funny sense she'd been following told her they were getting closer to Clayne. Much closer. He'd slowed down—or stopped. He was just up ahead.

Danica stopped and turned to look at Tony. She couldn't see much in the dark. "We're catching up to Clayne, so we don't have time to talk about what you saw right now. All you need to know is that he's going to get Beth back for you safe and sound. That's the only thing you need to care about."

Tony swallowed hard, then nodded. "Okay."

She turned back around and pulled her Glock. Behind her, she heard Tony do the same.

Up ahead, she heard someone crashing through the trees. It was faint, but getting louder with every passing second. She started forward, moving as quietly as she could. Tony did his best to imitate her.

If she didn't know better, she'd swear she had a radar detector in her head, one that blinked faster the closer she got to Clayne. He couldn't be more than a hundred feet away.

Just then, a howl so familiar that it couldn't belong to anyone but the man she loved split the night air, and her feet almost faltered. There was an answering yowl and a thud, as if two huge bodies had slammed into each other. That was quickly followed by growling, crashing, and a woman's scream that sounded like it came straight out of a horror movie.

Danica ignored the fight or flight instinct telling her to run the other way and hurried in Clayne's direction.

The cat shifter was closing in on Beth, his hooked claws extended and swiping toward her back, a feral grin on his bearded face, when Clayne burst out of the trees. He didn't know who was more shocked—Beth or McDermott. He put his money on Tony's wife. She'd been so focused on running away from her kidnapper that she didn't even see Clayne until he was practically on top of her. She tried to stop but slipped and fell. On the up side, she avoided the killer's razor-sharp claws. On the down side, it put her in what could be an even more dangerous position—in between two shifters intent on killing each other.

Clayne leaped over Beth. He might not have as much momentum as the cat shifter, but he outweighed McDermott by thirty or forty pounds. Plus, he had the element of surprise.

They hit each other so violently it should have broken bones and knocked them both unconscious, but it didn't. Clayne hit the ground with a thud and a howl that probably sent every animal within miles running in fear. Every animal but the fucking cat shifter. He was on Clayne like lightning, raking at him with those vicious claws, aiming anywhere and everywhere he could.

Despite being quick, however, the other shifter wasn't a trained fighter. He depended solely on his instincts, which gave Clayne an advantage. He'd spent countless hours fighting with another feline shifter who was faster—and far more intelligent—than this one. And the one thing sparring with Ivy had taught him—don't try and out-speed a cat shifter.

Clayne rushed McDermott, letting the other shifter slice his chest with those sickle-like claws. The wound hurt but wouldn't be fatal. It was a small price to pay to get close to the cat. Once he did, he grabbed McDermott's shoulders in a crushing grip, letting his own claws sink in deep. Then he head butted him with all the force he had. The crunch, not to mention the caterwaul of pain that came with it, was damn satisfying.

If McDermott was skilled at hand-to-hand combat, he would have immediately retaliated. But he didn't counterattack. Instead, he responded like the pussy he was and lifted his hands to protect his face.

Clayne ripped his claws from McDermott's shoulders, ready to tear out his throat, but a flash of movement off to the side caught his attention. That was the only opening the cat shifter needed. He twisted aside and tore up the hill in the same direction he'd come.

Every fiber in Clayne's body wanted to go after the man, but he couldn't leave Beth alone. What if McDermott doubled back around?

Suppressing a growl of rage, Clayne ran over to where Beth still sat on the ground. She stared at him wide-eyed, fear in her eyes. Shit, she was probably as terrified of him as she was of McDermott.

He started to shift back, but stopped when someone ran out of the trees into the clearing. He spun around, teeth bared, claws extended, but it was only Danica. She took one look at him and Beth before sweeping the uphill perimeter of the clearing with her pistol. Damn, Clayne had forgotten how fast she was at assessing situations.

She fired off three shots at McDermott's shadowy form as he disappeared up the hill but didn't hit him.

Tony emerged from the forest a few steps behind Danica. He stood there, his gaze fixed on Beth as if he couldn't quite believe she really was safe and unharmed.

"Beth!" Tony dropped to his knees beside his wife and pulled her into his arms. "Oh God, I thought I'd lost you. Are you okay? Did he hurt you?"

Beth was sobbing too much to answer. But Clayne could see the slashes on her arms and legs from where the cat shifter had used his claws on her. That was when

Clayne realized Beth was only wearing a man's pajama top that hung to her knees. Shit, she'd been running in this rocky landscape without shoes. He didn't have to look at her feet to know they were a mess.

But she was alive and that was the important thing. That didn't do anything to assuage the fury welling up inside him. He bit back a growl and turned to head uphill. Danica was immediately at his side, her face as dark and angry as his.

"Stay with them," he ordered.

Tony drew his gun. "We're okay. Go with him, Danica."

Danica was barely able to keep up with Clayne as he climbed the rocky slope. And that was only because he was moving slowly enough to let her. "Did you injure him enough to slow him down?"

"I smashed in his face and about ripped out his shoulder muscles," Clayne said softly.

For a guy with claws and fangs that could rip a regular person to shreds, Clayne had a habit of using his head when he really wanted to damage someone. "Did you head butt him?"

"I might have."

Usually, she got on his case when he did things like that, but it might actually help them this time. "So, I take it he can't breathe too well, huh?"

"Probably not," Clayne said. "What are you thinking?"

"That we need to stop him before he gets to the highway north of here. If his breathing is as screwed up as you say, you should be able to get ahead of him without him picking up your scent and herd him back this way."

Clayne frowned. "Toward you? No way. I don't want him anywhere near you."

She swore. He could be so damn hardheaded sometimes. "Clayne, on the map there was a camping area up near the peak. I don't want him anywhere near there when we take him down. Herd him back to me."

"If I do that, you won't know where's he's coming from until the last second, you know that, right?"

"But I'll know where you are, so I'll keep shifting left or right based on your position."

Clayne didn't ask how she knew where he'd be. He simply took for granted that she could. She'd always liked that about him. He never doubted her.

"I still don't like it, but I see your point." He stopped and caught her arm, bringing her to a halt. "Just be careful. This guy isn't like any of the trained killers we've faced before. There's no telling what he'll do when he's cornered."

"All the more reason to herd him in my direction," she said. "Besides, I'll be downwind of him. He won't be able to smell me until it's too late. If that nose of his is even still working."

Clayne's fingers gently grazed her cheek, and then he was gone, moving up the hill like the graceful, powerful animal he was. *Her* graceful, powerful animal.

Danica followed at a steady pace, staying slightly to the west in response to that subconscious locator she didn't understand but accepted. If they were right about the killer's location, Clayne should be turning him in her direction soon.

She was halfway up the hill when she felt more than heard soft, careful footsteps moving toward her from

the west. She spun to face that direction, her gun at the
ready. Had McDermott somehow gotten down here
without her hearing him? He must have caught her scent
because those had been the quiet steps of an animal on
the prowl, not one running for his life.

Years of training with Clayne kicked in. She needed
to find a clearing where she could see the shifter coming at her. It was the exact opposite of what instinct
told a person facing a psycho killer to do, but hiding
from a shifter was never an option. They'd always sniff
you out.

Danica hurried to higher ground, her heart thudding
in her chest. Whoever came at her from the west would
have to cover at least fifteen feet of open space to get to
her. She dropped to one knee and scanned the tree line
hoping to catch sight of movement when a loud noise to
her right had her turning her .40 caliber in that direction
just as a man came hurtling down the slope at her.

He slid to a stop about thirty feet away. Blood covered his face and ran down the front of his shirt, but it
was his curved claws that held her attention. They were
so sharp and white they almost gleamed in the darkness.

McDermott's wild-looking gaze went from the gun in
her hand to her face, then back again as if he was trying
to calculate whether he could jump her before she could
get a shot off.

She caught a flash of movement out of the corner
of her eye that desperately made her want to check
behind her again, but she didn't dare take her eyes off
McDermott. Clayne crested the slope behind him and
came to a stop before slowly moving to the side so he'd
be out of Danica's line of fire.

"Doesn't look good that way, Ray," he said softly.

McDermott threw a quick glance at Clayne, sizing him up.

"You don't have to do this," Clayne told him. "You could give yourself up."

The cat shifter ignored the offer, slowly sweeping his gaze back to Danica. He darted a quick look to her left, then her right, before focusing on something to her left again. Dammit, was there someone back there or not? But if there was, Clayne would know it.

McDermott leaped at her so fast she barely had time to react. She squeezed the trigger, putting two rounds through his chest even as she rolled to the side. Two more loud shots rang out, echoing in the darkness. Just because Clayne hadn't had his weapon out when he crested the hill didn't mean he couldn't get it out when he needed it.

Danica glanced briefly at the shifter to make sure he was down, then swept the edge of the tree line with her gaze, looking for whatever she'd seen earlier.

Clayne was immediately at her side, his .45 targeted at the same general patch of undergrowth that held her attention. "What is it?"

"I don't know. Maybe nothing." Maybe she was just so keyed up she was seeing things. "Smell anything?"

"Just him." Clayne jerked his head at the body on the ground. "His scent is everywhere."

She shrugged and holstered her weapon. Clayne did the same, then fell into step beside her as she walked over to McDermott's body. The shifter didn't look nearly as intimidating now without his claws and fangs, both of which had retracted in death. Without them, he almost looked pathetic. She dropped to one knee to check for a pulse.

"It's hard to believe this is the guy who killed six men and ran us ragged," she said.

"Nobody looks tough with four bullet holes in him," Clayne told her.

She supposed not. "You'd better call in the cleanup team. The FBI will be here soon."

Clayne took out his DCO-issued satellite phone and switched it out of standby mode, then dialed. "Yeah, it's done," he said to whoever was on the other end. "You think you can find me, or should I come and get you?" He waited for an answer, then grunted and hung up. "Effing great."

"What's wrong?" she asked.

"John sent Foley and Hightower."

Danica tried hard not to smile. The DCO director had a strange sense of humor when it came to personnel management. If there was one person at the DCO that Clayne hated—besides Dick—it was Foley.

"You want me to wait here for them instead?" she asked.

He shook his head. "No. It's better if you deal with Carhart. You might want to check on Tony and Beth, too. They're probably both freaked right now, and you have it all over me when it comes to handling stuff like that."

Danica thought he'd say that. Clayne was good at saving people, but talking to them afterward wasn't his thing.

She reached up to examine the four ragged claw marks across his chest. They'd stopped bleeding, but were definitely going to leave scars. Then again, he had lots of those.

She gently pressed her hand to the wounds, right over his heart. "Thank you."

"For what?"

"For everything," she said. "For coming out here on this case, for saving Beth, for giving me a chance to fix something I'd screwed up, for still being willing to… love me."

She said the last part so softly she wasn't even sure Clayne could hear it with his exceptional ears. Or if he'd admit it if he had. Guys like him had a hard time with that itty-bitty four-letter word.

He didn't say anything, just pulled her into his arms for a long, hard kiss.

"Don't bring the feds up here too quickly," he said when he lifted his head. "This is Foley we're talking about. He couldn't find his ass with both hands. I may have to go get him."

Danica smiled. She almost wished she could stay and watch Clayne and Foley bitch at each other. Then it would really be like old times.

Foley and Hightower got there surprisingly fast—thanks to GPS, Clayne was sure. He resisted the urge to say something snide to Foley and simply watched the two men work instead. The faster they got done, the faster they'd be out of here.

The DCO didn't like the idea of leaving shifter DNA around where anyone could stumble across it, so while Foley injected the shifter with a drug that would make

McDermott's body go really ripe really fast, consequently making an autopsy useless, Hightower transferred the man's fingerprints to a .38 Special and left it on the ground next to the body, then applied gunshot residue to his hands.

Watching a cleanup team work always gave him the sinking feeling that the DCO could make anybody they wanted look guilty for just about anything. It made him glad he worked for the good guys.

When he was done, Hightower fitted a metal glove—for lack of a better word—to the shifter's right hand. Only there were four sickle-shaped metal claws where the fingers should be. It looked like something a comic book freak into Wolverine would wear to one of those crazy-ass conventions.

"What the hell is that?" Clayne asked.

Hightower grinned at him, his teeth white against his dark skin. "Nice, huh? I made it myself—with some tips from the techs. The claws will match the wound patterns in the previous victims exactly."

The DCO thought of everything. The FBI would go nuts if they couldn't figure out how McDermott had slain his victims. Hightower had given them that answer wrapped with a bow. The scary part was that Hightower looked proud of his handiwork.

"You really need a hobby, Hightower."

The other agent just chuckled.

The feds showed up a few minutes after Foley and Hightower left. Clayne hung around just long enough to tell them what happened—"McDermott came at us and we had no choice but to shoot him"—then high-tailed it down to the trailhead.

The area was teeming with police, FBI agents, park rangers, medical personnel, and reporters. He looked for Danica in all the confusion and found her talking to Carhart. As usual, he was pissed as hell. Clearly, he wasn't buying her story about getting a last-minute tip on McDermott and their crappy cell phone reception.

The vein in Carhart's temple practically pulsed with anger. "You were supposed to control the situation."

"I tried, sir, but—"

"I heard you the first time, Agent Beckett. You heard a woman's screams and had to move," he cut in. "But I'm not buying it, and I'm not going to forget it."

Danica opened her mouth, but whether it was to beg Carhart to reconsider or tell him to go to hell, Clayne would never know because the asswipe stormed off before she could get the words out.

"Want me to go smack Carhart around a little bit for you?" Clayne asked in her ear.

"If I didn't know you were serious, I'd take you up on that."

Damn, she never let him have any fun. "Carhart's probably full of hot air anyway."

"I'm not so sure about that. I disobeyed orders and embarrassed him. He meant what he said. He's not going to let it go."

"You helped catch a serial killer. That has to count for something."

"Not enough. But on the bright side, now I won't have to request a transfer to the DC office." She gave him a small smile. "Come on. Let's go see how Beth is."

Clayne would rather not face Tony and his wife after what they'd seen, but he couldn't avoid them forever.

They were Danica's friends. He followed her over to the ambulance where an EMT was bandaging Beth's feet.

"That'll do it for now, but you're going to need stitches when we get you to the hospital," the paramedic said as she finished up.

Beth made a face at that but didn't argue.

"Can you give us a few minutes?" Tony asked the EMT.

The woman glanced at Clayne and Danica, then nodded and walked off.

Clayne tried to hang back, but Danica took his hand and tugged him forward. He waited for Beth to stiffen or cringe and shout, "Monster!" But she simply hugged the blanket close around her shoulders and leaned into the comfort of her husband's embrace.

"You're pretty damn tough, running barefoot on this terrain," Clayne said.

"Not tough enough," she said quietly. "He would have caught me if it weren't for you."

Beth looked at Tony, something unspoken passing between them. Tony pressed a kiss to her forehead, then looked up at Clayne. "Beth and I had a lot of time to talk after you and Danica went after that…thing. We both saw some stuff that didn't make sense, but neither of us are going to say anything about that in our statements. As far as I'm concerned, you tangled with McDermott, giving me time to get my wife to safety, then you and Danica took him down."

Beth pushed her curly hair back from her face. "And I'll just play the emotionally distraught victim and say I don't remember what I saw." She took Clayne's hand and gave it a squeeze. "You saved my life tonight. Because of that, I'll have a lot less nightmares knowing there's someone like you out there to protect us from someone like him."

Clayne didn't quite know what to say. He was pretty sure he blushed a little. Luckily, Tony saved him from embarrassing himself.

"I saw you talking to Carhart," he said to Danica. "Everything okay?"

She recapped the conversation, adding, "I think I might be looking at a suspension."

Tony swore under his breath. "I'll talk to Carhart, and if I can't get him to see reason, then I'll go over his head."

Danica smiled. "I appreciate the offer, but as vindictive as Carhart is, he'd probably only suspend you, too. And that's not going to happen."

Tony regarded her thoughtfully. "What are you going to do then? Go back to Homeland?" He glanced pointedly at Clayne. "Or whatever organization it is you used to work for."

"I don't know about that," Danica said. "But now that Clayne and I are together, I am going to be moving back to DC."

Tony exchanged looks with Beth, who grinned. "We kinda figured that."

She looked as if she would have said more, but the EMT chose that moment to come back.

"We really should get you to the hospital, Mrs. Moretti."

Beth sighed. "Okay, okay." She looked at Danica. "Stop by the house before you and Clayne leave?"

"We will," Danica promised.

Tony waited while they loaded Beth into the

ambulance, then jumped in after her. Clayne watched as it drove away, then turned to Danica. Some of her hair had come loose from her bun and he had to resist the urge to tuck it behind her ear.

"Coming back to the DCO isn't a bad idea, you know," he said. "I don't officially have a partner, and I know John'd love to have you back."

"Dick wouldn't," she pointed out.

"So we get rid of him." When she frowned, he corrected himself. "Or at least get rid of the evidence he has."

She wasn't sure if that would be enough.

Chapter 11

WALKING INTO CLAYNE'S GEORGETOWN APARTMENT was like going back in time. Two years, to be exact. Everything looked precisely as it had the last time Danica had been there, right down to the throw pillows lying on the floor where Clayne had carelessly tossed them out of the way when they'd made love on the couch the night before Dick had torn their lives apart.

She swallowed hard and turned away. Clayne was standing in the entryway, still holding their bags. She knew from the pain in his beautiful dark eyes that somehow he'd figured out what she was thinking.

"When you left, it was like half my soul was gone." He set down the bags. "Surviving was the best I could do."

The words brought tears to her eyes and she closed the distance between them to throw her arms around his neck and hug him tight. He hugged her back just as fiercely, a man who was finally whole again.

"I felt the same way," she whispered.

Going up on tiptoe, she kissed him hard on the mouth, trying to express all the emotions she couldn't find words for right now. It must have been enough for Clayne, because he kissed her with just as much passion. Suddenly, the quickie they'd had that morning before leaving for the airport to tide them over felt like a lifetime ago. Taking his hands in hers, she tugged him toward the bedroom. She wasn't sure how it happened, but somehow they left a trail of clothing from the front door to the foot of his bed—which had been left unmade. Damn, he really had gone to hell without her, hadn't he?

Clayne scooped her up and set her down in the center of it, then stood back and caressed her naked body with his gleaming gold eyes. The desire reflected there was almost enough to set her on fire and it was all she could do to lie there and not spontaneously combust when he climbed in bed with a low, sexy growl and gently nibbled his way up her leg.

She grabbed hold of the sheet on either side of her, forcing herself to stay still as his mouth found its way along her calf to the sensitive skin of her inner thigh and finally to her pussy. By the time he got to her clit, all bets were off. The things the man could do with his tongue. *Daaaammmn*.

"You keeping doing what you're doing and I'm going to come," she warned him.

Clayne stopped long enough to flash her a sexy smile. "And that's a problem?"

He didn't wait for an answer, but buried his face between her legs again and went right back to licking her clit. Danica let her head drop back on the bed with a whimper. Clayne knew how to make her lose control like no one else, and two years since doing it hadn't made him forget how. If anything, he seemed to be even better at it now. Then again, maybe it was because she'd been forced to live with nothing more than her vibrator for the last two years—which was no substitute for a talented tongue.

She reached down with one hand and buried her

fingers in his hair, holding him right where she wanted him, though she doubted he intended to go anywhere. Clayne was one of those men who put a woman first. Making her come hard was as pleasurable to him as the great sex that would come next.

He always seemed to know exactly how long to torment her with his tongue, too. And how long to draw out her climax. Which usually meant until the sensations became so incredible that the lines between pleasure and pain blurred. Then and only then did he stop.

Her head lolled back, too heavy to lift. After an orgasm like that, she could barely think much less move.

Clayne's mouth moved gently up and down her inner thighs, nibbling and kissing first one, then the other. When she finally found the energy to open her eyes and look at him, he was grazing his slightly extended fangs against her tender skin. The feel of them sent little shock waves through her.

"I love making you come like that."

The deep rumble of his voice elicited an answering tremor between her legs, and she moaned. "I'm sort of fond of it myself."

He chuckled and pressed another kiss to her thigh. "I'll be right back. Don't go anywhere."

Danica opened her mouth to say something teasing in reply, but the sight of his well-muscled ass made speaking completely impossible. While she didn't mind the view, she did wonder where he was off to. She found out a few moments later when he came back with a condom in his hand.

She propped herself up on her elbows, watching as he slowly rolled the thin rubber over his hardness. Clayne might be impulsive, reckless, and quick to anger, but when it came to loving her, he always took his time. While that was a good thing, right now it was driving her crazy. She had to bite her lip to keep from telling him to hurry up.

"Get on your hands and knees," he commanded softly.

He didn't need to tell her twice. Doggie-style—or rather, wolf-style, as she liked to call it—was her favorite position. Heat throbbing between her legs, she rolled over and snuggled down low in the warm bedding that smelled overwhelmingly of her lover, then turned to throw him a sultry look over her shoulder.

Clayne groaned. "You have no idea what you do to me, do you?"

"If it's anything close to what seeing you kneeling there like that does to me, then yeah, I think I do," she told him.

His gold eyes gleamed even brighter at that, and a shiver ran through Danica as he climbed onto the bed behind her. He grasped her hips in his big hands, teasing her with his hardness before plunging into her. Even though they'd already made love several times since their reunion, the feel of him buried deep inside still made her gasp.

Clayne moved slowly, the rhythmic motion of his hips sending little ripples of pleasure through her with each thrust. Danica rocked back against him, matching her tempo to his and making them both moan.

Wrapping one arm around her, he grabbed a handful of her hair and tugged her head back to expose her neck. The dominant move would have been enough to make her melt all by itself, but then he leaned forward to gently nip her shoulder with his fangs. Considering his teeth were so sharp, it should have hurt, but it didn't. In fact, the opposite was true. Dear God, she actually got dizzy from how good it felt.

That, combined with his powerful thrusts, pushed her over the edge so hard and so fast she couldn't have stopped herself from coming even if she'd wanted to.

Clayne's hand tightening in her hair, as well as the sinfully sexy growl in her ear, told her he'd found his own release, and the knowledge only made her own orgasm that much more intense.

It was only afterward, as they lay side by side in each other's arms, that it hit her. She was finally back in Clayne's bed where she belonged. And nothing was going to take her away from him again.

—⁓—

"The way I see it, we have three options," Clayne said.

Danica leaned back against one of the throw pillows she'd put back on the couch and eyed him over the rim of her glass of diet soda. "Options for what?"

He reached for his fourth slice of the pizza they'd had delivered and bit into it. "Neutralizing Dick."

Ah. Knowing Clayne, she had a feeling what one of those options was. And while she probably knew what the second one was, she wasn't sure what option three might be.

"One, we kill him and dispose of his body where no one will ever find it," Clayne said, ticking it off on his finger. "Two, we steal the evidence he has on me. And three, we get new identities and run away together."

She stared at him, wondering if he was serious about running away with her. Dear God, he was. Why in the world had she ever walked away from a man like him?

"What?" Clayne asked.

She laughed, unable to help herself. "Nothing. It's just that I'm touched you'd run away with me. It's the most romantic thing anyone's ever offered to do for me."

He frowned. "I thought my offer to kill Dick would have been the bigger sacrifice."

"Considering you'd rather kill Dick than look at him again, not really." She reached over to pull off a piece of pepperoni—one of the three meat toppings Clayne liked on his pizza—and popped it into her mouth. "If I said that was what we should do, you'd have the job done by sunrise and come back with a bag of bagels for breakfast."

"I do like a good bagel," he agreed. "So, what's it going to be? If you say kill the little weasel, I'll even grab some of that strawberry-flavored cream cheese you love so much."

There were probably some who'd think it was sweet that Clayne was willing to do something as extreme as murdering a man so they could be together. It sounded so very Romeo and Juliet. But Danica wasn't one of those women. While Dick might be the nastiest a-hole she'd ever met, she didn't have a right to decide whether he lived or died.

"I think we should try to get the evidence back first. If that doesn't work, we can consider running away. Option one just isn't even on the table, okay?"

Clayne didn't exactly look happy about it, but he nodded.

She sipped her diet soda. "Where would he keep incriminating stuff like that anyway? His office?"

Clayne took another bite of pizza and chewed as he considered that. "I don't think so. It'd be too easy for someone to stumble across it there."

"You're probably right. His home then?"

Clayne finished his slice of pizza and wiped has hands on a napkin. "Only one way to find out. Let's go break in."

Danica blinked. "Now? Don't you think we should come up with a plan first?"

"That is the plan."

"Yeah, I know. I meant maybe we should think this out a little bit more."

He let out a snort. "Please. It's not like we're breaking into Fort Knox. How hard can it be?"

A forty-minute drive and one look at Dick's upscale apartment building proved Danica's point.

"There's no way we can get in there," she told Clayne.

"Sure we can," he insisted.

Clayne was good at a lot of things, but skulking around wasn't one of them. "You've never slipped past anyone in your life. Bash them over the head, yes. But stealth past someone? I don't think so. And what if he has the stuff in a wall safe? What are you going to do, rip it out and carry it down in the elevator?"

He let out a heavy sigh. "Okay, maybe you're right. But Ivy could do it."

It was Danica's turn to frown. "Ivy Halliwell?"

"It's Donovan now. She got married. But yeah."

Danica knew the feline shifter from her days at the DCO but didn't remember much about her. "If we ask for her help, we're going to have to tell her everything, including what Dick has on you. Are you sure we can trust her?"

"Besides you, she's probably the only other person I trust."

After calling Ivy to let her know they were coming, Clayne brought Danica up to speed on what had been going on with the cat shifter since Danica had left. It turned out that the feline shifter had a new partner now. The previous one—Jeff—had ended up being even more of an asshole than he seemed. According to Clayne, Jeff had tried to sexually assault Ivy while on a mission. After getting fired from the DCO, he promptly joined up with some guy named Stutmeir. Long story short, Ivy and her new partner—who later became her husband— found Jeff when they were sent to take down Stutmeir, and Ivy killed Jeff in self-defense.

"Wait a minute," Danica said. "The DCO allows partners to get married now?"

She really wanted to know more about the mission and this Stutmeir guy. At the moment, however, she was more interested in the DCO's no-fraternization policy.

Clayne shook his head as he pulled into the underground parking garage near Ivy's apartment building.

"Hell, no. Ivy and Landon are just much better at hiding their relationship than we were. Besides me, Kendra is the only other person at the DCO who knows."

A tall, good-looking, dark-haired guy answered the door when Clayne rang the bell. He glanced at Danica curiously before his gaze went back to Clayne. "Hey." He opened the door wider. "Come on in."

Clayne put his hand on Danica's back, urging her

ahead of him. "Sorry to come by so late, but I need to talk to you and Ivy. Is she here?"

"Yeah, she's in the bedroom."

The man gave a shout to let Ivy know they were there, then turned back to give Danica another curious look.

"Oh, sorry," Clayne mumbled as if realizing he hadn't introduced her. "Danica, this is Landon Donovan, Ivy's husband. Landon, Danica Beckett, my…old partner from the DCO."

Surprise flickered across Landon's face again, but he quickly hid it as he held out his hand. "Ivy's mentioned you. Nice to meet you."

She smiled. "Same here."

Danica turned to see Ivy saunter into the room. She was definitely a cat shifter, no doubt about it—that slinky walk was a dead giveaway.

The other woman's eyes went wide at the sight of her. "Danica?" She threw a quick look at Clayne, then swung her gaze back to Danica. "I didn't know you were back."

Danica wasn't big on hugs, but Ivy didn't give her any choice. One moment the feline shifter was standing three feet away, the next she had her arms around Danica like they were long-lost college roommates.

Ivy pulled away to give her a thoughtful look. "God, how long has it been?"

Before Danica could answer, Ivy leaned close again. Only instead of hugging her this time, the feline shifter sniffed her. Danica was so startled she didn't have a chance to react. By the time she recovered, Ivy had turned her focus on Clayne. Something unspoken passed between them before he finally nodded.

"Why didn't you ever say anything?" Ivy asked.

Clayne gave her a sheepish look. If Danica didn't know better, she'd think he was blushing. "It was complicated."

Huh?

Danica glanced at Landon to see him staring at his wife with an expression of total confusion. *Join the club, buddy.*

He looked from Ivy to Clayne, then back again. "What am I missing here?"

When Ivy didn't answer, he looked at Danica for help. She could only shrug.

"Were you two sleeping together back when you were partners?" Ivy asked Clayne.

Danica blinked. *How the hell?*

"Yeah," he said. "Unfortunately, we weren't very good at keeping it a secret."

Ivy shook her head, her eyes full of understanding. "I can't believe I didn't figure it out. Now I see why you had to leave the DCO. But not why you two broke up. How did you two get back together anyway?"

"I was out in Sacramento tracking down a rogue shifter turned serial killer," Clayne said. "Danica was the FBI agent working the case."

"Huh. Well, if you weren't working at the DCO, why didn't you keep dating?" Ivy groaned. "Sorry. Curiosity and the cat in me. You don't have to answer that."

Clayne gave Danica a small smile. "Actually, that's kinda what we wanted to talk to you and Landon about."

"Okay. Now I am really curious." Ivy gestured to the big sectional couch. "Come sit."

Danica and Clayne took one end of the couch, while Ivy and Landon sat on the other.

"Before we get into why we're here, I need to ask you something," Danica said to Ivy. "How did you know that Clayne and I were a couple?"

Ivy's lips curved. "I smelled Clayne all over you when we hugged."

Danica knew feline shifters had an incredible sense of smell, but she didn't know they could discern that two people had sex. "How did you know we hadn't, I don't know, hugged, let's say? Or stood close together on the Metro?"

"The scent was too strong for casual contact like that. It's a unique blend of pheromones and…other things."

Danica felt her face heat. A shifter could smell all that? She looked up to see Clayne grinning at her in a very knowing way.

"The big giveaway, though?" Ivy continued. "He left little bite marks on the curve of your neck. I'm not that up on wolf shifter mating behavior, but I think he was marking you as his."

Danica clamped a hand to her neck, jaw dropping. She'd felt Clayne nip her when they'd made love, but she hadn't realized he'd left marks.

"May I use your bathroom?" she asked Ivy.

The feline shifter uncurled herself from the couch. "Sure. Come on, I'll show you where it is."

Danica followed but not before throwing Clayne an accusing look.

"Don't worry." Ivy smiled as she switched on the bathroom light. "They're not that bad. No one else would even see them unless they really looked."

After Ivy left, Danica leaned close to the mirror and tugged the collar of her shirt to the side. Sure enough, there was a tiny collection of bite marks on the curve of her neck. They weren't all that visible, she supposed. Actually, they looked kind of sexy, in that I'm-dating-a-wolf-shifter way.

She rubbed her fingers lightly over the marks. Clayne had nipped her during sex before, lots of times, but he'd never left a mark—not one. Why do it now?

Because he's in love with you.

Her heart did a backflip. True, Clayne hadn't said the words, but maybe in his mind, he'd done one better by marking her as his.

She supposed that made her his...*mate*. The word made her smile. She liked the sound of it.

Laughter from the living room pulled Danica back to the here and now. She took one more look at the light pink teeth marks, then straightened her T-shirt and left the bathroom.

Clayne cut his chuckle short as Danica sat down beside him. Crap, maybe she shouldn't have made such a big deal about the love bites he'd given her. How could she tell him he was welcome to nibble on her neck whenever he felt like it with Ivy and Landon sitting there?

She put her hand on his jean-clad thigh and squeezed firmly. Clayne's eyes flickered gold. Yeah, that got the message through.

"Did you tell them?" she asked him.

He shook his head. "I wanted to wait for you."

"Well, she's here now," Landon pointed out. "Don't leave us hanging."

Clayne took a deep breath and let it out slowly. "Dick was the one who realized we were sleeping together."

"Why am I not surprised?" Ivy muttered.

"But instead of reassigning us to other teams or even straight out firing one or both of us, he blackmailed Danica into leaving the DCO and breaking up with me."

Landon's brows drew together. "Blackmailed her how?"

Clayne glanced at Ivy. "Remember I told you that I didn't come from a very good background?" When she nodded, he continued. "What I didn't tell you was that I was in jail when Dick recruited me."

"In jail for what?" Landon asked.

The muscle in Clayne's jaw flexed. "Murder."

"Stop saying it was murder. It was justifiable homicide," Danica corrected. "Not to mention self-defense. Because I'm sure those men would have killed you once they found out you weren't down with their plan."

When Ivy and Landon gave her curious looks, she explained the story about the little girls Clayne had saved from the sex slave trade, as well as Dick's subsequent visit to Clayne when he was in jail. "Dick said he'd make sure the evidence disappeared, but instead he kept it. Since he had no way of knowing Clayne and I would be teamed up together, maybe he simply held on to it to keep Clayne under his thumb."

Beside her, Clayne snorted.

"Regardless, if the stuff on that videotape gets out, Clayne could go to prison for a long time," she finished. "Maybe the rest of his life."

Ivy muttered something about Dick living up to his name. "What do you need us to do? Whatever it is, the answer is yes."

"You may regret you said that," Clayne said. "We need you to break into Dick's apartment and steal the evidence."

"We'd do it ourselves, but he lives in a fancy building with security cameras and twenty-four-hour guards," Danica added. "Breaking and entering isn't our specialty."

Landon frowned. "Hold on a minute. If Dick was the one who brought you into the DCO, why screw with you like this?"

Clayne's mouth tightened. "Because he's always wanted the shifter program to fail and figured that with Danica out of my life, I'd lose it and give the powers that be a reason to shut down that part of the DCO."

"That's messed up." Landon shook his head. "Does John know about any of this?"

"No," Clayne said. "At least I don't think so. Besides, it's not like John could keep me out of jail if the evidence found its way onto some DA's desk."

"I don't know about that," Ivy said. "John has a lot of influence in a lot of places."

Landon frowned. "But he's also a straight shooter. I don't think he'd use his authority to keep one of his people out of jail if the evidence showed that's where he should be."

"But Clayne had to kill those men," Danica insisted.

"I know, but Landon's right," Ivy said. "Are you willing to take the chance John'd see it the same way? He's the kind of man who'd want to see this worked out in the justice system. We can't go to him"

Clayne looked from her to Landon. "Does this mean you're still in?"

"Hooah." Landon grinned. "Ivy and I still owe you one, remember?"

—∞—

"What's taking them so long?" Danica demanded.

She glanced at her watch for what felt like the hundredth time since Ivy and Landon had gone into Dick's apartment building over an hour ago. She and Clayne had been sitting on the place the entire time.

Clayne glanced out the car window. He looked as worried as she was. "I don't know, but if they're not out in ten minutes, I'm going in."

Danica turned her gaze back to the posh high-rise apartment building. "Ivy and Landon are good friends. Not everyone would've agreed to help us."

Clayne sat back in the seat, his gaze still trained on the building across the street. "Sometimes I think Ivy was the only thing that kept me sane after you left. If it hadn't been for her, I might have done all the horrible things Dick hoped I would."

Danica didn't believe that, but she was glad Ivy had been there for him all the same. Something in Clayne's voice made her wonder just how good a friend Ivy'd been, though. It would probably be better not to know, but she had to ask.

"Did you and Ivy…?"

Clayne turned his head to look at her, his eyes unfathomable in the near darkness. "Did we what?"

"Did you…sleep together?"

Danica held her breath. She told herself she wouldn't be angry if they had. She'd dumped him. It was only natural he'd try to move on. So she definitely wouldn't be angry. She couldn't promise she wouldn't be jealous, though.

"No, we didn't sleep together," he said quietly. "Not for lack of trying on my part, though."

Danica didn't say anything. Processing the fact that he'd wanted to sleep with the beautiful feline shifter was about all she could manage right now.

"But Ivy only wanted to be friends," he continued. "Then Landon came into the picture and… Let's just say things were ugly for a while."

Danica didn't have to ask what he meant by that. She could imagine.

"If you only knew the things I did and said to them." He shook his head. "I couldn't understand how she could want to be with a human. I thought he'd hurt her like you hurt me. And I didn't want her to hurt like that." He let out a snort. "My intentions almost sound noble when I say it like that, but honestly? I was the one who didn't want to get hurt again. I guess I thought that if I stuck to my own kind I wouldn't."

His own kind. Meaning a shifter like him.

"I thought Ivy would help me get over you, but I was wrong," he admitted. "I would have ended up hurting her without meaning to because she wasn't you. None of them were. I don't think I ever would have gotten over you, Danica."

He'd said none of them, meaning there'd been other women besides Ivy. Other women he *had* slept with. She wanted to be jealous, but her heart ached too much. Tears suddenly clogged her throat. God, she hated what she'd done to him. And she hated Dick even more for making her do it.

She opened her mouth to tell him again how sorry she was, but he leaned over and silenced her with a hot, hard kiss. She buried her fingers in his hair, forgetting about the past and all the pain she'd caused him. She was back now, and that was all that mattered.

A knock on the side window made Danica jump, and she pulled away to see Ivy and Landon standing beside the car. Clayne muttered something under his breath and rolled down the window.

"Did you get it?"

Ivy shook her head. "It wasn't there. The place is clean."

Clayne swore. "So, where the hell would he keep it?"

"Kendra might know," Ivy said. "She's been working with Dick longer than any of us."

That made sense. But while Danica trusted Kendra, she didn't like the idea of someone else knowing about this—more chance of it getting back to Dick. On the other hand, she and Clayne didn't have much choice.

Clayne hesitated, but then gave Ivy a nod. "Okay."

The cat shifter pulled out her cell phone. "I'll ask her to meet us at our place."

———⁓———

Clayne and Landon were raiding the fridge when Kendra arrived. Danica looked up from setting the table as the blond walked in. She stopped in her tracks when she saw Danica.

"Hey! I didn't know you were back."

Clayne wrapped an arm around Danica's waist, popping a cherry tomato in her mouth before she could answer. "It's complicated."

"We'll explain over dinner," Ivy said, walking past Kendra to help Landon in the kitchen.

"Dick wouldn't keep anything that sensitive in his

office," Kendra said matter-of-factly as they ate. The fact that Clayne had a dark secret in his past didn't seem to faze Kendra in the least. Nor did the fact that they were asking for her help to essentially steal something from the DCO deputy director. "If it's anywhere," she added, "it's at the DCO's records repository."

"What repository?" Clayne asked.

She scowled at him over the rim of her glass. "The one where all the crap you field agents bring back gets stored. You know—the computer disks, the spy gear, the weapons, the mountains of files and classified documents?" When they stared at her blankly, Kendra sighed. "We scan the critical records into our computer database, but most of the stuff—boxes and boxes of hard copy files, various digital media that just isn't important enough to waste time on, not to mention all the miscellaneous hardware crap—that all has to get stored somewhere. We might be a high-speed covert ops organization, but we're still part of the U.S. government. We don't throw anything away. What, did you think all that crap ended up in my office? I'm organized, but not that organized. Besides, you guys bring back enough stuff on a daily basis to fill up a couple moving trucks."

Ivy helped herself to more salad, then handed the serving bowl to her husband. "Where is this repository?"

Kendra sipped her iced tea. "Outside Crystal City. You've probably driven past it a hundred times without noticing it." She twirled some spaghetti around her fork. "I've been there more than a few times, dropping off classified packages for John and Dick."

Landon's brows drew together. "Do you seriously think

Dick would keep his blackmail material in an agency storage facility? I mean, that's pretty freaking ballsy."

"Landon has a point," Ivy said.

"I don't think you realize how secure this place is," Kendra said. "Dick is the only other person in the DCO besides John with unescorted access to the vault, which means he doesn't have to worry about anybody else sniffing around. And since the place is so big, it's not like someone is just going to stumble across the evidence by accident. A person would have to know what they're looking for and where it's located."

"How big are we talking about?" Danica asked.

Kendra shrugged. "I've only been inside with John twice, and I didn't get to wander around on my own. But still, the part I saw was huge. You could fit a basketball court or two in there and have room left over for handball. The place is filled with so many filing cabinets and storage lockers that you could hide a body in there and nobody would know it."

That raised a lot of eyebrows. Across from Danica, Ivy and Landon nodded. Even Clayne seemed to think Kendra was onto something.

"That's where we should look next," Ivy said.

"Hold on a minute," Danica said. "Are you seriously saying that we're all going to break into a DCO warehouse protected by God knows how many security guards?"

Ivy shook her head. "Of course not. It won't be all of us. Just Kendra, Landon, and me."

Kendra's head jerked up. "Me? Why me?"

"Because you know your way around the place," Ivy

told her. "Landon and I can get inside, but we'll need you to find the evidence."

Kendra groaned. "Okay, I guess I walked right into that one. One stipulation—if I get caught and John fires me, I'm moving into your guest room."

"If we get caught, getting fired will be the least of your worries," Ivy said. "We'll probably be shipped off to prison."

"If they don't just shoot us on sight," Landon pointed out.

Kendra made a face at him. "Thank you. I feel so much better about it now."

Danica didn't blame Kendra. She had more than a few reservations about the plan, too. From the scowl on Clayne's face, so did he.

"None of you are going to get arrested or shot, because you're not going in there," he said. "I am."

Danica snapped her head around to gape at him. "You're joking, right?"

"No," he said. "If anyone's going to get arrested for breaking into a guarded government facility, it should be me. I'm the one Dick has incriminating evidence on, not Ivy or Landon or Kendra. Or you."

Danica bit her tongue. How could she argue with him for wanting to protect his friends—or her? "Then I'm going with you."

He gave her a hard look. "No, you're not."

Two could play at that staring contest. "Yes, I am."

"Neither of you are going," Ivy said firmly. "Clayne, I know how you feel, I really do. Please don't take this the wrong way, but this isn't your kind of op. There won't be any shooting or kicking in doors or punching anyone. The place will likely be full of sensors, alarms, and roving guard. This will be a pure stealth mission, which isn't exactly your area of expertise. You need to let us do this."

Clayne was silent, but Danica could tell from the tightness of his jaw that he didn't like it. "Okay," he finally agreed. "But if you get caught, I'm breaking you out of prison and we're all going on the run."

Danica was the only one besides Clayne who didn't laugh.

Chapter 12

LANDON GAVE THE HALLWAY BELOW THEM ANOTHER scan with the thermal sensor before grabbing the rope to lower Ivy down. The scanner would have alerted him if anyone was moving around down there. This backed up what they already knew: the guards swept through this side of the corridor about every thirty-eight minutes. If everyone kept to their normal schedules, that gave him, Ivy, and Kendra about thirty minutes to get down to the corridor, slip into the medium-level security computer server room three doors down, then get through there into the main vault. All they had to do then was find the evidence against Clayne—if it was there—and get back out before the guards came by on their next sweep and noticed the skylight in the roof had been propped open.

Piece of cake.

Ivy was down the rope in seconds and heading for the server room before he even got Kendra rigged up for her trip down. She slid down almost as fast as Ivy. Damn, he was starting to think that maybe John was wasting her talents. She had the makings of a good field operative.

He looked around the dark roof one more time before following Kendra down. He gave the rope a tug, yanking it down after him. Leaving the skylight ajar was bad enough. There was no way he could leave a big rope hanging down. That would be just too damn obvious. When it was time to go, Ivy would tie the rope to her belt, then he'd boost her up and wait for her to scramble out the skylight and lower the rope down for him and Kendra. As exit strategies went, it wasn't complicated, but those were usually the best kind.

By the time he got to the server room, Ivy and Kendra were already busy pulling up the covers on the floor housing the bundles of wires and cables that ran under the quietly humming computers. Landon grimaced at the mess Ivy'd made of the keypad to the right of the door. The cover was dangling from a lone wire, bypass leads attached to the circuitry. Once they left the room, they'd pull the bypass lead off and put the cover back on, good as new. But if a guard walked by right then, he wasn't going to miss that someone had tampered with the keypad. Yet another reason to get out fast.

When he and Ivy had broken into the construction company late last night, it was to get a look at the floor plan of the repository before and after the DCO renovations. Finding the right ones had taken a while, but without the schematics, they never would have known there was a gap the size of an air vent in the floor between the server room and the vault below it.

He crouched down, looking over Ivy's shoulder as she and Kendra crawled around the cables and wires. "Please tell me they haven't closed up that gap we saw."

"It doesn't look like it." Ivy grinned at him. "Get down here and help."

Landon lowered himself into the crawl space with them and immediately saw what had made Ivy so happy. Attached to the concrete floor underneath the cables was a three-foot square piece of plywood right where the hole was supposed to be. He had to move some wiring

around, but he got the plywood up easily. Underneath
it, there was hole big enough for even a guy his size to
squeeze through.

"We have a little over twenty minutes," he reminded
Ivy and Kendra as they dropped down into the vault.

Landon climbed in after them and swore. There were
rows upon rows of filing cabinets and storage lockers.
Shit, this place really was huge.

"I hope you know how to use the cataloging system,
Kendra, or there's no way we're going to find that evidence," he said.

"We'll find it," Kendra said firmly.

Landon wasn't quite as confident, but he didn't say
anything as he followed them over to the computer on
the console against the far wall. According to Kendra,
there was a searchable database of everything that was
stored in the vault. Only two people had access to use
it—John and Dick. Fortunately, Kendra had John's
password. Apparently, the DCO director never hid it
from her when she'd come in here with him.

Kendra logged on to the system, then started searching.

"Anything I can do to help?" he asked.

Kendra didn't take her eyes off the screen. "Not
until I figure out where Dick hid the evidence. You can
look for the video if you want. Maybe you'll stumble
across it."

He was man enough to recognize when he was being
told to get out of the way and stop being a nuisance.
"Make it fast," he said. "We've got less than twenty
minutes now."

Landon watched Kendra scroll through the database
for a few seconds. If he was stuck waiting, he might as

well have a look around. Hell, maybe Kendra was right and he'd stumble over Dick's evidence on Clayne.

Landon wandered over to the first filing cabinet and opened the top drawer. Inside were neat rows of folders, each marked with an alphanumeric tag on the upper right-hand corner. He picked one and thumbed through it. The pages inside were covered in some kind of foreign language he didn't recognize. He put the folder back and closed the drawer, then glanced at his watch.

"Eighteen minutes," he told Ivy and Kendra.

He moved down the row of filing cabinets, picked one, and opened the top drawer, then grabbed a folder at random. At least this one was in English.

It was an after-action report describing how the CIA had captured a man in September 2002. The man, a freelance American assassin, had been in the process of carrying out a job for the Russian mob when a CIA field team had stumbled onto him. The interesting part of the report was that the man was a shifter—apparently the first one the DCO had ever encountered. The shifter, known only as Adam, had been hired to kill a Ukrainian oil tycoon attending a diplomatic function in the States. The CIA stopped him, but the effort it took to bring down the shifter—in the words of the lone field agent who'd survived—was extraordinary.

Landon threw a quick glance at Ivy and Kendra. Ivy was rifling through a filing cabinet as Kendra called out numbers. He checked the time.

"Twelve minutes," he told them, then went back to skimming the report.

It essentially told the story of how the DCO

Committee had decided to bring Adam on as an operative. Not everyone was thrilled about the idea, but
they finally agreed to do it, making all traces of Adam's
capture by the CIA disappear.

The file described how a team was built around
Adam, with the express purpose of both supporting
him and making the shifter disappear if anything went
wrong. *Nothing new there*, Landon thought, remembering his first briefing with John when the man had
informed him that one of his jobs would be to kill Ivy if
it ever looked like she might be captured.

Within a year after starting the shifter program, Adam
had gone rogue, murdering most of his own team before
being killed. Some members of the Committee—with
Dick Coleman leading the charge—wanted the shifter
program canceled and the shifters already identified ex-
terminated. The report didn't give details, but somehow
John had stopped them.

Landon checked his watch. Five minutes. He looked
up to see Ivy hurrying from one file cabinet to the next
as Kendra called out numbers.

He'd never have time to read the rest of the file and
still look around. But the stuff in his hand was too good
to leave behind, so Landon shoved it in his bag, then
moved on to the next cabinet.

He skimmed as many files as he could. Damn, the entire existence of the DCO was spread out in these cabinets.

Then Landon saw a word in the next folder that
stopped him cold—Stutmeir—the name of the former
East German intelligence officer who developed the hybrid strain and had Ivy tortured. He narrowed his eyes.
What the hell?

There were no dates in the file, but from what he could tell, someone in the DCO had been in contact with Stutmeir well before he started kidnapping scientists and making hybrids. If Landon didn't know better, he'd say Stutmeir had *worked* for the DCO at some point. But why hadn't this come up during their initial briefing on the man? John had acted as if he'd never heard of Stutmeir before then.

"Okay, hon," Ivy called from the other side of the room. "We've got what we need. Let's go."

He closed the file and shoved it in his pack with the other one. He'd read it later.

Landon's head whirled like a tornado as they left the repository. While he was damn happy they'd gotten the evidence against Clayne, all he wanted to do was get a closer look at the files he'd stolen. The DCO obviously had a history with Stutmeir, and Landon wanted to know exactly what it was. But even more importantly, he wanted to know why John had never told them.

~~~

Clayne and Danica took the evidence—a VHS videotape and the original arrest report—to a deserted warehouse near the Port of Baltimore. The report contained written transcripts of what was on the tape, detailed forensic analyses, as well as the original evidence itself— fingerprints, blood, hair, fibers, and glass fragments taken from the crime scene—all of which were in neatly labeled plastic evidence bags.

Clayne built a fire in a fifty-five-gallon drum the city's homeless probably used for heat in the winter.

Then he slowly tossed each piece of damning evidence, one article at a time, and watched it burn.

Neither of them spoke until every last piece of paper had turned to ash and they were in his Charger heading back to his place.

"Do you think Dick has copies of that stuff anywhere else?" Danica asked softly.

Clayne considered the possibility. "Maybe." He shrugged. "Even if he did, they'd only be copies, like you said. A good lawyer would have a field day with the chain of custody and pointing out how the video could have been manipulated prior to Dick copying it. And he wouldn't have any of the actual physical evidence. Without that, none of it would hold up in court."

At least he hoped it wouldn't.

"You're probably right." Danica leaned back against the headrest with a sigh. "I guess now all we have to worry about is that FBI review board."

He gave her a sidelong glance. "Not if you resign from the Bureau and come back to work for the DCO."

She snorted. "I'm sure Dick would be completely on board with that."

"Screw Dick," he growled. "He doesn't have anything to hold over our heads anymore."

Danica was silent. "The DCO still has that stupid policy about partners not getting romantically involved."

"We can do what Ivy and Landon do when they're at work."

She gave him a wry smile. "Do you honestly think you can pretend that we're just professional partners again? Dick knew we were sleeping together before, and he'll know it now. He'd have me fired in the first week for violating DCO policy."

He scowled as he pulled into the parking space that came with his apartment and cut the engine. She was right. He'd never been any good at pretending.

Danica reached out to lace her fingers with his. "Where I work isn't important, babe. What's important is that we're together."

Clayne leaned over to kiss her tenderly on the mouth. For the first time in what felt like forever, he was actually looking forward to tomorrow, and the day after that, and the next one after that. The woman he loved more than anything was back in his life for good, and nothing was going to take her away from him again.

Chapter 13

DANICA WOKE THE NEXT DAY TO THE EARLY MORNING sun shining through the curtains. She smiled and snuggled up against Clayne's warm body, more than willing to stay right where she was for the rest of the day. It was the weekend and she was due some extra sleep. Between tracking McDermott, the flight to DC, and getting back the evidence Dick had been holding over Clayne's head for years, she was exhausted.

Then again, she might also be tired because Clayne was determined to make up for lost time when it came to sex. Not that she was complaining. Yeah, he was wearing her out, but she was happy.

She turned her head on the pillow, watching Clayne sleep peacefully beside her. His hair had fallen across his forehead and she had to resist the urge to reach out and brush it back. She felt like pinching herself to make sure all this was real. She had found something special with him and lost it, only to find it again. How had she gotten so lucky?

As much as she wanted to stay in bed with him for the rest of the day, the endorphin high she was on forced her to get up and do something. Like go for a run. It was either that or jump Clayne, and he needed the sleep maybe even more than she did. She'd leave him a note telling him where she'd gone.

She eased out of bed carefully so she wouldn't wake

him, then tiptoed over to the suitcases she'd yet to un-
pack and dug through them for her running clothes.
She hadn't gone on a serious run since before the serial
killer case had landed in her lap. That was a long time
for her.

She'd already put on her yoga pants and sports bra
and was slipping into her shirt when the bed creaked
behind her.

"Where are you going?" Clayne asked, his voice
husky with sleep.

She pulled her hair up in a ponytail as she turned to
give him a smile. "Jogging. I'll be back in a little while."

"Wait up. I'll go with you."

He tried to claw his way out of the blankets, but she
threw them back over him and sat down on the edge of
the bed.

"Since when did you start running?" she asked as she
put on her shoes.

"I run all the time." When she lifted a brow, he added,
"I chase bad guys, don't I?"

"Not the same thing." She finished tying her sneak-
ers, then leaned over to kiss him. "Stay in bed. You were
pretty energetic last night. I know you must be tired."

Clayne grinned. "Maybe a little tired. But in a good
way." He ran his finger down her cheek. "Don't be
too long."

"I won't." She kissed him again, long and slow.
Okay, if she didn't leave right now, she'd never go for
that run. She pulled away, forcing herself to her feet,
then grabbed her cell phone from the nightstand. "I'll
call when I'm on my way back so you can warm up the
shower for me."

A grin spread across his face. "Don't tire yourself out too much. I have plans for that body of yours."

Mmm. That was something to look forward to after a run—even better than a warm shower. "I'll hold you to that."

Clayne chuckled.

Once outside, she headed for one of the running paths that ran along the Potomac, then set the music on her phone, turned up the volume, and gave herself permission to zone out and enjoy the scenic view of downtown DC. But rather than losing herself in Lady Gaga's lyrics, she thought about Clayne. Who was waiting for her back at his apartment right now with a warm shower and a hot body. The image made heat pool between her thighs.

Danica made it a mile more before turning around. Running was highly overrated anyway.

She was still fantasizing about making love in the shower with Clayne when another jogger came around the curve in the path from the opposite direction. She didn't pay much attention to him, other than to note that he ran really freaking fast. It wasn't until she got close enough to see his face that something seemed familiar about the guy. She took in his angular features and sandy blond hair, trying to place him, but couldn't.

He slowed his steps to a more leisurely jog the closer he got. Did he think he recognized her, too?

It wasn't until he was almost even with her that she finally remembered where she'd seen his face—on a guy she and Clayne had put four bullet holes in back in Sacramento.

Crap.

Danica tried to dart around him, but the shifter was

too fast. He lunged at her with a growl, grabbing her arm and jabbing something into her chest. The pain was horrendous and completely debilitating, and she only had a fraction of a second to think about Clayne waiting for her back at his apartment before everything went black.

Clayne was lying in bed thinking about how he and Danica would spend the day. Sex to start, for sure. Then maybe breakfast at a diner he knew nearby. Then… Who cared? They had the whole day to themselves. He was still grinning when his cell phone rang.

He grabbed his cell from the nightstand, his grin broadening when he saw Danica's name on the call display. Maybe she'd decided a run wasn't the kind of exercise she'd been looking for.

He thumbed the answer button. "On your way back already? What, you miss me?"

There was silence on the other end of the line, then a low, rough, all-too-familiar laugh. "Does she miss you? Probably. But on her way back? Don't think so. I'm afraid your woman is going to be a bit late for breakfast. Or whatever it is you leidolfs do in the morning."

Clayne jerked upright in bed, terror stabbing him like a knife. He had no idea how it could be possible, but the voice on the other end of the line belonged to the same psycho he'd talked to in the FBI's field office in Sacramento. The same psycho who'd viciously killed six men. The same psycho they'd shot four times. And he had Danica's phone.

"What kind of game do you want to play now?"

Clayne snarled. "I killed you once already. You want me to do it again?"

A short, harsh laugh. "I guess cats really are terrible at playing dead, aren't they? Then again, we do have nine lives. But don't worry, there's no game this time. No clues to figure out, no deadline to race against. I just called to tell you that I'm going to kill your woman—slowly and painfully. And there's not a damn thing you can do about it. I'll make sure her body is easy to find, though. I owe you that much after all the fun we had together. You lose, Leidolf."

Then he hung up.

Clayne's claws were digging into his palms before he even knew they were out. He threw back the blanket and grabbed his jeans from the floor where he'd left them the night before, yanking them on as fast as he could. His hands shook so much he could barely button it. He forced himself to calm down as he shoved his feet into his boots, forced himself to override the fear welling up and threatening to overwhelm him. He couldn't lose Danica now, not after all this.

Where had she said she was going running? She hadn't. Where could she have gone running? Anywhere. But he could track her—he knew her scent and could follow it anywhere.

He put on a fresh T-shirt and ran out the door. He picked up her scent immediately. He sprinted down the sidewalk, weaving in and out of the people in his path like it was a slalom course.

He veered onto the running path. Why the hell hadn't he gone with Danica? When he got her back, he'd go jogging with her three times a day if she wanted.

If he got her back.

The word echoed in his mind, mocking him as his boots pounded the pavement.

Clayne didn't even know how far he'd run before her scent disappeared.

He skidded to a stop and backed up until he found it again. Then he dropped to one knee and sniffed the ground. She'd been lying right here. But at least there was no sign of blood.

He sniffed again. McDermott's scent was there, too, overlaying hers. How the hell could that be? He and Danica had each put two large caliber bullets through his chest. He knew for a fact that both of Danica's had pierced the shifter's heart. Not even a hybrid could live through that.

Clayne straightened and started down the running trail again, following McDermott's scent instead of Danica's this time. It led to an empty parking lot a hundred feet away, then stopped. He spun in a circle, fear rearing up again, roaring loud and long. Danica was gone and he had no way to find her—not in time. McDermott would torture her; then he would kill her, just like he killed those men out in California. An image of her lying in a pool of blood with her throat ripped out flashed before his eyes, and a growl rumbled low in his throat.

He forced the animal down. His human side—his human intellect—was the only thing that would save her now.

He sucked in a deep breath, then took out the cell phone he barely remembered sliding in the pocket of his jeans on the way out the door. He scrolled through his list of contacts until he came to Ivy and Landon's number, his thumb hovering over the screen. What help could they give him? He didn't even have any clues to follow this time. All he knew was that McDermott wasn't dead and that he had Danica.

Clayne scrolled down the screen until he came to Kendra's number. If anyone could help him find Danica, it would be her.

"Hello," Kendra mumbled, her voice groggy with sleep.

He skipped the pleasantries. "It's Clayne. I need you to trace Danica's cell phone."

There was silence on the other end, then Kendra's voice came back, sharper and more focused. "Her cell phone? Did she…leave you again?"

He swore. "No, she didn't leave me. Can you trace it or not?"

"Not from home. I have to go to the office. It'll take me about twenty minutes to get there, though."

"Shit," he muttered. "That's too long."

"Clayne, you're scaring me here. What's wrong?"

He didn't have time for this. "I need to find Danica's cell phone. Please tell me you can do that."

"I can call the twenty-four-hour mission hotline and get the duty officer to run it, but if I do it that way, everyone will know about it," she said. "Including Dick."

"Do it," Clayne told her.

If it got him a location on Danica, he'd deal with Dick later.

"Stay on the line," Kendra told him. "I'm going to put you on hold."

A minute went by, then another. A pair of joggers passed, giving him a wide birth.

"Okay," Kendra said. "They ran her cell. No luck."

"What do you mean?" Clayne barked. "I thought you guys could track those things."

"We can. But not if the person powers down the phone or yanks out the SIM card." Kendra let out a breath. "What's going on, Clayne? Is Danica in trouble?"

Clayne didn't answer. He lowered the phone and stared off into the distance. That son of a bitch had known Clayne would try to track Danica's cell.

No scent to follow, no cell phone signal to lock in on, no clues to figure out. There was nothing left to tell him where she was. The need to howl out all his rage was so overwhelming he almost threw back his head right there in the middle of the trail.

But as a gut-wrenching pain began to settle in his stomach, a little voice in his head told him that wasn't true. There was a way to track her.

Kendra was yelling at him over the phone, trying to get his attention. He hung up on her and shoved his cell back in his pocket.

Clayne took a deep breath and closed his eyes. He forced himself to relax, trying to sense Danica like he'd done when they'd been chasing McDermott in the forest that night. But for whatever reason, he couldn't feel her. He turned his body one way, then the other like an antenna hoping to improve his reception. It didn't help. Maybe Danica was already too far away for him to pick her up? But he refused to go down that road. If he did, it would mean he wouldn't find her at all.

He focused harder, pushing his awareness out—like he did when he wanted to pick a particular scent out of a crowd. But again, it didn't work.

Dammit! Why had this been so easy when he'd chased McDermott through the freaking forest?

Because he'd let his inner wolf out and given it free reign.

Clayne shifted, right there in the middle of the running path. Anyone that got too close was going to be in for one hell of a scare. Fangs, claws, features—he let it all go.

Every sound was suddenly louder, every smell more intense. The vibrations of cars and trucks moving on a road a mile away found their way through the earth and up the soles of his feet to his head, where he cataloged and analyzed them. If he opened his eyes, the blue of the sky would be more vivid, the horizon farther away.

But none of those senses mattered. He was only interested in the sensation that told him where Danica was.

When he finally felt it, he almost dropped to his knees and wept. How could he have missed it?

He turned slowly until he was facing in her direction, then opened his eyes. He was facing almost due east, into the heart of DC. A laugh, mixed with equal parts growl, escaped his lips.

I'm coming, Danica. Just hold on.

Danica woke to a strange echoing sound filling her ears. What the hell was that noise? And why did her chest hurt so damn much?

She tried to lift her hand to rub the area and ease the pain there, but her arm felt like it was too heavy to pick up. She tried her other arm but couldn't move that one, either. That was when it came back to her—waking up beside Clayne, going running on the trail, seeing McDermott.

Her eyes snapped open and she jumped up—or tried to. That was when she realized she was tied down to something. She jerked hard, but her arms and legs were immobilized. There were ropes wrapped around her wrists and forearms. No, not ropes. Yellow, heavy duty extension cords. She was tied to a cheap metal armchair.

That didn't explain the pain in her chest. It felt as if she'd been hit with a stun gun. Which made sense. McDermott liked to subdue his victims that way.

Where was that sick bastard anyway?

Danica lifted her head to find the cat shifter sitting in a matching chair a few feet away, his long legs stretched out in front of him. She had shot him twice—in the heart. How the hell could he be alive? It was impossible, but it was true. He'd gotten rid of the beard and cut his hair shorter, but it was him.

"You should see the look on your face, Agent Beckett," he said. "It's absolutely priceless."

He pulled his legs in, then leaned forward to rest his forearms on his knees, and she felt her stomach quiver in fear as he focused his predatory eyes on her. The only reason she wasn't dead already was because he had something far worse in mind for her, she was sure.

"Of course it doesn't compare to the one you had on your face when you first saw me on that running path. It was like you'd seen a ghost. Though I guess from your point of view, I am a ghost." He sat back, regarding her like she was an amusing puppy. "Nothing to say. What's the matter? Cat got your tongue?"

He laughed at his own joke.

That was when Danica realized she wasn't gagged. She darted a quick look around, ready to start screaming her head off.

"Don't bother," McDermott said, reading her mind. "No one will hear you." He jerked his chin to the concrete wall on her right. "That constant hum you hear from that direction? That's I-395, just a block or two over." He jerked his thumb over his shoulder to another concrete wall. "That's a Metro station over there, with a couple million tons of concrete between us." Then he pointed straight up. "And that way? More concrete. We're about four floors below street level. You could scream until your vocal cords fell out and no one would hear you. Which is good, since that's exactly what I intend for you to do before I kill you. I want to make sure your furry boyfriend knows exactly how bad it was for you—when he finally finds you."

Danica could have lost it then. She certainly would have been well within her rights as a normal human being faced with a psychopathic serial killer. But she bit her tongue. She'd learned something important when she'd joined the DCO—don't ever let a shifter know how scared you are.

So she quelled her fear, squeezed it into a tiny ball, and put it somewhere out of sight. She needed to keep her cool. When she didn't come back, Clayne would call her. And when she didn't answer her phone, he'd come looking for her. If she held on long enough, he would find her. She knew that in her heart. He had found Beth in the middle of a national forest—he'd find her in the middle of a concrete one.

She looked around at the place this crazy killer had

brought her. He'd said they were in between I-395 and a Metro station. That meant they were in DC proper. She'd never been to this place, though.

She turned back to McDermott. "Where am I?"

If the cat shifter was disappointed that she didn't respond to his threats, he didn't let it show. Instead, he grinned. "You'll love the irony here. Someday very soon, this construction site will be the National Law Enforcement Memorial Museum. It will be dedicated to all the heroic men and women who have died in the line of duty, protecting the world from bad guys like me."

She wasn't sure what kind of response McDermott expected from her, but he probably didn't expect her to laugh. In fact, from the way his eyes narrowed, she was sure he didn't.

"I get the symbolism here, I really do," she said. "But the joke would have worked out much better if you hadn't gotten me fired from the FBI."

He stared at her as if trying to figure out if she was lying. "You're shitting me, right?"

She shook her head. "No. I'm officially suspended pending a review board. See, my boss was quite upset that I killed you before he had a chance to play big man in charge."

Danica thought McDermott would bite—okay, bad choice of words—but instead he waggled a finger at her. "Shame on you." He got up from his chair and walked over to circle behind her. "You're thinking that if you keep me talking for a while, your wolf in shining armor will come loping down here to save you."

He gripped her shoulders with both hands and gave them a squeeze, letting his claws dig in. She bit back a cry of pain. She wouldn't give him the satisfaction of a response.

"It's not going to work." He put his mouth next to her ear. "Remember the four floors of concrete? Your furry lover boy could be standing right above us and never get a single whiff of your sexy scent." He put his nose in her neck and inhaled deeply to emphasize his point. "I called him, you know. I didn't give him any clues on how he might find you, though. So trust me, there won't be a happy ending to this story."

Hope kindled in her heart. Clayne didn't need to smell her to find her, but the cat shifter didn't realize that.

"If that's the case, there's no reason you can't satisfy my curiosity about a few things before you kill me."

That came out so calmly, she was almost proud of herself.

McDermott circled around in front of her, then leaned in and inhaled deeply again. "Mmm. I can definitely see why your wolf lover keeps you around. You're ballsy, and you smell like peaches—with a hint of filet mignon." He gave her a chilling grin that made her shiver. "Lucky for you I like to play with my food. So ask your questions. I'll keep answering until I get bored. Then I'll start tearing your skin off in little strips."

Danica didn't even try to control her heart as it started to race out of control. There was no way to handle a threat like that calmly.

McDermott went back to his chair and sat down. "I can hear your heart pounding, little rabbit. Better ask me your questions quick, or I might change my mind and start toying with you right now."

Right then, Danica had a hard time concentrating.

All she could think about were those razor sharp claws ripping into her skin. Even worse, she imagined what it would be like when Clayne found her mutilated body. It would drive him so insane he might never recover.

She was on the verge of hyperventilating when a calming sensation appeared out of nowhere. She knew at once what it was. Clayne was out there, still far away, but closer than he'd been before she became aware of him. He would find her—she just had to keep McDermott talking. She took a breath, then another one. She pushed the fear away until her heart became her own again.

"Why aren't you dead?" she asked.

She expected him to say something about shifter physiology, and that a cat shifter actually did have nine lives. But instead he completely surprised her.

"Because you never shot me. You shot my twin brother."

Clayne had been tempted to run to downtown DC from the Potomac running path where he'd picked up Danica's location. But he got a grip and sprinted back to his apartment to grab his car.

He let his innate sense of direction guide him downtown. Past the White House, he pulled out on K Street and started weaving his way east toward Union Station until he reached 6th. There, the sensation was so strong that he pulled over to the curb in a no-parking zone and started hoofing it. His car was going to get towed with one hundred percent certainty, but he didn't care. He needed to be on foot to truly feel where he needed to go. He got a lot of odd looks from tourists out sightseeing, but he didn't care about that, either. However, he did his best to keep his canines covered and his fists clenched. A big guy running down the sidewalk was one thing, but a big guy with claws and fangs was something completely different.

When he got to the Judiciary Square Metro Station, his inner GPS told him he was close, but no matter which direction he went, he couldn't seem to pinpoint exactly which way to go. He'd take a step one way and his sense of her would strengthen. But three more steps and it'd practically disappear. When he moved the other way, he couldn't even find the place where he'd sensed it so strongly before. Nothing he did seemed to help.

He was so frustrated he felt like howling.

He was thinking he'd made a huge mistake, that he wasn't getting any closer to the woman he loved when his internal compass finally pointed him in the right direction—a construction site under the buildings. He didn't need to go left or right—he needed to go down.

But how?

One quick lap around the block and he found what he was looking for off F Street. He checked to make sure no one was watching—just tourists more interested in their maps than in the people around them—before ducking under the tarp covering the entrance.

Danica's delectable scent hit him the moment he stepped inside. *Just a few more seconds, sweetheart. I'm almost there.*

"This is so fucking perfect. With all your forensics, your FBI profilers, and your pet wolf to hunt for you, you still never for a single second thought there might have been two of us."

Danica shook her head. "That can't be right. Clayne would have smelled the difference if there were two of you."

"You'd think so, wouldn't you?" McDermott slouched back in his chair. "But don't be too hard on your boyfriend. It turns out that shifter twins share everything—looks, fingerprints, scent, even sociopathic tendencies. There's no way to tell us apart." He held up a finger. "That isn't quite true. There was one very distinct difference between me and my brother. Ray was an idiot, whereas I'm not. The ultimate case of environment over heredity."

She'd been trying to think of some way to keep him talking, but it never occurred to her to appeal to his vanity. "You two weren't raised together?"

"No. We were placed into foster care when we were still young. I was adopted shortly after and was raised by a family that had the money to pay for a good education along with everything else they could buy. Poor Ray, on the other hand, bounced from one foster family to the next his entire childhood. He never even graduated from high school. To say that he had a checkered past would be an understatement."

"How did you find each other?"

Clayne was near—she could feel it. She just had to keep this guy talking a little while longer.

"Ray liked to kill people, but he was messy about it," the cat shifter said.

Danica didn't say anything. She had no doubt this guy liked to kill people, too. He was just a lot better at cleaning it up.

"He got his picture in a Denver newspaper by claiming to have witnessed a murder he committed, only he said it was a mountain lion attack," McDermott explained. "I recognized him and tracked him down. I'm guessing that's how you tracked him down as well?"

At Danica's nod, the cat shifter continued. "I helped him find a new home, paid his bills, tried to curb some of his baser instincts. I showed him how to hunt his victims without leaving any clues. It worked for a little while, but environment won out in the end." McDermott sighed. "It turns out that his little brush with the law—the one where he'd pretended to be a witness—had really twisted the sick bastard. He decided he liked watching the cops find his kills. I guess you could say he was a sadistic voyeur."

Danica could think of a lot of things she could say besides that—like how he could have turned Ray into the police—but she didn't think that'd go over very well. "So, when he wanted to kill openly, you decided to help him."

The cat shifter grinned. "Damn, you are a clever little rabbit. It's too bad I can't keep you. Brains like that, with a body to match—a rare combination." He sighed. "But yes, I decided to help him. If we were going to kill people, we should at least make it interesting. I came up with the hunting idea. I picked the targets, the hunting grounds, where to dump the bodies."

"And Ray did the killing?"

"We all do what we're good at I guess." McDermott got up and walked over to stand in front of her. There was a feral glint in his eye that worried her. Like suddenly he'd grown bored with the conversation. "I enjoyed the mental part of the game more, especially once your wolf lover joined the hunt. I didn't expect you to find us when we grabbed that FBI agent's wife, though. I suppose I underestimated you. And poor Ray paid for it with his life. Not that I cared. He was getting to be a pain in the ass anyway. I have to admit, I thought there for a second you were going to catch me, too."

Danica frowned. "That was you I sensed in the woods just before we shot your brother, wasn't it?"

He leaned in close, taking a long, lingering sniff of her neck. Their conversation was coming to an end, she could feel it. She should have been terrified, but for some stupid reason, she wasn't. Maybe because she knew in her heart that Clayne would be there in time—that he was already there.

McDermott pulled back, eyes narrowed. "Are you sure you don't have a little animal in you? That would explain how you figured out I was in the woods the other night, and how you're controlling your fear now when all the men my brother and I hunted were practically pissing their pants at this point."

"No, I'm not a shifter. But there is something that makes me different. Special, even."

For the first time since she'd awakened to find herself tied to a chair hoping to live a little longer, the killer seemed off-balance. If you're not like me, why do you think you're special?"

"I'm special because my mate is a wolf shifter."

The cold swagger returned to his glimmering eyes. "Having sex with a shifter doesn't make you special. If that's the case, there are a lot of prostitutes out there who could consider themselves special."

"I'm not special because I slept with Clayne," she explained. "I'm special because I'm mated to him. There's a difference. I doubt you'd understand, but there's a bond between us, a bond that only exists between a wolf and his mate. And that bond means he always knows where I am, and I always know where he is."

McDermott smirked. "Damn, I know you're desperate, but that's the biggest pile of shit I've ever heard. As you've probably already guessed, I love games, so I'll bite. If you always know where your mate is, then tell me—where is he?"

Danica smiled. "Behind you."

Once underground, Clayne could no longer pick up Danica's scent. Or McDermott's. But he could hear them talking. Then again, if he couldn't smell anything, neither could McDermott, and Clayne had no problem using that to his advantage.

And he'd take any advantage he could get—since he realized about five minutes ago that his Colt was sitting in the nightstand next to his bed. But that's what happens when a serial killer grabs the woman you love. You stop thinking about slowing down to get your man-made weapon and instead bring the ones God and nature had given you.

Clayne forced himself to move slowly as he left the

stairwell and silently made his way through the construction debris, Danica's voice guiding him.

Stay calm and keep the asshole talking and focused on you, babe. I'm right here.

He stopped at the corner of a floor-to-ceiling metal utility panel. It stuck out far enough for most of his six feet six inches, two-hundred-plus pounds to stay hidden behind while he got a good view of the room. To see if McDermott had his back to Clayne. If not...

Clayne was just about to take a peek when Danica's words stopped him. At first, he assumed she was giving the shifter a dose of FBI psychobabble—connect with your kidnapper and all that shit. But she was talking about being his mate and knowing exactly where he was. And him knowing where she was.

Clayne didn't stop to think about how insane that claim made her sound. He simply accepted it and stepped out from his hiding place. If Danica somehow knew he was there, she would have found a way to warn him if the coast wasn't clear.

He bit back a growl. McDermott was standing less than ten feet from him, his back to Clayne. He couldn't see Danica with the cat shifter blocking his view, but he could tell she was tied to a chair, and that there was only a foot of space separating her and the killer. That was too close. If McDermott heard him, he could slash Danica's throat with those wicked claws of his before Clayne closed the distance between them.

Shit. For the first time in his life, he couldn't attack when every fiber of his being was howling at him to do just that. But he couldn't. Not if it would risk Danica's life.

But then Danica gave him that one thing he desperately needed—a distraction.

When McDermott asked where her wolf lover was, she gave that little laugh she did sometimes—sort of a cute snort—and told him that Clayne was right behind him. He rushed McDermott just as the cat shifter's instincts warned him he was screwed.

Clayne swung for the back of McDermott's neck with a deep, rumbling growl. He was going for a killing blow, but he'd settle for anything that got the other shifter away from Danica. Because McDermott twisted at the last second, the blow didn't end him, but it still tossed him halfway across the room and bounced him off a wall.

Clayne risked taking his eyes off McDermott just long enough to check on Danica.

"He has a stun gun," she warned. "Be careful."

Not exactly the romantic line he'd been expecting, but then Danica had never been one for the damsel-in-distress routine.

He turned back to McDermott to see the shifter already on his feet, eyeing both him and the path to the exit. The guy looked different without the beard and the wild hair, but it was him—there was no mistaking the scent.

Clayne closed on him with a growl of pure hatred. He rarely had to find a reason to get violent, but seeing Danica tied to a chair and knowing what this son of bitch had intended to do to her gave him an urge to destroy like he'd never felt before.

That mindless rage almost got him killed.

The cat shifter moved faster than Clayne could follow, dropping into a crouch, then sweeping his leg around and taking Clayne's out from under him. Clayne landed on his back so hard the air burst from his lungs and his head bounced off the floor.

Blackness studded with stars dimmed his vision, but McDermott didn't give Clayne time to recover as he jumped on top of him and started swinging. Clayne barely got his hands up in time to fend off the swinging claws that came at him like a collection of razor blades.

Clayne heard Danica shouting at him to get up as claws ripped into his forearms. If McDermott succeeded in slipping inside his defenses, the fight would be over before it started.

But no matter how much his head hurt, Clayne wasn't going to just lie there and take this ass whooping like a piece of meat.

Lacking any better alternative, he brought both knees up like he was going to do some crunches and slammed them into the cat shifter's back. The force of his knees smashing into McDermott shoved the killer forward a little, just enough to momentarily slow the cat shifter's slashing strikes.

That was the reprieve Clayne needed. He tensed his gut as if he was going to drive his knees into McDermott yet again, and when the shifter moved away from what he thought was an oncoming strike, Clayne instead threw a quick jab at his jaw. The punch didn't have a lot of power behind it—not with him lying on the floor like he was—but he had the advantage of surprise. The punch snapped McDermott's head back, and Clayne quickly followed up with a right-handed swipe at his attacker's face, raking his claws across the shifter's left cheek and eye. He felt them dig in with a satisfying resistance. That earned him a crazed yowl of pain and gave him a chance to finally throw the killer off his chest.

Clayne wanted to immediately leap to the offensive while his attacker was off balance. But his animal instinct wouldn't let him. Above all, he had to protect Danica.

Instead of throwing himself at the cat shifter, Clayne did a backward roll, coming to his feet directly between McDermott and Danica.

The other shifter slowly pushed himself to his feet and wiped away the blood that was running down his face.

Clayne was bleeding, too, but slashed arms weren't enough to hinder him, so he ignored them.

"Can you get free?" he asked Danica without looking back.

"I don't think so," she said. "Don't worry about me. Focus on protecting yourself. You know he's not the guy we shot, right? It's his twin brother."

Um, he actually hadn't realized that—he'd been a little too busy getting his ass kicked. But now that she said it, that explained things. He'd thought shifter twins were a genetic impossibility.

"Be careful," she warned. "He knows how to fight."

Clayne wanted to make a smart-ass comment about that being obvious, but he didn't have time. The cat shifter was already circling around to work his way toward the exit.

Clayne automatically moved to intercept him, but then hesitated. Protecting Danica was his first priority.

McDermott suddenly stopped and reversed course, like he was going to circle back toward Danica. But then, without warning, he leaped at Clayne, lashing out with a kick. Clayne blocked it, but just barely.

They traded punches and kicks, using their claws to rip at each other in between. McDermott was faster than he was, and it was all Clayne could do to protect himself. Worse, the speed disparity was only part of it. Clayne was also at another major disadvantage—he had to focus on protecting Danica. McDermott knew that, too, and used it to his advantage. Every time he feigned a move toward her, Clayne disengaged to get in front of her, which was when the cat shifter would land a blow. It didn't take long before Clayne was bleeding from more places than he could count. Chest, shoulders, back, thighs—nothing major yet, but at this rate, it was just a matter of time.

"That's right, pup. You can't win this," McDermott taunted. "And as soon as I put you down like the mutt you are, I'm going to skin your wolf bitch. Too bad you won't be alive to hear her scream."

Rage exploded in Clayne's head like a supernova, and he let out a deafening roar that echoed off the walls as he launched himself at McDermott. He grabbed the bastard's shirt in both hands, digging his claws deep into the other shifter's chest as he shoved him across the room. McDermott dug his own claws into Clayne's shoulders and pushed back against him, trying to halt his slide across the floor. But Clayne ignored the pain and kept shoving until he got the killer away from Danica.

Barely able to see through the red haze of fury that surrounded him, Clayne allowed instinct to take over and did the first violent thing that came into his head—he stopped pushing and smashed his forehead into the asshole's face. He ignored the extremely pleasant crunching sound and pulled the bastard off his feet, slinging him halfway across the room.

Unfortunately, in his anger, he forgot where Danica was, and ended up slamming her with a couple hundred pounds of cat shifter.

Shit.

Fortunately, the chair took the brunt of the impact, but both the cat shifter and his woman went down in a heap.

He rushed over to check on Danica, but she waved him off. "I'm fine."

Clayne hesitated. She had to be hurting—the blow had crushed the chair she'd been strapped to like it was a kid's toy. A few feet away, McDermott slowly rolled onto his back.

"I'm fine," she repeated. "Go!"

Clayne leaped over her, and the tangle of chair and power cords she was still wrapped up in, and threw himself on McDermott, ready to deliver some of the same punishment the son of a bitch had given him when he'd been in that position. But before he could get in the first blow, the greasy cat shifter somehow twisted around and slipped right out from under him to head for the exit.

Growling in frustration, Clayne scrambled after. There was no way he was going to let this piece of shit get away this time.

He caught up in a few strides. Sinking his claws into McDermott's shoulder, Clayne spun him around and bared his teeth, preparing to go for his throat.

The cat shifter brought up his right hand, the stun gun crackling with sparks.

Shit.

Danica had warned him about the weapon, but McDermott had still suckered him like a chump. Clayne had to jerk his upper body backward like a limbo dancer to avoid taking the tip of the hand-sized cattle prod right in the face. A shifter his size could handle a lot of punishment, but a million volts could incapacitate anyone.

Clayne grabbed McDermott's wrist and twisted it, trying to keep the stun gun away from him at the same time he threw the cat shifter over his hip. They both landed on the floor beside Danica. She was frantically working herself loose of the extension cords binding her.

McDermott immediately jumped Clayne, shoving the stun gun in his face again. Clayne swore, grabbing his wrist just in time. Another few inches and the shifter would have fried him.

The cat shifter hissed and sunk the claws of one hand into the wounds on Clayne's forearm. Clayne grit his teeth against the fire shooting up his arm.

"That's right, mutt," McDermott snarled. "First you, then your bitch. I wonder how long it will take to kill her if I zap her over and over with this thing?"

Clayne opened his mouth to tell him to go fuck himself, but Danica cut him off.

"Guess you'll never know, asshole."

The cat shifter suddenly arched up, yowling in pain.

Clayne didn't have a clue what happened, but he wasn't going to waste the first clear shot he'd gotten to end this fight. The moment McDermott pulled away, he wrenched the stun gun to the side and lunged at the shifter's throat with his free hand. Then he dug in his claws and ripped.

The amount of blood that sprayed out was enough

to tell Clayne he'd done more than enough damage, but that didn't mean he was done. The bastard had just threatened to torture the woman who meant everything to him to death with a stun gun. Just killing McDermott wasn't enough anymore.

Clayne jumped to his feet, pulling the other shifter with him. Then he shoved him across the floor and slammed him against the wall. McDermott thudded into the concrete with a satisfying crunch.

"You can stop now, Clayne," Danica's calm, soothing voice intruded from somewhere nearby. "He's dead."

Clayne let go of the cat shifter and took a step back, watching as the killer fell limply to the floor. Then he looked over to see Danica lying on her side on the floor. Her legs and one arm were still tied to the remnants of the chair, but she'd somehow worked her other arm loose. There were red marks on her skin where the extension cords had been. The sight made him so furious, he almost picked up McDermott and bashed him against the wall again.

Danica must have read his mind because she motioned him toward her. "He's dead, remember? Maybe you could just untie me instead?"

Shit.

He started to hurry over so he could do just that, but stopped when he saw the piece of metal sticking out of the back of McDermott's leg. It was the arm of the chair. That's why McDermott had screamed the way he had. Danica had somehow gotten herself loose, dragged herself and what was left of the chair half a dozen feet, then skewered the bastard through the thick muscles of his hamstrings.

He shook his head. Damn, she was amazing.

Suddenly remembering she was still waiting for him to untie her, Clayne ran to her side and dropped down to start working on the knots. The freaking cords were so tight it was almost impossible to get his claws under them to free her. How the hell had she managed?

He hadn't realized he was growling until she told him to stop. "Clayne, I'm fine. Better than you, in fact. Just get me untied so I can take a look at those wounds."

It took him a couple minutes, but he finally got her loose. Then he pulled her into his arms and squeezed the hell out of her.

"Whoa," she squeaked out. "Trying to breathe here."

Cursing his thoughtlessness, he relaxed his grip. He buried his face in her hair, breathing her in. He wasn't sure he was ever going to be able to let her out of his sight again.

Danica pulled away so she could examine the wounds on his arms, chest, and shoulders. He frowned when she gently touched his neck—he hadn't even noticed those.

But he couldn't care less about himself. He cupped her face. "Never mind that. What about you. Are you okay?"

She covered his hand with her own. "I told you, I'm fine. I can't believe you did that, though."

"Did what?" he asked. "Found you in time? Or killed that sick bastard?"

Her lips curved. "I never doubted you'd find me. I also knew that when you did, that asshole's days were done."

He frowned. "What then?"

"I can't believe you threw that bastard at me."

Oh yeah, that. He gave her a sheepish look. "Sorry. I was sort of in the middle of fighting, remember?"

She ran her fingers over the slashes on his arm, a smile playing at the corners of her mouth again. "Is that what you were doing? I think the chair your mate was tied to gets as much credit as you do."

Clayne stared at her. *Mate.* That wasn't the first time Danica had ever use that word. He'd heard it when she was talking to McDermott—when she said she was special because her mate was a wolf shifter.

"Mate?" He said the word softly, tentatively, afraid if he actually said it out loud, she'd backtrack and change her mind.

She grinned. "Yeah…mate. You don't mind if I use that word, do you?"

"No, I don't mind." He returned her smile. "I like it."

"Good."

Reaching up, she slid her fingers in his hair and pulled him down for a long, lingering kiss that made him wish they weren't in the middle of whatever this underground building was with a dead shifter lying a few feet away.

They were still sitting on the floor like that when a dozen gun-toting DCO agents rushed into the building, Ivy and Landon leading the way.

The DCO medic insisted on checking Danica out even though she'd told the man repeatedly that his time would be better spent looking at Clayne. But her mate was on the other side of the room giving John a situation report. So she bit her tongue and sat there like a good patient while the medic took her vitals.

She glanced at Ivy. The feline shifter had been hovering over Danica with a concerned look on her face ever since she and the other DCO agents had arrived. Though whether she was more worried about Danica's injuries or Dick showing up at the scene, Danica wasn't sure. She wasn't too thrilled to see him there herself.

According to Ivy, Kendra had freaked out when Clayne called, asking to track Danica's cell phone, and had immediately called a code red alert after he'd hung up on her.

Danica saw Ivy throw a quick look at her husband. He was standing with Clayne and John, a frown on his face.

"Ivy, I'm fine," she told the shifter. "Go check on Clayne."

When Ivy made no move to go, Danica sighed. "Ivy, I'm fine. Really." She eyeballed the medic, who obviously wasn't going to leave until he'd examined every single inch of her. "Tell her I'm fine."

"I'm sure you are," Ivy said, not giving the man a chance to answer. "But Clayne is worried about you, so we're checking and double-checking for his sake."

Danica stifled a groan. She supposed she couldn't fault them for caring. The medic left to check on Clayne's injuries just as Dick came over.

"I'd like to talk with Agent Beckett," he said to Ivy, then added, "alone."

Ivy gave Danica a questioning look. Danica nodded. She was going to have to deal with Dick sooner or later. After Ivy left, she turned to Dick.

"What do you want?"

Just because she'd known that this head-butting contest was bound to happen at some point didn't mean she had to be polite about it.

Dick didn't bat an eye. His voice low and threatening, he practically sneered. "I knew you didn't have it in you to stay away, even when it was for your own good—or your boyfriend's, at least."

She gave him a frosty smile. "Maybe I'm just in town on vacation."

He shook his head. "How stupid do you think I am? I told you to leave DC and never come back or contact Buchanan. But you just had to do it, didn't you? Well, I hope you enjoyed your time together, because you've just sent your boyfriend to prison."

The man was so smug it was sickening. Time to use their trump card and find out if Dick had backup copies of the evidence. She hadn't been this terrified of McDermott—or whatever his name had been.

"I don't know what you're talking about," she said.

Dick's eyes narrowed. "Don't try and play games with me. You're not very good at it. You know full well what I'm talking about. As soon as I leave here, I'm going to go get that evidence and give it to the Eerie County Attorney. He'll have Clayne in lockup by tonight."

That evidence. Like it was a singular stash of stuff.

"I don't know what evidence you're referring to." She folded her arms and put on her best FBI face. "You should be careful threatening people when you don't have anything to back it up. Some people might take it the wrong way," she looked pointedly at Clayne, "and rip your face off."

Dick stared at her dumbfoundingly for a moment before it dawned on him. Rage twisted his features. "You bitch. You broke into the DCO repository, didn't you?"

"I don't know what you're talking about," she said.

"Bullshit," he ground out as he pulled out his phone. "I'm going to have both of you arrested."

Danica took a step a closer. "Go ahead. Try it. You won't find a single piece of evidence tying us to this repository of yours."

Dick glared at her, speechless. Then his gaze swung to Ivy and Landon. When he turned back to Danica, his eyes were cold. "You got them to do it for you, didn't you?"

Fear shot through Danica, but she quickly covered it up. "I have no idea what you're talking about. But supposing there was a repository, and someone like Ivy and Landon had broken into it, they wouldn't leave any evidence behind to put them there, and you know it."

The vein in his temple pulsed so hard she thought his head might explode. But then he smirked.

"You might have won this round, but you haven't won the war. The shifter program is headed for serious changes. It's just a matter of time before the DCO won't need psychos like Buchanan anymore. Sooner or later, he's going to end up in jail where he belongs—or put down."

What the hell did he mean by the shifter program changing? Danica wanted to ask but wouldn't give him the satisfaction. Besides, he wouldn't tell her anyway.

Danica lifted her chin. "Or maybe the DCO will finally realize they don't need a back-stabbing little prick like you. And you'll be the one who ends up in jail where you belong."

Dick's face turned an unhealthy shade of red, and for a moment Danica thought he was going to lose it right there in front of everyone. But instead, he turned and stormed off without another word. It was almost anticlimactic. She'd been waiting for him to say something like *I'll get you my pretty, and your pesky wolf, too.* She had to fight the urge to cheer and shout, *Take that, you dickweed.*

A strong arm encircled her waist, turning her around. "I wanted to come over the minute I saw you with Dick, but Ivy and Landon told me you had this," Clayne said. "Everything okay?"

She nodded. "Yeah. Dick just about had a cow when he realized we stole the evidence he had against you. Based on his reaction, I'm pretty sure he doesn't have backup copies, so I think we're good."

Clayne sighed and closed his eyes for a moment. When he opened them again, he surprised her by kissing her. Danica quickly looked around, wondering just how many people had seen their little PDA. But everyone was busy doing something else. Even John was politely looking the other way. It wasn't as if they had to keep their relationship secret—as if they could—since she wasn't working for the DCO now, but Clayne didn't normally like an audience for this kind of stuff.

He brushed back some stray hair that had escaped from her ponytail just as John came over. Her old boss gave her a smile.

"Sorry to interrupt," he said.

Danica returned his grin. "You're not. I was just about to talk Clayne into letting the medic take a look at him."

"Ah. Well, good luck with that," he said. "Clayne told me about the review board. I'll take care of it."

She shook her head. "I appreciate the offer, but I can't let you do that."

He waved his hand. "It's the least I can do after what you did to help Clayne catch a pair of serial killers. And for finding your way back into his life. I only wish I could have figured out a way to make it happen sooner."

She shot Clayne a look. He seemed just as surprised as she was. "You knew," she said to John. "About us, I mean?"

His mouth curved. "I had my suspicions."

"You never said anything."

"Because I think the policy is ridiculous. If a team gets the job done, I don't care what their relationship is outside of work." He glanced at Ivy and Landon, and Danica wondered if he knew about them, too. Or just had his suspicions. But he turned back to her and Clayne before she could decide. "You know, I heard there's an opening in the Bureau's DC office, if you're interested. Though I'd like to borrow you every now and then for an odd job, if you don't mind working with Clayne again?"

She laughed. "I'd love to." And Clayne looked thrilled. "Dick might have an issue with it, though. It'll be hard to look the other way now that Clayne and I are living together."

John's mouth tightened. "Like I said, you'll be working for the FBI. It's none of Dick's business."

"Deal," she said. "Thank you, John. For everything."

John nodded and told them to take some time off, then gave Ivy and Landon a wave and left.

"I guess that's John's way of saying we have some vacation time coming." Clayne flashed her a grin.

"So, what do you think we should do with all that time off, partner?"

Danica liked the word *partner* almost as much as she liked the word *mate*. She gestured to his arms. "First, we're going to the training complex to get those looked at since you refused to let the medic look at them."

The medic looked like he'd tried to bandage the worst of them, but no doubt Clayne had been his normal fussy self and scared the poor man off. The wounds on his arms had stopped bleeding, but they still looked horrible to her. The DCO had a medical facility out at the training complex—people were always getting themselves hurt out there. Maybe Clayne would accept medical attention if she were there.

She braced herself for resistance—this was Clayne they were talking about. But he surprised her by nodding. "Okay, whatever you say."

He took her hand and started toward the exit, but she hung back. "Are you okay?"

She wasn't kidding. This wasn't like him. And he had hit his head really hard during the fight with the other shifter.

"Yeah, I'm okay. I was just agreeing with you— about getting looked at."

"But you never listen to me about stuff like that."

"That was before." He took her hands in his. "Things are different now."

She thought she understood, with this whole *mate* thing and all, but she still had to ask, just to make sure he wasn't loopy from a concussion.

"Different how?"

"Well, when you're in love with someone, you have

to do things they want you to do, to make them happy—
even if you don't think it's necessary."

Now it was her turn to be surprised. "Love?"

His very sexy lips curved into a smile—a casual,
confident smile. "Yeah…love. You don't mind if I use
that word, do you?"

She laughed and shook her head. "No, I don't mind
at all. I like it."

"Good." He pulled her close, sealing the word with a
kiss. "Because I love you like crazy. It might have taken
a while for us to get it right, but now that we have, I plan
to tell you frequently how much I love you."

Danica told herself she wouldn't cry. It just didn't
seem right to cry over something so mushy, considering
that she was this tough FBI agent who'd survived being
kidnapped by a psychotic werecat serial killer.

But she failed miserably as tears started trickling
down her cheeks.

Clayne reached up to gently wipe them away.
Considering that his were the hands of a man who could
do such an extraordinary amount of violence and harm
when he wanted, his touch was incredibly tender.

"Come on. Let's get me fixed up so I can take you
home and show you exactly how much I love you,"
he said.

Danica let him lead her toward the stairs, but after a
few steps, she tugged him to a stop. "I almost forgot. I
love you, too."

Chapter 14

"DO YOU HAVE ANY MORE ICE?" KENDRA ASKED, sticking her head around the corner into the kitchen. "The guys dumped the last of the stuff from the ice bucket into their beer cooler."

Danica shook her head. She had the feeling that was going to happen. Considering that beer didn't taste any better cold than it did warm, she didn't know why they bothered.

"There's a cooler of fresh ice hidden behind the shower curtain in the guest bathroom. I put it there when Clayne wasn't looking. There're more wine coolers in there, too."

Kendra grinned. "Thanks, Danica. You're brilliant."

Danica laughed and checked on the chicken wings in the oven. They had another few minutes, so she leaned back against the counter and caught her breath.

Things had been crazy since she had moved back, and this thank-you party she and Clayne had ended up hosting was just the start. Their lives were probably a little too busy to be trying to pull this kind of party off, but they owed Kendra, Ivy, and Landon big time for getting that evidence Dick had on Clayne. If they hadn't, she and Clayne might be living in Bora Bora right now under assumed names.

Danica would have invited John if she thought he would have accepted the invitation. She and Clayne owed him just as much for their newfound happiness, not to mention getting her a job at the FBI's DC office. Tony had told her Carhart just about popped a blood vessel when he'd found out she'd been transferred. She would love to have seen the look on his face. Then again, she'd rather not deal with that idiot.

"Too bad you couldn't tell him you killed the Hunter twice," Kendra said when the subject came up after Danica joined the rest of the party out on the deck.

"No, thanks," Clayne said, answering for her as he reached for another chicken wing. "Let's just keep that hidden in the DCO files forever."

Danica nibbled on a chicken wing as she listened to Clayne tell their guests how hard it had been to take down the shifter who'd kidnapped her. He'd told them the story before, but they listened anyway. Well, Ivy and Kendra were listening—Landon was staring off into space.

"Everything okay, Landon?" she asked when Clayne paused to take a breath.

It took a second for her question to get through to the soldier-turned-covert agent. He gave himself a shake. "What?"

Ivy whacked him on the shoulder. "You zoned out."

He gave them a sheepish look and swigged his beer. "Sorry. Clayne was putting me to sleep. I've only heard the story about five times now."

His wife frowned. "Nice try. You were thinking about that stuff you found in the repository again, weren't you?"

Clayne reached for his beer. "What stuff?"

"Nothing." Landon sat back and put his arm around his wife's shoulders. "Just some old records."

"Bullshit," Clayne said. "If you're still thinking about it, it's more than just some old records. Spill it—what'd you see?"

Landon exchanged looks with Ivy. "Tell them," she urged. "If you're right about this, they should know."

He took another swallow of beer while he thought about it. "I found a bunch of files on Stutmeir."

Danica vaguely remembered Clayne mentioning the name when he'd told her about Ivy's capture and the off-the-books-rescue effort he, Landon, and Kendra—along with Landon's Special Forces buddies—had mounted to get her back.

"So?" Clayne said. "The DCO probably has a whole wing of the repository set aside for the guy and his damn hybrids."

Landon shook his head. "That's the problem. The files I read weren't new. They were at least two years old."

Kendra's eyes went wide. "What?"

"Wait a minute." Clayne frowned. "You're saying the DCO was previously involved with that psycho and forgot to mention it?"

Ivy nodded. "There's more."

"I didn't have a chance to read it while I was there, so I stole the file. Since then, Ivy and I have been poring over every word," Landon explained. "The scariest part is a funds transfer document that makes it look like the DCO gave Stutmeir an assload of money. Maybe enough to fund his hybrid research."

Danica was speechless.

"Well, crap," Kendra said.

"No kidding," Clayne agreed. "I know I don't trust most of the people in charge at the DCO, but I have a hard time believing they'd do something like this. Not even Dick is that screwed up."

"We don't know that they did," Landon said. "All I can say for sure is that we have a document showing the DCO transferred a large sum of money to Stutmeir, but it didn't say what it was for. We're guessing on a lot of this."

"But you have to admit, the timing is damn coincidental," Danica pointed out. "Clayne told me about the hybrids. It would have taken a lot of cash to get a program like that up and running."

Landon didn't say anything.

Ivy tilted her head to look at him. "Tell them the rest."

The muscle in his jaw ticked.

Okay, that had Danica even more worried.

"The funds transfer document had three approval signatures on it. Dick's, some member of the Committee we didn't recognize, and…John's."

Danica almost choked on her wine cooler. "John?"

"I can't believe that," Kendra said. "John would never be involved in something like that."

"I don't like to think so, either," Landon said. "Look. I'm not saying I know what it means. All I'm saying is that his name and what looks like his signature are on a document giving money to someone named Stutmeir."

Clayne shook his head. "Damn, Landon. You really know how to throw a wet blanket on a party."

"Maybe the money was for something else," Danica suggested.

John had done so much for her and Clayne. She couldn't believe he was involved in something so underhanded.

"Maybe," Landon agreed, but he didn't sound convinced.

Or maybe not. "The other day Dick said something odd to me when he found out he wasn't going to be able to put Clayne in prison. He said the shifter program is going to change and that the DCO wouldn't need shifters like Clayne anymore. If the DCO did fund the hybrid research, maybe that's what he meant."

Ivy grimaced. "I guess the real question is, what do we do about all this stuff we think we know?"

"There isn't anything we can do," Landon said. "We don't know enough right now. We could break into the repository again and look for more information, but now that Dick knows we broke in, they're going to put in a whole new security system that we don't know anything about. Hell, I wouldn't be surprised if Dick goes in and gets rid of anything he thinks might be incriminating. I think we're just going to have to watch our backs and make sure we know who we can trust."

"I know who I trust." Clayne laced his fingers with Danica's, his thumb brushing the diamond engagement ring he'd given her the same day he rescued her from a demented serial killer. "Danica and the three of you."

Danica sighed. Five people in an organization as big as the DCO wasn't much, but for now, it would have to be enough.

Ivy, Landon, and Kendra stayed a little while longer, but after that bombshell, no one seemed to be in the mood to hang around and party. Clayne had a pensive look on his face as they cleaned up.

Danica set the chip and dip bowl on the counter and took his hands in hers. "Hey. I know you're worried about that stuff Landon told us, but we're finally back together, and that's the important thing. If the DCO is making hybrids, we'll deal with it. Right now, we have more important stuff to focus on—like planning our wedding."

Clayne grinned. "I was thinking about that. If we leave now, we could be in Vegas by morning. We could get married in the Elvis chapel as the sun comes up."

She laughed and went up on tiptoe to kiss him. "That's not bad as a backup plan, but I have something else in mind."

"Like what?"

"Like a big church wedding."

He made a face. Danica laughed. She might have to talk him into it, but he was going to look so damn sexy in a tux. Just like he had on that mission in Mexico all those years ago when she'd first realized she was falling in love with him.

Epilogue

Somewhere South of Khorugh, Tajikistan

MINKA REFUSED TO SCREAM ANYMORE.

She sat on the floor with her back against the wall of a small, cold, concrete room while three men threw sharp stones at her. The doctors who had made her into the animal she was stood behind them, writing down their observations in little notebooks and recording her reactions with their cameras.

"Hit her harder," one of the doctors said in his strange accent. "We need to see her instinctive reactions. Force her to respond."

She covered her face and head with her arms, turning into the wall to protect herself. But the stones found vulnerable spots anyway, drawing blood, causing pain. She bit her lip and tried to make herself a smaller target. She would not scream anymore, no matter how hard they hit her. Because when she did, the men would laugh. And when they did that, something in her would snap and she wouldn't be able to stop the thing inside her from coming out.

Minka knew because she had tried with all her heart and soul to keep the beast contained. But it was hard. Most of time, it was impossible. When she was scared, in pain or angry, it simply came out.

The doctors knew this and used it against her. To test her, they said.

So, as hard as she tried, this time proved to be no different.

A large stone clipped the back of her head, smashing a finger at the same time. The pain was so intense she screamed. As it morphed into a hissing snarl, she whipped around, catching the next incoming rock in mid-flight and flinging it back at the man who had thrown it.

The stone struck him between the eyes, knocking him to the floor. She leaped across the room before he'd even hit the floor, intending to slash and tear with her long, sharp claws, but the chain around her ankle snapped taut and she crashed to the floor like she had every other time before.

The pain in her leg paled in comparison to the pain of failure.

She looked up and growled her hatred at the four remaining men. The man she had struck with the stone would not be getting up—ever. His two friends looked at her with undisguised hatred on their faces, but the doctors were smiling and praising her instincts, her reaction time, and her aggression.

Minka lowered her gaze to the dead man on the floor and wished it was her lying there instead. She didn't want to kill anyone, not even these men who hurt her. But she had no choice. The animal inside her wanted to kill all the time.

"Why did you do this to me?" she demanded, the sound of her own voice still strange to her when she was like this.

One of the doctors—the older one who seemed to be in charge—stepped closer. He stayed behind the two men who had been throwing stones, careful to stay well out of her reach.

"We told you before," he said. "We did this to make you better."

Better? How was this better? "But I did not want to be like this!"

The other doctor came closer. He was younger, braver, and more foolhardy. Minka did not like the way he looked at her.

"You should be happy," he told her. "You are our greatest success to date. Many men and women before you died in horrible pain so that we could create you." He turned to the other doctor. "You'd think she would show some gratitude after all we've done for her."

The older doctor regarded her thoughtfully. "Perhaps we should show her the videos of our previous attempts so she can see how lucky she is."

"That might work," his partner agreed. "Perhaps the video of that little girl in Canada."

Minka's eyes widened. "You did this to a little girl?" She hissed, jerking against the chain anchored to the wall.

"We thought that administering the DNA infusion just prior to puberty would improve our chances of success," the older doctor explained. "That hypothesis proved dramatically incorrect. The poor girl died in tremendous pain. Or at least she appeared to be in tremendous pain. She died before we could learn exactly what happened to her body."

Minka leaped again. She was all too willing to maim herself to get her claws into these men. For the first time, she actually wished her claws were longer and less curved. Then she might have been able to at least scratch him.

"You're monsters," she growled.

But the men only laughed and walked out, leaving her alone with her thoughts and her cursed body. They had wanted to see her perform, and she had.

Her hair fell over her shoulder as she lowered her head. She watched through tears as her wicked, curved claws retracted. She wondered where they went and how it was possible for claws that long to disappear inside her small fingers.

But she knew the answer to that question. She had said it herself when she had called the two doctors monsters.

She was a monster now, too.

Here's a sneak peek at book 3 in Paige Tyler's hot X-Ops series:

Her Wild Hero

THE FLIGHT DOWN TO COSTA RICA WAS PURE HELL. Instead of the roomy C-17 or C-5 Declan MacBride had expected, they'd been stuck in the cargo area of a smaller C-130 plane that was mostly filled with pallets of equipment and supplies. He and the rest of the team had been relegated to two sets of drop-down benches wedged between pallets of bottled water. Worse, the two rows of uncomfortable seats were facing each other. Brent, Gavin, and Kendra were on one side, while he and Tate were on the other. Which meant he had to look at her the whole way. There was a time when he would have thought spending an entire day gazing at Kendra was time well spent, but being forced into close proximity with her now made him mad as hell.

Or maybe he was still just pissed off at Tate. He and the former U.S. Marshal had gotten into it pretty good before leaving the tarmac at Anacostia-Bolling.

"Why the hell is Kendra coming with us?" Declan had demanded when he finally got Tate alone. "There's no reason for us to be going down there, but there's even less for her. She doesn't even add anything to the team."

Unless you counted long blond hair, big blue eyes, and the sexiest butt he'd ever seen.

"Look, I know you don't want to be around Kendra," Tate said. "I'm not thrilled at the idea of her tagging along with us either, but John wants her to get some field time on a low-risk mission—sort of a reward for all the hard work she's been doing."

Declan swore. "You know that's crazy, right? There's no such thing as a low-risk mission, not when every third person in the place we're going carries a weapon. Is John willing to let her—or one of us—get killed just so he can give her a freaking *reward*?"

"No one's going to get killed," Tate shot back. "And unless you want to quit the DCO in protest, there's only one option—shut up and soldier on."

"I'm a forest ranger, not a soldier."

"Yeah? Well, go over there and take a look in your rucksack. I'm pretty sure forest rangers don't carry the amount of weaponry you have shoved in that bag."

Tate was right, dammit, but Declan still growled in frustration.

His friend sighed. "I know the situation sucks, but it is what it is. You have to get your head right or somebody is going to get hurt. But it won't be because of Kendra, it'll be because of you."

That had pretty much been the end of the conversation. Tate had left Declan there staring at the cracked asphalt of the runway, wondering how he was going to handle two weeks in the same jungle as Kendra.

But no answer had been forthcoming then, and twenty hours later as he sat wedged into the too-small strap seat, he still didn't have one.

Being so close to her shouldn't bother him. He'd
gotten over his crush on her and moved on. As he stole
occasional glances at her, he knew that was a crock of
shit. He'd tried, he really had. But since deciding four
months ago that enough was enough and it was past
time he stop pining for a woman who refused to even
acknowledge his existence, he'd been miserable as hell.

He bit back a growl. Damn, he was pathetic. But there
was something about Kendra that attracted him like a
bear to honey. He might have chuckled at the analogy if
it wasn't so damn fitting.

Kendra had already been firmly established with the
Department of Covert Operations when he'd shown up
seven years ago. Back then, she'd mostly shadowed the
training officers and watched—taking notes, making
her quiet observations and recommendations directly
to the trainers. At the time, Declan had been coming
off the disaster that was his relationship with Karen,
so he hadn't been interested in getting involved with
any woman. Plus, he'd been consumed with trying to
fit in with his team and learn everything they had to
teach him. He had no military training to fall back on,
so there'd been a lot to learn. By the time he'd gotten
his head above water, he already had it bad for the be-
havioral scientist.

Unfortunately, he couldn't string together two sen-
tences whenever he was around her. He wasn't a Romeo
with the ladies by any stretch of the imagination, but
he'd never gotten tongue-tied around women—not even
his former fiancée. But it wasn't hard to see why Kendra
had that effect on him. She was beautiful and smart,
made him smile like no other woman ever had, made the

camouflage uniform she was wearing look way sexier than it should, and she smelled delicious as hell.

His nose usually wasn't that good—mostly because he never used it—except when it came to Kendra. Then it worked just fine. Sometimes he could pick up her scent from the far side of the DCO training complex. Sitting this close to her now, it was the only thing he could smell, and it was overwhelming. He closed his eyes, hoping to block out her scent, but it was useless. Her pheromones surrounded him, holding him prisoner and refusing to let go.

He'd tried to catch Kendra's eye for years and fallen flat on his face every time. Because she was too busy obsessing over that jerk, Clayne Buchanan. It had taken Declan a while, but he finally realized he was wasting his time—and his life—waiting for her and had decided to move on.

And it had been working. He'd gotten to the point where he didn't think about her 24/7, didn't subconsciously sniff the air to catch her scent the minute he drove onto the DCO complex. He'd even dated a few women he thought might have long-term potential. There might not be that same animal attraction he felt with Kendra, and he'd have to hide his shifter side, but that wasn't too high a price to pay to be normal, right?

Before today he thought he'd been well on his way to forgetting about Kendra and getting on with his so-called life. Then John had decided to send her on this mission and everything Declan thought was in the past came right back and smacked him in the face.

For the first time in forever, he felt like putting his fist through a wall. But as he felt his anger rise again, he realized he wasn't angry at John, or Tate, or even Kendra. He was mad at himself for being so screwed up that the mere thought of being in the same jungle as the blond-haired, blue-eyed beauty could get him so twisted up in knots.

Damn, he really was pathetic.

HER WILD HERO
COMING MAY 2015

Enjoy a sneak peek at
Paige Tyler's brand-new series:

Hungry Like the Wolf

GAGE DIXON STRAINED AGAINST THE HEAVY BARBELL, relishing the resistance as the stacked metal plates on either end of the solid steel bar made the whole thing flex. The bar quivered slightly as it reached that sweet spot of the lift where his pecs stopped doing all the work and his triceps and shoulders kicked in. But he'd already been punishing his body for over an hour, and this time the bar momentarily stopped moving upward, gravity insisting that down would be a much better—and easier—direction to go.

He grit his teeth, let out a growl, and forced his muscles to keep pushing until his arms locked out straight. He racked the load with a clatter of metal on metal. Even then, the bar still bowed and flexed—loading 525 pounds on a barbell would do that.

Gage sat up and looked around the small weight room he and the other members of the Dallas Police SWAT team had set up. It wouldn't measure up to any of the fancy gyms in the area, but considering they'd paid out of their own pockets for the mirrors, heavy-duty lifting equipment, and free weights, it wasn't too shabby. It would have been nice if it were bigger, though. The presence of the four other men reminded him just how small the room was.

Then again, his men made most rooms seem small—special weapons and tactics (SWAT) teams tended to attract big, muscular men, and his particular team happened to be bigger than most. No surprise there either—alpha werewolves were always big as hell.

Gage wiped the sweat off his face with the back of his arm and took a moment to appreciate the relative peace and quiet. Regardless of the room's size, it was rare for there to be only a handful of men in it. But with half the team out helping run weapon qualifications at the police academy and most of the others out conducting joint training with the ATF, the compound was practically empty.

Across the room, Diego Martinez spotted for his best friend and teammate, Hale Delaney, as the man tried to go for a personal record on the other bench press. At the same time, Gage's two assistant squad leaders, Mike Taylor and Xander Riggs, were hanging upside down from the ceiling-mounted chin-up bars, seeing who could do the most crunches. Alphas didn't need much of an excuse to turn everything they did into a competition.

They hadn't gotten around to cutting an opening for the air-conditioning units they'd bought for the room yet, so it was pretty warm. Which meant that all of them were sweating like crazy even though they weren't wearing shirts.

Gage was wondering if he should spring for some gym towels when he heard the sound of fast-moving boots coming down the hallway.

The other werewolves' keen hearing had also picked up the sound, and everyone was looking toward the doorway expectantly by the time McCall poked his head around the corner.

"Got a bad one, Sergeant," he said to Gage. "Hostage situation over on Belmont. Multiple injuries, at least two dozen hostages. Five shooters being reported."

"Well, there goes the workout," Delaney muttered, getting up from the bench.

"Gear up," Gage ordered. "I want us out of here in less than five minutes."

Gage was only thirty seconds behind the rest of the team, but by the time he got to the second floor of the admin building, the other four men were already gearing up. He joined them as they yanked on navy blue T-shirts, matching military-style uniforms, and black boots. Then came the heavy black Kevlar vests, with tactical web pouches attached. The sounds of Velcro being yanked open filled the room as they adjusted their vests, ammo pouches, and holsters to a snug fit. The gear wasn't the most comfortable stuff to wear, especially during the hot Texas summers, but it came with being in SWAT.

McCall met them heading down the stairs, tossing Martinez and Delaney their military grade M4 carbines, while giving Gage more details on the situation. The kidnappers were serious—there were cops and civilians already on the way to the hospital.

As they moved outside, Gage's men carefully checked their weapons, yanking slides and bolts back to inspect chambers, then dropping magazines and clips to check their loads before slamming them in with a firm click.

While they'd been working out in the weight room, there had been a lighthearted sense of competition about them. They'd even joked and laughed while they'd gotten dressed. But as they moved toward the operations vehicle and the white SUV that McCall had ready and running for them, the tone had changed. A charged intensity filled the air, the kind you sometimes feel right before lightning strikes.

They were heading out to face a group of men who'd already shown a willingness to shoot cops and innocents. They likely wouldn't hesitate to shoot a SWAT officer, given the chance.

Everyone turned to look at Gage just before climbing into the vehicles. He glanced at his watch—barely over three minutes since the call had come in. Good.

"We're going in a little undermanned on this one," he announced, though it wasn't something that needed to be said. "There's a department negotiator heading for the scene, and we'll give him every chance to get control of this situation. You heard what McCall said, so you know as well as I do how this one is likely going to turn out. These men are killers, so if we have to go in, don't take any chances. Hit them hard and fast, and let's get everyone out of there alive and in one piece—us included."

With that, Gage climbed into the passenger seat of the white SUV, and Martinez had it moving for the gates before he even got his seat belt on.

"Hey, Mac. We got something."

Mackenzie Stone jerked her gaze away from the

fenced-in compound and its collection of mismatched concrete buildings. In the driver's seat of the *Dallas Daily Star*
undercover van, her photographer, tech guy, assistant, and
all-around best friend Zak Gibson yanked the buds from
his ears and switched the police scanner on the dash to the
external speakers. The blare of a fast-talking dispatcher
spouting code numbers and addresses filled the van.

He glanced over his shoulder at her. "There's a hostage situation over on Belmont Street and the on-scene
commander has requested SWAT to respond."

About damn time. "Excellent. Let's go." She climbed
around the console and into the passenger seat as he
cranked the engine. "It'll take a while for them to gear
up. If we hurry, we can get there before they do."

She and Zak had been slowly roasting in this dang
surveillance van for two days in a row trying to figure
out how to get inside the SWAT team's inner sanctum.
She'd been so close to walking up to the gate and ringing the freaking bell. It probably wouldn't have gotten
her anywhere, but right about now she was willing to
try anything.

Mac clicked her seat belt into place just as Zak
slammed on the brakes. She was thrown against the
restraint, then flung back. "What the hell?"

Zak pointed at the monstrous vehicle barreling
through the gate, cutting them off. A white SUV bearing
a matching SWAT insignia followed, lights flashing as
it raced down the road.

"How is that even possible? They just got the call,"
she said to Zak.

"Fast response time?"

She snorted. Just one more thing that didn't add up

about the Dallas Police Department's SWAT team. She considered scrapping the idea of following them in favor of sneaking into the compound and snooping around, but the gate had already closed. Inside, a cop the size of a linebacker scanned the fence line, then headed back into the building. Just her luck, one of them had stayed behind.

Damn.

She tucked her long, dark hair behind her ear and sank back in the seat. She wouldn't have to be so underhanded about this whole thing if the police department had agreed to a ride-along with SWAT. Or at the very least, an interview with their commander. Why wouldn't they want her to do a story about the team unless they were hiding something?

Investigating cops who might be corrupt was never a good idea. But she'd earned her reputation by sticking her nose in places other investigative journalists were too afraid to go. She went wherever the story took her and never flinched when things got rough. She'd helped to make the *Dallas Daily Star* synonymous with fearless, Pulitzer-worthy journalism. So when she'd told her editor she wanted to go after SWAT, he gave the okay. Even if he did think she was wasting her time. There wasn't a division in the Dallas Police Department that had a better—or cleaner—reputation than SWAT.

It didn't help her cause any that everyone except the criminals SWAT put in prison thought the tactical team was damn near perfect. They'd taken on some of the toughest and most ruthless crooks, gangbangers, and cartel goons in the city. You name the bad guys, Dallas SWAT had taken them on and taken them down. Considering the load of major shit storms the group had been involved in, they had a ridiculously low number of complaints filed against them. There'd been allegations, but nothing had ever come of them—not since the new team leader, Sergeant Gage Dixon, had taken over eight years ago. Since then, the SWAT team had been beyond perfect.

By itself, that was enough to make her suspicious. All organizations tended to screw up occasionally, no matter how dedicated and capable they were. But that rule didn't seem to apply to the Dallas PD SWAT.

The police chief held them up as an example for the rest of the department to emulate, and for reasons she couldn't figure out, the other divisions seemed eager to try. The mayor even used their exploits to roast other civic leaders across Texas and the southwest. Hell, even the Girl Scouts wanted to be associated with them, and SWAT was happy to oblige by lending their muscle-bound presence to the annual cookie sale kickoff every winter. As far as everyone in Dallas was concerned, the SWAT team was better than sliced bread, PB&J with the crusts cut off, and sex in an air-conditioned room—combined.

"Just what do you expect to find, Mac? That they don't floss after eating popcorn?" her editor had asked in his deep Texas drawl. "Maybe the Dallas PD finally got something right for once. Maybe this city just has the best damn SWAT team in the country."

Mac had good reason to believe the SWAT team was crooked and a danger to everyone around them. But she had to be damn careful how she sold it to her editor. She had a hard time believing the story, and she'd heard it firsthand from an eyewitness named Marvin Cole.

Marvin was a two-time loser currently out on bail awaiting trial, this time for kidnapping, assault, and resisting arrest. Normally, Mac wouldn't have given the guy the time it took to call security to escort him out of the building. But then he had something on the one group of people in Dallas who were damn near untouchable—SWAT.

She was intrigued, so she'd bought him a cup of coffee. She figured it was sour grapes—they had busted his ass, after all—but she pretended to pay attention as Marvin described how two big SWAT guys had smashed in the reinforced door of his secret hideout, tossed him around like a rag doll, and took the kid he'd been holding for ransom.

She didn't exactly swoon from excitement, but then Marvin described how one of the SWAT officers had growled like an animal, then grabbed him and shoved him up against the wall, holding him there with one hand as his feet dangled above the floor. The only reason that got her attention was because Marvin weighed about 350 pounds—and most of it was muscle. Still, SWAT guys were big and tough—everyone knew that. Marvin must have seen how skeptical she was because he opened his shirt and showed her the two sets of four parallel scratches gouged in the muscles of his enormous chest. He looked as if he'd been clawed by a big animal.

"Son of a bitch did that with his bare hands. I lived on the streets my whole life so I know when someone's messed up," he said as he slowly buttoned his shirt and sat down. "Those SWAT dudes that everyone's so freaking impressed with? They're on something."

She lifted a brow. "You mean like steroids?"

Marvin shook his head. "Hell no, lady. Shit, I take steroids and I ain't never acted like that. No, those cats are on something really serious. Something that makes them crazy strong."

The idea that SWAT members were on some kind of designer drug was insane, but Marvin wasn't making up the ragged marks on his chest.

Well, today she was going to talk to the elusive SWAT commander even if she had to take the man hostage.

Okay, maybe not. But she *was* going to talk to him, damn it.

HUNGRY LIKE THE WOLF
COMING JANUARY 2015

Acknowledgments

I hope you enjoyed *Her Lone Wolf* as much as you enjoyed *Her Perfect Mate*, the first book in the X-Ops series. After reading the first book, everyone wanted to know who the hunky wolf shifter Clayne Buchanan was going to end up with. I hope his story met your expectations!

This whole series would not be possible without some very incredible people: my hubby of course; my agent, Bob Mecoy; my editor and go-to person at Sourcebooks, Cat Clyne (who loves this series as much as I do and is always a phone call or email away whenever I need something); and all the other amazing people at Sourcebooks, including Todd, Amelia, Rachel, and their crazy-talented art department. The covers they make for me are seriously droolworthy!

Because I could never leave out my readers, a huge thank you to everyone who has read my books and Snoopy Danced right along with me with every new release. That includes the fantastic girls on my Street Team. You rock!

And a very special shout-out to our favorite restaurant, P.F. Chang's, where hubby and I bat ideas back and forth about story lines and come up with all of our best ideas!

Hope you enjoy the third X-Ops book, *Her Wild Hero,* coming spring 2015, and look forward to reading the rest of the series as much as I look forward to sharing it with you.

And if you love a man in uniform as much as I do, make sure you look for *Hungry Like the Wolf,* the first book in my new series coming from Sourcebooks, SWAT (Special Wolf Alpha Team), available in digital and paperback online and in bookstores everywhere January 2015!

Happy Reading!

About the Author

Paige Tyler is the *USA Today* bestselling author of sexy romantic fiction. She and her very own military hero (also known as her husband) live on the beautiful Florida coast with their adorable fur baby (also known as their dog). Paige graduated with a degree in education but decided to pursue her passion and write books about hunky alpha males and the kick-butt heroines who fall in love with them. Visit www.paigetylertheauthor.com.

She's also on Facebook, Twitter, Instagram, Tumblr, and Pinterest.

Her Perfect Mate

X-Ops

by Paige Tyler

USA Today bestselling author

—∿∿—

He's a high-octane Special Ops pro

When Special Forces Captain Landon Donovan is pulled from an op in Afghanistan, he is surprised to discover he's been hand-picked for a special assignment with the Department of Covert Operations (DCO), a secret division he's never heard of. Terrorists are kidnapping biologists and he and his partner have to stop them. But his new partner is a beautiful, sexy woman who looks like she couldn't hurt a fly—never mind take down a terrorist.

She's not your average Covert Operative

Ivy Halliwell is no kitten. She's a feline shifter, and more dangerous than she looks. She's worked with a string of hotheaded military guys who've underestimated her special skills in the past. But when she's partnered with special agent Donovan, a man sexy enough to make any girl purr, things begin to heat up…

—∿∿—

Praise for *Her Perfect Mate*:

"A wild, hot, and sexy ride from beginning to end!"
—Terry Spear, *USA Today* bestselling author

For more Paige Tyler, visit:

www.sourcebooks.com

Her Wild Hero

X-Ops

by Paige Tyler

USA Today bestselling author

––⁓––

The third book in the hot, pulse-pounding paranormal romantic suspense X-Ops series from *USA Today* bestselling author Paige Tyler.

Department of Covert Operations training officer Kendra Carlsen has been begging her boss to let her go into the field for years. When he finally agrees to send her along on a training exercise in Costa Rica, she's thrilled.

Bear-shifter Declan MacBride, on the other hand, is anything but pleased. He's been crushing on Kendra since he started working at the DCO seven years ago. Spending two weeks in the same jungle with her is putting a serious strain on him.

When the team gets ambushed, Kendra and Declan are forced to depend on each other. But the bear-shifter soon discovers that fighting bloodthirsty enemies isn't nearly as hard as fighting his attraction to the beautiful woman he'll do anything to protect.

––⁓––

Praise for *Her Perfect Mate*:

"Absolutely perfect. One of the best books I've read in years." —Kate Douglas, bestselling author of the Wolf Tales and Spirit Wild series

For more Paige Tyler, visit:

www.sourcebooks.com

Hungry Like the Wolf

SWAT

by Paige Tyler

USA Today bestselling author

She's convinced they're hiding something

The team of sharpshooters is elite and ultra-secretive—they are also the darlings of Dallas. This doesn't sit well with investigative journalist Mackenzie Stone. They must be hiding something…and she's determined to find out what.

He's as alpha as a man can get

Gage Dixon, the SWAT team commander, is six-plus feet of pure muscle and keeps his team tight and on target. When he is tasked to let the persistent—and gorgeous—journalist shadow the team for a story, he has one mission: protect the pack's secrets.

He'll do everything he can to protect his secret

But keeping Mac at a distance proves difficult. She's smart, sexy, and just smells so damn good. As she digs, she's getting closer to the truth—and closer to his heart. Will Gage guard their secret at the expense of his own happiness? Or will he choose love and make her his own...

For more Paige Tyler, visit:

www.sourcebooks.com

Full Throttle

Black Knights Inc.

by Julie Ann Walker

New York Times and *USA Today* bestselling author

Steady hands, cool head…

Carlos "Steady" Soto's nerves of steel have served him well at the covert government defense firm of Black Knights Inc. But nothing has prepared him for the emotional roller coaster of guarding the woman he once loved and lost.

Will all he's got be enough?

Abby Thompson is content to leave politics and international intrigue to her father—the President of the United States—until she's taken hostage half a world away, and she fears her father's policy of not negotiating with terrorists will be her death sentence. There's one glimmer of hope: the man whose heart she broke, but she can never tell him why…

As they race through the jungle in a bid for safety, the heat simmering between Steady and Abby could mean a second chance for them—*if* they make it out alive…

Praise for Julie Ann Walker:

"Romantic suspense at its best." —*Night Owl Reviews*, 5 Stars, Reviewer Top Pick, *Born Wild*

For more Julie Ann Walker, visit:

www.sourcebooks.com